The Rain Thieves

William Ball

PARADOX ENTERPRISES
New Zealand

Paradox Enterprises Publishing

This edition published in April 2015.

ISBN 978-0-473-31936-6 Print
ISBN 978-0-473-31937-3 Epub
ISBN 978-0-473-31938-0 Kindle

Original Cover Design by Jan Morrison

Dedication

To my grandaugher Ellen
– better late than never.

Prologue

"It's time." The woman tapped send on her PSim.
Picking up the gift from her sister, she put it and a few
other 'treasures' into a large carrying bag on her desk.
"After twenty years as a meteorologist, ten in the same
office, you'd think I would have accumulated more than
a single bag full of things." She zipped it shut, swung it
onto her shoulder, turned out the light, closed the door
and headed for the car park. Tomorrow she'd be heading
for the Farm.

Chapter One
Every story begins somewhere.

Elle grimaced. The first hint of sunrise was more than an hour away. The heat had insidiously eased itself into her dream of being lost in a vast, featureless landscape, pinned under a canopy of unforgiving light. When she woke up, this dream would be easy to interpret. But others were not so obvious, like the ones where she was drowning. When she had told Noah about the drowning dreams, he had grinned and assured her that drowning was very unlikely to happen, but to be safe, she should perhaps avoid taking baths. To a child of the Dry, drowning did not seem even remotely possible, and the idea of there being enough water to drown in was not at all unpleasant.

Nights, especially during the winter months, brought some relief, but as soon as the sun rose the oppressive heat returned. In her thirteen plus years of life she'd experienced the bone shattering cold and mind numbing heat of the Wastelands. What she had never experienced was rain. Unless obscured by a dust storm, in her world the daytime sky was incandescent blue, ringed by a brownish haze that hugged the horizon. In her world, the nights were a festival of pin-pricked points of light. And when the full moon rose, her world was dressed in infinite shades of grey. In her world, the dry earth was ankle deep dust – dull, rust red – and the migration of seasons was nearly non-existent. In her world, water was an elusive chimera, a mirage at the bottom of the garden. To bathe, to be able to completely submerge oneself in water, was both rare and intensely pleasurable and, as with all rare and pleasurable things, an immensely anticipated event. In her world, one learned at great cost that no water source was secure. Fear that the Dry would claim the last vestiges of the remaining rivers, lakes, wells and springs was never far from either her thoughts or her dreams.

What woke Elle was not the dream. Rather it was the sensation that the sounds coming from outside had rearranged themselves. Something was moving in the yard under her window. Not an unusual event one would suppose, living on a farm as she did. But here, on this farm, life was not as abundant as it had been in the Before Times. There was very little wildlife, a much diminished morning chorus and no domestic animals wandering about. Rural people like Elle were highly sensitive to certain sounds, certain rhythms, because an unexpected noise could herald the approach of murderous intentions. Although in recent years such a threat of sudden death had become diminished, when the familiar background noises were disturbed or altered in an unanticipated way it still focused her attention. It was a matter of survival. The coming of the Dry had seen to that.

Despite the fact that none of the farm's alarms had been triggered, any unexplained sound was worth investigating. Besides, she suspected the heat would ensure there would be little chance of a return to sleep. Quietly she slipped from her bed and began to dress. In a more affluent time, the figure standing there in the moonlight would have been judged to be an underfed child. Elle did not live in affluent times. Though tall and thin, all arms and legs, she possessed a wiry, strong body and was as agile as a whip. Her skin, burnt a deep brown, had the smooth sheen of youth. Except for her height, the casual observer saw a rather ordinary looking, gangly child, neither plain nor pretty, that could easily be absorbed unnoticed in a crowd of children. Until she turned to look at you. There was something about her eyes and the way she stared that caused adults to hesitate when they met her for the first time. Some even felt the need to step back to gain a greater distance between them. These were not the eyes of a child, even one born of the Dry. A predator's perhaps, or those of a person much, much older who had lived through things no adult, much less a child, should have experienced. With deep squint lines at the corners and narrowed by bright sunlight, her eyes were never at rest. Gazing out from beneath a dishevelled mop of thick, black hair, they absorbed, gathered, studied, catalogued and analysed everything they saw.

In less than a minute she was up and dressed. All her clothes were cast-offs and there weren't many to choose from. With a cat's grace, a rifle in hand and a knife at her waist, she disarmed the house security system and slunk out the back door into a yard awash with moonlight to see what it was that had woken her.

Pausing to tuck into her shirt the ring that hung about her neck, she drew the night air into her lungs and then slowly let it out. It tasted, as it always did, of dust. She moved toward the source of the sound, hugging the wall of the house. Her bare feet sank into the soft dust. It covered her toes and deadened her footsteps. Whatever was out there, she was confident, would not hear her approach. She crept up to the corner of the house and carefully tilted her head just enough to allow her to see whether anything was there. A solitary shade tree stood on this side of the house. In the soft grey light she could make out its broad canopy and the amorphous shape that sat beneath it on her 'thinking' log. This was her place, the one place she came to when things were not going well for her, when she wanted to be alone or when she had an important decision to make. Just as she was about to take another step, a familiar voice greeted her.

"Good morning Elle. Having trouble sleeping?" It was her grandfather, Noah. It had always been this way. Successfully stealing up on others was a skill she enjoyed and employed often. She was a superb tracker and hunter with the ability to stalk game over open country. It was a different story when it came to her grandfather. Elle had never been able to sneak up on him. He seemed to know exactly what she was up to or about to do. It was as though Noah could sense the approaching presence of not only her but others as well. Her mother said that he was a family throwback to a time when humans were not so tame, back to a time when this land was young, alive and green, a time when the first people still roamed unencumbered and strange monstrous creatures preyed upon the careless. Some believed his soul had been forever disfigured by the Scavengers. Others believed he just enjoyed being in a perpetual foul mood. He was a curmudgeon, who found little pleasure in the company of others. To Elle, he was just her grandfather, her best friend and the one who had taught her to ride, to shoot, to hunt, to defend herself and to survive living in the wastelands. He was a huge, powerful man with a head and chest full of hair that remained black and disobedient despite his years. He had big hands, breathtaking reflexes, a volatile temper and a deep rumbling voice. He also possessed an uncompromising stubbornness, a trait it seems he had bequeathed to all his offspring, especially Elle. In spite of his many perceived flaws, his formidable temper had never been directed at Elle or her mother. She had no memory of not being welcomed into either his arms or lap. For her, his massive frame had always been there, just as much a part of her unchangeable world as the heat, the cold, the dust and brilliant, cloudless skies.

Noah had been gone for more than a week. This was not unusual. Often, without explanation and for no reason anyone could discern, he would saddle up and go. One time, her mother had told her, right after Elle was born, he had got up from the breakfast table and left, saying only that there was some unfinished business he had to attend to. He hadn't returned for nearly a year. Now he was back from another trip and hadn't even bothered to go into the house or care for his horse. She heard a soft snort from Blue who, having recognized her smell, let it be known that he wasn't happy. The horse, saddled and sweaty, stood waiting impatiently by the hitching rail. Not attending to his horse immediately was out of character for Noah, something she had never seen him do before. "A man who doesn't care for his animal had better get used to walking," he told her whenever he saw a horse being poorly treated.

She joined him on the log. Although the moon was very nearly full, his face remained in shadow, too dark for her to see it clearly. Elle knew him well enough to know he was troubled. She slipped her hand into his.

"What's wrong, Old Man?" she inquired. She knew calling him an Old Man was usually a sure way to get him to bite with a sharp retort, but not this time.

"We've got a problem." Noah never talked to her like a child. He treated her as he would any adult and she took this for granted. Not counting three older cousins, the youngest being sixteen, there were no other children on the farm nor any living close enough to compare her life to theirs. Like so many things, she accepted that that was the way it was and 'the way it was' was normal.

Trying to match the serious tone in his voice, she asked, "What problem?"

Turning to look at her, he said, "The pump at Miner's Hat has been damaged pretty badly. Found the whole upper section smashed on the ground. I suspect that storm we had a couple of weeks back knocked it off its perch. In addition, and I won't know until I get the pump going again, there are signs the spring might be going dry."

For hundreds of kilometres around, all sources of water were known to the family. Miner's Hat was a year-round spring just south of the farm and the only reliable supply out that way for more than fifty kilometres. The Farm had a well near the house and two springs within easy walking distance. Other than that, in any direction, there were only three other dependable water sources within a day's ride. Broken Wagon Wheel was a few hours ride due east. Ride another couple of hours and you would come upon what had once been a mighty river. Water from the northern lakes had stopped flowing within its borders long before she was born. Now it was nothing but one long dusty wadi that wound its way to the sea. Ben's Keep was up north past the road that led out of the valley. Close enough to the farm to be useful but far enough from the Northern settlements to make it reasonably safe to visit. Take that same road westward and, several hours later, you'd come upon Lone Willow Spring situated just over the hill that marked the end of the valley. Outside of those, the next closest source of water was further east and would take two days of hard riding to reach. Up north, over 400 kilometres away, was the southern tip of what remained of a once huge, inland, freshwater lake – a dangerous place for any outsider brave enough to venture there alone. There were a few more water sources westward but they were rarely visited.

At Miner's Hat, the water delivered by the windmill's efforts fed into a series of channels that irrigated over fifty hectares of ring-fenced grassland. Its loss would be disastrous, not only for the family's own animals, but for the wildlife out that way as well.

"Does that mean the stock will have to be moved to the Lone Willow Spring or Ben's Keep?"

"No point," replied her grandfather. "There is scarcely enough for the animals we already have there."

"What are we going to do then?" asked Elle.

With a shrug of his shoulders followed by a long sigh, her grandfather turned his face away. For the first time she could remember, he looked old and tired. The wastelands never made living easy. After a long pause, he said, "After breakfast we'll load the wagon and the boy and I will head back to see if the windmill is repairable. Other than that, Elle, I just don't know."

If Elle had been a different kind of child, one raised perhaps in comfort, she might well have cried at the sadness and regret in her grandfather's voice. There would be no tears from her though. She had been raised tough. The Dry saw to that, and any comfort she did experience was never taken for granted.

Under the boughs of the tree, in the stillness that comes in the hours before dawn, they talked some more of what could be done. Noah estimated that the trip out and back, plus the time he expected it would take for him and the boy to effect repairs, could be up to five days, maybe four if everything went well. Once the windmill was repaired, they'd soon know the condition of the spring. If water flowed, the boy would be sent back while Noah and Blue would set out to check the remaining water sources that lay much further south from the farm. It was always good to have a plan 'B' and, if possible, a plan 'C'. If things didn't go well, he would need the boy's help herding the animals back to the farm. The 'boy' was Chook, the youngest of Elle's cousins and deaf since birth. Elle saw no reason why she shouldn't accompany them and, if everything did go as hoped, she'd continue on with her grandfather leaving Chook to return to the Farm because it wouldn't take two people to bring back a wagon. Given a choice of staying put on the farm or roughing it in the wastelands, Elle would be gone before breakfast.

Noah removed a massive watch from his vest and looked at the time. Not that he needed to, the position of the stars and the hint of light along the eastern horizon told him what it was. It was more of an 'ending' ritual than anything else. In this case, the end of this particular line of conversation. The watch was returned to the safety to his pocket. In her minds' eye she could see every scratch and dent on the watch and remembered the story of where and how it got them, especially the pronounced indentation near the winding knob. She had not expected it to be so heavy and watching it fall from her grasp was one of her earliest childhood memories.

They decided the news could wait until the rest of family were awake since the time of the telling would not change anything. Whether Elle went to Miner's Hat was not Noah's decision – that would be her mother, Nora's.

They both got up. Blue had been patient long enough. All that needed to be said had been said; besides, the sun was just beginning to show itself and it was already too hot for idle conversation.

By the time they'd finished settling Blue in his stall, providing water and feed, brushing off a week's worth of dust and putting away the tack, the rest of the family was up and in the kitchen. The smells of breakfast had reminded the two in the barn that they were hungry. As soon as she stepped into the kitchen and saw the six empty places at the table, Elle remembered that two of her cousins and their families had left the day before. Seeing Noah had temporarily erased all the excitement of yesterday's departure.

The physical world had drastically altered since the coming of the Dry, but the basic needs of humanity had not. Accompanied by their parents, the two oldest of Elle's male cousins were off to meet and marry two sisters who lived in a small community about two hundred and fifty kilometres east of the Farm. Nearly three years ago the families involved had gathered together to agree upon and set a date for a double wedding. Technically it was not an arranged marriage. An arranged marriage is bounded by custom and implies there are 'other' choices. For Elle's cousins, their prospective brides were the only young women available within a two week's ride from the Farm. Isolated communities and families such as Elle's understood that an opportunity for their younger members to find a spouse, a companion, was vital. In the Dry, adults were considered old in their fifties. Infant mortality was high and even if they were lucky enough to avoid death in those first months, children frequently failed to reach maturity. Disease, famine, violence, adversity of all kinds claimed them. Women faced all these tragedies as well, but there was one reserved for them alone. As it had been with Elle's grandmother, women frequently died in childbirth, taking two lives instead of one. Life had become extremely hard since the coming of the Dry and harder still if one lived alone. Therefore few, if given the chance, remained unmarried. For reasons of his own, Elle's grandfather had.

Noah had known he would miss the boys' departure. That was regrettable, but the problems with the windmill at Miner's Hat had set his priorities. They would understand. While his desire for solitude remained personal and could be deferred, protecting the family and securing supplies of water lay at the core of all his endeavours. Besides, barring a calamity, Noah would be seeing the younger of the two in a few weeks anyway. Owing to the distance, the difficulties, the dangers and the ceremonial obligations that came with binding two families together, he could count on a month passing before they returned along with the youngest boy's new bride. In a ritual born of necessity, the older son would remain behind, a child in exchange for a child, a life for a life. After the harvest, Noah would take the opportunity to travel out to see how the newly wedded couple were faring. Maybe bring a larger gift than custom required by way of an apology for not saying farewell.

Once the family sat down and began to eat, Noah, signing for Chook's benefit as he spoke, elaborated on what he had told Elle earlier. The land south of Miner's Hat, as far as he had ridden, was continuing to die, becoming even more desolate. Though he allowed it to remain unspoken the family knew that even if the problems at Miner's Hat were overcome this time, it only postponed the inevitable. Just as in much of the vast wastelands that surrounded the farm, a time would come when there would be nothing out there but sand, rocks and heat. Their beloved farm had benefited from being ideally located close to several springs, but it was no more assured of a future than any other place where water once had flowed.

Time and options seemed to be running out for Elle's family despite nearly five generations of efforts and sacrifices. They could leave, as had the other families that had once lived in the valley, but where would they go? Except for a few isolated communities such as theirs, the five hundred kilometres in any direction from the Farm was nearly devoid of life and the water it depended upon. Traders, the occasional drifter, the rare and unexpected visit from a family friend and Noah's incessant outward journeys kept them up-to-date on communities and events far from the Farm. These pockets of families were dotted all across the country; like the Farm, each huddled around a water source. However, with the continued failure of these sources, each passing year saw more of these wastelands communities abandoned. Nearly all the larger settlements were located along the newly established seashore or in or around the remnants of an abandoned city upon which they could scavenge. Others huddled near the vestiges of the once mighty fresh water lakes, relocating their villages, towns and farms every few years. The need to be close to water was both psychological as well as practical.

Then there were the stories of people living in the far north and south of the continents. The lands that bordered Arctic and Antarctic regions had become the recipients of water from the glaciers and ice fields that embraced them. Owing to the comparatively harsh winters and cool summers, there was little evaporation, so both large and small, but relatively stable, bodies of fresh water formed wherever a big enough depression permitted. There were even rivers. However, the surrounding lands were extremely poor and sparse, comprised mostly of glacial shale, sand and bogs. The soil was thin and did not take kindly to being disturbed. Even so, the milder temperatures and the presence of so much fresh water offset these disadvantages. Thousands from the wastelands had migrated there, forming communities, building ramshackle dwellings and sheltering behind makeshift palisades for fear that what they had could be taken from them by newly arrived immigrants.

Even if the windmill at Miner's Hat had not failed, the morning conversation would have invariably found its way to the subject of water. Water, more precisely its reliability, always crept into any conversation. Elle's eyes rolled up toward the ceiling, a sure sign of boredom. "Yes, we need water. Yes, we will die along with our loved ones without it. And yes, the world will come to an end. We know all this." Of course, none of this was said out loud; that would have caused her nothing but trouble. And yet, she did so long for a conversation that didn't include water or the Farm. That had to be one of the reasons she enjoyed being in the wastelands with Noah. Out there, a diversion from her daily chores, they talked about almost anything but the Farm and water. She was just about to announce that she wanted to be excused when her cousin began to sign for attention.

Chook, who 'spoke' even less than her grandfather, signed, "I want to go to the mountains."

Knowing what this meant, the conversation around the table froze into stunned silence; all eyes turned to look at the boy, waiting.

He started to sign again. "Why not? I could go to the mountains. Everyone knows that's where it all started."

No one spoke at first. Her grandfather looked down at his plate, took a drink of what passed for coffee, but said nothing.

The kitchen was so quiet you could hear the fire crackle in the stove, the chickens squawk outside and a breeze rattle the chimes on the porch. Her father cleared his throat and was about to say something when he was interrupted by Nora.

Her voice was measured. You could feel the repressed anger when she said and signed, "If the Miner's Hat spring has failed, things here could become untenable. That's true. But it is equally true we are shorthanded. Until the rest of the family returns, outside of fixing the windmill, there are more than enough things around the Farm that have to be done in preparation for the coming harvest. There will be no further talk about anyone going to the mountains."

Chook repeated his desire to at least go and have a look. He'd be back before the harvest, and besides, he saw no reason to hang around the farm just so he could watch everything dry up and blow away. If the mountains held the answers, why not go? It would be better than sitting here, waiting.

That was about the longest string of signs Elle had ever seen him make and she didn't know what astonished her more, the conversation about that-which-shall-never-be-spoken, or that it was Chook who had brought up the forbidden subject.

No sooner had Chook finished than Nora, who rarely raised her voice even when provoked, rose from her chair, towered over the seated Chook and, with hands that frantically flailed the air in front of her, began to berate him for even suggesting such a crazy idea. No longer attempting to hide her anger, her voice was edged with incredulous indignation and the hands were signing so fast they were almost a blur. Such a sudden and unexpected outburst startled everyone at the table. Nora had many of her mother's qualities and was said to look a good deal like her. Right at this moment, however, no one was left in any doubt that she was also her father's child.

As tall as her husband, Jacob, big boned like her father, Nora, Noah's youngest daughter, was a formidable woman when crossed. Her temper could be inspiring. The face Elle saw frightened her. This was not the face that bent to kiss her good night. Nora had recognized the look on her father's face and knew that all it would take was the smallest of nudges to send him off on one of his adventures.

"Are you out of your mind?" she said. "Are things not bad enough that you suddenly have a death wish as well? Do you really think, even if both Noah and Jacob went with you, it would make a speck of difference? Even the Traders won't go there. Since the coming of the Dry, how many others have gone to the mountains? How many? A hundred? A thousand? Tens of thousands? How many returned? Only one that I know of and he came back speaking rubbish. Silver clouds and snakes striking everyone dead where they stood, everyone but him it would seem." Rounding on her husband when it looked like he was about to intervene, "And don't for a moment try, Jacob, to persuade me otherwise or attempt to calm me down. You're the one who found that poor deranged fool hanging in the barn like a sack of potatoes. He'd killed himself within a week of his arrival."

Glaring at each of the men in turn she continued, "Whatever it was he really saw, whatever it was that he did or did not do, whatever was done to him, we may never know, but what we do know is that it drove the poor sod to kill himself." She turned her attention back to Chook, who was now visibly shaken. "And just what is it we are supposed to do when you've gone? Wait here with the rest of the family for your return? Do you really think Noah would let you go alone? He'd jump at any opportunity to get away from here and out into the wastelands. And your parents, do you really think that once they found you'd gone, they wouldn't set out after you? And then there is your brother, how could he stay behind? Don't think for a moment that he wouldn't leave his bride. After all, he wouldn't want to be left behind, now would he? It would be an adventure, certainly better than working on some dying farm."

Chook winced as if struck when Nora signed 'dying farm'.

"The sad thing is, you probably wouldn't even get near the mountains anyway. What if there are still Scavengers out there? What is it with you men? Why are you so eager to lose your lives? Aren't things ever bad enough for men to not try to make them worse?" Pain flowed into her voice as she turned to look at Noah, beseeching him, "Dad, kill this idea here and now. Do not let it live a second longer, for you of all people know that it's a fool's errand."

Then, as suddenly as it had started, it was over. The storm in her mother's eyes faded away leaving her looking tired and defeated. She sank back into her chair and then reached up with her hand to touch the scar that ran along the side of her forehead before letting it drop onto her stomach. There, beneath the table, out of sight, it gently touched her belly making a couple of small circular motions before returning to the table.

Seeing the stunned looks on the men's faces Elle thought to herself, now that was a diversion. Not another word was spoken for the remainder of the meal. Breakfast sat in Elle's stomach like so many small stones, making her realize that you should be careful for what you wish for. On finishing, each person, avoiding eye contact, sheepishly got up. In silence they scraped their plates clean and using the smallest amount of water, washed and rinsed them. The water and waste, collected in a bucket below the sink, would be used later to feed the animals. After they had completed cleaning up they went their separate ways. What more could be said? They all knew the same stories.

What Nora had said, however, was only partially true. In the early years, thousands of soldiers, adventurers, sinners and saints, had at various times gone to the mountains to seek the rain. Very few ever returned. And of those that did, just like the man in the barn, many seemed to have been driven insane by the experience. All that had occurred long before Nora's birth. Considering the distance and the terrain, the man of Nora's memory was perhaps nothing more than another poor delusional soul from the wastelands. He might have never been even close to the mountains because they had long ago stopped being a destination, becoming instead a thing of myth. People, while willing to speak of the need for water, felt uneasy if there was any reference to the mountains. So they just stopped talking about them. And this unease didn't stop there. Other subjects were either ignored or seldom discussed. Anything to do with the Before Times, the cloudless skies, the Dry, the Sorrow or the Scavengers was often left unsaid. What was the point? Were these things not common knowledge? So why speak of them, if doing so brought nothing but pain and feelings of being powerless? Everywhere, the rains had stopped and nothing mankind had tried since had brought them back. Still, it was not altogether impossible that the man in the barn had been to the mountains. Although he'd never said as much, if anyone had been to the mountains and returned, sane, it would be her grandfather.

Elle walked outside to find a bit of privacy after her mother's tirade. She, like everyone else in the family, had heard countless times the stories of the coming of the Dry and so knew them by heart. How cities, towns and villages were either engulfed by the rising seas, abandoned from lack of water or consumed by fires. How minor infections turned septic and previously vanquished scourges reappeared along with pandemic diseases that scythed through the weak and strong alike. How fires raged everywhere. The sky, the very air one breathed, filled with soot and ash, clogging the lungs, smothering the old, the young and the unlucky. How, at night, no horizon lacked the glow of fires. How the displaced and homeless multitudes lined the roads with their graves. But not all who died did so from thirst, hunger, fire or disease. What the conflagration of nature did not bring, mankind had been happy to provide. Without the rains, anywhere there was water, even a suspicion of water, was besieged. Water was the single most important commodity of exchange. With the coming of the Dry, it was power. It was wealth. It was life. Armies, rabble, mobs fought desperately to possess it. No quarter was asked nor given. Those who won, for a time, lived. Those who lost, died. And, most discomforting of all, her mother had spoken of the unspeakable. She spoke of the Scavengers. Even her grandfather refused to use the word, so distasteful were they to him.

Once again on her 'thinking' log, she sought solace from the persistent restlessness she was feeling. All morning she'd been turning over and over again what had been said, and not said, at breakfast. Thoughts darted about in her head like frenzied animals looking for a place to settle. Something had awakened after a long slumber and now was trying to make its presence known but it remained just out of her grasp. A foot absentmindedly swung back and forth, carving a shallow groove in the moist earth as she listened to the gurgle of water flowing from a pipe that encircled the base of the tree. The tree was the family's one extravagance when it came to frugality with water. Over time, keeping it alive and healthy had somehow been interwoven with the family's own fortune. It was the one place visitors would come, just to stand in the shade beneath its canopy. Somewhere among its branches a bird sang but there was no reply to its challenge. This year, visitors of any description had become almost non-existent. It had been nearly three months since anyone had stopped, even a Trader. Still, should they come, every visitor would be given all the water they could carry and all the food Elle's family could spare. In contrast to most people from the road, her family were a people of wealth, of abundance and, because of this, not all who came to the Farm did so peacefully. Sometimes the generosity was paid back in violence and malice. But for now, the farm had as much water as they needed for the gardens, their few animals and the fields under cultivation. Nevertheless, in spite of all their efforts, the yields from the fields were smaller each year; the quantity of fruit and vegetables was less. The work to get anything to grow became harder. It was as if the soil itself, tired and hungry, was yielding to the despair of the Dry.

The broken windmill, the Farm's isolation, her mother's anger and a thousand other pieces of information tucked away somewhere deep in her mind suddenly fell into place: the Farm was dying.

The restlessness condensed onto a single thought. She might be only thirteen, a bit less than a month away from her fourteenth birthday, but the times had not allowed her to be a child or spend much time thinking of childish things. It was clear that her grandfather and her parents had been preparing her for this all her life.

Called by her mother to come and help load the wagon, Elle spent the next hour tramping back and forth from the barn and house with the rest of the family, shifting food, camping gear, spare parts for the windmill and the farm's portable forge. Finally, with Chook on one end and Elle on the other, they lugged the last item from the barn. It was the dirty, smelly and unwieldy, but all-important tarpaulin and it resisted their combined efforts to be lifted up and on to the wagon. Attracted by the grunts and expletives, Noah reached down to give the struggling pair a helping hand. In the wastelands, the only shade you could depend on was the one you brought yourself. Satisfied there was nothing else that needed to be loaded, they now turned their attention to the task of securing the load and hitching up Calli and Sue, two of the four remaining draft horses. Having left the others to finish, Nora reappeared with a canvas bag containing prepared food which she placed on the seat next to Noah and Chook. Not wishing to delay their departure any longer than necessary, Noah had decided that they would eat lunch on the road. All they had to do now was wait while Jacob did his final inspection.

All eyes followed Jacob as he circled the wagon, meticulously checking each of the tie downs. There were no roads to Miner's Hat, only rough open country. Hard enough for a man on horseback, it would not take much for a wagon, especially one so heavily loaded, to break an axle or damage the cargo if its load should shift. Elle was bemused by her father's thorough attention to each of the knots. Those were her knots and nobody, not even Noah, could have done a better job. Nevertheless her father was a notoriously cautious man. He was also gentle and easy going and, as far as she knew, never raised his voice, although she was sure there were times when both she and her mother had given him reason to do so. In all the years of her life, it had been her mother who disciplined her, never her father. She could only recall seeing him get angry once and once was enough. Her grandfather was bigger and stronger than Jacob, but the man, a visitor, who had shown an unacceptable disrespect towards her mother, would not have noticed the difference. Without a word, Jacob had walked up to the man and dropped him with one blow. Although Elle had thought the man deserved it, she was taken aback when her mother rounded on her husband while the man's friend tried to revive his unconscious companion. It took Elle a moment to realize it wasn't because Jacob had hit him, rather her mother had been about to do the same and now had missed the opportunity.

Satisfied, Jacob stepped up on a spoke of the wheel to shake each of their hands and wished them a safe journey. Noah, having said his goodbye, reached into his pocket and pulled out the great watch, announcing to all that they were running late. He mounted Blue and then nodded to Chook. A flick of reins and the two horses leaned into their harnesses.

From the porch, Elle watched the wagon until it crested the rise and was lost from sight. She was not going with them. In secret she did not want to. There had been a change of plans. She had been in the process of conjuring up a believable excuse when her mother had unwittingly interceded on her behalf, thus preventing Elle from lying to her grandfather. Nora was obviously still very agitated with the lot of them and was making sure that the males of the family knew this. So, when Noah asked why Elle was standing around and not getting ready to leave, he was informed that she was not going.

Daring her father to contradict her, Nora said, "There's too much work that needs doing here. The two of you, I am sure, are capable of doing what needs to be done without some female slowing you down."

He'd no difficulty reading his daughter's mood. The tone of her voice, the way she emphasized the word female, and the expression on her face radiated defiance and anger and reminded him so much of her mother. But he had no idea what really lay at the core of her anger. It had to be more than what had happened at breakfast. Whatever it was, he felt that it was best to just leave it alone. Five days away might be long enough. He glanced over at Chook and Jacob, hoping to glean at least a bit of support from the other men, but none would be forthcoming from that quarter. With both hands shoved deeply into his pockets, Chook was trying to make himself as small and as silent as possible. He might have been only sixteen but he was wise enough to know when to remain silent. Jacob had found something riveting on the ground which seemed to require all his attention.

So Elle stayed behind, allowing her to implement her own plans without betraying her grandfather's trust.

Later, with the morning's chores completed, she went inside, letting the door slam shut behind her. The noise echoed throughout the house. Since she didn't hear either of her parents yell out, "Don't slam the door," the house was empty. Not for long though; it was nearing lunch time. Soon she would have to start setting out the leftovers from last night's dinner for the three of them. She grabbed a breakfast biscuit from the breadbin and spread a dollop of butter on it before taking a bite. A bit dry, she thought. After lunch they'd be going to the pigs or crumbled up to be mixed with whatever they had for dinner. No food ever went to waste. She pushed open the door and stepped into the dining room.

A brilliant light filled the room, greeting her as it poured from the skylight overhead. The room was hot, stuffy and had an air of abandonment. This is where all the family ghosts come when the living are asleep, mused Elle. Maybe it was the room's size, the huge dining table and all those empty chairs that made the place feel so forlorn. Nowadays, the dining room did not get used much. Instead, the family ate at the table in the kitchen. It just felt cosier there, less intimidating. She shoved the last of the biscuit into her mouth, wiping the buttery crumbs on her pants as she walked over to the 'Wall'. Soon two more names will be added, she thought, the wives of her cousins. Elle stepped back to better take in the whole painting. She never tired of looking at the family's tree that adorned Nadia's Wall.

Chapter Two

Without family, friends, what are we?

The first time you stood in front of Nadia's wall you could not help but be humbled and awed into silence. The 'Wall' was initially created by Nadia, the middle child of Atticus and Zee, Elle's great-great grandparents and the founders of the Farm. Rebellious to the last days of her life, she, unlike her sisters and their families, never actually lived on the Farm. After her death, the Wall lay dormant until Nora, Elle's mother, came of age and took up the brush many years later. As testament to her heritage, the mural lost none of the magic bestowed upon it by Nadia's brush. Art, the skill of rendering the world on canvas, flowed though both women. Tradition held that Elle would follow her mother. For her part, she hoped that when that time came the muse that guided their hands would somehow make its presence known in hers. As yet, her muse was nowhere to be seen.

The Wall was a thing of rare beauty, as magnificent as it was immense and as richly detailed as the pages of a monk's illustrated manuscript. It filled every millimetre of the available space, from floor to ceiling, from wall to wall. Strong vibrant colours surged along its broad surface to mingle with softer tones, a symphony of light and dark shadows.

Elle moved toward the wall and instinctively began to look for her name. Among its branches and foliage all the members of the family were represented in caricature along with the date they were born and when they died. Her finger hovered over the mural, following her life line up until it moved just out of convenient reach. Arm extended, the pointing finger held its position as her eyes continued to trace the line upward and slightly to the left through all the other lives. It ended at her name and the figure of a young girl sitting precariously on a twig with legs dangling in the air. She grinned at her mother's interpretation of her daughter. Seeing her name and the figure next to it always gave her a warm feeling all over. She stepped back so as to be able to read the names of the Farm's founders. All had life lines denoting descendants; all that is, but one: Scout, the 'lost' sister. A solitary figure of a woman rested against the letter 'T' and seemed to be staring across to where Atticus sat with Zee in the fold of one of the tree's massive roots. The family assumed that the woman next to the 'T' was Scout but, like so many things concerning the Wall, one could not be sure. Nadia had refused to explain her work. There was no death date next to Scout's name and no life line. Nadia's rules for the 'Wall': no body, no date, no children, no life line. Elle's eyes searched for and found Nadia's name and that of Noah's father. He too had no death date and was the only one without a likeness somewhere nearby, just a hint of an outline of someone peering out from the shadow of a leaf. Nadia never could bring herself to paint the face of her husband, as if in doing so she would be accepting that he was dead.

There were so many names at the beginning. Elle looked over to Zee's side of the family. All those brothers and sisters and all their children; the Sorrow, the Scavengers and the Dry had claimed them all. Following the lines back down to the beginning, she traced the life lines of Atticus and Zee's daughters and their children's and their children's children. Again the Sorrow, the Scavengers and the Dry had made their presence felt. Of all the life lines rising up from the base of the tree, of all its many branches, there were only six in her generation. The Wall showed that Noah was the last of his generation and, of hers, she was the only girl.

Looking at the names of her generation, she thought of what her mother had said about the mountains, the dangers involved and the fruitless efforts of so many. If she carried out her idea, it was possible she might not live to see the names of the new wives inscribed next to those of her cousins. She stepped further back so as to see all the others, a living tribute to the history of her family. The artistic hands of the two women had recorded them all and of them all, only a handful remained living. So few, among the so many, and yet, once your name was placed on the Wall you would not be forgotten. You would be remembered. That was a kind of immortality. Perhaps not as satisfying as being alive, but surely, for the living, it's good to know that you will be remembered and that your life mattered.

Some say that the tree outside her window was the original source for the inspiration. But no one really knew for certain how the idea of the family tree came into being or why this dining room wall had become a kind of obsession for Noah's mother. It was not as if it was planned or discussed, far from it. Nadia had not been known to plan or discuss anything about what she was up to or what tomorrow might hold. She had not dwelt upon the past nor had she been overly worried about the future. It was not in her nature. The present, the here-and-now, was more than sufficient for her. As far as she was concerned, there was not enough time in a day to get done what needed to be done. As a child, she had had an irrepressible need to scurry through the day, cramming as much as she could into it. Even when seated she'd wriggled, fidgeted and squirmed. She'd collected friends like others might collect stuffed toys and, as with the pied piper, they'd felt compelled to follow her wherever she went. And as no place or thing held her interest for long – there was always somewhere else she wanted to be – they evolved into something akin to a travelling circus. And like the circus, the clothes they wore and all that surrounded them was festooned with bright colours.

Her nomadic wanderlust was a bone of contention, causing much distress to the rest of the family. This was especially true for Atticus who wanted all her children living close by, and under protection. But the goals of a husband, children, a fixed address, were never hers. This had been true before the rains stopped when the world in which they lived was still reasonably secure. Now, each departure filled those on the Farm with apprehension, each return was a temporary release. Perhaps once or twice a year Nadia, her 'man' – she never allowed anyone to refer to him as her husband – and a horde of various 'gypsy' friends would descend on the settlement in a fleet of flamboyantly painted 'house' buses. Each and every visit, but one, was a festival. The Farm's routines would be set aside, and for a time, there would be loud music, lots of laughter, heaps of food, drink and many hours of catching up. Such times together always flew. Despite the family's bribes, pleadings and attempts to instill guilt, trying to turn this visit into something permanent, one morning the visit would end. The front yard would be transformed into a place of bedlam. In amongst long goodbyes, kisses, well wishes, hugs, promises to return and tears, bags, boxes and crates were packed, loaded and stowed. Minutes later, amidst a din of musical horns, shouts and frantic waves, they'd be gone. There'd be silence once more. The Farm held little interest for either Nadia or her companions. Before the dust from their departure had time to settle, those who remained would drift off to resume their labours.

But no matter how brief the visit, somewhere in the interim of arrival and departure the Wall would change.

This pictorial history of the family began on the second day of Nadia's first visit to the Farm after it was known that the rains had stopped; the coming of the Dry. Looking at the dining room's vast blank wall, Nadia called out to her mother, "Do you mind if I do something to this? I feel it needs its own voice." Not at all sure just what her daughter meant, Atticus simply replied that that was what walls were for, to do something with. Over the ensuing years Atticus would agree to almost any request that might somehow delay the inevitable departure of her itinerant daughter. Nadia, using a piece of charcoal fixed to the tip of a stick of kindling, started to sketch. Wide sweeping arcs and lines streaked across the face of the wall. From that moment on, during all her too-infrequent visits, the wall was her place of residence. Unless pulled by family obligation and protocol, this was where she worked, ate and slept. Colourful images emerged from the tip of her brushes and then vanished. Sometime a whole scene disappeared beneath their strokes to be replaced by yet another. Nothing was safe. An epic battle of heroic dimensions raged across the wall and within Nadia. This was not just a war of light and shadow, shades and tints, it was an attempt to harness the fury whelming up within her. Colours cried out against the loss of all the could-have-beens, the should-have-beens. The vivid colours strove to thwart an achromatic, waterless world. On the wall, Nadia's painting defied the reality outside. Here there were scenes where water did not just flow in abundance. It gushed. The scent of flowers hung in the air, the soil's moist softness yielded easily to the touch. Birds, mammals, amphibians, reptiles, insects, drew breath and lived again. The Wall resonated with songs of nature. Upon the birth of her son, Noah, and the death of her father, the tree found its way on to the wall and the names of the family began to appear. The Wall had become a visual requiem and symbol of renewal. Noah told Elle it was his mother's magnum opus, an unfinished testament to her family and, so long as a single member lived, it would remain unfinished waiting for another hand's brush stroke.

Sometimes when Elle stood before Nadia's tree, it revealed little secrets, something new tucked away within its nooks and crannies. She'd never divulged this to anyone, especially her grandfather, but there were times when she felt that it was as if the Wall did not always need the aid of a living hand. Like now. Way up along the left hand edge, a few millimetres from the girl on the twig, leaning slightly forward as if engaged in a private conversation, stood what? An apparition? A spectre? Or was it her sister? Whatever it was supposed to be, she was certain that it had not been there moments before. Or had it? A trick of the light perhaps? Was this some recent rework by her mother and if so, why? Elle dragged over a chair for a closer look. There was the translucent figure in the shape of a young girl with what looked like some kind of snake coiled about her feet. Strange, very, very strange and a little bit creepy. What in the world was my mother thinking when she painted this? Elle wondered and absentmindedly fingered the ring that hung about her neck, a habit she had acquired when retreating into thought. I bet Noah would know the story behind it. Getting him to tell me is another story, because everyone in the family avoids talking about my sister.

Like the Wall, Noah was a wealth of information. A host of secrets were stored away in the vast labyrinth of his mind, waiting for someone like Elle to come along to tease them out. How she loved discovering them, and none more than the stories of the early years after the coming of the Dry and her wayward ancestors. Often during a cold winter's night she'd snuggle up against his bulk while they sat on one of the aging couches in front of the fire and thumb through the photo albums of those earlier times. Like actors in a beloved and familiar play, all the family was there, a cast of hundreds, a menagerie of personalities: Atticus, tall and aristocratic; Zee, looking like a bear that had just woken up; their three girls and their families; Zee's brothers, sisters, and their families, and many, many friends. Ironically, upon the arrival of the Dry, three generations had come to live on this long abandoned, sprawling complex of a defunct end-of-days cult. Noah told Elle that his grandfather, Zee, often commented about the doomsday cult and their building of the Farm; that it was all in the timing.

The whole family and some close friends ultimately came to live on the Farm. All, that is, except Nadia and her crowd of 'gypsies'. Considering what was happening out there in the rest of world they seemed a happy bunch. Dressed in an array of rich vivid colours, smiling faces posed for the camera in front of garishly painted buses looked up at Elle from the photos. To Elle in her own drab attire, the world of her great-grandmother seemed unimaginably bright and festive, a world far removed from hers. Noah had a story for each of the photos: the place where it was taken, who the people were, their 'special' skill and what they had been doing. A whole history contained within the covers of a few worn albums. The best part for Elle, however, was the story of her grandfather's birth. He'd tell of how his father had been told by his mother, in no uncertain terms, that the baby was going to be born at the Farm and that was that. When the contractions began two weeks earlier than expected, what had been a leisurely meander became a race against the forces of nature. Followed by the other buses filled with companions, theirs tore through the back roads. While at the rear of the bus in the 'master bedroom', with the help of several women friends, Noah's mother struggled at every twist and turn to stop from being thrown from the bed. His father, not renowned for calm and restraint, refused, with threats of personal injury, anyone who suggested they could drive for a while. Thirteen hours later, with a hiss of steam pouring from the radiator, the flapping of a disintegrated rear tyre, cries from a newborn and the shouts from the back, "It's a boy", the bus pulled into the front yard. Noah had indeed been born on the Farm... just.

After such an intrepid birth, Noah told her of those 'happy times'. How he and two later siblings lived on the road for the next twenty years with his parents and their friends. Avoiding the inherent dangers and chaos of the larger cities when they could, they wandered over an ever increasingly fractured landscape. Behind the safety of the bus's barred windows, he saw and later recorded, through the lens of his father's digital camera, how the absence of rain changed the way people went about living. He looked on while the demands on the remaining rivers exceeded their capacity to help relieve the people's thirst. Hardship, privation and displacement oppressed the majority, inconvenienced the powerful and pursued the wealthy. He watched as death from starvation became common, though not as common as death from violence. The very young and the old suffered disproportionately. Infant mortality soared. Armed gangs of young men, when not fighting one another, preyed upon the tide of humanity that choked the roads leading away from the once great metropolises. Held in Noah's hands, the camera's unerring eye recorded the sad pageantry that unfolded before him.

In those earlier years, amazingly, through sheer force of will, the government and its institutions provided the country a degree of stability. Although all communication beyond the western mountain ranges that divided the nation had been lost, the people east of the ranges somehow managed to avoid the turmoil that engulfed much of the rest of the world and had weathered the initial onslaught of the tens of thousands of people seeking refuge from their own deprivations and miseries. They had successfully fought a war with their southern neighbour and secured an alliance with their northern to share the dwindling resources of the lakes and rivers that straddled their common borders. All along the eastern and southern coastlines, the government frantically installed solar desalination plants, knowing that they could not possibly meet the needs of so many. All this was recorded by the camera. Including Noah's contributions, there were 31 albums in all, beginning with childhood photos of Atticus and her sister Scout and ending with Noah at nineteen, with a collection of friends, preparing to return to the Farm for a visit.

Through Noah, Elle came to know all the members of the family and the many friends that were included within the family circle. He was the only remaining bridge that linked the Farm's past to the present. Elle would choose an album and it would lie open on Noah's lap for her perusal and bemusement. Each page brought with it an assortment of visual rewards and a mixture of emotions. Joy, sadness, regret and pleasure, in their turn, vied within her for expression. It didn't matter how often she sat with him on that dilapidated couch, she never tired of reliving the past or hearing his stories and the inevitable allegories that accompanied them. Of all the albums, her favourites were of Noah in the early years that showed his parents and their friends enclosed by their buses, camping, repairing, dancing around a fire or setting up their trading stalls in town centres, along broad highways and intersections. He told her that, to support their way of life, they had evolved into itinerant traders like the tinkers of old. He would tell Elle how he and his younger brother and sister and the other children from the buses were sent out to forage for fuel and other necessities. The children quickly learned that there was always somebody, in spite of pleading poverty, who had something to trade. All they had to do was find that person and then, having found them, produce something they wanted more than the fuel or other treasures in their possession. Paper money held only a modest value. It had been replaced by bartering or precious gems, silver and, above all, gold. In the midst of all this misery, gold retained its mythical hold on people and Noah's family always seemed to have had ready access to it. Of all the photos, her favourite showed a motley row of kids proudly standing behind various shaped containers and other 'finds', the results of a day's successful foraging. It was not difficult to pick out her granddad. At thirteen, the same age as Elle was now, it was easy to see in Noah his father's ethnic legacy and prodigious height. He was already taller than most men but lean as a rail. The muscles would come later during harder times.

In the twenty-fifth year of what became known as the Dry, everything changed. Noah was almost twenty when those comparatively good years for his family and all those who had survived the tumultuous earlier times came to an abrupt end. So did the photos.

With one last look at the Wall, Elle turned and went back into the kitchen. As there were still a few things that needed attending to before lunch, Elle wasted no time in laying out the table before going outside. A sure way of drawing unwanted attention from either parent was to have not completed an assigned chore. As to the translucent figure and the snake on the wall, she'd keep quiet. This was not a time to risk complicating things. Outside, along with the unavoidable sweat flies, a swarm of gnats danced above her. In a science book on insects she had read that they would be all males using her as a staging post while waiting for a female to show up. "Best of luck, guys," she said, slipping a well-worn hat onto her head as she moved toward the barn. The gnats followed, ever hopeful.

The Farm's buildings, with their metre-thick, rammed earth walls, heavy timbered rafters and interlocking slate roofing tiles, had weathered the worst of those earlier years. The Farm was in a shallow valley surrounded by low hills and bisected by a single four lane highway that went from one end to the other. Before the Dry a hundred families had lived there, sharing the small river that flowed through its length. Outside the valley, thousands more families dotted the surrounding countryside. They were a mixed bag. Some were market gardeners and orchardists; a few came only during the summer, while others lived on their 'life-style' blocks but commuted to the big city some two hours' drive up north or to one of the towns nearby. By the fifth year of the Dry only the farming families and a few of the hardier life-stylers remained; by the tenth year only those with springs or deep wells were left. The rest had vanished, often leaving with only what could be stuffed into a car or truck. The abandoned houses became home to the wildlife and places for the remaining kids to play.

In the barn and out of the bright light, Elle stood for a moment to let her eyes adjust to the dim interior. Drawing in a deep breath through her nose, she savoured the odour. Nothing else in her experience smelled quite like the barn. It was all suspended dust, fresh dung, hay, leather and animals. The horses and the house cow leaned out over their stalls and greeted her. When she was much younger and there were still a few farming and life-styler families living near enough to visit, the barn had been where all the kids ended up playing, down among the stables and up high in lofts. Owing to the inconvenience, danger and the distance travelled, families would sometimes stay for a few days. It gave Elle and her cousins the opportunity to play with someone other than each other. Should the visit coincide with the arrival of Traders, there would inevitably be a party with music and dancing. Somehow the mere presence of the Traders was an excuse for everyone, including the adults, to set aside the seriousness associated with the times.

For Elle, such visits were a combination of excitement and discomfort in equal measure. Excitement because there was the occasional girl; discomfort, because on the Farm she was frequently left to her own devices by her cousins. The sudden arrival of a girl, especially one attired in her Sunday best dress, caused a degree of social uncertainty. What was she supposed to do with something dressed like that? But, as with children throughout the ages, this uncertainty never lasted long. If nothing else, their respective isolation incurred a fascination about these other kids. Curiosity about one another would invariably overcome their shyness and soon she, her cousins, and the other visiting kids would range around the Farm, playing and having a great time. And the dresses, if they survived the initial encounters intact, were soon exchanged for something more durable.

For the adults, the visits were not just about the pleasure of friends and company; they also confirmed that they were not alone. The first hours of any visit involved discovering what each family had in the way of information. The status of water, food, safety, health came first, followed by what Noah called domestic issues: the state and wellbeing of the family which invariably descended into general gossip; the glue that binds a community together. Ultimately, in amongst the noise of rambling conversations, came the business of the day. "Do you have something you need or want to trade?" This question always came up, especially if there were Traders present. Then there was, "I require help." This could be nothing more than the need for a certain skill or a few extra hands for a day or two. It could also mean that a family's efforts to survive were failing. Depending on what could be done with the resources on hand without jeopardizing others, the question for many came down to, "Will you be going or will you be staying?" Later, before the evening shadows grew too long, the families sat down to eat at long tables in the courtyard. There was a strong human need to hear, to be heard. Between bites and sips, and the occasional burst of laughter, the hum of conversation continued unabated. All but Noah had their stories to tell.

Later still, by the light of lanterns, under the influence of home brewed beer and full stomachs, people's normal caution relaxed and tongues loosened. Thinking the children were asleep, they'd begin to share what Noah called their 'war stories'. It is a human affliction, where fragments of memory, of their own and others', an indiscriminate blending of fact and fiction, were welded into personal narratives that gave reason and order to their lives. They spoke of the good times, the bad times, the worst times, the times yet to come and even of the times Before, when rain fell everywhere in abundance and the world was green. Eventually all conversations drifted into one of two directions. One revolved around the stories about the 'who', and the 'why' that lay behind the coming of the Dry. The truth was that no one knew why the rains had stopped and those that had known were most likely dead, but that never stopped anyone from speculating. The other stories, usually told in hushed whispers as if fearing to be overheard, were of the Sorrows, the Scavengers and the Western Mountains. These stories, the source of nightmares for the listening children and dread for their parents, were unlike those of the Before Times. These stories were not some imaginary tales; these nightmares were told by those who had survived them. There was another topic but it only came up if Noah or the Traders were not present. Then the visitors might speak of the part Noah and the Traders played during those terrifying years following the arrival of the Scavengers. But when any of them were present, good manners, respect and a just a hint of fear ensured their silence.

Squeezed in amongst the older kids, Elle hid in the dark listening to the anger and despair in the adult voices. Why they spoke of the loss of the Before Time puzzled her. None of those present, including Noah, had lived back then so why speak as if they had? Like her, they were children of the Dry. It made no sense. Perhaps it was then that she began to understand that the past always lives in the present. Their stories of loss, Nadia's mural, Noah's tales of his youth, were just a means of using the past to explain the present.

After a while conversations drained away as people retreated into their own thoughts. Tired and sleepy, they allowed silence to engulf them. All had in common the history of the Dry and the longing for the rains to return. When the last of the adults had moved off to bed, Elle would creep from her hiding place, leaving the company of any remaining children, to seek out her grandfather. Most times she'd him find sitting on their 'thinking' log staring out into the blackness or up at the stars. If he was alone, which was most often the case, Elle would join him without a word, inviting one of his arms to encircle her for warmth and comfort. He never seemed to mind telling her of his time on the bus with family and friends, but he was reluctant to speak of those later years. Long ago he'd concluded that words could not change what is past nor mitigate the rage within.

Chapter Three

It is the decisions we make that determine what we become.

Lunch that afternoon was a sombre and silent affair. The three sat eating, engrossed in their own thoughts. Nora was angry at herself and not just for letting Noah and Chook leave without making up. She should never have lost her temper that way and certainly not in front of the kids. She knew all too well how life can be snatched away quickly and without warning, that each good-bye could be the last. Jacob was also angry at himself. Noah and Chook should have delayed their departure until tomorrow morning. The wagon needed some work, nothing serious, but still, problems could occur and Blue needed at least another day's rest. He was a powerful animal, jet black with a thick neck and chest. The horse would do whatever Noah asked of it, but Blue, like his master, was no longer young. A week in the Dry was hard on any animal, even one as robust as Blue.

Elle shared her father's interest in Blue's wellbeing and hoped that Noah would not push him too hard. And not just from the standpoint of the animal's welfare. It suited her that they take it slow and easy. It would suit her even more if, when the terrain permitted, both Noah and Chook walked part of the way. This was quite common on long treks in the wastelands. It also had the added benefit of extending the time it would take to reach the spring. With luck, taking into account the work that Noah said needed to be done to effect the repair of the windmill and possibly the pump, they might allow themselves and the horses a day of leisure before returning home. Elle was sure both were quite happy to give Nora an extra day to overcome her anger. If they did all that she hoped they would do, she'd have five, maybe even six, days in her favour. Longer if Noah took Blue and left Chook to return home alone. All of this, Elle calculated, would be to her advantage. However, she remained apprehensive, fearing she might have raised her grandfather's suspicion by not loudly protesting when permission to accompany him was declined.

That left the question; what about her parents? Elle's mother was a woman of the Dry and, being so, would be torn between adhering to custom and staying on the Farm or setting out in pursuit. She was betting that her mother, with some persuading from her father, would stay home. What about her Dad? Remembering how he reacted when her mother berated the men at breakfast, it was hard to imagine him as a young man in the wastelands with her grandfather, hunting down Scavengers. But he, too, was of the Dry. Experience had taught him to be practical and realistic, weighing the options before acting. Her father was no fool and very capable when it came to horses and machines, but he was foremost a farmer. She, in the way only a young person can, reasoned that he would be no match for her in the wastelands. Had not Noah trained her in its ways?

Besides, even if the wastelands surrounding the Farm seemed quiet these days, devoid of any real danger, he still would not take the risk and leave Nora alone, no matter how capable her mother was in defending herself. No, once he'd examined his options he'd choose to wait for Chook and Noah's return and it would be her grandfather, maybe with Chook for company, who would come after her. He was the only person who could put a halt to her plans. Even then, Noah might find it too risky to set off after her with a horse that had been worked in the wastelands for more than two weeks running. The Dry rewarded caution. This was what Elle was counting on. Her parents would be restrained by their indoctrination and the protocols enforced by custom. If they acted as she hoped, she'd have the time she needed.

Time, however, was seldom Elle's ally. It always seemed at odds with her. When out in the wastelands on her own or with her grandfather, time evaporated. On the Farm, it seemed to almost stand still. She looked at a shadow and then up at the sun. Except today, when she needed time to slow to a crawl, it was racing ahead, mocking her. She shrugged at her own impatience. There was a lot that had to be done before she was called in for dinner. She could not see her parents which meant they couldn't see her. Out of sight, out of mind. But she knew where they were. Her dad was off working on a failed water supply pipe that fed one of the fields. Sounds carried an amazing distance in the hot air. She could hear him and guessed he was having a bit of difficulty. Like all the family, his language could be quite colourful at times. Her mother, screened by a row of ripening corn, was dutifully occupied in the garden nearest the house. Elle had her own assigned tasks and, providing it appeared as though she was doing her share, she would be left to her own devices. She again heard her Dad damn something for eternity. I'm glad Noah isn't here, she thought.

If you are an honest person, one who is not given to deceit, it is extremely difficult to lie effectively, especially to someone who is paying attention. It doesn't matter how hard you try to conceal whatever it is you want to hide; your behaviour changes and people with a certain kind of talent will notice and become curious, suspicious. Her grandfather had this finely tuned and rather unnerving talent of being able to detect the smallest variation in a person's normal routine or manner. Unlike Elle's parents, who were busy with their own thoughts, Noah would have noticed something was ever so slightly different about his granddaughter. Once his suspicion was aroused, he would have been compelled to investigate. And any investigation by him would have immediately revealed what it was she was trying to hide. What made it worse, if asked a direct question, Elle was completely incapable of lying, to anyone. Even a raised eyebrow was enough for Elle to confess every misdeed of the day. Considering how often her mischievousness led her into difficulty, this trait would seem to have been a near fatal flaw. However, Noah was not there and her parents were immersed in the running of the Farm, so she was free to prepare for her journey unmolested and undetected.

In the Dry, water was life; so water was her first priority. But water was also very heavy. With the weight of all the other 'stuff' she would be taking, 200 litres would be her limit; about four days' supply, five, maybe six, if she travelled mostly at night. A person could go up to two weeks without food but, in the wastelands, few lasted for more than a day without water. Horses fared no better, requiring each day ten times more than a human.

The Farm was not in want of water or water containers. Over the years, anything that could hold water was kept and stored. What she needed, though, were a few large containers that could be lifted without too much of a struggle when full, were easy to secure and that would not cause discomfort for the horses. They also had to be tough enough for the rigors of the journey, not breaking or leaking. Fortunately, she had just what was required, a bit of Before Time technology. She took down four shapeless leather swags from their pegs, old-world high-tech at its best. Each was lined with an impervious material that had the pliability of a soft plastic. Any liquid stored in it tasted as fresh as it did the day it went in, even months later. Better yet, they each held 30 litres when full, weighed 33 kilos, and, like a big floppy bladder, sat nicely across a horse's haunch. 33 kilos was just on the limit of what she could lift over her head. Now all she needed was to collect a number of smaller containers that would be easier to handle, drink from and use to fill the larger ones.

Next on her list was food for herself and fodder for the horses. Unlike water, most of the supplies she was about to take could not easily be replaced until the coming harvest. The cupboard had already been raided once. Along with a quantity of supplies meant for the 'binding' feast, the wedding party had taken enough provisions to see them and their horses to their destination and back. Reciprocity, good manners, custom, call it what you will, dictated they should not be a burden to their host. One should never invoke an obligation upon another without an equal or greater obligation offered in return. This 'custom' was now troubling Elle. Taking supplies for the eight weeks journey was theft. Rationalizing that the amount would be less than she would use if she stayed did not ease her sense of guilt. It was stealing. And to make it worse, it was stealing from her family. However, it was a guilt she'd bear until it was repaid. With that thought, she began selecting what she would be taking.

Unlike the wedding party, who had taken one of the Farm's two freight wagons, she couldn't possibly carry the supplies she needed for the journey with just two horses. She would have to rely on finding grazing for the horses and her skills as a hunter. Too bad they weren't carnivorous. They might occasionally go hungry, but they'd be unlikely to starve. She smiled at the thought of meat-eating horses and some of the possible consequences. Not one of your better ideas, Elle.

Not wanting to explain to her parents why she was standing in the middle of the garden with her arms full of vegetables, Elle snuck into the cool-store and took enough fresh food for the first four days. After that, what the heat hadn't ruined, the flies would have. She filled the packs with only those foods that could survive the Dry without spoiling. This meant a lot of dried or salted meats, beans, fruits and vegetables. While it was possible some of it could be eaten without cooking, it was not a good idea. Boiling water not only made the food edible, it also killed a lot of nasty things that would otherwise cause a great deal of unpleasantness. However, water had to be used prudently. Noah relentlessly harped on water preservation to the point that it was ingrained into every aspect of her way of life. "Even if you are standing up to your chin in it, he'd say, don't ever waste water. One day you might find that, in order to survive, you will have to drink your own pee." Grinning, he continued, "From experience, might I suggest to you do everything you can to avoid that necessity?" She packed salt. The body needed salt nearly as much as water. This was one of many things people had forgotten when the Dry first came and a number of lives were lost before that knowledge was regained. It had been her grandfather who pointed out that she might be made up of more than 60% water, but it was salty water, the same as a tear.

In the Before Times, tucked away safely and comfortably in their homes, many people were obsessed with the idea of being armed. According to Noah, "They were fat, paranoid and a bigger danger to themselves and their family than any intruder." Times had changed. No one was considered paranoid if they thought there were people out to kill them. There were. At any given moment, one could be fighting for their lives and those of their loved ones. This was true on the Farm, in the vastness of the wastelands and in any of the larger settlements.

All around the Farm, guns were strategically placed within easy access. Even the long-drop had a carbine with four full clips sitting next to what served as toilet paper. Figuring she might need all the fire power she could muster in addition to her own rifle, she added two handguns from the armoury located in the basement of the house, a short barrelled military type semi-automatic and several boxes of cartridges for each of the weapons.

To make sure that her theft would go undetected by her parents, Elle arranged the row of boxes to look just they had before. It would have been easier if she had taken what was needed from some of the less obscure storage places, but she wanted to avoid anyone asking questions about a missing firearm and its associated ammunition. Weapons were placed where they were for a reason and that reason still existed. She closed the door on the armoury and went over to the family 'vault'. There, she filled two small leather bags with gold coins. One thing that had not changed since the coming of the Dry was the value of this yellow metal in matters of payment for goods and services rendered. And people still killed for it.

Finished, she made her way upstairs to her bedroom without being seen. Even though it was unlikely anyone would enter her room without permission, she carefully shoved the bags of weapons, ammunition and gold well out of sight under her bed.

She would have liked to have taken Noah's most cherished weapon, but stealing it was not going to happen. Not just because of manners enforced by custom – you did not take the weapon of another. Even to ask was considered a serious breach of social etiquette. Now if it was offered, that was another story. But, she smiled to herself, it is one hell of a weapon. Even in the Before Times, long before the coming of the Dry, this particular rifle would have been exceedingly rare. According to her father, the rifle was able to kill at such a great distance that Noah needed to load the barrel with salt so the meat wouldn't spoil before he got to it. Elle could only manage a weak grin and a groan at the often repeated story of the weapon's lethal efficiency. With a scope, her rifle was accurate to about five hundred metres. Noah said that if he could see the target, he could hit it. "The greater the distance, the safer the shooter," was another of her grandfather's sayings and there had been times when this had proven true for him.

By the time she was called to come in for dinner, Elle was nearly ready. She just needed to finish packing some of her personal belongings, retrieve the weapons from under the bed, load the horses and go. She looked over at the sun. In another hour it would be dark. For once the sun and time had co-operated, as she had needed every minute given.

Dinner was pretty much the same fare as always. Variety had died along with so many other things that had been taken as given before the coming of the Dry. Other than the freshness of the garden vegetables and the culinary skills of her mother, it was not much different from what she had hidden in the barn and what would be her daily fare for the next two months. Later in the year, although most would be set aside for canning, there would be heaps of fresh fruit; but that was a month or more away. Something to look forward to when I get back, she thought.

Just as at lunch, everyone ignored the events at breakfast and treated Nora's outburst as if it had never taken place. The conversation at the kitchen table returned to normal, even if a bit restrained. Elle was surprised how hungry she was. Maybe carrying the guilt she felt on her shoulders all day was a lot of work, or maybe it was trying to keep a secret from her parents. Whatever it was, she was starving. With some assistance from her father, she made sure there would be no leftovers this time. Considering the embattled and hurried morning, it had been a good day. The repairs to the water supply had been successful, a good omen perhaps for Miner's Hat? The fields of grain and other crops, though small, were progressing nicely, promising a good yield later this year. A bountiful crop meant plenty of flour, which suggested fresh scones, pancakes and bread as well as pies and cakes. Elle could almost see her father salivate at the mere thought of his wife's baking. The garden was also coming along nicely. The recently installed drip system enabled better usage of the 'house' water. With a little luck, there should be a bit more to eat this winter than beans. The term 'with a little luck' was a ubiquitous phrase for them. Luck was often the only thing that separated the family from being alive or being dead.

Towards the end of the meal, that pleasant time when stomachs were full, Jacob began to speculate on just how far Noah and Chook had gotten. As it was unlikely they would travel without stopping, he felt they were probably at the Spencers' Graves.

The Spencers, according to the Traders' gossip, were from a settlement north-west of the Farm, more than three weeks away by horse. Some nine years ago, Noah and Jacob had discovered the family of eight clustered together under a large overhanging rock that had once shaded a pool of water fed by the creek that used to flow there. But it and the creek had dried up long ago. To the men looking down from their mounts, it first appeared as if the family had just sat down to wait for death. However, upon closer inspection, the men saw signs that the women and children had been killed, most likely by their men folk. Dying of thirst was very unpleasant. Not wishing to leave them exposed like they were, the pair dismounted and buried the family in shallow pits near where they lay. Perhaps, not knowing the area, the family had gotten lost, an easy thing to do out in these wastelands.

"A pity," Elle's father said between mouthfuls, "though it too has since gone dry, a clearly marked well bubbled away less than five hundred metres from where they sat." In the earlier years of the Dry, it was the realization that the rains were never going to return that drove people to commit suicide. Later it was those who had survived the horrors of the Sorrow and the Scavengers. Even now, visitors, if asked, confirmed that individuals, families and even small communities still found it easier to take their lives than to continue the struggle against the Dry. Thinking of her own family's determination to survive, Elle was incapable of understanding the depth of despair that drove parents to take the lives of their children before taking their own. It was not in her temperament to yield.

An hour before the moon reached its highest point in the sky, Elle lay awake in bed. She felt stillness encircle the house. The only sound was the soft tinkling of the chimes that hung on the back porch being disturbed by a passing breeze. Other than the lone 'night light' at the head of the stairs, the house lay in darkness. Exhausted from another day of labour, her parents were deep in sleep in their bedroom on the other side of the mezzanine. They were always tired. No matter had hard they worked, there was an endless list of jobs and seldom enough time to do them, even in depth of winter. The Farm did have electricity. A luxury that was derived from the slowly fading banks of photo electric skin panels on the roofs and an old diesel backup generator. The aging array of batteries stacked along the wall in the basement leading to the armoury and vault supplied the Farm with power and lights. And there were lanterns and a few hand-held sun-lights. But sun-lights didn't last long, lanterns burned precious fuel and lights used power that would be needed during the day. So unless something couldn't wait until morning, the family went to bed soon after the sun set and got up when it rose.

Although Elle often read for an hour or two by the weak light of a very small lamp, rising just before first light was a pattern she knew intimately. Through parted curtains she had been watching the moon rise, a near perfect orb of burnished silver. It would be full in two days. She slipped out of bed and stood up fully clothed save for her boots. She would slip these on once outside. Around the Farm she tended to wear the soft moccasins her father made for her and the family. They were plain, unadorned and shapeless. Functional was the word Jacob used to describe them. The boots had been a much sought-after gift from Noah a few months back. Like nearly everything she owned, the boots had once belonged to someone else. Sensing it was better if she did not inquire too closely as to their origin, she thanked him. It was best to keep such thoughts to herself as there were already too many ghosts. The boots appeared almost new, if a bit neglected. These were the first real boots she had ever owned, and she had spent hours in her room cleaning and polishing them.

"Leather's a living thing," her grandfather had warned, "and it needs lots of care to be kept supple."

They were a bit big but she was assured by one and all that she would grow into them.

She retrieved the weapons from their hiding place and took a knife from the wall next to her bed and strapped it to her waist. Modelled after an old frontiersman's hunting knife, the long broad blade with two serpents running down its thick span was made of something from the Before Time. Not metal, akin to glass perhaps or ceramic, it never required sharpening and was tougher than steel. The handle was made from an unidentified green material that could have been some kind of plastic but Noah wasn't so sure. The knife was over 70 years old, had lain in the wastelands for several decades, and yet no marks or sign of wear showed on the handle's smooth glossy surface. That was not all. When she had found the knife, the handle seemed to have been designed to fit a bigger hand. Now, it fitted her slender hand as if it were custom made. She gave the handle a reassuring pat and took no notice of the soft coloured ripples that emanated from her touch. And why should she? A good deal of the Before Time stuff made little or no sense to those of the Dry.

Opening the drawer of her bed table, she withdrew her most prized possession; a ring suspended from a braided thong. She'd placed it in the drawer after Noah left, thinking that she would leave it behind, but had a change of heart. The ring would be coming with her. Like the knife handle, no one had ever been able to identify the green stone or explain why it seemed to shimmer, even in a darkened room. And like the handle, everyone assumed that it was just another bit of lost technology from the Before Times. She slipped the looped thong over her head and felt the ring's weight and its coolness against her bare skin. The contact with her skin caused a near imperceptible disturbance, a shiver that danced along the surface of the stone. Both of these items had originally belonged to her great-great-grandmother, who had given them to Noah's father. Now they belonged to her. Every time she picked them up to wear she remembered how they came into her possession.

She'd been out hunting with her grandfather. After six days, their little excursion out in the wastelands was proving to be a disappointment. Travelling within the contours of the Knobblies, a cluster of rolling hills two days out from the Farm, they again found no spoors of animals larger than a rabbit and if they had wanted to hunt rabbits they could have done that by sitting in a chair near the house garden. One more day it was decided and, if they found nothing, they would head home. It was then that they stumbled across the bodies. The two men lay in the hollow of an old stream bed and appeared to be locked in a lover's embrace. Even now, after seventy years, it was not uncommon to find the dead like this out in the wastelands. Because of the lack of moisture in the air and the heat, bodies did not often putrefy, they desiccated. With so few predators, once robbed of their water, the dead, if left undisturbed, could end up as these two; mummified. By the type and state of their clothing they had been dead for a very long time, perhaps decades. They certainly had not been dressed for a lengthy stay in the desert.

"Scavengers or townies?" asked Elle.

"Not sure. They aren't dressed like Scavengers or like us, so I guess they were most likely townies," replied Noah. The emphasis placed on the world Scavenger did not go unnoticed by Elle. Just saying that word made him look as if he had tasted something foul and unclean.

While Noah kept watch, Elle dismounted to inspect the bodies. Survivors of the Dry seldom lost an opportunity for recovering spoils, even from the dead. Elle knelt beside them, giving no more thought to the task than one would turning over a stone. Her first impression was that neither man had much in the way of value, certainly nothing obviously worth dying for. But it wasn't difficult to guess how they died: both had long bladed knives embedded deep into their respective chests. Inflicting each other with those kinds of wounds, both of them would have bled out quickly, dying within a minute or two. Using primarily her left hand, she pulled the bodies apart and a cloud of fine dust rose up followed by a musty odour from the separated carcasses. The dust particles irritated her nose, which provoked a series of violent sneezes. She stood up to get away from the dust and tried to suppress another round of sneezing with little success. Pulling off the kerchief from around her neck, Elle wiped her nose.

A wide grin spread across Noah's face. "Need any help?" he asked, his grin visibly increasing in size.

"Nope!" came a rather clipped reply. Not wishing to start another sneezing attack, she covered her nose with the kerchief and kicked at the intertwined corpses until they fell apart. With the two skeletal remains more or less separated, Elle, with her nose still covered, knelt down again for a better look.

One of the weapons was a common kitchen knife, not of any real value but she would keep it anyway. The other knife was something different altogether. Grasping the handle, she gave it a sharp twist as she pulled it from the desiccated body. It was heavy, the rear and front bolster had to be made of gold, and very well balanced. She knew knives and this was a thing of rare beauty. In the right hands, it would also be deadly. It had been made by a master of the craft. She placed the knife carefully beside her on the ground and then reached over to retrieve the kitchen knife. It was firmly wedged between a set of ribs, requiring Elle to yank the handle up and down a couple of times before she was able to wrench the blade free. As she did this, something caught the light as it rolled out from under the mummified remains, coming to a stop near the toe of her moccasin.

It was a ring. She picked it up and gave it a wipe with her kerchief. The thing was massive, big enough to fit Noah's finger, and judging by its weight, like the bolster on the knife, it must have been made of solid gold. Two snakes formed the circle with a curious looking stone held by their gaping mouths. She turned and held it for Noah to see. It had to be the gaudiest piece of jewellery Elle had ever seen. Even so, gaudy or not, the presence of the ring and the knife certainly made the deaths understandable. Despite their tawdry appearances, the expertise of craftsmen involved was unmistakeable. Noah leaned down and beckoned to his granddaughter. She placed the ring and the knife into his waiting open hand. To Elle, the knife and ring were treasures from the Before Times. To her grandfather, they were much, much more, for he had recognized them and knew both their origin and their history.

Straightening up, he examined both carefully. There was no mistaking them. They had once belonged to his father, a 'mock' wedding gift from his mother's parents. The items had been with his father when he and a family friend vanished while away on a foraging trip. No traces of either of them or their bus were ever found. As now, it was a violent time, and abductions, hijackings, and murders were endemic. No one and nowhere were safe. Back then, even the Farm came under attack.

Noah dismounted to stand by his granddaughter. Looking at the scattered remains of the two men, it seemed reasonable to Noah that one, maybe even both of these men, had taken part in his father's death.

"How do you know they are not your dad and his friend?" asked Elle, unaware of the implications of that question.

Noah showed no irritation in his reply. "Elle, use your brain. You've seen photos of my dad. He was taller than me and I don't think either of these men would have reached my shoulders. As to the other being his friend, it's highly unlikely." A sad smile appeared as the image of him and his parents standing there together in front of the bus flickered briefly in his mind. In a wistful voice filled with regret, he said, "He was very tall man. My mother's nickname for him was 'Treetop Lover'." He kicked one of the heads hard enough to have it disintegrate into several pieces. With contempt in his voice he said, "Neither of these men was my dad's friend."

Not for the last time, Noah found himself musing on the circumstances surrounding a person's death out in the wastelands. But if these two were the ones responsible, how nicely ironic, he thought, and so appropriate; murderers, murdered by their own hand. Then loud enough for Elle to hear, "It could almost make you believe in a just world. Almost… but not quite."

He put an arm around Elle and returned the ring and knife to her. "Supposedly they were made by my grandmother's twin sister, Scout. She gave them to my grandmother shortly before the Dry began. If I remember correctly, my grandmother said that Scout referred to them as 'The Inseparable Twins', but I have no idea why. I don't think anyone did, not even my grandmother. Be that as it may, since I don't like wearing rings and I already have a good knife, you keep them. Who knows, considering the improbability of such a find, maybe you're the one they were meant for. After all, you're a twin just like my grandmother." As soon as those words were out of his mouth he wished he was able to claw them back. Elle looked at him with those eyes of hers. Drawing in a deep breath, he squeezed her shoulder and remounted Blue. Looking down he said, "Sorry Elle."

She'd shrugged. "It's all right Granddad, no harm intended, no harm done." She had no memory of her sister and even when asked, the family avoided talking about her. Why, Elle did not know.

In the hallway, she temporarily deactivated the Farm's security alarm, giving herself ninety minutes before it rearmed itself. Then she grabbed her hat from the peg before heading outside. Closing the door with exaggerated care, she turned and stepped out into a yard draped with the soft light of a nearly full moon. Stopping to slip on her boots as quickly and quietly as possible, she started toward the barn. Not a sound accompanied her. Other than the omnipresent buzzing and chirps of the night's insects, the yard was deadly silent. They had had a dog once, but it had died when she was seven. Teddy would have barked as he had done every time she tried to sneak out of the house at night, waking the whole family. He was silent now, buried beside her 'thinking' log.

In the barn, Elle greeted and then hurriedly saddled her horse. This was going to be a long hard journey. Leaving little to chance, she had divided everything into two nearly equal piles earlier in the day. This would ensure that, in the event one animal was lost along with its cargo, the other would still be carrying a portion of all that was necessary. Knowing there would be little room for her for a few days, Elle placed the provisions, water and feed from the smaller of the two piles, as well as the extra weapons and ammunition, carefully onto her horse, ensuring the load was evenly distributed. It was important that the loads were also comfortable to carry.

Like most of the things she valued, the horse had been a gift from her grandfather upon his return after a year's absence. Though Elle was too young to remember, she had heard her father tell the story so often it seemed as if she did. She had been playing on the front porch when this massive man rode into the yard leading a young filly. Without a word this strange man climbed down from his mount and, taking her into his arms, lifted Elle up and onto the young horse's back. Once the man was sure the little girl was unlikely to fall off, he said, in that now familiar deep voice, "You both were born on the same day and in the same year, so I think it's fitting that you two belong together. Happy birthday, Elle." They had never been separated since. No one but Elle could ride her and Elle would ride no other. The mare had grown into a stout, barrel-chested, surefooted, loyal consort and according to her grandfather the ugliest mount he had ever seen, hence her name – "Bellita", little beauty, shortened to Belle by Elle and the family.

Nearly finished with readying Belle, she slipped one of the bags of gold coins and a few well-chosen books into a pocket of the saddle bag that straddled the animal's backside. "Never leave the Farm without a few books and a bit of gold," was a family axiom and as axioms go, the family had found this one useful. Elle

63

next turned her attention to the horse in the adjacent stall. Buck, a chestnut gelding, had all the attributes one looked for in a farm horse. He was as big as Blue, strong, reliable, hard-working, and often doubled as a pack horse during their forays in the wastelands. Although not very bright, Buck was one of the Farm's draft horses. Expensive to keep, they were nevertheless essential for the running of the Farm. But since planting was all done and the harvest was a couple of months away, his presence wouldn't be missed in the day-to-day running of the Farm. She retrieved an old, much abused, pack saddle from the tack room. There were others hanging there that were newer and in better shape, but this one had special meaning. It had been made by her grandfather shortly after he arrived to live on the farm and was as familiar to her as was Belle. The number of times she had helped Noah load it up for trips to the wastelands was countless. Now that she was going on her own, she got comfort from the thought that this particular piece of history would accompany her.

Buck stood patiently as Elle struggled, first with the pack saddle and then with the remainder of the provisions, water, feed, a couple of books and the remaining bag of gold. It amazed her how Buck's additional height made the work of loading that much harder. She was already bushed and hadn't even left the barn.

Within an hour Elle was ready. A rifle in one hand, Belle's reins in the other and Buck's lead tied to Belle's tail, she started toward the barn doors. Her parents' horses, the last on the Farm, snorted and moved uneasily as the small party departed. The occupants of the house slept undisturbed. The moon's strong light coated the grounds outside in soft greys as three long, ghostly shadows moved across the yard. Elle stopped at the gate to look back on the only home she had ever known. She turned and took the first step. Better get going, she thought. Over two thousand kilometres there and back.

Chapter Four

Without water there is no life

For this enterprise to be successful Elle needed a lot of luck, and everyone, especially Noah, had to play the parts she had given them. If they did, she might have a five day head start before they figured out where she was headed and came after her. By then it would be too late. In the wastelands, not even Noah would be able to catch up with her. Five days would ensure that she avoided the humiliation of being dragged back to the Farm like some spoiled, wayward child. It would bad enough facing her parents. Her cousins? A shiver ran the full length of her back at the thought of what they would have to say about an aborted attempt to reach the mountains. Whatever it took, she vowed, her cousins could never be given that opportunity.

To help ensure she got the five days she needed, Elle would not take the safest route westward, the highway just north of the Farm. Her plan was far riskier. She would head for The Maiden Springs. A difficult ride over open, rugged terrain, it normally took a good four days from the Farm, but she would need to do it in less than that. From there, once the horses were watered and had a chance to feed on the surrounding grass, she would turn west toward Red Rim Springs, another two days further on. After that, the countryside would be a lot easier for her and the horses. A short distance from the springs was a paved road that eventually met with the highway that led to the mountains. There was one major drawback with this plan – the distance. Should both springs prove to be dry, she would have lost the gamble. Even if she was able to reach another water source, it would be at the cost of at least one of the horses, possibly both. There was water for four days, six if she stretched it. In the heat of the Dry, a horse needed a minimum of twenty litres of water per day. A human, if very careful, could get by on less than four.

"What is the matter with you?" she muttered. "We haven't been on the road for more than an hour and already you've got us all dying of thirst. You're pathetic." She grinned. "Yeah, I am." Elle shook herself free of all the 'what-ifs', and quickened her pace. "The future," as Noah said, "belongs to no one." It was just over five hours before the moon would set and a bit more than seven hours before the sun would rise. In that in-between time, the wastelands, even with its canopy of stars, was a very dark place to be. To play it safe, she would stop and wait for the sun to reappear. And when it did, her parents would go into her room and find that she was gone. Elle wanted to be more than forty kilometres from home by then. Even though the contents of the letter left on the bed gave no indication of where she was headed, they would know.

As long as there was moonlight Elle had no intention of stopping to rest. For four hours she and her companions trekked across the wastelands. On a small mound surrounding a shallow basin, she paused and, not for the first time, wished she was sitting on Belle and not walking beside her. The moon hovered near the horizon. Taking the opportunity before it got too dark, Elle gave each of the horses a drink. In doing so, she looked back over the direction they'd come. Elle had never experienced a large body of water. Most sources she was familiar with were deep wells accessible only by a rope and bucket. Of the springs, the biggest she'd ever seen was no more than a couple of dozen metres across and maybe two in depth. Others were no bigger than a wash tub, while some were nothing more than a small ribbon of water. So the moon's light falling across the landscape did not give her the impression that she stood in the middle of a shimmering lake as it might have to those of the Before Times. Even though a lake had existed there once, a hundred years ago, the scene around her conjured up nothing other than what it was, the wastelands awash with the fading moonlight. The only water in this basin now was strapped to the backs of these horses standing patiently beside her.

The heat of the previous day radiated from the surrounding rocks and soil, ensuring the night was little better than the day. Hatless, wearing a faded sleeveless singlet, a pair of oversized men's shorts, boots to mid-calf, a knife at her waist, a rifle slung across her shoulder and a ring suspended by a cord around her neck, Elle stood stock still, letting the pitifully weak breeze play across her exposed skin. It brought only the slightest relief. The singlet showed the exertion of the last few hours; under her arms and down her back were dried patches of encrusted salt. The air was so devoid of moisture sweat evaporated almost instantly. Except during the winter nights, clothes were seldom worn for warmth and the need for modesty was unknown to Elle. They were worn for protection, protection from the sun, protection from a hostile wastelands, protection from the insects. Even naturally dark skinned people avoided, as much as possible, being out in the open without adequate protection. But right now, that problem was a few more hours away. In another hour the moon would disappear, leaving her in the dark. Before then she wanted to find a place to stop until sunrise. During that time they'd all get some rest, have something to eat and drink. She might even be able to grab a bit of shuteye.

Deciding that she was wasting time, Elle pulled on the horse's reins, descended the mound and minutes later had left the dead lake behind. Her imagination seemed inordinately active tonight. It was not as if she had never wandered the wastelands in the dark before but, for reasons of its own, her mind was busy constructing potential dangers that lingered in wait within every shadow and behind every rock formation. Suddenly Elle burst out laughing. She'd just realized she had been gripping the rifle strap so tightly that her hand was growing numb. The unexpected noise startled the horses, causing them to dance around a bit. All thoughts of hidden danger evaporated as she attempted to calm and reassure them that there was nothing to be concerned about. Once she regained control, Elle reached out to stroke Belle's muzzle. The horse's warm breath on her extended hand was comforting and eased a bit of the tension that had been building up unnoticed. She looked around again, "What am I doing out here, Belle? Am I crazy?" Her mother's face came into her mind. "My Mom is going to kill me."

It was now getting dark as only the wastelands can. Noah had told her of people who had gone mad out here. "Keeping one's own company is not something most folks care for or are equipped to do," he had said. "We're no different than horses in that respect. They and we crave companionship, family. Those that don't are a danger to everyone. They go rogue and end up killing themselves or others."

Elle had not been not convinced. "You spend a lot of time out here alone and you're not mad or rogue."

"Oh I wouldn't be so sure about that, Elle," was Noah's response. Grinning at her puzzled expression he continued. "I sometimes suspect being a bit mad and paranoid kind of helps, because it's not a good idea to become too comfortable or too complacent. To do that and then start thinking you're alone out here, that mistake could be fatal. The wastelands are never as empty as they look."

Suddenly the phrase from an old tattered magazine she'd once read popped into her head. 'The fact that I'm paranoid doesn't mean there aren't people plotting to kill me.' "Now where did that come from?" said Elle to her two rather puzzled companions. "Maybe I'm a little mad as well, but I'm not alone, am I?" She gave each of the animals a reassuring pat.

Sunrise found Elle and her horses resting in the shadow of a small ridge. In the dark, the animals had been relieved of their packs, watered, fed and brushed clean of salt, sweat and dust before Elle attended to her own needs. Noah would be proud. The meal of fresh bread folded around a slice of some meat was eaten with the single-mindedness of the famished. Finished, she took a swig from her canteen and laid down on her bedroll where she soon fell asleep.

Later, fully awake and feeling the results of walking all night, Elle rubbed her sore feet. She loved the boots, but they were not designed to walk in for any great distance. The moccasins, on the other hand, with their double layer soles, were. Discounting her little kip, Elle had been awake for a full day and night and on the move since leaving the Farm. What she wanted was nothing more than to lie right back down and get a bit more sleep. That wasn't going to happen. These first few days were critical, so sleep would have to wait.

Patting her beloved boots, Elle stored them away, along with her shorts and singlet, and retrieved her moccasins, pants and a long sleeve shirt. Dressed, it was time to go as the sun was already eroding what shade they had and there was a lot more ground to cover before the heat of midday drove them to find some shelter. Luckily, Elle had travelled this way several times before and knew a good place to stop. And once there she just might, while waiting for heat of the day to pass, find the time for a nap. Until then, there were quite a few kilometres of walking before they reached Ash Valley.

The building sat on a barren knob of rocky ground surrounded by and separated from the rest of the lakefront properties by a crumbling parking lot. Noah had told her that it was this isolation that probably saved it from the fire that swept through here decades ago. Elle was unimpressed. Even in its prime, the building would not have been much to look at. Circled by a concrete patio, the featureless cinderblock and tile structure once provided its patrons with changing rooms, toilets, a snack bar and a view of what had been a lake. For the newly arrived, the building would now provide a temporary shelter from the sun. Elle stepped up on the patio and peered inside. It was as she remembered from her last visit. Except for the damage inflicted by time and a wandering vandal or two, it was in rather good condition – quite remarkable, considering the desolation and destruction that surrounded it.

Why is it, when sleep is wanted most, it doesn't easily come. Crumpled, grimy and moody, Elle rested on her bedroll, watching the sun's light inch its way slowly across the far wall. A few discarded pages of Before Time newsprint lay beside her. One benefit of the absence of rain was that it ensured even the frail things like newspapers could survive, even after all this time. It was not unusual to find a newspaper, or at least some of its pages, strewn across the floor in an abandoned building like this. Sometimes you'd find a pile stacked in a corner or boxed up, waiting perhaps for the recycling truck that never came. She'd read a bit earlier, before trying to get some sleep, but found nothing of interest other than a rather superficial article about the rising acid levels in the oceans and the effect they 'might' have on the dwindling fish stock. One of Noah's stories of his travel in the bus concerned the abandoned fishing fleets, rusting hulks, moored and forgotten alongside equally abandoned and forgotten wharfs. According to him and some books she'd read from the Before Times, the world's oceans' ecosystems were in dire straits well before the coming of the Dry. There were lots of jellyfish it seemed, but little else. She tucked her hands behind her head and wondered if there were any whales left.

With the demise of the worldwide communication networks, printing presses of sorts had had a revival in the various settlements, providing their population with an abridged form of a newspaper. Once in a while one of them, having passed through any number of hands, would find its way westward and show up on the Farm. The newspapers of the Dry were noticeably different from their Before Time predecessors. The print paper was of very poor quality; they contained no more than a dozen printed pages, had little advertisement and fewer photos, none of which were in colour, and covered mostly local news with a few items from further afield, often unfounded speculation, according to Noah. Elle was amused at how the subject matter remained much the same, as if the Dry had never happened. Maybe people were more interested in crime, personal tragedies and the seedier side of politics, than in, as her mother believed, more 'weighty' subjects.

Finally giving up on getting any real sleep, she stood up. Time to get on the road again.

She emerged from the building, leading the horses from its dilapidated interior. The nap, what there was of it, had done little to refresh her. Outside, the sun's glare from the concrete momentarily blinded her and caused her to collide with the metal barrier separating the grounds of the kiosk from the parking area. An involuntary yelp escaped from Elle's lips as she squatted on the ground to vigorously rub the injured shin. The edge of the barrier had cut through the pants' leg and into her skin below the right knee. "Damn, damn damn," she muttered, getting back up to sit on the offending barrier. "These first few days are critical and here I am, not a full day from home, and I have already managed to nearly cripple myself." With the pants' leg pulled up she probed the damaged area with a finger, a tiny cut oozing an equally tiny amount of blood. It wasn't going to cripple her but the bang on the shin was going to leave a very nice bruise. "I've had worse," she said, remembering the numerous injuries she'd inflicted on herself over the years. She continued to sit on the rail to let the throbbing subside a bit more. Raising her hand to shield her eyes, she looked out over a land the colour of grey ash that stretched in every direction to the horizon.

The sun was past its high mark but any real relief was hours away. The horses followed Elle down the knob, through the car park and onto the road. Caught by gusts of wind, whirls of the grey ash chased after them. Fire, heat and wind, the Dry's ubiquitous holocaust, created the wastelands. Without water, fire cannot be contained. Driven by ferocious winds, fire devoured everything; forcing people to flee their cities, their towns, their homes and farms. As the effects of the Dry entrenched itself in the very fabric of the land, there were times the whole world seemed to be in flames. Even now the effects of its rampage were evident everywhere. The Dry, this merciless Dry, was still defined by fire and water, too much of the one, never enough of the other.

On the crest of hill, just clear of Ash Valley, Elle stopped for a moment to look back at the small dot that was the cinder block shelter before continuing along the road that headed in the general direction of The Maiden. The land in the Before Times had been divided, partitioned, blocked off by a dizzying array of fences. Stone, brick, steel, timber and hedge – all were used to define the boundaries of both the rich and the poor. The fires, time and mayhem had found ways to remove them. Freed of ownership, the land was open again. A traveller could go where they would without fear of encountering a single fence or locked gate. But what a price had been extracted for this privilege, this convenience. A journey across the open wastelands might be unhindered by either fences or locked gates but the Dry had made sure that it was arduous and time consuming. And yet, there were those who sought the wastelands' harsh unrestricted emptiness in exchange for anonymity. Some travellers craved the assurance that they would pass unobserved. Roads, highways, came into being without fences or gates. They were designed for swift and unhindered travel. However, unlike the open wastelands, their paths were fixed. Weighing her options, speed versus obscurity, she chose the road. Though fragmented, broken, and encumbered by sand and debris it remained the easiest and quickest means of traversing from one point to another. Pursuit would come from the east when it came and then only when they knew what path she had taken. Until then, to best use the time she had, the roads were the best choice. She swung west.

The fire that consumed Ash Valley had raced along the lands on both sides of the road but not as intensely. Surprisingly there were areas it had missed altogether. Not that it mattered; the only difference was that, instead of charred stumps, there were skeletal remains of dead trees. Unlike the valley with its lake, this part of the road meandered through what had been rich fertile farm land, although, looking around, there was little in the way of visible evidence to say this was so. Years before the Dry, the lands here were being devastated by drought. By the time the fires came, there was little left to feed upon. Now the empty land stretched out before her, all the way to the horizon, with only the occasional ruin or the bleached corpse of a dead tree to disrupt the dull monotony. And it was dull. An abandoned city was different. They were filled with all kinds of interesting things. Here, there was nothing to look at, nothing to tease her curiosity. This sterile landscape was proving to be not just boring but mind numbingly so. And the heat not only beat down upon the trio, it rose from the asphalt, penetrating the soles of her moccasins and playing havoc with the horse's unshod hooves, forcing them to walk along the uneven shoulder of the road as they had done since early morning. Only when the surface cooled late in the day would they move back on. The salt flies, the midges and the dust mites milled around her and the horses, making a nuisance of themselves, making her wish that a strong breeze would spring up and flush them away. Then there would only be the dust kicked by her and the horses and the wind to contend with.

All this inconvenience stemmed from the need to be on the move. Under normal circumstances in the wastelands, you'd find a nice shady place well out of the sun and not venture out again for the next three hours. This was hard on her and on the animals but she promised herself that she'd make it up to them later tonight after the moon had set. A town, not a very big one, was just over the shallow hills that lay in front of her. She had been through there several times with Noah and so knew it well enough to find a place to stop before nightfall. They could make camp there for a couple of hours or so before setting out again.

This was the closest town west of the Farm and yet her grandfather always rode straight through without stopping. Why, he never said, and she never asked. She understood him well enough to know that some things remained private and personal.

Along with a few looted vehicles, dead trees lined the highway on either side and marked the beginning of the town. Soon buildings began to appear, hugging tightly to the roadside. If you disregarded the broken windows, absent doors and the general sense of abandonment, a few of the buildings had survived pretty much as their owners had left them. Others, however, appeared shattered, as if an explosion had blown away the outer walls allowing the collapsing roofs to fall on the debris below. Some stood like skeletons with nothing left but the frames. Most were nothing more than tangled rubble, a single vertical slab of concrete, a steel support or prefabricated column. The town and its buildings were of little interest to Elle. In small towns like this one, it was highly probable that nothing of value remained. They were usually emptied long before she was born. And even if there was the odd trinket, she had neither the time nor the desire to linger in the town longer than necessary.

Even if she did not know why her grandfather avoided stopping here, there was the heightened risk of harm associated with built up areas, especially if you were on your own, and Elle had a problem with 'sleeping with the dead'. It was one of her rules, maybe not an unbreakable one but a rule nevertheless. Unlike the open wastelands, town and cities were notorious for their ability to hide their dead and so, if possible, she'd avoided camping in places where there were obvious signs of death. Not that death was unfamiliar. Nor was she concerned about the likes of spirits, ghosts or gods. Aside from last night's momentary discomfort, she knew such things did not and could not exist. But she also knew that some people needed to believe in such things, for the world was a cold and pitiless place with an endless array of devices at its disposal to bring pain and death. Believing in ghosts might help somehow, but she had no idea how. Maybe those who still believed that there was a broader purpose to life needed the idea of an afterlife of some kind. For Elle and her family, the Dry had brought with it an end to such beliefs. Not wanting to lie with the dead was, then, more of a personal preference than some sort of superstition or phobia. "Let the dead lie with the dead but not with me," was her motto.

The moon made its appearance along the edge of a cloudless, bright blue sky. One more night and you'll be full, thought Elle. When very young, she had seldom missed the opportunity to sit with her mother on the thinking log to watch the full moon rise. It was their special time, a private thing between mother and daughter. When or why they'd stopped, she couldn't really remember, but she guessed that her frequent trips into the wastelands with her grandfather had broken the rhythm. Miss one or two, why not three or four? Why that particular fragment of memory had suddenly come into her head puzzled Elle. Along with the memory came the thought that her mother might have been hurt by Elle's breaking their private time without so much as a word of regret. Funny, she had completely forgotten about that routine of theirs.

In the remaining light Elle started to look for a place to camp. Bone tired, the last thing she needed or wanted was to be caught in the open fumbling around in the dark. It had been a long, long day, proceeded by an equally long night. She couldn't remember the last time she'd been this weary. Not counting her two previous failed attempts to grab a bit of sleep, she had been awake now since yesterday morning, about 36 hours. She looked back at Belle, "Of course, I'm not riding. I'm walking, aren't I, old girl?" What she needed was some food, hot food, and some sleep. She'd make sure that she got the hot meal but the only sleep she'd be getting tonight was that little wedge of time between moonset and sunrise. With the sun a finger's thickness from the horizon and the town a couple of kilometres back, a road branched off the main highway. A house, a single dwelling, could be seen at the end of a twisting driveway sitting on the side of a hill. "Bet it had a great view in the Before Times." Since Elle judged it was not that far off and it was elevated, with unrestricted views, and stood alone, it was worth a look. Twenty minutes later, standing in front of what must have been a very impressive house in its time, Elle felt relieved. It was just what she needed.

She manoeuvred the horses up the sloping driveway and into the house, coming to a halt in what had been the main living room. The last of the daylight spilled through the vacant windows into the room, giving it a golden hue. This was Elle's favourite time; for a few short minutes the whole world lost its harshness and became soft and bathed in warm honey. It was beautiful. While exploring the rest of the ground floor to make sure it was secure, she watched the sky darken and thought how nice it would be if that soft golden light could stay this way a little longer. But her grandfather had said that much of its beauty was in its brevity. "Otherwise our senses become dulled and we stop seeing." Elle was never sure if it was only the late evening's light he was referring to.

Large enough to suit her purposes, the room, like the rest of the house, was gutted, picked clean. On the far side, the wall with the view had been nearly torn away leaving nothing but open space. She walked over to the room's edge to look down into the front yard. There, off to the right, down a flight of flagstones and surrounded by a rusting, shoulder-high fence, was what remained of a swimming pool. A pleasurable shiver ran down the length of her spine. Imagining its purpose was more than Elle's life experience could grasp. It was just incomprehensible. All the water it once contained was there just so people could take a swim or splash about and nothing else. Ideal! thought Elle, as a host of images cascaded through her mind's eye. Yep, ideal. She jerked herself loose from her thoughts of the people playing around a pool filled to overflowing with cool, clear fresh water. But this is not getting you guys out of your gear is it? Years of training ensured removing the horses' packs, cleaning the sweat from their backs, getting them watered and fed was done with the least amount of effort and time. The same efficiencies were applied to her own needs. With the last threads of the light fading into black and the moon high overhead, Elle sat in front of the house's crumbling hearth encouraging the beginnings of a fire with a few slender offerings. Once it got going, she shielded the light of the fire with a blanket.

Despite her previous failed attempts, after a big mug of bush tea and a hot camp stew eaten from a battered pot, Elle was asleep, full and content with her first day. Normally a very light sleeper and easily woken, the recent combined effects of stress, sleep deprivation, a full stomach and physical fatigue plunged Elle into a deep dream-filled sleep.

Arched across the sky a star-speckled ribbon of silver rippled as if caught by a gust of wind. From beneath a sea of silvery liquid light, she fought for breath and the surface. Elle struggled to wake. So deep, so absorbed within her dream, only the restless movements of the horses finally caused her to wake up. For several minutes Elle lay confused, disoriented. She sat up but it took some time before she could focus her thoughts and eyes. The fire was out, the sun was long gone and the moon was high overhead.

"Bloody hell, what's the matter with me?" muttered Elle as she tried standing on unresponsive legs. "I've way overslept." A quick glance at the moon's position informed her that at least three hours had passed since sunset. She'd slept more than planned and had lost time she could ill afford. It did not matter to her that the best training in the world could not prevent an exhausted young body from demanding sleep. What Elle had wanted and what her body had needed had been at odds.

Using the light of the moon, she watered the horses. Leaving their feed bags in place, she ate the rest of the stew cold from the pot. Licking the last morsel from the spoon, Elle felt anger whelm up inside her. "Bloody hell!" she said again, "How could I have been so stupid? I can't afford to lose this much time." Fortunately the moonlight was even better than having a lantern. It made getting the horses ready a lot easier. If she had slept much longer, she'd have been loading up in the dark because it was risky just having a fire. Walking around with a lantern was out of the question. Out in the wastelands, any light could be seen for kilometres and there were things other than her grandfather that she needed to hide from.

She worked methodically, making herself slow down as she lifted the packs into place, checking the binding straps and ensuring the loads on each horse were secure and evenly distributed. There was not yet room for her to ride but by tomorrow two days' worth of water would have been consumed, allowing her space, an anticipated joy. Any horseman worthy of the name found no pleasure in walking. Ready for the last bundle, Elle went over to retrieve it when a glimmer of light caught her attention. From a corner of the room amongst a pile of debris where she'd stored her gear, something was reflecting the moon's light. Elle stopped and went over to investigate, expecting nothing more than a shard of glass. Reaching down to shift bits of refuse away, Elle exposed an intact picture frame. She couldn't tell whether it was a real photograph or a frozen image on a PSim. It was too dark to see clearly so, saving it for later, she stuffed the frame into the remaining bag before hoisting it onto Buck. "Done. Now let's get out of here before we waste any more time," said Elle to the two non-verbal members of her party.

Out of the house and into the night, almost breaking into a run, they hurried down the driveway to the road leading out of town. The time lost in sleep was only half regretted. Unlike a few hours before, there was definitely a spring in her step giving her confidence that the lost time would be made up. Even the horses seemed to have benefited from the extra hour of rest.

By midnight they'd reached the junction that would lead to The Maiden. Turning left, they were again heading southwest. It was going to be another long night for all of them. No stopping until the moon set and it got too dark to see. Then, as soon as there was enough light to avoid running into something, they would be off again and wouldn't stop until noon. They'd rest for no more than two hours and, despite the heat, set off again. The time she'd slept away had to be made up and not just to get as far from the Farm as possible. Under the best of circumstances four days in the wastelands was hard on both animal and human. They would all need a good long rest by the time they reached The Maiden. By extending their marching they'd not only make up the lost time but gain a bit as well. Being on schedule or a bit ahead was vital. She did not want to cut short their time at The Maiden because there was all the water they could drink, grass for the horses and a shady tree for her to sleep under. That is, if the springs still ran clear.

Chapter Five

Few of life's plans proceed as envisioned.

Elle kept her resolution. That night and for the next two days, she followed a punishing routine. Keep on the move from sunset to moonset; find a place to camp, care for the horses, then, if it was possible, build a fire that was undetectable to the outside world, treat herself to a hot meal, and grab what sleep she could. In the grey light of predawn, load up and go till the sun's heat drove them to cover. Once in the shade, the same routine was followed. Two hours past midday, the threesome would set out again. The only alteration to the routine came on the morning of the third day. Enough water and provisions had been consumed by then to allow Elle room to ride. However, in order to save her horses, the pace she wanted to maintain meant she spent as much time walking at their side as she did riding Belle.

On a whim and as a means to save some time, Elle veered onto a gravelled road that took her further south than the previous times she'd been this way with Noah. This was new territory, a part of the country she had never seen, not that it mattered. The wastelands did not have much scenic variation. Astride Belle, Elle and her companions made their way down the road that wound through a grove of dead trees. Bleached white, they had once formed a green, leafy shield around an abandoned fishing cottage and boatshed. The canopy was long gone;

sun's light poured through their bare branches unabated. The sight of the cottage was welcome. It's late enough in the day and I'm not likely to find better; we'll camp here, thought Elle as she ran a knowledgeable eye over the place. The cottage itself was ruled out as too confining, but the boatshed would be fine.

The shed sat on high piles over a river that no longer existed. Checking to be sure the floor was sound, Elle led the horses in and stripped, cleaned, watered and fed them. She left the entrance doors wide open and then proceeded to do the same with doors that faced the empty river bed. Just as she didn't think her preference for not sleeping with the dead was superstitious, Elle did not consider herself claustrophobic. It was a preference, that's all. It just felt more comfortable with the doors open. Besides, she'd close them come nightfall, a little more than an hour away. Before then, there were things that needed doing.

Little in Elle's life helped her to comprehend how beautiful this place had once been or the joy and pleasures it had brought its owners. Their memories were of long tranquil summers spent along a slow flowing, fish-rich river, fed by the melting snows from the northern mountains. True, the summers were hotter, the winters milder and they had not been ignorant of the difficulties elsewhere, but here there were still fish to catch, berries to pick, wild animals to watch, shaded areas in which to sit, and a river to swim in. Elle had no such memories. The Dry, the wastelands, a sweltering sky were her world. To the ever practical Elle, this cottage, this shed would be only a memory of a place to rest while keeping out of the sun. However, should she wish, she would recall every aspect of it. Like her grandfather, Elle had a unique genetic quirk that enabled her to retain the smallest detail of nearly everything that she had seen or experienced. Her mother claimed that Elle remembered everything and forgot nothing, except when it came to her chores. Elle smiled, she could picture her mother with that look of frustration at how easily her daughter could be distracted from her assigned tasks.

The horses cared for and the first real meal of the day just coming to a simmer over the open fire, Elle sat at the end of the boat ramp with her feet dangling in the air. Her mind wandered, leaping from one thought to another, presenting a whole cavalcade of images of family, the Farm, the wastelands. She found herself missing Noah, her parents and even her cousins. If there was any good that came from the coming of the Dry, it had to be the strength people found in family and friends. For many, scattered and isolated, it was virtually the only human contact and companionship they would have for months at a time.

A bird was singing somewhere off to her left. She smiled. Her dad had almost ruined her enjoyment of listening to birds calling out by explaining, "they sing to attract a female and warn all males 'go away, this place is mine'." Well this place might be his but there was a bit of wildlife about. Marks in the soil told her of hunters and prey. This had to mean a source of water was somewhere hereabouts, even if only a trickle. She stored that information away for future reference.

Suddenly Elle recalled the object she'd taken from the house two days ago. Jumping up, she went over to the packs, located the one she wanted and opened it. After fossicking around, she withdrew the picture frame. A little worse for wear and covered in dust and grime that obscured the image, there was no doubt the frame held a real photo like the ones in the albums back home. Amazingly the glass was not broken and the contents it protected appeared undamaged. She spat on the glass and with the hem of her shirt wrapped around a finger, began removing years of filth. There was so much accumulated dirt, however, that her efforts just ended up smearing mud about the glass surface. She freed her finger, reached back into the bag and removed a folded length of cloth. Then, after dripping water from the canteen on the cloth, she began again.

She smelled something burning. "Damn!" Putting the partly cleaned picture frame down, an annoyed Elle rushed over to a very smoky pot in an attempt to save her dinner. The stew was not completely ruined, but it was a waste of fresh vegetables. Later, after eating the remains of her burnt offerings, Elle retrieved the picture and again sat down, facing out into the river bed, and continued to wipe the glass. After a few minutes, her efforts were rewarded. Though slightly faded, the colours sliding toward a bluish tinge, it was clean enough for her to see a full length photo of four smiling, round faces looking back at her. A mom, dad and their two children? To Elle they looked unnaturally pale and plump, much like the faces her father would occasionally fashion for her using wax from a candle. Then there were the clothes. She had seen clothes like theirs before in magazines and other photos while scavenging in deserted houses over the years. How could anyone bear to wear so much stuff? You wouldn't catch me dead in an outfit like that, she thought. The girl, standing in front of the woman whose hand rested on the child's shoulder, appeared slightly younger than Elle, maybe ten or even twelve. She wore a large straw hat, sunglasses, a sleeveless dress with a ribbon tied around the waist, pink socks and black shoes.

Elle abruptly put the photo against the wall, got up from the boat ramp, picked up her rifle and walked into the cottage. From past experience, it was a sure bet the cabin had a mirror and with luck, she would find it undamaged or at least a sizeable fragment somewhere inside. Like all abandoned houses, this one had been heavily vandalized. Windows and cupboards had been smashed, broken or removed along with anything else of value. Elle started her search. Room by room, she inspected each one, paying special attention to those places where such things were kept. At the back of the house, a long corridor led into a small bedroom. Its door was propped up against a wall, minus all its hinges and door knob. Metal was precious. This was the last room and it was, like the rest of the cottage, empty. Whoever they were, they had been thorough. She felt surprised at her disappointment. The driving reason behind why she wanted to find one was a mystery. Like a lost word on the tongue's tip, the desire hung there.

As she began to leave the room, on impulse, she turned the door around. Suddenly Elle found herself staring at the reflection in the mirror of a tall, rake-handle thin, dark-skinned girl with a battered hat pulled level with her eyes, wearing filthy over-sized pants, a shirt that didn't fit and a belt with obviously added holes to accommodate a very narrow waist upon which hung a knife whose scabbard ended nearly at her knees. There were deep lines across her forehead and at the corners of her eyes and mouth. To her astonishment, Elle found herself mentally comparing the girl in the mirror with the girl in the photo. They looked nothing alike and yet, in a way, they did. Elle had no real understanding of just how different their two worlds were. Two worlds, two children: one most likely dead now but from a living world, the other alive but in a dying one.

This is foolish, I've wasted enough time, she thought. What I need now is to get some sleep. Returning the door to its original position, Elle left the cottage and headed back to the boatshed. The sun sat low in the sky. If she was going to take a nap, she had better do it now. A little over an hour was all that she had, no more. By then the sun would be setting, giving enough daylight time to load up. Tonight the moon would be full, rising just before the sun set so there would be no delay waiting in darkness before setting off. Elle had kept up this punishing routine not only because she wanted to stay well ahead of any possible pursuit. There were good reasons to reach The Maiden before sunrise. The spring was at least six, maybe seven hours from here. If she left at sunset she would have nearly nine hours before sunrise, eight if you counted the false dawn.

After checking the horses, Elle returned to where she'd placed the photo and picked it up. Looking again at this well fed family in the picture, she cautiously wrapped it in the cloth she had used to clean it and carefully returned it to the safety of the pack. That done, ensuring she was concealed from uninvited visitors, Elle curled up and fell asleep. The drowning dreams soon came as they sometimes did when she was out in the wastelands. This time, however, they were much more vivid and detailed, with the result that when she awoke it was with a lingering taste of fear.

In spite of all her efforts over the three days, Elle arrived late. The moon hugged the horizon, rendering the world below in many shades of grey. It would set a few minutes before sunrise, but by then the sun's presence would already be seen all along the eastern perimeter. She had at most an hour to safely do what she needed to get done. She would have preferred more time. The Maiden, nestled within a wide natural hollow, lay just over a cluster of hills about five hundred metres in front of her and was the only water for many kilometres around for humans and animals alike.

Having left the horses back in a wash, she rested in amongst a tangle of dead and fallen trees, scanning the hills for movement. If Noah was there waiting for her, there was nothing she could do about what would happen next. If, however, there was anyone other than Noah camped at the spring and there were more than one of them, someone would most certainly be sitting up there on the highest summit right now. Or that's what I'd do, thought Elle. If they were there and were doing their job, she'd be spotted the minute she stepped out in the open. In the wastelands, being observed could be deadly. The shortest route to the top was off to the left, but that way was devoid of anything remotely useful to cover her advance. The right side was only marginally better, although there did seem to be a few strategically placed rocky outcrops protruding from the bare soil that could come in handy. She could hide and move within their shadows, but she'd have to make up her mind soon. There was not much time before the full morning sun presented itself. Elle lowered her head, resting it on the rifle in her hands. Over the last three days she'd gotten precious little of the sleep she craved. Along with the drowning dreams, that girl in the photo had plagued her sleep in ways that were unfamiliar and discomforting. What she really wanted to do was continue to lie there and sleep, but that was not an option.

Having decided the terrain to her right was the best on offer, Elle crawled out from her hiding place. The light from the moon caused any unevenness of the ground, rock or dead scrub to cast long, dark grey shadows, creating hundreds of hiding places. With an earth-coloured camouflage blanket tied around her neck to cover her back, Elle began the arduous task of slowly ascending the hill. The trick in reaching the top unseen had two aspects. If someone was up there, they did not know anyone was at the bottom. And, unless they were under attack, even the best sentries became bored and started to relax over a long period of time, even if they had someone to talk to. On the other hand, if anyone was up there, Elle did not know where they were. Finding the sentry would take time. But what was there to worry about? Did she not excel at playing this game?

The first Nathan knew he was no longer alone was when he heard the distinct 'click' of a firearm's hammer being pulled back and a muffled voice, just loud enough for his ears only, saying, "Sit as you are, don't move". No threat was made but the tone of the voice left Nathan in no doubt of the consequences if he did not obey. He quickly suppressed the urge to turn his head in the direction of the voice or reach for his rifle, suspecting any such movement would get him killed. But, what to do? If he didn't comply and was shot, at least the camp would be warned. A small sacrifice, considering what could happen if they weren't. His dilemma was whether to sacrifice his life for many.

Elle could see him struggling, trying to decide. She'd help. "I am not a Scavenger or part of a gang. If I were you would be dead already and the camp below would be under attack."

The young man sat motionless and waited. The voice was that of girl, a young girl, and, as far as he knew, Scavengers didn't come in that particular gender. He nodded, but didn't relax.

What followed next was a series of instructions given at just above a whisper. "Put your hands on your head with your fingers interlocked. Now, very slowly, stand up, turn around and face away from my voice. Now, step away from your rifle. Now, very slowly undress using only your left hand. Now, move away from your clothing and keep your back toward me."

He was surprised by how hard it was to disrobe with only one hand but Nathan completed each task as commanded by his unseen companion and soon stood in nothing but his underpants and boots. The first light of the sun struck the ridge and he still had no idea who the voice behind him belonged to. Nathan saw the shadow of his mysterious captor fall across the rocks in front of him as Elle emerged from her hiding place less than a metre from where he had been sitting.

She took a step forward, never taking her eyes off him, and stooped down to inspect his clothes. Satisfied they did not contain any potential danger she tossed them to him but kept the heavy cloak. She had seen cloaks like this before. Noah had one and she knew who wore them.

"Don't turn around. Get dressed but again use only the left hand and keep the right hand on your head."

Reaching down, Nathan picked up a stone and hid it within the folds of his pants.

As he did so, the voice spoke in a tone leaving no room for denial.

"Please put it back. I'm sure you don't want me to break my rule of not killing anyone before breakfast."

He couldn't help but admire her skill. Dropping the stone, he dressed as he had been told, with one hand. As he straightened up he automatically started to use both hands do up his belt only to be cautioned to "put the hand back on your head." He did, although he found it even more difficult to do up a belt with one hand than to undo it. The sun was now fully up and Nathan was beginning to feel that that he might actually get out of this alive.

Elle took a couple of steps back to make sure that she was out of reach if he should suddenly turn and try to grab her. "Are you a Trader?" she asked.

"Yes!" There was no mistaking the pride in his prompt reply.

Elle knew a great deal about the Traders. Until a few years ago, Traders had been frequent visitors to the Farm. However, since late last year there had been none. To her, swap the buses for wagons and they appeared very much like the people in her grandfather's old photo albums. In anticipation of a visit, he would entertain her with stories about them, their adventures as well as those of his parents and their gypsy friends. To be a friend of a Trader was to secure a sanctuary for the rest of your life. Though they belonged to a kind of family clan, these large extended families seldom travelled as one, preferring instead to mix and match. Later she understood that it was the younger folk who preferred it that way as it gave them the opportunity to travel with someone that wasn't a sibling or first cousin.

Being matriarchal, it was their custom that only a woman who had given birth and raised the child to adulthood could own a wagon or lead a 'family'. When more than one wagon travelled together, the leader would usually be the oldest of the women. Any woman who owned a wagon was referred to as Mother unless you were on very familiar terms with them; then you could call them by their given name. Elle thought it sounded a lot like her own family when it came to running the Farm.

Although she felt the warning unnecessary, Noah had advised her to never lie when speaking to a Trader. To lie at any time, without just cause, is seldom an attractive or desirable characteristic. In the case of Traders, a person caught in a lie would not be welcome in their presence again. Also, never barter. They considered it demeaning. If a person thought a quoted price was too high, they could say so, but no more. A Trader would inform you whether they wished to continue to trade or not. In Noah's experience, Traders were honest people and could be trusted, even with one's life. In the affairs of business, he'd never felt he had been cheated. So, as he advised her, unless she was willing to risk her life needlessly, she should never question their integrity. To Elle, it seemed that her grandfather and the rest of the family shared a lot of characteristics with these people.

One of the Traders' more curious customs was not that each wagon had a name, rather the name of every family member associated with that wagon, especially if they were born in it, began with the same first letter as that of the wagon. Her grandfather confessed that he had no idea when or how the custom had started and wasn't convinced that even the Traders knew for certain. The idea that her great-grandmother, Nadia, was one of the original Trader matrons pleased Elle. The fact that you have nothing to do with what happened before your birth is certainly true. Nevertheless, Elle thought that springing from such a lineage was gratifying and more than a bit exciting. Since the name painted on the bus pictured in photos was *Nemesis*, it explained why both her grandfather's and mother's names began with the letter 'N'. However, as Nora's daughter, why was she called Elle? Because she was born on the Farm and not in a wagon? But all her family had been born on the Farm.

The Traders had evolved from a people like her great-grandmother in the Before Times who had chosen a wandering way of life. Elle knew it would be a mistake to think of them as a kind of regressive gypsy group. Itinerant and flamboyant they might be, but much of the similarity ended there. Interwoven with artists, academics and a spattering of scientists, they were, for the most part, closeted geeks – technocrats, who used the mobility that a world-wide communication net and computers offered to them. They could and did wander where they would. Their travelling homes were their work places. With the coming of the Dry, trading and their acquired skills became a means rather than an end in maintaining their way of life. By using and then expanding their technological skills they linked themselves into a kind of amorphous union. It was this union that enabled them to survive throughout the worst parts of the Dry, the Sorrow and the onslaught of the Scavengers.

Elle had spent many a wakeful night imagining what it would be like to travel with them and enjoyed knowing she was linked by blood to these mysterious people who now and again stopped by. That they were kin certainly explained the way they greeted the family.

Another thing she knew about the Traders; they had two sets of attire. The colourful and flamboyant clothing like the ones she'd seen in the photos was reserved for trading and general mixing with non-Traders. At other times, usually when on the road and out of sight of non-traders, they wore simpler practical garb whose main distinctive article of clothing was a long, loose-fitting, earthy brown cloak with a pointed cowl, much like the monks wore few hundred years back. Out in the wastelands it offered protection from the sun during the day, warmth on winter nights and a degree of camouflage. It was his last article of clothing that had alerted her to the young man's possible identity.

However, the possession of a Trader's cloak did not a Trader make. In the wastelands, to assume that which was not proven was risky and best avoided.

With her face in the shadows of first light, Elle asked, "Ready to go down so I can meet everyone? But please, be a good boy, no signals. We've come this far without a messy incident, so let's keep it that way."

Smiling in spite of his predicament and at being called 'boy', Nathan answered with a nod of his head.

"Then you'll need this," remarked Elle as she threw the cloak high over his head to make it difficult for him to catch and easy for her to snatch up his rifle.

This redirection did not go unnoticed. "You're a very clever little girl." Once again, he found himself admiring her skill. "The question is who's trained you?" He put the cloak on and started to bring the cowl forward when a sharp rebuke stopped him.

"Keep it down."

As his hands fell back to his sides, he turned his head just enough to see his captor silhouetted in the sun's glare. He saw the outlines of a very tall and extremely thin girl and, as his eyes adjusted to the morning light allowing him to see into the shadow covering her face, a pair of predator-like eyes. "Truly, an undomesticated animal," he thought. His attention went to the unwavering rifle aimed at his back.

"If you're done, turn your head back to the front. Put your hands back on your head, fingers interlocked. Walk slowly in front of me. Do not stumble or make any movement I could misinterpret. Make no sound or call out. If you and your people are Traders, you have nothing to fear from me. If not..." Elle did not finish the sentence.

They started their descent to The Maiden. Nathan wanted to laugh at how ridiculous this would appear to his friends and family; captured by a girl. Should he survive, he was in no doubt they would never let him forget. He predicted that within a year this story would be told around every Trader's campfire – how an underfed girl, poorly dressed in ill-fitting clothes, had caught him completely off guard and then, adding insult to injury, marched him down the hill for all to see. If it had not been for those eyes, he might have risked taking a chance to disarm her, but those eyes persuaded him against such an action.

Still mostly in shadow, the camp and the adjacent spring were clearly visible from the hill's summit. The camp was coming to life. People were awake and moving about in that slow, early morning fashion. Voices called out to one another. Children were busy getting in the way, as were the dogs. There were half a dozen wagons parked front to back, forming a wide circle with the camp's main fire being prodded to life at its centre. The smaller cooking fires were also being rekindled beside each of the wagons. More than thirty horses were off to one side in a sling corral. The total number of souls was hard to tell as some had not yet emerged, but those she could see were more than she had been accustomed to for some time. In a single glance, Elle took it all in, noting and remembering everything she saw. If this wasn't a Trader's camp and things turned nasty, she knew the position of every person who might be a threat and the order in which she would kill them without a second thought.

About a quarter of the way down to the camp, Elle suddenly lifted her head the way an animal does when it first detects the presence, the mere hint of an unexpected smell or, as in this case, sound. She became aware of music. It was coming from a smallish figure, dressed in a cloak with the cowl pulled fully forward, winding its way up toward them. Elle had never heard anything like it in all her short life. It was as painfully beautiful as it was sad, making her feel desperately alone. The hooded figure, engrossed in its own concentrated musicality, continued up the path leading to the summit, totally unaware of the two, who in the next few minutes would be blocking his ascent.

Head bent, with eyes content to watch the path move beneath his feet, Nic played a tune whose origins were old long before the coming of the Dry. It spoke of things lost and of hope gone. When Nathan's feet came into his view, the music stopped. The boy of sixteen, removing the harmonica from his lips, pushed back his cowl with his free hand and looked up.

What began as a smile of recognition quickly turned into a rapid succession of puzzlement, concern and finally understanding, as a girl's voice whispered, "Don't move! Put your hands at your sides and please, nothing unexpected."

He didn't move. She motioned impatiently with her rifle and Nic slowly began to raise his arms.

"Are you daft? Put them down and keep them at your side," she snapped. "Move off the trail a little more so I can see you better." Nic complied. "Now take your rifle off of your shoulder with your left hand. Do it slowly and then lower it to the ground. Keep your hands away from the trigger."

While looking at Nathan's face for a signal, Nic did as he was told.

"Now turn around slowly and then the both of you start walking toward your camp."

A single raised eyebrow from Nathan signalled his younger brother to do nothing for the moment. The boy turned, leading off, and the other two followed.

Picking up the rifle as she passed, Elle stayed close enough to the older of the two not to be seen should any of the people happen to look up and see them descending, but far enough back to stay well out of his reach should the older boy try to catch her off guard. Wanting to hear more of the boy's music, Elle asked him to play again. Within the first five bars Elle knew she had made a serious mistake. The camp, to the casual observer, seemed unchanged but to Elle's eyes a subtle transformation began occurring. Movements became more deliberate. The children had become quieter and began to disperse. Just as she had seen her own family do when strangers arrived unannounced, she observed two men stop what they had been doing and climb into the nearest wagons.

"Stop playing. Stop walking," demanded Elle. "Both of you put your hands onto your heads, finger interlocked. Stand side by side and, I am asking very graciously, please do not move. You, the older one, call out to the camp. Tell them to stand still with their hands out in front. Tell the two men to come out of the wagons."

Despite the extreme danger they were all apparently in, Nathan once more found himself unable to stop feeling admiration toward this kid. She had known, as soon as Nic had started to play, that it was a tune to warn the camp. Nathan was a Trader, a good judge of people; he would do as she requested.

Nic's mother Nicole turned her head in the direction of the hill where her youngest had gone a few minutes earlier to relieve Nathan. Instead of seeing him nearing the top, she saw that they were both coming down. She was thinking they had better have a very good reason for leaving the summit unattended when the tune from her son's harmonica alerted them to danger. There were things out in the wastelands that even the Traders had reasons to fear. The coded musical alert stopped as soon as it started, but it had been enough. People had begun to move to their prearranged positions when they heard Nathan ordering them to stand where they were with hands exposed in front of them. This they did, for the moment at least.

The boys' mother was the anointed senior leader of these Traders and it was she who stepped forward and called out to her sons who were clearly visible, kneeling with their hands on their heads.

"What do you want?"

Again it was Nathan who spoke. "Sit down with your hands on your heads. And the men in the wagons are to come out with their weapons above their heads, place the weapons where she can see them and then join the rest of you on the ground. Please do as she says." Without prompting he added, "I don't think we're in danger."

Elle gave Nathan a tap on the head with the barrel of the rifle. "That's enough ad-libbing."

Nathan gave a nod and went silent. From one of the wagons, a tall, raw-boned man descended and walked over to stand by the woman who had called out. From the other, a man of similar composition also came out. They sat down and as they did, so did the others.

"Ok, we're seated; our hands are on our heads; now, may I ask who has my sons?" inquired Nicole.

After a short pause Nathan called back. "She said her name is Elle, the daughter of Nora, the granddaughter of Noah."

Immediately the fear evaporated and all the adults commenced to roar with laugher.

"Elle, come out from behind my sons and stop scaring the daylights out of us. I'm Nicole, Noah's daughter, Nora's sister and I am your aunt, the one who sold Noah your birthday horse."

Without permission people started getting up and walking up to meet the startled boys who remained kneeling in front of a now very bewildered and sheepish Elle. She would remember every single moment of the day that was to follow for the rest of her life. In minutes she was surrounded by a host of people. Everyone, it seemed, wanted to touch and hug her. Without a word, they took possession of the three rifles, her blanket and shoulder pack. Each of her hands was soon entwined firmly in the hands of a child, both of whom began to giggle incessantly. The dogs leaped about, desperately trying to join in. The two boys, chastened by the fact they had been captured by a scrawny girl of thirteen, were sent off to retrieve her horses when she had protested, in vain, that before anything else she needed to go and get them. With Elle in tow, confined in the middle of some twenty Traders singing a rather silly ditty about a boy who had lost his donkey, they headed back down and into the presence of the waiting Nicole.

Chapter Six
The best of times often arrives unannounced.

The joy of these people was infectious. The grin that had started as a bemused smile just kept growing until it could grow no more. Nothing like this had ever happened to her before. It was way beyond anything else she had ever experienced. When the crowd reached the edge of the camp they came to a halt and the singing and laughter stopped. Except for a number of suppressed giggles, it was quiet. Elle felt many hands gently pushing her forward until she stood in front of Nicole. As she had been taught, she extended both arms with palms up and hands open while looking straight into the woman's eyes. Then, with all the seriousness she could muster at such a moment, she said, "Good fortune to you, Mother." The next thing Elle knew she was enclosed within two massive strong arms and pressed into equally massive breasts so hard that she was unable to draw a breath.

"Bloody hell, girl, for a time back there you frightened me so much I almost wet myself. We thought you were a Scavenger."

With that, everyone again roared with laughter and Elle found herself being alternately patted on the back, hugged and kissed by all and sundry.

Breakfast and the lunch that followed were experiences she warmed to easily. Unlike in her home at mealtime, often a quiet affair, the only time there was anything like silence here – and even then the younger ones were having a go at one another – was during the blessing of the gathering by Nicole. The Traders made a lot of noise, talked over each other, and every word had an accompanying hand gesture. It had been about a year since they had seen Noah so there was a lot to catch up on. They wanted all the news of the Farm, her mother, Noah and the rest of the family. When they learned that her cousins had gone off to get married, she was bombarded with questions, demanding every gram of gossip concerning the coming nuptials. Not once did anyone ask why she was here on her own.

Food-piled stoneware plates moved up and down the tables at blinding speeds with everyone taking from them as they passed. As was their custom, she was offered and had accepted a place of honour. Even so, if it had not been for Nathan and Nic sitting on either side, she was sure she would have gone hungry during both meals. The boys slowed the speed of the dishes as they flew past. Even for the Traders, times were hard and food was seldom plentiful. Today, however, was a celebration. Noah's granddaughter was among them for the first time. To not offer their best would have been unacceptable, an unpardonable breach of good manners.

Elle was enthralled. She had thought she had eaten most every kind of animal and plant life there was in these regions, but some of the meat and vegetables and their preparation were beyond anything she had experienced before. She found it was very fortunate there was plenty of water, beer and bread available because some of the dishes served during lunch required copious amounts to quench the fire they had ignited in her mouth.

In the way the Traders spoke of her grandfather, it was obvious they held him in highest regard and it made her wonder just how much of his life he'd kept secret from her and if there were more revelations to come. When she returned to the Farm there were so many questions she wanted to ask him, starting with whether he had been with these people during the year he was gone and why?

After breakfast, accompanied by a few companions, Elle took a look around the spring. This was not the first time she had visited The Maiden. Its softness filled her with a sense of what the world must have been like before the Dry, when rain fell freely and often. Feeling the grass underneath her feet and touching living trees brought immeasurable joy as well as its companion, sorrow. In the world she inhabited, you couldn't feel the one without the other. We've lost so much, she thought, so very, very much.

The Maiden was indeed a thing of beauty. It was comprised of three smallish pools that linked to a fourth. Nearly seven metres across, it was the source of the spring. The first time she camped here with her grandfather, he had explained how all the pools were enclosed by sandstone hollowed out and worn smooth by the flow of water for "countless thousands of years and," with a hint of a smile, "the occasional human hand." A creek ran from the last and smallest of the pools, flowing into and feeding the whole Maiden basin. Trees hugged the perimeter of each pool, shading the water beneath. Cooled by shallow puddles, flat sandstone surfaces provided places of rest. Roots dipped into and ran along the walls of the various pools. Unlike in the wastelands, the air felt thicker, sweeter and was filled with sound of birds and insects calling from their hiding places within the canopy above.

With a hunter's eyes, Elle saw evidence of animal life everywhere she looked. In spite of the appetites of the Trader's horses and the local wildlife, much of the grass in The Maiden was lush and thick, providing confirmation yet again that these remaining water sources were sanctuaries from the forces of the Dry. The scattered remains of the spring's previous occupants, long abandoned, were evidence that it had been so for many generations before the coming of the Dry. Noah said the spring had always provided a sense of wellbeing for those who visited. This was especially true after the Dry. Then it became a point of destination for many, a reprieve from the realities of the wastelands. Sadly, all that had ended over 40 years ago. "Since then, only people like us come here, and then it's only to visit." There was no need to elaborate why that was so. Water did make life possible but it did not discriminate between the different life forms attracted to it.

Her companions were two small girls and Nic, who had been at her side since he and his brother returned to the camp with her horses. Elle decided that this trio had appointed themselves her guardians and all-round dogs' bodies. Throughout the morning and into the afternoon she had not been able to do a single thing for herself. The horses had never had it so good. The Trader children had bid for turns at feeding, watering and grooming the animals. Elle, watching her horses feed, realized that this was perhaps the first time Buck had ever grazed in such a lush meadow. She expressed some concern regarding this matter to Nic who told her not to worry. The kids would keep an eye on him. Traders knew how to care for horses, he reassured her. The various water containers had been emptied, cleaned and refilled for her early start the following morning. All her bags had been unpacked, sorted, cleaned and repacked. When they came across the old photo, Nic had held it up, inquiring who they were. That was a question she couldn't answer, saying only, "It was something I found a couple of days back and felt like keeping." Elle gently retrieved the photo from his hands, rewrapped it and put it back in her pack without any understanding as to why she felt the need to keep it safe and near her.

Suddenly finding herself alone with Nic, and filled to the brim from lunch, Elle saw that the Traders had something in common with the Farm; everyone had jobs that had to be done, even on a day that had been declared a celebration. The two children, who had dogged her since they took her hands on the hill, had disappeared for the moment. She decided to take advantage of this inattention, telling Nic she was going for a swim. To be immersed in cool spring-fed waters might only occur once or twice a year for her, so an opportunity like this would not be allowed to pass. Before entering any spring, it was customary to completely wash oneself from head to toe before entering. This not only ensured that the water did not become contaminated, it was a ritual of respect in this hard thirsty land. The first step in the ritual was the special attention paid to the left hand for it was the left hand that assisted in the more unpleasant aspects of human toiletry. The left hand was also the one which was used to touch what would be considered tainted, or unclean, such as the corpse of a human. To touch anyone with the left hand or offer it in assistance to anyone, even family and friends, was interpreted as, at best a social slip, at worst, a hostile act of discourtesy. Women menstruating, people with open infected wounds or ill were not allowed to enter a spring at all. A pregnant woman on the other hand was always given first right of entry.

With bucket in hand filled with water, Elle proceeded to walk a ways from the pools to look for a place to wash. Nic, with his bucket, walked beside her. Finding a spot to their liking they began to undress. Elle normally would have stripped down to bathe with no concern at all as to who was in her presence. Suddenly, in the company of Nic, she felt uncomfortable, shy, in doing so. However, the lure of the cool spring water was stronger than this newly acquired inhibition. They bathed and then raced each other, leaping into liquid joy. The water was surprisingly cold, raising goose bumps everywhere. She gave a little shudder and was about to look around to see where Nic went, when his grinning head popped up beside her, water cascading down his face.

"Where is everyone else?" asked Elle. "I thought there would be standing room only."

"Oh, we've been here three days already and Mom thought you'd like a little time on your own," replied Nic before diving underwater again.

As soon as he resurfaced she asked, mockingly, "Then why are you here?"

"Lifeguard," he said before disappearing under the water again. The two children, who had been watching from behind a tree, loudly announced that they were her lifeguards too, and then dove in. "So much for a little privacy," thought Elle as the girls began splashing her and then Nic, when he resurfaced.

Had she been on her own, she would have stayed in the pool till her skin shrivelled. Long before then and far too soon, they were called for the evening meal. The foursome reluctantly emerged from the water. She was surprised at how famished she felt as she headed over to where she had left her clothing. To her astonishment, the clothes were gone, as was her rifle, knife and, most disturbingly, her ring. In their place lay a clean Trader's cloak. Ignoring the barely suppressed sniggers from the children and Nic, she put on the cloak and then allowed them to lead her over to where the rest had gathered for their final meal of the day. "I'll deal with you all later," she said, smiling mischievously at them. "I have some games of my own you know."

She would never be given the opportunity.

Arriving with her entourage, Elle came upon the Traders standing in a row obscuring the setting of the evening's meal. As she approached, encouraged by Nic and the children, they parted allowing exposure of a single place setting. There were her missing boots, rifle and knife. Next to it, on a pile of neatly folded clothes, sat her ring. No one said a thing as she walked up and took the ring, placing it once again securely around her neck. Not a sound from the Traders as she again stooped to pick up the clothes. A shirt, a pair of pants, socks, a leather belt stitched with hundreds of coloured glass beads and underwear.... Underwear! The only underwear Elle had were some hand-me-downs from her male cousins. They were nothing like these. These felt as if water was running through her fingers and they were new. They were all new, none of the clothes had been worn by anyone else and they were hers.

She could not stop the tears; they came, as did a cry of pain. She sobbed. She wailed. Her shoulders shook as the tears became a torrent down her face. Her nose began to run. If that was not enough, Nic started to play that melody he had played this morning while coming up the hill to relieve his brother. Everyone began to sing the first verses of, 'The Trader's Lament'. The words, the music tore at her heart. While they sang, cried and laughed, under Nicole's guidance, several women removed Elle's robe and began to dress her. When they finished, Nicole took her by the hand and led her to the head of the table, the place of highest honour.

Nicole stood on Elle's right side and raised her hand. The music and singing stopped as the rest of the Traders moved to take up their places around the table. Once that was done, Nicole began the blessing of the evening meal. "For all of those who preceded us, we remember you as a promise kept. For all those who are here and those of us who are absent, we remember you as a promise in keeping. For all those not yet born, we remember you as a promise in the making. In all of our names, we wait and wish for the rains to return." Finished, Nicole asked Elle to sit.

Elle, in a muddled state of bewilderment, allowed Nicole's hand to push her gently down until she was seated.

Giving Elle's shoulder a reassuring squeeze, Nicole scooped a small spoonful of food from one of the serving platters and put it on Elle's plate, saying, "With this, I recognize you." She then left to take her place at the other end of the table.

Her husband, taking her place, repeated the placing of the food onto Elle's plate and the phrase, "With this, I recognize you." He then left, and was replaced by another member of the family and then another and then another. Even the two children came, bowed, and then solemnly mimicked the adults and repeated the actions of their elders. Returning to their respective places they sat, waiting.

Elle's emotions were nearing breaking point. She found it hard to breathe. Her heart was beating so hard in her chest she felt faint. Confused, she thought, what I am supposed to do? They are all looking at me. Seeing Nic mimic eating with his fingers, Elle took some food between the fingers of her right hand, put it into her mouth and chewed. The Traders erupted in joyous applause as they started to fill their own plates.

Elle suspected every person there that evening had their own story of hardship and loss. These times were harsh, brutal and, far too often, fatal. She looked around at their faces in the fading light as they ate. Like her, these people had strong connections to family and friends and in this they counted themselves fortunate. They too travelled with good companions. Focusing on Nic and Nathan, she found herself a bit puzzled. Although it had been several years since they had visited the Farm, she hadn't recognized either of them at first. They had changed so much. Had she as well? Elle found herself thinking of her family back at the Farm and these people here. It was hard for her to reconcile such differences. Noah once told her "Each of us is defined by the family and friends we choose to be with." Remembering her own family and then looking at the people sitting around her, Elle felt a warm glow within her. "Is this how I am defined?" She smiled at the thought.

As the meal moved toward its conclusion, people left, returning with musical instruments. One by one they joined the others, following the lead of those playing, and the ranks of musicians swelled. Those who did not play clapped and sang. The songs were of far off places, of past adventures, of loves lost and gained, of regret and joy and of the coming of the rain. To Elle's surprise, she knew them all. Her mother had sung them all to her ever since she could remember. Elle recalled how often she had heard her mother singing. She sang in the fields, in the garden, in the house, but most of all, when Elle was younger or ill, she remembered her mother's songs as she fell asleep. These were her mother's songs. Were these her mother's people?

Elle sang. Her voice, the voice of youth, was clear and strong. It soared, taking the highest notes and flying with them. She danced. Tentative, awkward at first, she danced. She leaped, whirled. The music entered her. It found home. She flew. Nic and Nathan danced with her, as did others. Her whole body rang like a bell struck by its clapper. She was in sympathy with the music. Such a people; such a night. For Elle, this was the place and time. This too she would remember up to the moment of her death. Yet, in the midst of such happiness, she wished her family was here to share this with her. It almost seemed wrong without them. Maybe one of them held a piece of knowledge that would explain why all this felt so familiar. Maybe one of them could explain who these strangers, these Traders, were and where, in their world, she fitted. Elle, at the age of thirteen, asked for the first time, "Just who am I?"

All too soon signs appeared that the gathering was coming to an end. Without Elle noticing, the sun had set hours ago. The moon had already breached the surrounding hills. The music continued but its tempo became more sedate as people drifted off. It was late and there were chores yet to be finished.

With her back resting against a wagon wheel, Elle watched. Wood brought in from the wastelands fed the evening fires. A man, who had earlier introduced himself as Nero, stopped to wish her a good night before heading up the hill to take his turn on the summit. The last of the meal's remains, save for a plate left for the relieved sentry, were carefully cleared, cleaned, packed and stored away. They would be leaving tomorrow morning in order to rendezvous with Traders who had been trading, ferreting and gathering salt from places far to the north. Once they'd joined up, all of them would be heading east to gather with other Traders. As the Dry bit into more of the surrounding landscape, the Traders would not be back this way for years. There was much to do.

Elle would also be leaving. A hand touched her softly on her shoulder. It was Nicole.

"Come," was all she said.

Elle rose to her feet and followed her over to where Nic and the kids had stored her packs. Turning to look at Elle, Nicole said, "My son tells me you have a photo of a family. May I see it?"

Of all the things that were possible for Nicole to ask of her, this was not what she had expected. A flood of questions came to her as she bent down to retrieve the photo. She wanted to ask why, but did not.

"Here," was all she said as she handed the photo over. Tentatively, Nicole took the photo as if it was a thing so delicate that a misjudged touch could destroy it. She lifted her lamp up to get more light onto it. As if in a trance Nicole unconsciously handed the lamp to Elle and then began to stroke the figure of the little girl in the photo.

Elle had seen the look on her aunt's face before. It was the same expression she'd often seen on adults when they were remembering loved ones they'd lost. It encompassed sadness, regret and resignation all at the same time. Nicole, as if returning from a great distance, looked at Elle and handed back the photo. Elle took it and, as she did so, felt Nicole's hands stroke her face as she had done with the photo of the young girl.

"Thank you, Elle." Without a word of explanation she turned and left, returning to the activities surrounding the wagons.

Elle stood alone in the darkness feeling bewildered. What was that all about? She wished again that Noah was here. He'd be able to explain what had just happened, she was sure of it.

The moon, now high overhead, warned Elle that it was late and if she was to get a good night's sleep she'd better do it now. She unfurled her bed roll, removed the boots, took off the knife and laid it next to the rifle. In the wastelands you were never safe. You might take off your boots or moccasins but you never got undressed. It had been a good day. As soon as her head came to rest on the bedroll Elle was asleep and, at first, could not have been more limp or relaxed if she had been a well fed cat. But then the dreams came.

Still dark, the morning, as she knew it would, started hectic, moved to chaotic, then crescendoed in frantic excitement. Food from last night was eaten cold and in haste; people hurried about; children got in the way; lost items were found and lost again; well-fed horses, intransigent after days out of harness, expressed their displeasure. It was a pandemonium of sight, motion and sound. To outsiders it would appear to be madness, ants in a disturbed melée. They would be wrong. Within the noise and bustle, tables were collapsed; things were packed, lifted and securely stored. Horses and people were readied for departure and the sun had yet to crest the eastern hills.

Woken by the early calls of greeting, Elle began her own preparation to leave. She had slept well. The impressions of her dreams lingered. Like the others, her breakfast consisted of scavenged leftovers from last night's meal, which she ate while packing up the horses. Belle and Buck, unlike their counter-parts by the wagons, seemed eager to be on their way. She observed that there was once again no room for her to ride. She put away the boots and took out the moccasins.

Someone cleared their throat behind her by way of announcing their presence. It was Nicole holding a small, thin leather cylinder, no longer than the palm of her hand.

"You'll need this." Indicating that they should sit down, Nicole undid the binding of one end of the cylinder, removed its cap and slid out a scroll. Using the flat surface of an exposed slab of sandstone, Nicole unrolled the scroll and then unfolded it several times. Just under a metre square, it lay on the rocky surface like a handkerchief until Nicole pressed a spot on one of the corners. Instantly the 'handkerchief' stiffened, becoming as rigid as a thick sheet of steel. It was a map and not just any map. This was a Traders' map. Elle had heard Noah describe them.

The Traders were renowned for their topographical skills and the beauty and care that went into each of their maps. In his study Noah had piles of the mass produced maps made in the Before Times, but they were nothing like this. Other than providing the location of mountains, roads and cities, the mass produced maps were of little use in the Dry. The landscape had altered so drastically most places were unrecognizable or gone completely. Some towns had been completely erased from place as well as memory. There were no forests or rivers of any kind. And more to the point, these maps were not central to the needs of those in the wastelands for they could not show where there was water. They did not have a key for shade, desirable camps sites, defensive positions, settlements or the whereabouts of caches of supplies hidden by the Traders. Nor did they show the routes taken by the Traders.

Ultra hi-tech, the Trader maps were a source of pride, crafted by their expert hands. There was nothing else like them. They were printed on a nearly indescribable material that itself was considered a technical marvel in the Before Times. It was said to be made from a combination of silk, cotton, plastic, linen and a metal alloy woven into fabric that would not tear, wear or wrinkle. It was as light as a breath of air from a new-born and accepted ink and paint like the finest canvas.

The map laid on the sandstone covered the westward portion of the wastelands she would be travelling after leaving the Maiden, but it did not include the mountains. Richly crafted, the map reminded Elle of Nadia's Wall. She was humbled by the privilege being extended to her. In so far as she knew, no one but Noah or a fellow Trader had ever been allowed to see such a precious thing or have one in their possession. For Elle to be given one in trust illustrated the immense respect and reverence these people held for her grandfather.

Nicole spoke. Her voice sounded sad. "This is all that we know of the lands west of here. I'll show you how to read the map for it is not as straightforward as it may appear." To ensure Elle had a thorough understanding of the meaning of the symbols and the embedded codes, Nicole queried her every step of the way. She needed to be sure Elle understood; there would be no second chance. She seemed surprised that Elle did not need to go over the map's encrypted details more than once. Elle truly was Nora's daughter. At last, satisfied that her niece was now sufficiently versed in reading a Trader's map, Nicole solemnly instructed her to destroy the map if it was ever in danger of falling into unsavoury hands. She could do this by pressing simultaneously on any two corners of the map. Although the material would remain, all the print on the map would instantly turn into dust. If there was no time for such niceties, she was to rotate the bottom cap a full turn and push hard. In five seconds, if anyone was holding it they would be killed by the explosion. There was no need to define who the unsavoury hands might belong to or what the instruction concerning the detonation of the cylinder implied. It was given in her tone of voice. For, even though the Traders' preferred routes, gathering points, water sources and hidden caches were encoded, both knew that time and determination would render up all the map's secrets.

Elle folded and rolled the map as instructed and then returned it to its leather cylinder. She was about to stand when Nicole reached out a hand, indicating that she should stay seated.

"At the spring I showed you on the map there are two graves located toward the northern side, a short distance from a cabin. Please visit them and perhaps leave a few flowers if any are growing in the vicinity. We would view it as a kind gesture."

Elle knew that this was not an unusual request. In and around towns or in the middle of the most desolate and hostile regions of the wastelands one came across graves. They were ubiquitous. The land was filled with the markers of those fortunate enough to have been buried in a marked grave. Her own family had such a place. From her bedroom window she could see over fifty markers, family and friends, a silent tribute to the harshness, the indifferent cruelty of these times. Considering the billions that once inhabited this planet, she wondered how many people lay unburied, unmarked, unremembered. Elle, now standing and holding Nicole's hands in hers, assured her that she would do as requested when someone called Nicole's name.

The Traders were ready to depart. None had asked her why she was there or her destination; by giving her the map they indicated that they knew where she was going and what that meant. They also knew Noah would be the one appointed to come after her. None would tell her not to go, although, from their experience, it would end in her dying. It was not the Trader's way. A person could not freely choose to come into this world, to be given life, but at some point they must begin to choose how they would live, as well as the rules they would live by. Even if these new friends might have wished it otherwise, Elle would go to the mountains, as was her prerogative. Noah would try to intervene, as was his.

Nic came up and took her hand in his, pressed his harmonica into it. Then as was the custom Elle knew so well, he pressed his nose against hers, taking in her breath. He stepped back saying "Remember me as I will remember you."

Next was Nathan, he reached up and removed the much battered hat from her head, replacing it with a new wide brim, rabbit felt hat he had hidden behind his back. Pressing their noses together, he softly said as he did so, "Remember me as I will remember you."

As he stepped back, his mother came forward taking Elle once again into those powerful arms and pulling her close. Elle could smell the wood smoke, the musky sweat and feel the warm softness emanating from this unusual woman. The woman kissed each of her closed eyes, tasting the salty tears that were beginning to form at their corners. Briefly pressing their noses, she released and pushed Elle back, holding her at arm length, looking into her face. "You are worth a life, Elle." With that Nicole gently took the ring from around Elle's neck, removed the leather thong and replaced it with a heavy chain of gold. Before returning it to her neck, the mother of Nic and Nathan then stepped back, saying as she did so, "Remember me as I will remember you."

Elle stood immobilised by the struggle between joy and sorrow. She was emotionally overwhelmed as each of the remaining Traders slowly came to wish her a goodbye in the same manner. Then it was over. They returned to their waiting mounts and wagons to begin their trek north.

Taking the horses' reins, Elle led Belle and Buck out of and away from The Maiden. In less than an hour the spring was returned to its non-human inhabitants.

Chapter Seven

You feel the cold after leaving the comfort of a warm fire and good friends.

Nursing a nasty gash after slamming into something in the dark, Elle sat in the dirt, her pants pushed down below her knees. This was going to slow things up a bit, she thought. In the moonlight, she couldn't see how bad it was; another drawback of travelling at night. The cut hurt, a pulsing pain, and she could feel the blood run freely down her leg. Exploring the wound just below her left hip, her fingers found an impressive wound about half the length of the palm of her hand. As bad as it felt, it didn't seem to impair her ability to walk. Being crippled out in the wastelands could be a death sentence. Other than stopping the bleeding, there was little she could do until morning. In the meantime, after covering the cut with a thick bandage from the 'green box' and tying a strip of cloth around her leg to hold it in place, she'd just have to put up with it. She pulled her pants back up thinking that, with all the obstacles that littered the wastelands, it could have been a lot worse. Always the optimist...

A few hours later, with the sun high enough for her to see, Elle selected an outcrop of rock big enough to cast a reasonable bit of shade to sit in and inspect her injury. The wound was ugly – whatever it was she'd walked into it had left a jagged tear – but not deep or bad enough to be concerned about. It wasn't going to kill her, at least not right away. If it got infected that would be another story with an unpleasant ending. She'd have to attend to it soon to make sure that didn't happen. Fortunately, that opportunity was close at hand. By midday she'd be at Red Rim.

As a water source, it didn't number among her favourites. Other than the well, Red Rim had few amenities. A pathetic dribble did emerge, sparingly, from a small, moss encrusted fissure near the mouth of the well, trickling down to flow into a shallow depression. There the water momentarily pooled before spilling along the solid rocky surface until absorbed by the surrounding sand. There was little noticeable vegetation and a fierce heat radiated off the imposing sandstone surface. There was a single source of shade that did not alleviate the discomfort of anyone who chose to linger. In spite of the existence of water from the 'pathetic dribble', the solid rocky floor prevented Red Rim from providing a haven for any substantial plant life. What there was, except for the green slime tracing the water's path, the local wildlife kept in check. The few patches of struggling weeds missed by the locals were soon dispatched by the two horses. The only distinguishing feature and the source of its name was a single, broad, blood-red band that ran horizontally the full length of a sheer wall of sandstone twenty or so metres in height and nearly a kilometre in length. The red band had been quite a tourist feature in the Before Times according to Noah. As far as Elle was concerned, if her grandfather had not been having her on and people really did come all the way out here to gawk at a wall of sandstone, they must have had far too much time on their hands.

One thing about the Dry; in most places there was always ample material lying about to make a fire. But first she'd take care of the horses before attending to that cut of hers. There was no need to rush. She would not be leaving Red Rim until well into afternoon, so there was plenty of time to make herself comfortable. Elle reached into one of the packs and retrieved a leather bucket, tied a rope to its handle and dropped it into the well to let it fill. She heard the splash of the bucket hitting the water. The well was too deep and too much in shadow to see either the water or the bucket. She waited, testing now and again to see if it was full by giving the rope a slight tug, until she was satisfied that the bucket was ready to pull up. She repeated the performance two more times before she had enough water for both the horses and herself. Leaving the horses to drink she began to forage in and around the well, picking up enough twigs and small branches to meet her needs. Soon, confined within a small ring of stone, a compact fire blazed away nicely. A cooking pot filled with water sat above the flames.

After leaving The Maiden, Elle had maintained a pace that was not going to wear the three of them out. However, an ever so trivial error on her part resulted in transforming a two day walk into one that had taken nearly three. A slight change in route, another whim, meant going through much more rugged terrain than had been anticipated. Apparently the Traders' map didn't take into account or have instructions on how to avoid the calamities of a whim.

Weary, Elle sat down and leaned against a shaded portion of the well to wait for the water to boil. Absentmindedly poking the accumulating embers with a stick, she mused over the meaning behind Nicole's interest in the photo. What is a life worth and who are those people in the photo? Did Nicole know them? She stirred the embers a bit more and then let the stick drop from her hand. Her head tilted back until it rested against the sandstone. She closed her eyes, soon nodding off only to be woken moments later by the rattling of the pot's lid. So violently was the water boiling, droplets hissed as they struck the coals, threatening to extinguish them. A few of the heated droplets landed on her pants leg penetrating to the bare skin. Elle leaped to her feet, dancing around trying to separate the cloth of the pants from her flesh. "Bloody hell, girl, if you don't watch out you'll end with a scalded leg as well." Grabbing a readymade branch she hooked the metal handle and manoeuvred the sputtering pot away from the fire. "What's wrong with you?" Elle admonished herself. "If Noah had seen you do that, he'd box your ears. You're acting like a plebe." Turning to the horses who were straining at their leads to gain a better glimpse of the commotion, she flicked a hand in their direction, snapping, "And what do you two think you're looking at. Back off." In truth, Noah would have laughed at her antics with the hot water; it was the use of the word 'plebe' that would have gotten her the box about the ears. Not a word to use lightly and certainly not in front of people like her parents or Noah. It was not only a very derogatory term, it was disrespectful to all those who had faced the wastelands for the first time.

Elle sat back down and removed her pants to inspect the newest damage she had inflicted on herself. She was relieved to find nothing more than a small pink patch of skin. The wound on her thigh was another matter. Whatever it was that she had stumbled into last night, it had not done her any favours. Caked and crusted around the injury, the blood had soaked into the pant leg. Feeling carefully around the opening of the cut she noted that, although it looked nasty, it was shallow. No deep tissue damage, which was good. Once it had healed, all she'd be left with, as reminder, would be an impressive scar to add to her collection. Looks like I'll be needing a stitch or two to close that, thought Elle as she dragged a pack over. From it she pulled a large green metal box. Painted on the lid and all four sides, though faded, the white circle with a distinctive red cross was clearly recognizable.

It was one of three first aid kits she had found under a pile of rubble in a demolished hospital while on a foraging adventure with Noah. He had nearly wept at the find. She grinned, remembering the look on her grandfather's face and the jig he did in what had been the hospital's lobby. His joy was understandable. You just didn't come across a sealed, field-level first aid kit. Along with the rest of the pre-Dry medical infrastructure, they had disappeared a long time ago. Nowadays, you would be lucky to find a serviceable tin box. As the finder, the family allowed her to keep the smallest of the three, a real gift, as it would prove over and over again. Noah kept one and the one nearly as big as a foot locker was kept on the Farm. For Elle, its contents were another example of the wealth of the Before Times.

Selecting a curved suture needle, she placed it into the pot along with a length of cotton string and a fold of white cloth and then slid the pot onto the fire. Closing and securing the lid of the green box, she returned it to the pack. Now all that was left to do was sit there and wait for the boiling water to do its job.

The coming of the Dry had destroyed much of the old world's knowledge. Few PSims worked. The same with computers and other advanced electronic devices. Even if one had a source of electrical power, however intermittent, once the devices failed, other than to swap parts and hope for the best, there was no means to repair them. Technology, when lost, stayed lost.

Books, real books, were scarce. Even in the Before Times, with the advent of the global library, the desire to own a physical book was not much in evidence. The coming of the Dry destroyed the global library. Physical books, already becoming rare, disappeared in the millions. Those not destroyed in the fires that swept the land in those early years were incinerated during the Troubles.

From the beginning, the Farm was a repository for the printed word. As far as her family was concerned, books, whether fact or fiction, were treasures to be guarded and kept safe. This was especially true of any book containing technical information or to do with science. The farm house groaned under the accumulated weight of so many books that Elle's mother complained there was room for little else. Everyone in the family was an avid reader, even her dad. Although he confined himself mostly to books related to farming and associated topics, the odd murder mystery did find its way into his 'to read' pile. But it was the classics of the Before Times he loved best. If she happened to find such a book during one of her wastelands excursions, Elle delighted in seeing her father's pleasure at being presented with one that was not yet a part of his collection. Elle's reading preference was more like her grandfather's: eclectic, wide ranging, with a strong fondness toward anything to do with hard science, especially medicine. Often you would find her in the kitchen with a book propped up on the table and a coerced cousin, subdued with threats of bodily harm, sitting patiently while being practiced on. She'd become the family medic and was reasonably deft in stitching up the results of their various misadventures. In this she was even better than Noah, who was ecstatic the first time he observed her wizardry at tying a surgical knot with a pair of small forceps.

This time after allowing the lid to rattle away for a few minutes, Elle gently removed the pot from the edge of the fire and set it aside to cool. Fully aware of the lethalness of infection, she plucked the cloth from the still simmering water and began tentatively to remove the blood, dirt and grime around the wound before closing it with several stitches. The Dry was not devoid of antibiotics and such, but without the facilities of the Before Times and the educated people that ran them, things just kept winding down. Things that once seemed so plentiful were now rare or gone altogether and they would not be coming back. Fortunately it had only been three days since her bath at The Maiden. There had been times... well, best not go there, she thought. Later, admiring her handiwork, Elle pulled on her old ill-fitting pants over the freshly bandaged leg and redid the belt. With luck – that phrase again – she had expunged any contaminate from the cut. She knew from past experience it'd heal quickly.

Fortunately for Elle, she had returned to wearing her original over-sized and worn garb. If she hadn't, the new pants would have been torn and soaked with her blood. Except for the gold chain, the hat and Nic's harmonica, the gifts from the Traders had been consigned to the safety of the pack that held the photo. They had taken on the status of treasures, totems, links to a day with the Traders and The Maiden. The hand-me-downs would serve well enough. She threw a few bits of waste wood onto the glowing embers, aware of hunger pangs.

At the end of yet another meagre but inspired meal she took the harmonica from her pocket and tried playing the instrument as she had seen Nic do. After blowing a few tentative notes, Elle, feeling a tiredness sweep over her, put the instrument away and allowed her body to slide down the wall. Slumped in a heap on the bare rock, she was soon asleep. Sometimes the body is unwilling to perform what the mind demands.

This time when the dreams came they were more intense and the most vivid yet. Surrounded by unintelligible whispering voices, with lungs hungry for air, she was drowning in a silvery sea. There were bright twinkling dots of light all around her. Clawing to the surface, Elle struggled to wake, screaming. Bolting upright, taking in great gulps of air, drenched in sweat, Elle looked frantically about, desperately trying to orient herself as wave after wave of fear surged through her. She cried out again, a wail, a witness to her own death. Then, with a deep breath followed by a shudder that shook her whole body, she was released. Slowly her surroundings came into focus. Her breathing slowed as her heartbeat became more regular. The dream had seemed so real.

She started to get up but her muscles would not obey and she collapsed back onto the rock. Every part of her body felt rigid and aching. The fire had gone out and the sun was well past midday. She must have been asleep a couple of hours. Rubbing her shoulders in an attempt to relieve their stiffness, Elle again took a stab at getting to her feet. This time she succeeded. Still feeling the effects of the dream and the stiffness, she gave the horses more water and then started to pack up. Because Red Rim was to have been only a short midday stop, it did not take long to break camp and load up. Tapping Belle gently on the nose by way of saying she was finished, Elle led her companions toward their next stop, Table Top. Feeling stiff from sleeping on the bare rocks, she mockingly scolded Belle saying, "What's done is done, but next time, girl, don't let me sleep on the ground. Just remind me that it takes only a minute to get the bedroll." Realizing she was walking slightly bent over from the muscle tightness in her back, Elle chuckled at the thought that this was how Noah often looked in the morning when camping in the wastelands. As to the dream, there would be plenty of time to brood about that during the night's trek.

Since Red Rim, Elle had taken up hunting. This was not entirely out of need to extend her provisions; the civility of the Traders had seen that she was well provided for. The truth was that if she was frugal and there was grazing along the way, there were enough provisions for another six weeks or better. It seemed, unbeknownst to Elle, the Traders had not only returned her gifts of food but had added an ample selection from their larder. When she discovered their generosity, it explained some of the giggles and secrecy of Nic and his two small co-conspirators when they insisted on helping her repack. So it wasn't the need for food that drove her to hunt, it was the craving for meat that wasn't salted or dried.

Animals of any kind were never plentiful, especially in the depth of the wastelands. At best a hunter might be presented with one opportunity every two days or so. During the last two weeks she'd seen a deer, an antelope and a goat, any one of which she could have killed with a single shot. Out in the wastelands, however, there were other things to consider besides the expense of a cartridge. The discharge from a rifle could be heard for kilometres away. This was not always a good thing. To anyone alone, even one with Elle's talents, remaining undetected, anonymous, was not only preferable, it was paramount. Aside from the fact that her grandfather might be in pursuit, to unnecessarily alert others by advertising her presence could invite an unwanted and deadly visit.

Before settling down for the evening, she had gotten herself in the habit of setting snares, small loops of wire, along with pieces of food for encouragement strategically placed along game runs she'd find near her camp site. When she was about to head out, she would inspect her handiwork for the fruits of her labour. Rabbits were the most likely victims along with the occasional ground squirrel and rat. Like her, they proved to be scrawny and tough. Nevertheless, with a few dried herbs and vegetables and provided she let them simmer for a while, they made a welcome change. She skinned, gutted and de-boned them on the spot, then rolled the meat up in their own hides for later. Although Elle did not always do what was most prudent, fires in the open and at night, like the sound of a rifle shot, should be avoided if possible. A cooked meal was always a welcome reward. So if she was camping in a confined place such as Red Rim, she'd roast the meat over a fire during her midday break. On the other hand, if she knew she would be in a place where the fire was unlikely to be observed, she'd wait until settling down at the end of a day's trek and treat herself to the luxury of a slow-cooked stew.

The coming of the Dry had removed any uncertainty about weather. One impenetrably vicious hot day flowed indistinguishably into the next, as monotonous as the banal scenery. The only variation was the thickness of the swarm of insects that gathered about your head and how hard the wind blew. Elle paused to take a drink from the canister at her side. The warm water tasted flat as if the life in it had been squeezed out. Sliding the canister back into its holster, she stood for a moment to scan the horizon. A week had passed since leaving The Maiden and the company of those strange and colourful Traders. What lay before her was another empty town of ruins. The skeletal remains of a roadside rest area and petrol station, a road coming from nowhere ending at a collapsed bridge, a bicycle without wheels leaning against what had been the entrance to a sports field, failed to trigger any interest. Even if she had not seen these particular sights before, they were familiar enough. Like the weather, the coming of the Dry had reduced each town to the same interchangeable shades of grey, dust and debris, and therefore she saw no reason to leave the road and travel along the town's main street. That was unfortunate but there were, of course, reasons to steer clear of such towns, just as there were reasons to avoid riding along a ridge, crossing an open field, following a river bed or travelling through a narrow pass or gorge. All had the potential to harbour unwelcome and deadly surprises. "Don't ever make it easy for them," Noah had instructed her. "There are people who would kill you with no more qualms than that of swatting a fly."

The Red Rim and Table Top wells were behind her. In another four days she would be at the boundary of her known world, the furthest she had ever been west and close to being halfway to her appointed destination.

Right after the harvest, Noah, doing one of his 'look and see' trips, had taken her on a wide loop westward. Elle had been excited. The journey was planned to take about a month, the longest she had ever been away from home in the wastelands. No farm chores, just thirty-plus days of riding, hunting, exploring and camping. Midway through and at the limit of their westward trek they'd stopped at a particular homestead for the night. Although she had never met them, there was a struggling farming family living there with kids near her own age and water from a well. According to Noah the family held rather strong religious beliefs and so he cautioned her to keep her opinions to herself. She was also instructed to politely decline any offer of food as hospitality would force them to give what they could not afford. They would only stay overnight to rest the horses and replenish their water canisters. The following morning they would take their leave and begin drifting homeward with plenty of time for additional hunting and exploring. Things had not gone as planned.

What had happened still haunted her and would remain indelibly fixed in her memory.

The map indicated the homestead lay along the most direct route to a number of springs, including the one with the graves that Nicole wanted her to visit. Elle knew she didn't have to go there; all that was needed was to take a little detour, skirt around the edges. "No harm done. No time lost. Except... Except what?" She stifled a laugh. "That I'm petrified?"

The sun was near its zenith when she arrived at the outskirts of the deserted homestead. It was with some trepidation that she had decided to confront her fear. Noah would have approved. With a rifle in hand, she left the horses tied to a stump and moved to a vantage point where she could see, without being seen. The farm house and its outbuildings were the only intact structures for kilometres around. If there was anyone anywhere near, even though the well was dry, this was the place they'd come to get out of the sun and rest. Therefore, a degree of precaution was warranted and, besides, getting herself needlessly killed by not being prudent would have disappointed her grandfather enormously.

The scene below looked undisturbed, pretty much as she remembered it from when she was here with Noah. Nothing moved save the dust being pushed along by a small breeze. She lay there for a moment more, suppressing the images that kept trying to invade her mind. Pursuit by the hounds of Hades could not have induced her to set foot in that house again. Exposed in the open, the sun beat down on her prone body. Sweat trickled down her face and down along her back where it collected into a puddle soaking the waistband of her pants. Disturbed by the heat and pestered by the flies, she thought, you can't lie here all day girl; there are things to do, as she got up to retrieve the horses. They'd stay in the barn.

The barn's interior was a welcome relief especially for the horses. Although it had a distinctive lean, it was sound enough for her purposes and, short of having a critical support knocked down, it was unlikely to come crashing down anytime soon. Stepping into its shadows she was instantly greeted by the familiar smell all barns had, even when abandoned and forgotten. It was a cross between hay, leather, dung, urine, dust and decay. Elle loved it and was just about to start the ritual of relieving the animals of their burden when she froze. Dung? Urine? Without giving away that anything was amiss, she drew in a deep breath through her nose. The barn's stale but pungent air was tinged with faint odours that shouldn't be there.

To afford her some protection, she moved Belle into one of the stalls and, while untying the straps in order to remove a pack, she scanned as much of the barn she could without appearing to be too investigative. She removed one of the packs and put it on the ground. Squatting on her haunches, fiddling with the pack, she listened. Other than the impatient movement of the waiting horses and the buzzing of the flies, the barn remained silent. Keeping her back pressed against the stall's wall, she moved back to its entrance and, hoping that she wouldn't get her head shot off, looked out. Something small scurried briefly along the far side of the barn before disappearing into one of a dozen holes strung along the baseboard. If there was anyone out there, they were certainly not revealing their presence. She waited a few more minutes before stepping out in the open.

There might not be anyone there now, but there had been. The smells told her that much. Knowing she had been remiss earlier, Elle carefully moved around the barn scrutinizing every square metre for the source of the smell as well as any other evidence that someone other than she and her grandfather had used it in the last two years. Funny how the mind works. Even when it knows that a careless misstep can bring death, it can be remarkably inattentive. Trying not to think about what was in the farm house had been distracting. Now alerted, she could see a number of changes. The thick dust on the barn's concrete floor had been disturbed. The coming and going of multiple boots, hooves and wagons had left their distinctive marks; scattered remains of hay had been pushed against the back wall; there were piles of horse dung in a couple of the stalls. She walked over and squatted down to inspect one of the dung piles. It looked dry, definitely nothing recent. Picking up one of the round balls with her left hand she rolled it between thumb and forefinger before she crushed it and then brought it closer to her nose to smell. About a month old she judged, maybe more.

She got up, using the straw in the stall to clean her hand, and moved about to search the rest of the barn. In the dust near the doors, several rings were visible. Barrels? Now who would store barrels of anything in the middle of nowhere and then take them away? She circumnavigated the barn's interior again to see if she'd missed anything. There was no evidence to suggest that anyone had been here in the last month or so. She walked over to the open doors and looked outside and over at the house. Nothing, not a thing. Any evidence out there would have been swept away by the winds. Perhaps, like her, the visitors had taken advantage of the barn's amenities and stopped to rest for a few days before proceeding on. It wouldn't have been convenient to stay longer with no water.

She went outside and walked all around the barn and then went back inside to retrace her steps, inspecting every shadowed corner to see if she had missed anything. Her final conclusion was that whoever it had been, they were long gone. Of course, there was always the house.

Elle went over to the barn doors to stare at the farmhouse but went no further. Had Noah been with her he would have scolded her for her timidity, warning her not be inhibited by fear or blinded by biases. She knew they were luxuries you could ill afford in the Dry and she should have shown a bit more courage and gone over to the house and looked inside. Instead she justified her inaction by the shortness of her intended stay.

Coming back inside, she finished removing the packs from Belle and then started on Buck. Using some of their precious water, she cleaned away the sweat and encrusted salt from their backs. Within half an hour, everyone, including herself, had been watered and fed.

There would be no stew today. The sooner she left this place the better as far as she was concerned. Having left the horses tethered near the back wall, Elle selected a stall that was relatively clean, laid out her bedroll and was soon fast asleep.

Through a hole in the roof, a single shaft of light tracked the sun's path as it crept slowly across the floor of the barn before travelling up the length of Elle's body coming to rest on her face. This silent, solitary event saved her. She was seldom a deep sleeper so the light's intruding rays had already begun to wake her. To be cast suddenly into shadow by the appearance of a figure caused her to become instantly awake and fully alert. The speed at which Elle sprang to her feet with her knife at the ready startled the figure, causing him to hesitate in delivering what should have been a fatal thrust. As it was, she felt the tip of his blade strike her in the chest with such force that she stumbled back against the wall and out of his immediate reach. This effectively enabled her to parry his second thrust, which threw him off balance allowing Elle to flick her blade upward in a short slashing movement that inflicted a deep gash along the forearm that held the knife. The surge of pain and her aggressive counter attack caused the man to stagger back. He looked mystified at the unexpected wound that had suddenly appeared and the blood that now flowed from it. He took another step back and then another. Clear of the confined space of the stall, he stopped. Taking advantage of the escape route provided by her assailant, Elle followed him out onto the open floor of the barn where there was room for her to manoeuvre as she had been trained. In the stall, had he pressed his attack, she would have been trapped, confined where size and reach gave him the edge. In the open, these advantages remained but were less crucial against the fighting skills she possessed.

The knife sat within the palm of her hand as though it was an extension of her body. Alert to his every move, Elle sized up her opponent. He was thin, incredibly dirty and emitted a sour smell. A head taller than she was, he wore a long dark coat that she suspected would hamper him in the coming fight. To her surprise he was also wearing a 'Kill Joy' vest, a true marvel of the Before Time. But he'd left it open down the front. She had to be careful, as there was no way her knife could penetrate a Kill Joy. Even with it unsealed, wearing the vest made killing him much more difficult. She looked at the man's knife. It looked heavy and cumbersome, suited more for butchering than fighting.

Poised to strike, she rose up onto her toes, keeping the blade centred on the man facing her. He looked at the cut that ran the length of his forearm and then at her. His face twisted with rage as he snarled, "You little shit!"

The voice was a surprise. Not deep and threatening as she had expected, but shrill and whiney. He closed in on her. She was ready, having observed the change in where his eyes were now focused and the subtle shift of his weight from his back foot onto his front. It told her how and where the attack would come. Again the shrill and whiney voice. "I'm going to kill you."

This time, using his height, he brought the knife down in a wide sweeping arc. She sprang to her left, ducking under the knife, allowing his blade to pass harmlessly across her back while striking out with her own blade. It sliced through the coat, cutting into his right hip just below the vest. Springing back and out of his reach, again in the ready position, she watched and waited for his next move. Crying out like an enraged animal the man spun around to face this rag tag of a girl, a girl who had spent many long hours training for just such an encounter as this. The man began to circle around to her left in an attempt to move away from the hand that held the knife. He looked into the young girl's eyes and was startled to see no fear, none at all. As he once more pressed forward, Elle heard Noah advising her in that quiet way of his. "Stay calm, stay ready and watch. Most will clearly signal what they are about to do. Never give your opponent time to think. Always press hard so as to force them into making a mistake. Don't waste time, knife fights aren't supposed to last long. You can't afford them to."

The man felt the blood run down his body, soaking his pant leg as it poured from the wound on his hip. He was losing a lot of blood. Numbness crept up from the wound on the hip and travelled along his chest. He was in trouble. Seeing the girl asleep, he had expected an easy kill, not to be fighting for his life.

The two fighters continued to circle, using the time to assess each other. His breath was loud and laboured. Hers remained slow, deep and steady. Elle again heard her grandfather's voice. "Stay calm. Watch. Let your face betray nothing. If they talk, let them talk, and listen to the voice. Its pitch will tell you a lot of what will happen next."

From the cut on his arm droplets of blood fell to the floor, leaving small red puddles in the dust. His hand was covered in blood, making the knife slippery and difficult to hold. Elle could see that the fight was nearing its end. Soon the man would bleed to death. She could hold back and wait. Again she heard Noah's voice. "Finish it." The man's movements slowed as his mind tried to grasp what was happening to him. Before he had time to move against her, Elle feinted to his knife's side and as he attempted to counter her, she swung under his arm, taking his knife hand by the wrist forcing it up and away while driving her blade in between the narrow gap provide by the open vest, just below the heart, with the blade tilted upward. She felt his death shudder as she jumped clear, poised for another strike. As if suddenly remembering something important, he reached behind his back and drew out a hand gun, but it was too late.

White eyed with fear, the horses danced about in their stalls as the man slumped to his knees, tilting to the side as he fell forward, coming to rest on his back. Uncomprehending eyes watched the disturbed dust spiral upward in a beam of light before glazing over. Air rushed from his lungs; a slight twitch of a leg then it was over.

Elle, after making sure he was dead, seized her rifle from the stall and quickly moved to the open door of the barn. Crouching down she peeked outside from the safety of the barn's wall. Where in the hell had he come from? The answer to that question lay in the dirt. Prints led from the house's front porch to the barn. She glanced back at the dead man. "Bloody hell, how could I have I been so stupid?" she muttered under her breath. "I should have checked that bloody house." Returning her gaze to the farm house, she saw no hint that anyone else was there. Could the dead man have been alone or, like her family when strangers came, was there someone covering him from a window? Nothing moved. If someone was there, she thought, they did not seem to have much curiosity. Surely by now they would be wondering what had happened and come to investigate. "Better to wait a bit more, but I can't wait forever."

Shielded by a barn wall, Elle stayed crouched beside its open door watching for some movement from the house. She concentrated on the front door, suppressing the constant urge to turn and look at the man she'd killed. Elle reached up to touch the ring around her neck, a long standing habit, and felt a sticky moistness. There was blood on her fingers. Only then did she realize she had been stabbed. The front of her shirt was soaked with blood, her blood. She quickly unbuttoned the shirt expecting the worst, only to expose a small puncture below her left breast which corresponded nicely with her heart and the nick she could see on the inside of the ring. She scrambled on all fours back to one of the packs from which she retrieved a clean cloth. As with the wound on her leg, Elle tore a length of cloth to be used to hold it in place and then folded what remained several time before placing it over the wound. It had been a lot easier to bind the leg than it was her chest. Finished, she buttoned the shirt. She crawled over and picked up the pistol from the floor and shoved it into the belt around her waist. Feeling her own frailty and life's arbitrariness, she glanced at the dead man once again.

Back at the barn door, she looked out. Seeing that nothing had changed, she took a moment to inspect her handiwork and saw that blood was beginning to seep through the bandage. It must be deeper than she'd thought. There was no time to attend to it now. It would have to wait its turn as there were other more pressing matters that needed her attention. The sun would set in a few hours. There were a number of things she was going to do have to do before then.

She let a few minutes slip by. The windows with the faded and torn curtains stared back at her, betraying nothing. She surveyed the porch knowing that, once she got there, the roof over the porch would neutralize anyone at a window upstairs. Steeling herself, she muttered under her breath, "Now or never." Elle shot out of the door and sprinted for the front porch. Moving low and fast in the evasive zigzag pattern she had been taught, she hit the porch at full speed, rolled up against the wall and into a squatting position, levelling the rifle at the adjacent window. Pausing to get her breath, she listened. Silence. Carefully she rose up just enough to peek into the front room through the broken frame of the window.

The last time she had been in this house was with her grandfather. Back then the only things in the house beside its occupants were an odd assortment of dilapidated living and dining room furniture. Now there was stuff stacked chest high all over the room but no sign of anyone. Shuffling under the window and over to the open door, she looked into what had been the house's main living room. The place was a mess. Dozens of different kinds of bags, packs and boxes were stacked everywhere. The only clear area was a path that led from the front door through the dining room to the kitchen and another to the bottom of the stairs. Keeping a watch on both the stairs and kitchen door, Elle stepped into the room and picked her way through the clutter into the kitchen. Running her eyes over the room, she knew her mother would be horrified at the state it was in. It was not just dirty; it set a standard of filth beyond anything Elle had ever seen before. Not on the floor, the counter top or the kitchen table was there a single, clean square centimetre of space. One thing was for sure, one man, no matter how much of a slob, could not have made all this mess. Unlike the farm house where the kitchen table was ringed with chairs, there were only four chairs at a table that could have easily held twice that many. Four chairs for four people, it's a good bet, thought Elle.

A strange noise, a kind of muffled, high pitched, keening sound, came from beyond the door that led out to the back of the house. Taking no chances this time, Elle sidled up to the window that looked onto the back yard. Like the house, the yard was littered with boxes, cartons and crates. A horse, still harnessed to a two wheeled farm cart, stood quietly drinking from a shallow trough. The sound came again. It did not come from anywhere in the yard or from the horse but from a large burlap bag on the back porch; and it was moving. Whatever it was, it wasn't going to try to kill her as long it was confined in that sack, so it could wait until she finished looking up stairs.

At the foot of the stairs, with the rifle held high to cover the landing at the top, Elle looked up, drew a very deep breath, thinking that she really, really didn't want to go up there. This unease, this fear had already nearly gotten her killed. "Do it." She started up the stairs by stepping on the part of the tread nearest the wall. The irony of trying to avoid a squeaky step amused her since it seemed rather pointless at the moment. If they weren't deaf as well as blind, anyone up there was ready and waiting. Again she muttered as she stepped onto the landing, "I really do not want to do this."

Except for the presence of more piles of boxes and packs similar to those downstairs, the hallway was just as she remembered. Switching the rifle to her left hand, Elle pulled the pistol from her waist band and slid the safety off. At close quarters, the hand gun would be more useful, less likely to be batted away. She crept down the hallway and pushed the first of the four doors open with the tip of her rifle.

Leaning against one of the walls in the largest of the four bedrooms, with eyes half closed, like waking and finding that it was nothing but a bad dream, she enjoyed the feeling of relief. On her last visit there had been no sense of relief. Then the bedrooms had contained the fly blown, rotting corpses of eight children and four adults. Elle had seen death before but finding these people as she did, two families, was horrifying. She'd been sent reeling from the house into her grandfather's arms. Not knowing what had frightened her, after instructing her to stay with the horses, Noah rushed into the house with gun drawn only to emerge a few minutes later, ashen faced. All Elle had wanted to do was to leave immediately, but her grandfather had cautioned her not to feel threatened. "The family is dead. There is nothing we can do for them now for what is done cannot be undone." He'd given her a hug and reminded her that they were alive, the horses needed to get out of the sun and they all needed a drink and something to eat.

In the barn, Elle had seen a farm cart pushed all the way to the back and suddenly understood what had been nagging at her ever since they had brought the horses in out of the sun. Seeing Noah coming through the barn door she called out to him, saying, "Noah, there's a farm cart in here and dung in all the stalls, so what happened to the animals? Do you think they just wandered off?" Noah remained silent, keeping his council. If the truth can bring no good, then it best not be spoken. While his granddaughter attended to the horses, he had gone out to have a look around. In the backyard of the house he had come upon a grisly sight. "What were these people thinking, to go and do this?" There was no need for Elle to know. She had seen enough of man's stupidity for the day.

To distract his granddaughter from asking any more questions, Noah had sent her to get some water from the well and bring it back into the barn. When the well's bucket came up empty, she called Noah. "There isn't any water, granddad."

"Perhaps not, but let's be sure." He tied a sling for her to sit in and lowered her down until she touched bottom.

"Dry as a bone down here." It only confirmed what he already suspected. No water, no life. Simple.

Why the people hadn't left was a question Elle could never find a satisfactory answer to. Her grandfather was no help. He had seen every manner of death. This was a sad thing but it paled into near insignificance when compared with what the Dry was capable of. That it was unnecessary and avoidable seemed cruel but in his experience people tended to act upon what they believed be true, even if it contravened all logic and reason. He was about to pull her up when Elle called out, "I can see stars." Elle had just discovered what every well digger knows – in a well, you can indeed look up and see the stars, nearly as clearly as you can during the night. Noah liked that about Elle; even now, she found the world amazing.

They'd spent the night in the barn and Elle slept spooned within the curve of her grandfather's body, as close as the night's warmth would permit. Every time she cried out in her sleep, Noah would pull her closer to him to let her know she was not alone.

But that was then and this is now. Elle headed back toward the stairs, having satisfied herself that the house was empty. She had confirmed that four men lived here and that one of them was staring up at the rafters in the barn. That left three more. She did not think it would be in her best interest to wait for their return and she had no intention of spending the night anywhere near here if at all possible.

Back at the foot of the stairs, the sound from the back porch could be heard again, reminding Elle about the moving sack. Might as well find out what's in it, she thought as she threaded her way through the living room and kitchen and onto the back porch. Something was definitely alive in there, and from the sounds it was making, it was not very happy. Elle squatted down and began cautiously untying the string that secured the mouth of the sack. No sooner had she undone the knot than a black and white blur leaped out, knocking her off balance, causing her to tumble off the porch and onto the ground, flat on her back. The suddenness of the 'attack' completely caught her off guard. Lying there, winded, too stunned to move, she looked up at the porch and into the face of a small, hairy, black and white dog staring down at her with boundless joy, extremely pleased with itself.

"Bloody hell!" was all Elle could say.

Chapter Eight

You can tell a lot about a person by looking at the friends they travel with.

Elle picked up her rifle as she got up from the ground and worked the lever several times to ensure it hadn't been damaged. It seemed ok. Ignoring the dog's enthusiasm at being released, Elle slid the safety on and reached down to retrieve the ejected cartridges. As she did so, seeing an opportunity, the dog leaped down from the porch and gave Elle a very wet lick across the face and mouth. Sputtering, trying to wipe dog drool off with the back of her hand, Elle stood up and looked down at the dog and grimaced. The dog wagged its tail, giving one sharp bark. "That's twice you've ambushed me." Glaring at the dog, she continued, "If you try that again, I'll have your raggedy ass carcass for lunch." The dog looked up, whined and then moved its head under the hand at her side making her jerk it out of its reach. "No. Go away. I have enough things going on here without a flea ridden dog jumping all over me."

Trying to ignore her new companion, Elle surveyed the back area of the house. "Why didn't I see those cart tracks from the ridge?" The dog perked up its ears and gave another sharp bark. "Quiet you, I can't think with you yelping in my ear like that." The dog lowered its ears, sat back on its haunches and was, for the moment, silent except for the thump, thump, thump of its tail against the ground. Elle walked past the horse and cart, away from the house, following the tracks. The dog got up and followed. After a few steps, part of the puzzle became clear. Off to the left, the house had an attached garage with its doors opening to the backyard. That explained why they'd stopped using the stables. The garage was closer to the house and would have made it more convenient to care for the horses and load and unload the cart and any pack animals they might have. As for not seeing any evidence of the house being occupied, that question too was answered. Like at the Farm, a river had once run close to the house. Whoever these people were, they had used the smooth flat bottom of the sandy river bed as their track, allowing them to emerge just behind the house. From the stables, the river's raised banks and the height of the house had blocked the evidence that it was occupied. Noah was right; you can never know the unknown. This time it had almost got her killed.

The horse, having drunk its fill, was getting impatient at being left in harness and unfed. Elle, with the dog following at her heels, walked over and began to remove the leather binding. The horse flinched at her touch so she made soft cooing sounds to reassure it that she meant no harm. She hurried. The sooner she was ready and away, the better. Letting the harness fall to the ground, Elle took up the reins and led her newly requisitioned horse to the barn. The uninvited dog followed closely behind.

Elle's entrance was greeted by the sound of flies buzzing over the coagulating blood. "Never takes them long. I wonder how they do it," she mused. "Flies and buzzards – a corpse's closest friends." The dog was about to follow Elle into the barn when it saw the dead man. It emitted a low guttural growl and backed out with its tail tucked between its legs. Looking over her shoulder at the sudden noise coming from the dog, Elle guessed that this animal had a distinct dislike of the man lying dead on the barn floor. A bit more history than being tied up in a sack I suspect, thought Elle, as she tied the fresh recruit in a stall beside the other two horses. "Don't look gift horses in the mouth," she remarked as they eyed the new arrival. There were scars in the soft fleshy area where the back legs met the belly and along its flanks. Spur and whip marks? No one used either in her family and she had seen none among the Traders. What kind of man would use such things? Shaking her head in disbelief she secured their new addition to a rail and opened a feed sack, giving each horse a full measure. "You guys are going to need this. I want to be a long way from here when his friends come home. So we won't be stopping until daybreak."

While the horses ate, Elle cleared a large circle of anything that might catch unintentionally alight before building a small fire on the concrete floor. This is becoming an unfortunate routine, she thought as she took out the pot and filled it with water. The bandage was soaked with blood. Taking a length of cloth, the needle and thread from the green box, she dropped them into the pot, along with a piece that would serve as the new bandage, and then waited. Fire in a barn was not a good idea but at least in here it would be hidden a bit. The disadvantage was she couldn't leave it and go do something else. She did, however, make quick trips outside to make sure the dead man's friends had not arrived.

After cleaning around the wound, she stuck the tip of her little finger in the hole and found that it went just past the nail. Inspecting the bloody tip, Elle felt a little queasy. That was close. Luckily, although it was deeper than she'd thought, unlike her leg, the wound would need only a couple of stitches to close it up. When the water began to bubble she took out the two bits of cloth and hung them over the fire to dry.

When the wound was stitched and bound up in a fresh bandage, she changed her shirt and ate. Scavengers were not known for being hygienic and that went for their knives, but she had done all that could be done to stop the wound from becoming infected. The horses were not the only ones who would not be stopping tonight. Crushing out the fire and dousing it with the water from the pot, Elle left for a better look at what was in the house. She wanted to inspect the contents in those bags and boxes as well as the stuff left in the cart. Whoever these men were, they wouldn't have hauled anything all this way if it did not have value. Few things of the Before Times could still be manufactured these days, and this was especially true in the settlements that dotted the wastelands. Therefore, in spite of her rising anxiety about the dead man's companions returning, she wasn't going to waste an opportunity to salvage something useful. Elle had once heard her grandfather tell her dad that, when it came to foraging, having her with him was better than having a ferret on a lead. Having seen photos of a ferret, she wasn't sure if this was meant as a compliment.

The contents of each of the boxes and bags she'd opened heightened the mystery of what was going on here. Along with several Kill Joy vests, there were dozens of dead PSims, electronic boards, integrated micro components, things with knobs, dials and switches, coils of wire, clothing, shoes and lots different kinds of tools of which the majority needed electricity to work. There was no electrical power here as far as she could see, not even a generator, but there was back at the Farm. If this had been a 'fishing' expedition, she would have found some way to drag every one of these things back to the Farm for her dad. He loved gadgetry of any description. And tools? He would be beside himself with this lot, for in this room alone was enough to fill the wagon outside to the brim. More to Elle's delight were the books. Stacked all around the room, stuffed in boxes and crammed into bags were hundreds and hundreds of books of all kinds. Many appeared to be manuals pertaining to military hardware, while others were an assortment of novels, history, biographies and science. Only on the Farm had she seen so many books in such good condition. In the cities, if lucky, she might find a few books that were still intact, but nothing like this.

Some were still in their original, clear protective wrappings. This house, for some unknown reason, had become a treasure trove.

In the Before Times, the literary bond that welded reader and author together was fragile. Not because people were illiterate or even disinterested. Nearly everyone owned PSims of one kind or another that linked the user to a global information and entertainment network. Everyone and everything was connected. But the passion for owning, for holding a book, for smelling the scent of print rising from its pages, for the solitude and the giddiness of anticipation in reading a well written story had been replaced by other distractions. In the Dry's aftermath, the tenuous affiliation dissolved as national institutions, those delicate interlinking bodies that bind a nation and its people, shattered under the onslaught. The PSims went silent. People on the brink of starvation, fighting for survival or marooned in the wastelands, were alone, abandoned. Literacy gave way to more immediate needs.

Elle hastily flipped through the pages of a few of the books stacked by the door, fervently wishing there was more time. Why was time so grievous an adversary? She bent over and picked up a book whose cover attracted her eye.

Her family were all avid readers. For Elle it was pure pleasure for she did not just read books; they were devoured. Long after the rest of the family had wearily dragged themselves off to bed she would be at the kitchen table, oil lamp turned low, reading. Driven by an insatiable hunger, she consumed classics, science, biographies, history and novels at a ferocious rate. She had turned her grandfather's advice – to never go anywhere without a book – into a creed. And with her prodigious memory, she retained it all. She was the family encyclopaedia. In amongst so many books, she couldn't help herself. Even though the shadows outside were lengthening, Elle rummaged through as many stacks, boxes and bags as she dared, selecting those that looked promising. One in particular, a compact edition, she tucked into her shirt pocket and another, *The Body Snatchers* by a guy named Jack Finney, into her back pocket. She had a weakness for sci-fi. The rest she stowed in a bag she had emptied. Even if there was not going to be room enough for her to ride, it would be worth every step she took.

The kitchen was next. The room contained worthless stacks of dilapidated military looking boxes, a mixture of rusting canned goods with unreadable labels or no labels at all, lumps of stuff with a healthy growth of mould and something that appeared to be an exotic life form pulsating in the back of the cupboard. Their parents would be so proud, she thought, looking at the mess. Where's the stove? The family that had lived there would have had one. So, if it isn't in the kitchen... Elle went through the door and stood on the back porch...it's out here someplace, I'll bet. On the far side of the farm cart, tucked up against the wall of the house under a tattered tarp, sat the farm's kitchen. The dog's explosion from its confinement and the confusion that followed her tumble from the porch had caused her to miss seeing this makeshift field kitchen. Now, however, it came under intense scrutiny.

The kitchen being outside did not seem at all odd. Inside, outside, since the Dry what did it matter where one did the cooking? Without electricity, all Before Time appliances were useless. The cast-iron wood-fired range had been produced in the Before Times in small numbers for those who were 'off the grid'. These days there were few items more valuable to a family. The Farm had two large, rather ornate stoves. A part of the original owners' self-reliance, they had been there when the Farm was purchased by Atticus and Zee. This one in the yard was a plain and much smaller, poor cousin but, except for a missing leg, it was in surprisingly good condition. It had two cooking plates and resembled the one the Traders had been using at The Maiden – obviously very portable. A very nice find, however it was what was on those rings that grabbed Elle's interest. There sat a cast-iron pot, a camp oven with a lid and a large heavy skillet plus a set of matching long handled utensils: a spoon, fork, tongs and spatula. Elle had never seen anything like this matched set of utensils. Nothing matched on the Farm, a world of one-offs. After checking that they were undamaged and serviceable, she carefully wrapped and stored them and the camp stove in another satchel 'liberated' from the house. The kitchen stove would be a bigger problem but it was not going to be left behind. A skinned knuckle and a pinched finger later, the stove had been dismantled into its components, bound and made ready to be loaded onto one of the horses. One more peace offering to the family for when I return home, she thought to herself. Knowing what her mother might be going through, a few more treasures of this order would be needed to even begin to placate her.

Now it was the cart's turn. A rifle, sheathed in a leather case, was fixed to the wagon's side within easy reach of the driver. It was a military style weapon, an automatic with lots of plastic; short and light with a high-powered scope. The Farm's arsenal contained a number of rifles like this one, but she had never seen them used. Bullets were expensive, so she had been taught by Noah to prefer a single shot weapon and make each bullet pay for itself. However, examining the size of its magazine, she was in no doubt that it could do a lot of damage in a very short period of time. As it was not in her nature to wantonly destroy anything, and not wanting to leave it for others to use, she slung the weapon onto her shoulder. She stepped on the hub of the cart wheel and pulled herself up to have a look inside. Near the driver's seat were several metal boxes that, going by the faded markings on their side, contained ammunition. She removed the locking seal from one and opened it. Inside, pristine and undisturbed, laid hundreds cartridges of the type used by the automatic rifle. Very curious, she thought. Where in the world did he get a hold of stuff like this? The Farm had lots of metal boxes like these but they had been emptied of their original items long before she was born.

Moving the boxes nearer the side of wagon, her attention was drawn to several dark crescent-shaped stains on the wagon's floor. It didn't take her long to realize that the marks were identical to the circles in the barn. More curious, she thought. At a loss as to why they would be carrying around two hundred litre metal drums, she climbed into the cart for a closer look. The black stuff was sticky and there was no mistaking the smell; fuel oil. Curious indeed but it looks like whatever they are doing with it, they aren't storing it here, she thought. Encouraged by her finds, she checked to see what else of value the cart had on offer. To her delight, there were a couple of sacks of grain and behind them two canisters of water. "Not a bad haul. A least the horses won't go hungry," she said, speaking to herself but loud enough to cause the dog to bark. Suppressing a need to yell at the dog to be quiet, she continued rummaging around to see what other surprises were lying in store. Under the driver's seat she found slabs of meat layered in salt next to another stack of military boxes like the ones in the kitchen. Not knowing the meat's origin or whether it was any good or not, Elle's first impulse was to leave it when a yelp from the dog gave her another idea.

The dog had re-joined her as soon as she left the barn to re-enter the house. With its tongue hanging out of the side of its mouth and the tail wagging furiously, it followed her from place to place and from bag to bag, occasionally having a look for itself. Now it sat by the wagon making a nuisance of itself by barking. As Elle pulled the meat clear from under the seat, the dog gave another yelp and, if it was possible, wagged its tail more vigorously with an expression that could only be interpreted as anticipation.

"Are you hungry?" asked Elle. With that the dog jumped up with it forepaws on the cart's wheel and yelped again. "OK," Elle slid the knife out and sliced off a large chunk and tossed it over the side. The dog sprang up, catching the meat in mid-air. It was in rapture, gulping down the offering in just a few bites, and began to whine for more. "It appears, my little furry friend, that you didn't get much to eat while in that sack." She cut off another piece and tossed it to the appreciative dog. Thinking that it might also be thirsty, Elle found a container and poured some water into it from the canister in the wagon. When she offered it to the dog it drank every drop. She then told the dog, who sat at her feet with great expectations of many good things to come, that it was fortunate there was water in that cart or it would've been out of luck. "It could be poisoned, so we'll wait a bit to see what happens to you before giving any to the horses."

Not checking the wagon before removing the horse made Elle angry. This continued lack of forethought, of not thinking things through, was uncharacteristic. She'd bumbled from one near disaster to another. It was as if a part of her brain had drifted off some place leaving the rest to fend for itself. This was not how she had been trained, and she could not help but feel that Noah would be disappointed. Not just because she had nearly gotten herself killed, but why. She should have checked the house, but hadn't. Still muttering to herself like some demented person, Elle returned to the barn to fetch the dead man's horse. The wagon could carry nearly as much as all three horses, but it would leave a trail that anyone could follow. But without a packsaddle there was no way a load could be secured to the horse. Fortunately, everything she needed lay in a heap in front of the wagon.

With a bit of judicious cutting, stitching and tying she managed to rig a reasonable pack sling. Elle stepped back to admire her handiwork. Not perfect but it would do the job until she found the time to create a makeshift packsaddle. Finished, she fitted the sling onto Ted's back – every horse should have a name – and began loading the stove, cooker, grain and other 'liberated' contraband, including all the Kill Joys.

Back at the barn, which the dog still refused to enter, Elle finally turned her attention to the man on the floor. So this is what a Scavenger looks like, she thought. This was the subject of nightmares. All her life, she had heard the stories of such men, the personification of evil. Her grandfather couldn't even pronounce the word without gagging. If this was indeed a Scavenger, he wasn't a very impressive demon. His clothes, an odd mixture of old and new, civilian and military, were ill-fitting and incredibly dirty. The boots were military, and although the leather was cracked in places, the soles looked almost new, as if they had just recently been taken out of their box. The face, relaxed in death, was unshaven, grimy and heavily lined as one who lived rough. He was balding, and what hair he did have was grey, filthy and matted. His mouth, lips pulled back into a grimace, revealed broken and blackened teeth. Elle could see that this man had not lived a gentle life.

She went through the pockets in the coat and pants, finding five gold coins. The coins, with the image of yin/yang on one side and the words "Lest we forget" on the other, were identical to the ones in her saddle bags. Next she turned the man over onto his face so she could remove the Kill Joy vest and, in doing so, found the empty holster. She took the holster and pushed the pistol she carried into it. Like the rifle, the Farm had a few of these in their arsenal, short barrelled semi-automatic, 18 bullets in the clip, only useful if your target is less than 30 metres away. "A nasty piece of work, good for nothing but killing people," was how her grandfather described such things. Nasty or not, it came loaded with two spare clips. Since it was small and light, Elle slid the holster onto her own belt. The vest joined the others on Ted.

Time was again not cooperating as she hurried to load the remaining packs onto Buck and Belle. She should have left long ago as the threat of the dead man's companions returning remained a reality. Once the sun set, there would be some five hours before the moon rose, a lot of time in the dark. With Buck and Ted completed and ready to go, she took the saddle from the stall, flung it up onto Belle and did up the cinch. Even though there would be no room for her for a day or two, she checked that it would bear her weight and then loaded up the last of the remaining gear.

In spite of her increasing anxiety, there was one last chore that needed to be done before leaving. Grasping the reins just below the bit, Elle manoeuvred Belle past where the man lay and stopped. She then took a coil of rope that hung from the saddle and went over to kneel beside the body. Disturbed, a thick mass of flies swarmed about them as she turned the cold and stiffening body on to its back. One end of the rope was looped about the ankles; the other was secured the saddle's horn. A sharp pull ensured that the rope wouldn't come adrift in transit causing her the unpleasantness of having to go back to retrieve a damaged corpse.

With a quick tour around the barn to see if anything had been forgotten, Elle led the three horses out, dragging the dead man behind them. The wind that often comes with the setting sun was just picking up, filling the air with dust. This could be good, annoying but good, she thought. They turned and headed toward the riverbed and down its banks. Moving away from the house, she followed its course for a few hundred metres until she rounded a bend. Out of sight of the homestead, she looked for and found a place that suited her purpose; a high bank with a large overhang. She dropped the reins, knowing that Belle and Buck would stop Ted from wandering off, and attempted to undo her knots. More time wasted. The man's weight had caused the knot to dig into the horn making it difficult to undo. Thankfully the legs were easier as she had used a simple shank knot.

After coiling up the rope and securing it to the saddle, she squatted next to the body and rolled it over until it pressed hard against the bank. Satisfied that was as far as it was going to go, she looked for and found a way up the bank and onto the overhang. On the third jump the ledge gave way and unexpectedly took her with it. The dog, which had trailed behind, came up and looked at Elle sprawled on the ground. Worried, the dog gave her a reassuring lick across the mouth. Taking a swing at the dog and missing, Elle got up muttering unpleasant things about the animal while slapping at the sand clinging to her clothing. "What is it with all this licking stuff?" The dog sat, thumping its tail in the dust, assured that it had done the right thing and then moved under her hand. Elle looked over at her handiwork and gave the dog a scratch behind the ear.

His boots stuck out but other than that, the body was completely covered. Elle went back up and, with more care, dislodged enough sand and dirt to finish burying him. A gust of wind stirred the sand around her. Glancing back along the way they'd come, she watched an approaching cloud of dust. "I think this is going to work for me," she told the dog. The walls of the river trapped the wind and, acting like a funnel, swept the dry sand before it. Recalling how the front yard looked upon her arrival, as if no one had been there for years, she hoped it would do the same for her. The dog looked at the approaching wind and whined. "Well I can't say they won't find him, but if this wind keeps up, it might buy us a little time."

She jumped down, gave the dog another scratch and started to lead the horses back to the settlement. The dog, enjoying the unexpected attention, thumped its tail a few times before wandering over to the mound of sand to squat down and pee. She smiled at its sign of contempt. "You really didn't like that guy very much did you?" With the sun just above the horizon, Elle turned into the wind and headed back toward the homestead. The dog took its place by her side. At least a few good things had come out of nearly getting killed. The additional horse meant that in a couple of days she would be able to ride unencumbered. They had more water, two twenty-five kg sacks of feed for the horses and a bit of food for the dog. The extra food and drink also added another week to their supplies.

Elle looked at the dog. That thing probably eats as much as I do, she thought. Perhaps sensing Elle's ongoing evaluation, the dog looked up as if to reassure her of its intrinsic value. But it was not really about the dog. The problems associated with keeping a dog, a pet, were not foremost in her mind and she certainly didn't want any more responsibilities than she already had.

On the way back she brooded over how close death had come. She touched her left breast and felt the bandage beneath her shirt. Nearly murdered, and for what? She had been asleep. He could have taken her alive without any problem. And if he had wanted her dead, why not just shoot her in the head; after all, he had a pistol. Why the knife? If there was an answer, it had died with him. Her grandfather had a reputation of being bad tempered, but in her experience, he'd had always been gentle and patient with her, the family and any animal, even the ones he'd hunted. And yet, she had no doubt he would have snatched this man's life from him without compulsion or remorse.

For Elle, this was the second life she had taken and, as before, there had been no other choice. The first time was when she and Noah had been fired upon while exploring the ruins of a city. One of the men must have been a little too eager and sprang the ambush too soon. His impatience cost him his life and that of two of his companions before those remaining broke off to fade away. Her grandfather, when she asked if they were Scavengers said, "No, they were opportunistic bottom feeders, common thugs. Scavengers are stone cold killers and would have waited." Elle had felt nothing about those deaths, perhaps because there's nothing personal about killing at a distance. Through the scope of a rifle, men are just an object. And because caution had prevented a closer examination, she did not have the opportunity to see the face of the person she'd killed, or look into their eyes, or even know if it was a man or a woman. This time it was different. She was close enough to smell him, to see his face and watch the eyes as they clouded over when he died. This time it was personal, and for the first time in many years, it was not Noah but her mother she wanted to talk to. The incomprehensible nature of humans' murderous intent was beyond her thirteen years of experience.

Out in front of the homestead, she left the horses ready and waiting while she had one last look to see if she had missed anything of value. In the fading light, she poked around the living room, opening more boxes and bags. In the corner near the front door, she came across what she first thought was a blanket crumpled up in a pile of other discarded garments. Thinking that a large heavy blanket would come in handy, she picked it up. It was, however, not a blanket but a Trader's travelling cloak. Holding it up at arm's length with both hands Elle saw that it would fit someone slightly bigger than her and that the person who had worn it was dead. Where the Trader's heart would have been was a set of holes, both front and back, encrusted in blood. She wouldn't leave this here but take it with her. After checking to see what else was in the pile, she carefully folded the garment and went back outside to the waiting animals.

Feeling the stress of pushing her luck, and fearing that any minute it would start to push back, Elle knew that unless she wanted to end up like the man under the sand, she had to go. If there had been more time, maybe she'd have been able to eradicate most of the evidence of her presence here. Or was she just kidding herself? Even if she had had a couple days, it just wasn't possible. Setting aside cleaning up the pools of blood, the ashes from the fire, the poop and piss from the horses, there was still the missing man, his horse, the harness, the stove, the supplies, and a dozen or so other things she'd liberated. So it would have been a waste of time trying to hide the fact that someone had been there. If they were Scavengers, the question would not be would they come after her, but rather would they look for their companion first? They probably knew this area better than her, especially west of here. That was a problem. But what if they didn't know which way she went? Like those back at the Farm, they could end up wasting a lot of time finding out. So the plan was to head east, back toward Table Top, for a reasonable distance; find some hard or rocky ground that would make tracking difficult and turn north. Stay on that course for a while before turning west. The trick wouldn't fool Noah, and it might not fool them for long. But if it granted her any extra lead time, it was worth the attempt.

The swirling dust kicked up by the wind and the absence of a moon made traversing the rough terrain treacherous for the horses, particularly with the heavy loads they carried. It increased the likelihood of a mishap becoming more serious than a shifting pack. But considering a possible alternative made the risk acceptable. To help she'd picked up a long stick and, using it like a blind person, walked and tapped non-stop until the moon rose as a thin crescent. It would be with them until sunrise. They stopped, and while everyone had a drink, even the dog, she checked the packs, paying special attention to Ted and the makeshift sling. She shivered. The wind had finally dropped away leaving the night air surprising chilly for this time of the year. She reached into the saddle bag and removed the Kill Joy vest she had set aside for herself. Of the seven it was the smallest, and once sealed, the material would attempt to conform to her body like a second layer of skin, or would have if she had been a tiny bit heftier. Next she took out the Trader's cloak given to her at the Maiden and slipped it over the vest. As she did so, she thought about the one she'd found at the house. No one at The Maiden had mentioned a Trader being killed. If they knew, she was sure they would have said something to her. So who did it belong to? Why was it at the house, and why would a Scavenger keep a Trader's cloak with bullet holes? The blood stain wasn't fresh but it wasn't old either, not much more than a couple of months at best. So many question and no answers; but she did feel a genuine relief at quitting that place, and not just because of the possibility of the dead man's friends returning. It held nothing but bad memories.

The moon's frail light allowed little more than the ability to see a hand before her face and the lie of the land immediately around her. The night sky and the compass on her wrist both said they were still heading westward. Just as she was about to start up again, the dog shot past her to take the lead. At first she almost laughed at the absurdity of it but, while she knew what direction they were heading and could recall what information there was on the Trader's map, what lay ten metres in front of them was a mystery. Turning to Belle she said, "I hope that animal knows where she's going, 'cause I sure don't." This was true. By the time the sun came up and gave her the opportunity to look around, there was no telling what she would see. A person could get themselves into a lot of trouble wandering the wastelands in the dark. At least, as long as she could see the tail of the dog, they weren't about to go over a cliff. So whether the dog knew what it was doing or not, it seemed content to lead the column, and the horses, as if this was how they had been doing it all their lives, seemed happy to follow. The only one not so content was Elle. She was fed up with walking, and figuring the additional weight of her scrawny body wouldn't even be noticed, stopped, threw away the stick and climbed up on poor old Buck. Despite being perched precariously high, straddling a sack of grain like a rooster on a roof, Elle regained that sense of security of being on a horse. It could have been the height or just a kind of satisfaction in the familiarity of a horse's rhythmic stride. Whatever it was, right now Elle needed all the satisfaction she could muster as her thoughts drifted back to the stall in the barn and the man who had come close to killing her.

Why had he made it personal? The family might treat her like an adult, and Noah might have trained her to not only survive but to prevail in this hostile, violent and unforgiving world, but it didn't really matter how she was treated; over the last two weeks, it had become very evident that she was not an adult. Things had not gone at all as planned. She was making too many mistakes. In many ways, living on the Farm, in the wastelands, might have made her seem older than her years, but no matter how much experience she had, her mind had its own clock, set its own time. She loved the things Noah had taught her about the wastelands and felt proud of the skills her training gave her. Without them she'd be the one lying dead in that barn instead of the man. Yet, she remained a child. A talented and very dangerous one to be sure, but a child nevertheless. Perhaps, in time she would become an adult, if such time was granted, because not many children of the Dry reached adulthood. She longed for the comfort and safety of her family. She needed them to help make sense of it all: the Traders, the man she had killed, the bloodstained cloak. It was a lot to carry in such a young head. Elle rubbed her temples, trying fruitlessly to relieve the building pressure within. To make matters worse, her chest had started to feel as if it were being slowly squeezed in a vise. Releasing a long sad sigh, she craned her head back to view the wide night sky. In six more days there would be a new moon.

Those who had lived in the Before Time could not possibly fathom the night sky Elle took for granted. With no artificial illumination to dilute its clarity, no clouds now that the wind had stopped, no clouds of dust, not even a wisp of veiled mist to obscure the heavens overhead, from horizon to horizon, stars – billions upon billions of stars – filled her sky. Cold, lifeless, indifferent, pin pricked holes of stellar light hung in a sky so devoid of atmospheric disturbance, so sterile, the stars didn't twinkle. Elle felt, if she was not careful, the stars would reach down and suck life's breath from her. At such times she became more sympathetic to Noah's observation that this desolate, empty land was far too big for one person. Even with the Trader's cloak, she still felt chilled and in the need of her family's warmth and the sound of their voices.

Remembering the harmonica, she stopped her train of horses and retrieved it from Belle's saddle bag before resuming her place on the grain sack. It was time to see if she could pick out a tune, even if an undesirable someone out there might be listening. With the first notes Elle knew she needed lots and lots of practice and that it was indeed a stupid thing to do. With some difficulty she pulled the cloak up high enough so that she could put the harmonica in the pocket of the vest. The dog, hearing the harmonica, turned its head in Elle's direction trying to discern the nature of such a sound. Distress? Pain? Flee? Fight? It decided it was none of these, but whatever it was, for the dog and the horses the dawn could not come soon enough.

The Dry had decimated all breeds of dogs leaving only two types: the wolf size, like Teddy on the Farm, and the coyote size, like the one walking in front of her. But unlike this one, whose coat was long, thick and matted, most dogs were normally very short and rather thin. How an animal survived in the Dry with all that hair showed an inconsistency in logic. It should have died from heat stroke or something similar. But there it was, very much alive, with white upon black markings like ones she'd seen in a book, herding sheep. This was the same book that claimed the 'dog' was most likely the first domesticated animal and thus a companion of the human species for well over twenty thousand years. Elle liked the idea of two adversarial species with innumerable dissimilarities finding a means to cooperate. But that was in a book. Other than the dogs that accompanied visitors or the Traders and 'old' Teddy, Elle had precious little experience with them. Horses were another matter. They were useful, a necessity. Dogs, from her current perspective, were a disposable, luxury item. More like a liability. And yet, there was an indefinable pleasure in trying to play the harmonica in the light of the stars under a frail sliver of moon while watching the dog, its restless tail and loping gait. For its part, for the first time in its short life, the dog felt safe.

They came to a paved road just as the false dawn gave way to the sunrise. The road was nearly one hundred metres across. Astride Buck, Elle looked to her left and then to her right. Obscured by drifting mounds of sand in spots, broken and fractured in others, this black, undulating band stretched out of sight in both directions. This was not the first time Elle had stood on one of these massive highways that crisscrossed the width and breadth of this continent. She had been on its smaller sister north of here that was almost as impressive. There was supposed to be a third somewhere farther south, but she had never been given the opportunity to see it. This one was called The Great Central Highway, and unlike the puny two-lane road that skulked through her valley, this behemoth literally carved its way through the landscape like a bulldozer until it reached the sea.

Leaning over to give Buck a scratch between the ears, Elle said, "The map shows this running all the way to the mountains, so I guess we'll be travelling on it for the rest of the way. It'll be a lot easier than travelling across open country."

Shafts of light from the rising sun struck her and her companions, casting elongated shadows along the road leading west, the start of another blistering hot day. With a slight nudge from the heels of her boots, click of the tongue and flick of the reins, Elle swung her company onto the road, and following their shadows' lead, headed west. It was time to start looking for a place to stop for the morning as it had been a very long night. The dog, having been somewhere investigating something or other, looked up and saw that it was being left behind. Abandoning whatever had drawn it away, it raced to rejoin them.

Chapter Nine
What is it about a friend that separates them from all others?

Fronted by acres of asphalt-covered car parks and embedded within a row of mock adobe-styled architecture sat a building, like its companions, covered with peeling and cracked earth brown stucco. It was one of those 'family' restaurant chains. Not the first of its kind she'd encountered; she'd seen and been in dozens of them. It seemed to have been a requirement to have at least one in each of the ubiquitous 'strip malls' that littered the perimeters of any arterial road. Each one, no matter where it was located, the theme, the food, the building, inside and out, would be nearly indistinguishable from any of its siblings. Coming from a world where most things were handmade one-offs, why this was desirable was never clear to Elle.

Set back a few metres to accommodate a patio, this one once had a floor-to-ceiling window running its full length, the remains of which, tiny cubes of glass, now littered the patio and its interior. She struggled to dismount with a modicum of grace from her elevated perch and failed. A droplet of blood formed from a small cut on the palm of her hand. "I can't even get off a horse without injuring myself," she muttered. Using the toe of her boot, she slid some of the offending glass out of the way before inspecting the opening to see if it would allow easy access and room to accommodate the horses.

The place was a shambles. Whatever the particular theme of this restaurant had been, it had been vandalized beyond recognition. But it was big enough to house them in relative comfort with the added bonus of a clear view of the highway in both directions.

As she'd already accumulated more than her share of cuts and bruises, and to avoid anyone else being pierced by a piece of glass or a protruding nail, she cleared a path to and through the window. Once inside, she kicked more shards and bits of debris aside to create a safe place for all of them. The dog, not waiting for an invitation, followed. Away from the sun's growing strength, Elle began the ritual of relieving the horses of their packs. Since the dog showed no sign of being poisoned, she gave the horses water from the Scavenger's canister and some grain. The dog, anticipating that it too was about to be fed, wagged its tail with great vigour. Elle cut a portion from the slab and, using a knife, scraped it clean of excess salt. Even though dogs required as much salt as humans, just like humans, too much was dangerous. Next time it would perhaps be better to soak the meat and wash out as much of the salt as possible before giving any more of it to the animal. As it was never wasted, she'd use the now 'salted' water for cooking.

After feeding the dog, the next thing was to give each of the horses a thorough brushing. Belle was first, and then Buck. Feeling guilty, she paid him special attention for having to carry her as well as his load. When Elle approached her new addition, the horse seemed unsure of the attention it was about to receive. At first the horse attempted to shy away, shivering and moving restlessly under the brush as it was stroked. But Elle had a way with horses. With each long slow soothing stroke of the brush, she cooed softly, reassuring Ted that he would come to no harm. Feeling the brush and listening to her soft voice, the animal soon warmed to this rather pleasant new sensation. By the time she had worked along his shoulders and down onto his chest the horse even started to lean into the brush, giving just the smallest quiver of pleasure. Finished, Elle gave the horse a pat on its neck. "Didn't anyone ever show you any lovin' before, fella'?" The Scavengers' reputation for cruelty toward their captives was well known. Feeling numerous raised welts from healed wounds beneath the horse's hair told Elle that it extended to the animals in their care as well.

The task of caring for the horses completed, she started to attend to her own needs. The efforts of the long night's trek, no sleep, little food and stumbling along in the dark, had been hard on them all. She was bone weary and wanted nothing more than something hot in her stomach and some sleep. The first she'd be able to do. The second, other than a brief nap, would have to wait as she was, again, pressed for time. To put as much distance between them and the homestead as she could, she'd have to push through the midday heat. Not what she desired, but a more attractive alternative than being caught. This effort meant she'd arrive at Alissa in the afternoon, with plenty of time, if it was unoccupied, to set up camp and prepare for the possible arrival of unwanted guests. If someone was there who took exception to her showing up...well, she was wearing a Kill Joy. Either way, as the moon would not rise until well past midnight and there was no desire on her part to blunder around in the dark again, at Alissa's she might find a way to get some needed sleep.

Right now, she wanted nothing more than to get something to eat. Noah had once told her, while demonstrating his proficiency, "the making of fire is as close to an ancient ritual as our people have." Foraging among the refuse, Elle collected shattered bits and pieces of timber for firewood which she then stacked up on the restaurant's forecourt. When she'd collected enough for her purpose, she fetched the hand axe from her saddle and began to split some of the brittle wood into kindling. Like much of her gear, the axe had been a gift from Noah, presented on her eighth birthday. He said he had found the neglected head behind one of the Farm's old sheds. It could easily be more than a hundred years old. The original handle had long since deteriorated to nothing so he had fashioned its replacement himself. While handing the present to her he had said, "Elle, a horse is a necessity and with a knife and an axe you can survive almost anywhere. Keep it with you. Take care of it and it will serve you well."

Elle returned the axe to its holster on the saddle and, squatting back down by the pile of fire wood, pulled the knife from its sheath with her right hand. With the left she selected a likely candidate from the pile of kindling for the next stage. The keenness of the knife's blade soon reduced the stick to a neat pile of fine shavings which were placed under a cradle of kindling. The task completed, she took her prized fire kit from the rucksack, a striker and flint, and set to work. Soon the tiniest whiff of smoke rose up from the shavings. Another thing you could be assured of; in the Dry, all wood was dry. Elle lowered her head, nearly touching the ground, and expelled the gentlest of breaths. A glow appeared. Another breath and the glow expanded. With the third breath, the glow flickered and then ignited, rewarding her with the eternal magic of flame.

The next minutes were a blur of activity. The new camp oven, with its marvellous lid and half-ring steel handle, was put to work. Water, a careful selection of dried, preserved, and salted provisions, a few herbs and the last of the rabbit were added to the pot. Table Top was the last time she had eaten anything, apart from quick snacks she had gobbled from the rucksack. This was to be a welcome change from hardtack; a good thick stew with lots of gravy. The dog, having finished the meat given to it, found a place beside Elle. It looked at the simmering pot, which soon emitted an enticing aroma, and then at Elle and then back at the pot. In between, it made loud slurping sounds with its tongue. This perceived expectation of good things to come prompted Elle to turn to the dog to inform it, in terms the animal could hopefully comprehend, "If you think you're getting any of this, you can think again. If you want any more food go outside and kill something 'cause you're not having any of mine."

Afterwards, not as contently full as she had planned, Elle looked over the top of the map to watch the dog trying to harvest the last tiny morsel remaining in the pot. "Bloody greedy mongrel," said Elle to a room full of animal indifference. The dog looked up at her voice to ensure there was no pending problem before returning to its happy task of licking the pot clean.

Going back to her study of the map, Elle could see that this highway ran very close to her destination. Maybe another twenty kilometres would put her in line with where the spring should be. And from the map, it did look like there was a turnoff for her to follow all the way there. With luck there might even be a sign pointing the way, although she had no idea what it would have been called before the Dry. Having decided on the route, Elle snuggled down in a hollow she'd made with the packs and allowed herself to drift into a shallow sleep. "I'll just take a wee kip," she told herself. Soon her breathing became slow and rhythmic and the lines along her forehead softened. That is until the dreams came flooding in. They distorted her expression, forcing her body to respond to their intensity. She trembled as if cold, struggling with the phantoms. Then they were gone, vanished. Her body became calm and relaxed again as she fell into a deeper slumber. But this time there was a difference. This time when she woke she remembered something about the dream along with the impressions of its fierceness. The rainless storm, vast, eternal, raging, an unstoppable juggernaut that darkened into an opaque mass as it swept over her, had eyes that looked into hers.

To add to the unease that the dream had left her in, Elle woke to find that the dog had managed to find a way to snuggle up without disturbing her. Although it was not an altogether unpleasant sensation, her first reaction was to yell, "Get off me you stupid mutt", but delivered in a tone that was neither convincing nor punitive enough to discourage the animal from trying again at the next opportunity. Still, this bothered Elle. She did not like to think it possible that the dog could have crept up as it did without waking her. This dented her pride a bit. Except perhaps for her grandfather, she'd thought herself immune to being surprised in such a manner, even by this manipulative and apparently cunning dog. As she tried to remove the evidence of the dog's closeness from her clothing by picking off each and every hair it had deposited, she consoled herself that she must have been really tired for this to have happened. It is doubtful if Elle understood the nature of this particular dog, but she had, without her permission, acquired a friend.

A quick glance at the length of the shadows outside told Elle that it was still a few hours before noon, which meant she had slept for nearly two hours, both a good and a bad thing. Knowing what was in store for them once outside, she again weighed up her options. While it was preferable not to travel in the heat of mid-day, the pressing concern of possible pursuers and the threat they imposed outweighed the disadvantages. If it was going to be hot for her, it would be hot for them as well. Even if they had correctly guessed her destination, she was certain they would not have been able to follow her and therefore would not know precisely what route she had taken. No, the real danger would be as she approached the spring. They could get there before her if they pushed their mounts hard enough. That was a risk she was not prepared to take. Her horses had to not only get her to the mountains but take her home again. She could hear her grandfather's voice in her head advising her to avoid the temptation of short term gains. "They're often too expensive to be of any good."

Her grandfather was an endless source of advice. For a man noted for his silence and keeping his own company, he seemed to make an exception with her. Around her he talked; a privilege given to none of the others, not even her mother. It was from him that she had learned how to read both the land and the people it contained. He had insight, an understanding of the way things were, the way people were. No matter how much one might wish otherwise, the world was dying. Noah knew this and accepted it but he'd not yield. He had remained alive when others had not. He was born into a world still rich with human life numbering in the billions. Now the world's population was less than one percent of what it had been and declining. At times she felt like an empty bucket that he was trying desperately to fill with all that he had learned, fearing as he did so that there was not going to be enough time.

Everything was a lesson with him. Once in the wastelands they had observed a hawk swoop down to nab a rabbit. He told her, as the pair rode by the feeding hawk, "Learn from the mistakes of others, Elle, because only the very lucky get a second chance out here. This," nodding at the dead rabbit, "is what happens when one has a momentary lapse of attention." It was a graphic illustration.

The image of the feeding bird of prey came to mind as she finished the last of her preparations for departure. The dog sat outside, waiting with irritating eagerness, its tail sweeping a clean half circle on the concrete. Elle, doing up the cinch on Buck, looked over at the dog. "Don't look so smug. I only fed you because, when I get a little short of victuals, I want you to be nice and plump." The dog's tail cleaned more vigorously. Elle took the reins of the horses and prepared to leave. In case the men were out there, instead of becoming an easy target by sitting high up on her horse, she'd use a trick her grandfather had shown her. Until they were clear of this built-up area she would walk wedged in between the horses. While it made it more difficult for anyone to draw a clear shot, the tactic did have an inherent problem – the ever present danger of being stepped on.

Chapter Ten

Hatred is born from unresolvable private grief.

The sun slid past its mid-day mark and heat reflected from every surface. Other than having to skirt around a collapsed overpass that blocked the full width of the highway and then pick her way through hundreds of abandoned vehicles, the morning had been thankfully uneventful. Driven from the tarmac, Elle, again perched high on Buck's back, travelled along the brick-hard median strip. Its surface was nearly as good, cooler and with no sticky tar to contend with. All the horses had to do was avoid stumbling into the drainage ditch or falling into one of the soak holes. The strip mall with its decaying adobe stucco proved to be the prelude to what had been a sizeable city in its day. The highway, like a great river, sliced through its centre, separating one half from the other. From what she could see from the sunken hollow of the median strip, this part had fared reasonably well during the years since the coming of the Dry. Certainly better than most other towns and cities she'd seen. A few buildings showed evidence of fire, but at least here they had somehow remained confined, local. For one reason or another, the infernos that swept through the surrounding lands had failed to penetrate this far. That might be because in the Before Times this was already an arid landscape where fires had been frequent visitors. The vegetation, trees, farms, golf courses, gardens, lawns were all confined within the limits set by the reach of a sprinkler or could survive the long periods between rain falls.

Of course, in the Dry, there were destructive forces besides heat, time and fire. There was the hand of man. As she looked around, it appeared the city had miraculously been spared the wrath of that particular species. But the lack of destruction didn't mean anything of value remained. Like everywhere else, along with the former inhabitants, it would have vanished. When the rains stopped, when the dams emptied, when aquifers went dry, when the municipal water ceased to flow, the people who worked and lived here, as they had done all over the country, simply left. Not always taking just what was theirs, they abandoned their homes and places of business. Over the years, even during the Sorrows, border wars and the ravages brought on by the Scavengers, Traders and other wastelands wanderers, when given the opportunity, would pick over whatever spoils remained. Elle had no doubt her grandfather would have been numbered among them. Sixty years later, what fires failed to consume and mobs, vandals and foragers hadn't destroyed or stolen, the Dry's merciless unrelenting heat hammered into submission, covering it all with a monochromatic, lifeless, grey dust.

Still this was an opportunity to explore a city that wasn't a pile of rubble and, under different circumstances, the impulse driven by an innate curiosity would have gotten the better of her. Alone and pursued, the risk of going 'a-wandering' wasn't worth it. She soothed her disappointment with the consolation that upon her return she'd take the time to see what secrets the city might yet yield. That was a promise. This being on her own was proving to be more of a nuisance than she had anticipated. If Noah were here it would be different. The Scavenger would never have been given the chance to get the drop on her and any pursuers would be under more danger than those pursued. The sudden realization that her supposed independence depended upon another was an unwelcomed revelation and further eroded her sense of self-esteem. She shook her head in an attempt to dislodge the image forming there of a weeping little girl hiding in her grandfather's arms.

Batting impatiently at the image and the circling flies with her free hand, she leaned back until she was looking straight up at the sky and yelled, "I know, I know, I should've checked the house."

With Noah's knowledge of the Before Times and its aftermath, the city's architecture and artefacts did not melt into a dirty brown blur. He had the ability to bring the most innocuous of items to life, giving it a kind of personality and animation all its own. Because of him the derelict water tower over to her right, announcing the entrance to the city, and a string of communication masts, were not an incomprehensible curiosity. She knew all about them. Dozens of the towers and hundreds of the masts would have dotted the city's landscape, providing landmarks, dependable water pressure and global telecommunication for its citizens. Although the masts were now silent, the water tower, a lone sentinel, with faded lettering giving a name to this part of city, had context. Through Noah she saw the Dry and the wastelands, both in detail and as a historical living event. It was he who explained that the present was nothing more than an accumulation of all that went before. So she also knew what likely fate had befallen this sole survivor's once numerous companions.

Here on the city's fringe, there were a few offices blocks or high-rise apartments but no fashionable boutiques or cafes. The ghostly remnants of fast food restaurants, factories, car lots, real estate brokers, small service businesses and petrol stations bordered and defined the roadside. Out of sight, away from the road and its industrial maze, was the domain of the suburban estates and their supporting malls. She couldn't see them but she knew they would be there, sprawling outward all the way to the horizon. Why anyone would want to live in a suburb was incomprehensible to her. In a city's heart, if it was as exciting as some of her books had indicated, perhaps; in the country on a farm, most certainly, but a suburb? Why? Suburban houses, from her understanding, confined to a tiny piece of dirt, circled by neighbours with equally tiny pieces of dirt, had neither the city's hurried intimacy nor the country's less inhibited freedoms. But according to Noah, millions had chosen to live that way.

The median strip disappeared when the road dipped and began to run between high concrete walls. Elle, the dog and the horses moved in and around the congestion caused by the numerous cars and trucks that clogged the highway and in and out of the shadows of the bridges overhead. Hemmed in and unable to see over the walls, she wished she'd gone around the city. Even if it had taken longer, she wouldn't have felt so vulnerable and exposed, and not just because of the increased risk of coming to harm. It was visceral. People who spent their lives isolated in the wastelands felt confined the moment their vistas contracted. It didn't help that the city stretched ahead for several kilometres more or that the horses' footfalls echoed off the surrounding concrete, exaggerating their presence.

There was one small consolation. She'd never before seen so many different kinds of vehicles jammed together in one small area. Like the photos in magazines, they resembled something akin to a huge used-car yard of the Before Times. There had to be over a thousand cars and trucks filling all the lanes of the highway, the shoulders and the off ramps in both directions. Before the walls obscured the view of the city, she'd seen hundreds more stranded along the service roads paralleling the highway and the connecting side streets. Trapped between the concrete walls and the vehicles, they had barely enough room to thread their way through the congestion. Why were there so many cars? In her experience vehicles weren't abandoned in a great clump like this. Normally they would have been taken by their owners or by dead-enders, those who were the last to flee. Only later, when they'd run out of fuel or had broken down, would they have been abandoned. This gave rise to another question; why were there bodies in some of the cars? Unless they were murdered, people didn't routinely die while sitting in a vehicle, and if the city was still largely inhabited, they certainly would not have been left there. Another small question; other than being sand blasted to bare metal, most of the vehicles, like the city, had escaped destruction. That, to her, was unprecedented. Any vehicle, left as these were, would have shown some sign of being vandalized.

Emerging from the dip in the highway and back out into the open, away from the confining walls, Elle noticed another oddity which prompted her to ask one last question. Looking up and down the line of vehicles; if this had happened long before her birth, shouldn't there be a bit more sand piled in and around them? This last question drew Elle's attention to a line of semi-truck and trailer units, so called road-trains, parked nose to tail along the road's outer verge. If they were abandoned at the same time as the city, shouldn't they share a kind of seamless uniformity with their surroundings? The thickness of windblown dust and sand should be the same on every object whether it was a car, truck or doorway. These road-trains did not share that uniformity. The dog whined and looked up at her. It didn't share her interest. It was hungry and so trotted off, weaving its way in and out of the line of cars, searching for something to eat.

Alerted that things were not quite right, Elle slid the rifle from its scabbard, dismounted and wedged herself between two cars before scanning the surrounding buildings to see if there was anything else that appeared out of sync. In the Dry nothing could be taken as mere coincidence. Someone had tampered with these trucks long after the city should have been deserted. She wanted a closer look. Using the horses again as shields she moved out from the protection of the cars and walked down the line of trucks. The fuel-cell packs were missing, fuel caps had been removed and left where they'd been dropped, and holes were punched into the underside of the fuel tanks. Although the pools had evaporated, there was evidence of spilled fuel, still sticky to the touch. Whenever she and Noah were on a walk-about, fuel-cell packs and fuel, especially diesel, were two of the items always on their 'essential' list. Looking at the empty fuel-cell cradles and punctured tanks, she saw that the Farm was not the only ones who had batteries and diesel on their essential list. This was perplexing and a little unnerving. Except for the Farm and the settlement she'd just left, there weren't any others she knew of within three weeks of here, and all of them had long since been abandoned. Whoever did this had a lot time and a lot of willing hands. Maybe it was the Traders on one of their foraging expeditions. Why not? She and Noah did. But what if it wasn't the Traders? Who would have had the numbers and the organisational skills to carry it off? She remembered the circles in the barn and the wagon. "This is not good," she murmured.

Instead of seeking shelter from the mid-day sun for her and the horses as she should have done, Elle kept walking up and down the line of trucks. About fifteen years ago the last of the Scavengers gangs were either hunted down and killed or scattered to all points of the compass. So if not the Traders or the Scavengers, who? Skiving off with a horde of fuel-cell packs was understandable, but the fuel? There shouldn't have been any or not enough to concern yourself with. It would have been siphoned off by a needy someone decades ago. Besides, over a relatively short time fuel deteriorates. Any dregs left in those tanks would have been useless. But someone had thought it was worth the effort. This was a puzzle fit for Noah.

The art of refining fuel was not a lost art. Fuel could be and was produced from a variety of sources. All that was needed was a sufficient concentration of people, technology and the appropriate raw material. Although, according to her dad, the resulting quantity, when compared to the effort required, was often disappointingly small. The same could be said of the batteries. This did not stop bigger settlements. Despite the cost, whether powered by methane, petrol or batteries, in the cities and towns the sight of cars, trucks and even the odd plane was not that unusual. Even the farm produced fuel and used the resulting blend of bio, ethanol and methane to run an old diesel generator, a couple of tractors and the old four-by-four truck. As far as the batteries were concerned, a whole room in the house was devoted to storing the electrical energy derived from the photo-electrical panels and the wind turbine. Considering the number of vehicles along this road and the number of ones that were powered by fuel-cells, you'd have to wonder just what these people were up to.

Now that she was aware of what to look for, the evidence of the visitors' thoroughness was impressive. Without exception, every vehicle she inspected, if powered by a combustion engine, had punctures in its fuel tanks; if powered by batteries, their cradles were empty. A glimmer of suspicion crept into her head. In the Dry, all things were in one way or another linked. The event at the homestead, the things strewn around the house, the black rings on the floor of the barn and the farm cart were somehow connected to the missing batteries and punctured fuel tanks. She'd bet all the gold in her packs that the drums were full of collected fuel.

Looking up at the sky in mock prayer, Elle said, "Noah, what is going on here? I thought you said that the Scavengers were all dead? Well, I think I've got news for you: it appears you may have missed a few."

Up the road, opposite an off-ramp, she could see four petrol stations, one occupying each corner of the intersection. "If I was looking for fuel and batteries, that's where I'd go." She flicked the reins, dismissing the possibility of being shot from her perch, and headed for the off-ramp. There she found all the evidence she needed to convince her that a well-organised effort had gone into retrieving any remnants of fuel. Each courtyard had been dug up, exposing the massive underground storage tanks. At one of the stations, however, things had definitely not gone according to plan, failing in a most spectacular fashion. One of the tanks had erupted in what had to have been an enormous explosion and fireball. The eruption had created a huge hole in the ground, buckled the station's thick concrete forecourt, toppled several support pillars and collapsed the roof. The resulting blast had also knocked down and set fire to everything within a fifty metre radius. Standing in amongst the wreckage Elle was certain that whoever they had been, they wouldn't have had time to be terrified before being vaporised. "I'll bet the survivors showed a bit more caution in any further endeavours."

To see what other surprises might be in store, she continued on foot along the service road to the next on-ramp where she came upon a fire truck turned onto its side. She had seen one similar to this and it had not been in a book. The town north-east of the Farm had one, minus the tyres, the engine, the drive train and anything made of brass, stranded in the fire station The one on its side in the middle of the road looked like someone had taken to it with a sledgehammer. Not only were the batteries gone and the fuel tank ruptured, the whole upper swivel water cannon looked like it had been dismantled and carried off. "Fuel, batteries that I understand but why in the world would anyone want a water cannon? And where is there enough water to use it?" With her curiosity fully aroused, she really wanted to see what else these people might have been up to, but it was getting late. Her enemy, time, was moving the sun across the sky. Keeping the rifle cradled in her arm, she clambered back on Buck. The heat was crushing out here in the open.

Contrary to her earlier plan to push on toward Alissa despite the heat, the animals needed rest, shade and water. Settled once more in the crux of the packs, she conceded, even if she pushed on, so much time had been lost it was unlikely that she'd make the spring within the needed safe margin. "What to do? Can't stay out here in the open, because right now I can't summon up enough moisture to spit; and I don't want to be in the city." Propped up against a pack, she pulled the map out to look for an alternative. She had already memorized the map but it didn't hurt to have another look. Also, like a book, there was something about holding the map that felt satisfying, reassuring. Her eyes traced the route she'd travelled. If stopping here within the city limits was not an option, she would have to find a place that was, and this, pointing at the symbol of an airport, would suit her needs perfectly.

Except where windblown sand covered the surface, the road remained as hot as a stove top. The oozing bitumen tar stuck to the horses' hooves forcing her to again seek the relative coolness of the median strip. The dog, coping as best it could, had lost much of its earlier zeal. Panting heavily and looking miserable in its thick coat, it flopped down in any available shade to wait for the others to catch up. What she wanted was to be clear of this city, but the vehicles continued to make it difficult for the horses and the ruins just continued on. Until they reached the airfield she could only sympathize with their discomfort.

Just when it seemed as if the city would go on forever, Elle was stopped by a collapsed overpass. Similar to the one they'd encountered at the city's entrance, the scattered debris across the highway blocked any further progress. There were a lot of things about this city that made Elle very uncomfortable. Two collapsed overpasses, one at each end of the city while those in between appeared fine, was not a coincidence. A close inspection of what remained of a concrete support confirmed her suspicion. Blast marks. Someone had blown this overpass up. Even if she had had the time, there was no need for her to go back to check the other overpass. This had been a trap.

She wasn't going to waste time sitting on Buck, figuring out why anyone would blow up two overpasses to trap a bunch of people in their cars, especially since the cars were still here. Something very bad had happened and she was sure her grandfather would know what it was. But Noah was not here to ask.

All she wanted was to get out of this city, find some shelter, feed, water and rest the animals. A skewed and battered sign on a metal arch over an off-ramp indicated the direction of the airport and the distance in kilometres. She sighed with relief. With a flick of the reins, Elle guided the horses up the damaged ramp and onto the road that lead away from the city and towards the airport.

The land surrounding the airport, even by the standard of the wastelands, was bland and stark. It was also unequivocally flat, with no mountains, not even a respectable hill. Large rectangular industrial buildings, like discarded tin boxes, squatted beside the road. Here and there a woody nub poked from the ground; all that remained of the few straggly trees and bushes, architectural afterthoughts that once grew in front of some of the buildings. Elle could well imagine how uninviting this place must have been, even in the Before Times. She manoeuvred the horses across an empty field, past tangled wire fences, twisted metal beams and the charred carcass of a large plane, before coming to a halt at the far end of the main runway. Five square kilometres of concrete stretched out before her to disappear into the heat haze. Aligning on the control tower, she urged the tired horses forward and was soon flanked by enormous warehouses, hangers, storage facilities and a terminal. Looking up at the looming tower she thought that, once the animals were settled, she'd see if the upper portion was accessible. If it was, she'd have an excellent panoramic view and the opportunity to see the lie of the land in the direction of Alissa's. It might even be fun to be so high up.

The airport was far bigger than she had expected to service a city of this size, and therein lay the problem of not knowing history and context. It had not been a great metropolis. It had no historical importance and possessed not a single museum, university, art gallery or theatre of note. A tourist unfortunate enough to find themselves stranded there would have wandered the streets without once pausing to take a photo. It truly was a forgettable city, filled, as it had been, with self-satisfied, boring, dull and uninteresting people. People who, even as the last wells ran dry, managed to delude themselves a little longer that the coming of the Dry was nothing more than one of nature's ordinary glitches, a momentary inconvenience. Science and curiosity were not listed as their strong points. The city did have, however, one indisputable advantage that saved it from obscurity when its mineral wealth had been exhausted. It was conveniently located. Through its innocuous city centre ran the transcontinental highway and railroad, and from the airport hundreds of flights landed and took off every day of the year, to and from every part of the country. Daily, thousands of transients stopped, if they were fortunate, just long enough to scurry along the terminal's corridors to catch another flight to somewhere else. When Noah was a child, this had ensured that it remained a very noisy and active place. Now, if you ignored the buzz of insects and whooshing of windblown sand, there was silence, the Dry's most prevalent feature.

Having never seen a transcontinental long-flight aircraft, the detour to the airport was a small concession to satisfy Elle's curiosity. She was not disappointed. Tethered to the terminal by walkways or skulking within the hangers' shadows, twenty or more giant birds sat. Even a broken back or the loss of a wing or a ruptured fuselage did not diminish the mystique of these behemoths. She understood the theory of flight, but theory alone could not override the suspicion that it was impossible these magnificent Before Time wonders had flown at twice the speed of sound with over a thousand passengers inside. The airport, the terminal, had been the pride of the city. Steel, glass and concrete, it was a statement to the rest of the country that they mattered, that they were not a staid but a creative people. The critics, however, disagreed, calling it, "a green-house filled with dead plastic plants and populated by churlish zombies." From a distance she could see the huge steel beams that had supported the roof, but the famed arched glass ceiling was gone.

Buoyed by her tourist-like excursion, Elle swung around the terminal to find access to the building's departure and arrival lounge. Somewhere in its interior she was confident would be a shaded nook just right to set up camp in. She was looking forward to getting something into her stomach and maybe having a little nap. Occupied with getting the horses inside without injury from the fallen glass and other scattered remains of the entrance, it took a few minutes to realize what littered the floor.

When she did, overwhelmed, her legs gave out from under her and she fell to the floor. "A Cleansing." She knew the word and what it meant, but that was not the same thing as being confronted by the results. The terminal was a huge building, maybe a kilometre long, and she was lying near its centre. The floor, as far as she could see, was covered with the remains of men, women and children, stacked two or three high in places. This was not a recent event, nor one in her lifetime. This had occurred in a time when her grandfather was young, younger than her mother. Years after the rains failed, when the vast majority of the nation's people fled eastward, there had been those who stayed in their cities and towns, huddled around their wells, refusing to believe that the rain had truly stopped. These were the people for whom the trap had been set.

The contents of her morning meal lay in a pool on the floor next to her. Sitting near the entrance, she would go no further; she would not bring the animals in because no one was going to rest nor eat nor drink here. She got to her feet with difficulty and staggered outside. It seemed that her life-force had simply drained away. Once outside she slumped against a concrete pillar and slid down to come to rest on the walkway. No flood of tears. No great anguish or grief. No rage. Elle felt nothing; it was as if that part of her mind that dealt with emotion, unable to comprehend the magnitude of what had happened, had shut down.

Like the small town west of the Farm, there were places Noah would refuse, without explanation, to go to or to stop to camp in. Although he would speak freely on almost any subject, there was one which he never would speak of. Her mother, father, aunts and uncles also would talk to Elle about anything she wished, anything but one. Traders, during a visit, were the same, as were strangers who came unannounced from the wastelands or friends on a visit. Except to acknowledge that they had taken place, no one talked about the Scavenger Wars, the Cleansings or the roles they had played during them. There were hints, fragments of stories, uncompleted sentences; but no one, no one but the children, in hushed whispers, spoke of those times. Elle had roamed the wastelands with her grandfather before she could talk or even walk. She had seen the skeletal remains of dozens of people and a few recently dead. Counting the one in the barn, by her own hands, she had now taken the life of two men. Death, in the Dry, in the wastelands, was as common as the flies that buzzed about her head. But she'd never seen anything approaching the likes of this. Was there any wonder that no one spoke of these things or the deep, abiding hatred Noah and the others felt toward the Scavengers?

Chapter Eleven

In the midst of danger, a fellow traveller can assist in an unanticipated way.

'Full Service Rest Stop', that's what the sign said, although a simple perusal of the rest stop's amenities indicated they were sorely limited. The toilet block was a pile of rubble; the café was a burned-out husk. The concrete picnic tables and the benches looked like someone had taken to them with a sledge hammer; the creek was dry, the trees were dead, but there was a large, roofed pavilion still standing all on its own. That it survived when its companions had not was in itself nothing short of a minor miracle.

Under cover and out of the direct sunlight, the horses wallowed in satisfied contentment, and why not? They were free of their packs and saddles, had been thoroughly brushed and were currently drinking their fill and munching their way through their own bag of grain. Whether the dog shared her fellow travellers' contented mental state was not verifiable at the moment because it was nowhere to be seen. Elle had not bothered with a fire as she was anxious to be on her way. Cooking, though pleasurable, was a time waster. Just as well she had a good set of teeth as she gnawed her way through a thick slice of jerky. The rifle lay in the crook of her arm and would remain there, and not because of what she had seen at the airport or the possibility that the friends of the man she'd killed could be coming after her, although the latter was reason enough. It was because this rest area had had a lot of visitors lately. From the evidence all around her, she'd guess there had been maybe twenty or more. A big crowd this far out in the wastelands.

A lot can be learned about people from the way they keep camp. The two things she learned about these particular campers were that they were unhygienic and unbelievably messy. Each of the five poorly constructed hearths was strewn with fragments of meals, bones, trash, empty cans and boxes similar to the ones she'd seen in the cart and the kitchen at the homestead. The site was littered with remnants of their stay from one end of the rest area to the other – definitely not a tidy people. To make matters worse, it seemed they didn't mind where they defecated or peed.

All of that was interesting, but not as interesting as some of the other pieces of information left by the visitors. Along with an assortment of boot and hoof prints were wheel marks from at least three large wagons. And it seemed they had not been overly worried about being detected. Aside from the fires, a sign on a post had been recently propped against a tree and used for a target. Automatically she counted the holes. Knowing the cost of a single reliable cartridge and how difficult they were to obtain, Elle concluded neither concealment nor frugality were held in high regard. Her gaze drifted over toward the far end of what had been the main parking lot. Seeing something that was odd enough to prick her curiosity, she walked over for a closer look.

Pressed into the dirt were the impressions of four rows of rings, indistinguishable from the ones she had seen in the barn and the cart, forty-three in all. Elle dipped a finger into a small reservoir of sticky black goo, a pool from spillage when the barrows were loaded off or onto the wagons perhaps, and put it to her nose. Diesel, it smelled like diesel.

Insistent barking from the dog interrupted Elle's investigation and train of thought. Something deep in the park's wooded reserve had triggered a very vocal response from the animal. Elle stood up, wiped the oily muck off her fingers onto her pants and released the safety on the rifle. Whatever it was, the dog was not letting up. From her position it was impossible to see through the trees. Though dead, they shielded the dog, and the object of its excitement, from her. With a quick glance around to ensure everything else was in order, she moved with caution in the direction of dog's barking.

Before she was half way the smell hit. No one, once they had been in the presence of a rotting corpse, would ever forget the stench. The dog, seeing Elle approach, stopped its barking but remained fixed, staring. Propped up in a sitting position with his back against a tree, legs splayed out in front, was a man riddled with bullet holes. Like the sign, he seemed to have been used for target practice. With the flies, the maggots, and the stink, Elle didn't want to get any closer. Unfortunately she was going to have to. The man was dressed in similar clothing to the one in the barn, but this one, unfortunately, had been wearing a Kill Joy. Having learned from her mistakes at the homestead, she was going to search the body.

While she leaned over him, the impulse to retch was nearly impossible to supress. The only saving grace, as she began her examination, was that the worst of the putrefaction had passed. The man had been dead for about two weeks. Just as with the man in the barn, there was nothing on the body to identify him, nothing to indicate who he was or what he had been up to before others had taken a distinct dislike toward him. Finished with her self-imposed examination, Elle had to grab the dog by the scruff of its neck and drag the animal away. For reasons of its own the dog did not want to leave and insisted on barking at the dead man all the back to the pavilion. Too bad the animal couldn't talk because it certainly acted like it knew and hated the man. Back under cover Elle finished her so-called meal and ignoring the horses' displeasure, packed up. There were getting to be too many coincidences.

A sign on the ground by the road had a faded inscription informing the visitor to the rest area they were nearing the gateway of a national park whose 'pristine forest' was 'one of nature's true wonders'. From her vantage point the 'pristine forest' was nothing more than a thousand square kilometres of desolate landscape. Not a sprig of green as far as the eye could see. The Dry and the resulting fires, driven by gale force winds, had seen to that. Photos in a magazine were her only link to what this place might have looked like nearly a hundred years ago, because this forest had been dying before the rains stopped. She took in a long breath, held it for a few seconds before letting it out. Alissa's spring was said to rival the Maiden. Located not that far away, it was hard to believe it had survived the holocaust when everything else had been consumed by the fires. She would know soon enough. Following the road with her eyes, she could just make out what could be an intersection and, according to the map, if it was, the connecting road would lead to the spring situated, like the Maiden, behind a series of low rolling hills.

The desolation was not noticeably different from all the other regions of the wastelands she had traversed except for the near absence of ruins. For Elle the loss of this forest did not register as deeply as it would have for her grandfather. It was just another stretch of the wasteland, oppressively dull, eliciting no interest. This was an advantage possessed by Elle's generation but not so for Noah. Noah, though born during the Dry, was not really a child of the Dry. He had memories of rivers, of green forests, of grassy fields, of abundant wildlife. Noah could and did, if only within himself, continually contrast this world with that of his childhood. The Dry, the wastelands, was Elle's only world. She had no other memories. The impact of the raging fires that had rendered this forest to ash and blackened stumps could not affect her as it would him. For Elle, this was her history as well as her present. No amount of reading or looking at photos could possibly match the memory of a walk beneath a mature canopy of trees. Books and such things cannot bequeath unto the reader the smells, the feel, the sounds of all that life.

They had to be getting close, because when she turned around she could see that portion of the road from where they started and the distance seemed about right. But she could be wrong. This part of the road was particularly hilly and, combined with the distortion from the heat haze, gauging distance was deceptive. When they crested a rise in the road, there it was – the intersection and a pair of off-ramps curving down to join the road below. But, there was a problem. The west bound ramp was completely gone, nothing but empty air, and a large segment of the east bound was missing. Fire or man-made damage? Elle gently pulled back on the reins, bringing the company to a halt. Leaning down she patted Buck's muscular neck while she considered what to do. First, there was the question of whether this was the road leading to the spring. If it wasn't, the damaged off-ramps wouldn't be her problem. She'd just need to go a bit farther and find the correct one. But what if this was the road she wanted? She looked around the intersection for clues, but the fires had left nothing in their wake to indicate where that particular road went. The turnoff was approximately the correct distance; it did lead off to the left in the general direction of where the spring was supposed to be and there were a series of low rolling hills not that far away. So, assuming this was the road to Alissa, the next question was how they were supposed to get down without getting injured.

The national forest had been designated a wildlife sanctuary and the road was elevated in places to allow animals to pass safely underneath. This intersection was just such a place. In other areas, the road was bordered on both sides by a sturdy animal-proof fence. Elle edged Buck over to the road's shoulder to see how steep the embankment was and if it was possible for the horses to navigate their way down. They could, she decided, but only without their packs. But that was only the beginning, and perhaps the easiest part. Once down, there was still the fence to get through, which could be difficult. Even when that was accomplished, how could she retrieve the packs without the use of the horses? Considering the time, she would most likely be loading up the animals in the dark. Elle pictured the five of them falling and shook her head to expunge the image, thinking that it was best not to imagine it.

She returned from inspecting the corridor, three metres wide by twenty long which linked the two halves of the off-ramp together, and hobbled Ted and Buck. A precaution – left to its own devices, a spooked horse can run a long way before being captured. Aside from the lost time, the prospect of retrieving damaged packs and other articles strewn across the countryside, possibly in the dark, was something Elle wanted to avoid. Hobbled, all a horse could do was prance about a bit. Belle would go first and, if all went well, she'd come back for the others. The dog demonstrated that it had no qualms or inhibitions. Having anticipated their destination, it had already crossed the narrow strip of road several times with impunity and now waited on the far side, tail thumping impatiently, wondering why it was taking so long for the others to join it.

Belle came across just as Elle had expected, sure footed, confident and without a bother. Surprisingly, so too did the new recruit who followed the young girl as if he had been born to the task. With two of the horses safely on the other side without incident, Elle turned her attention to her father's farm horse, good old reliable Buck. Steady as rock. She knelt down and removed the hobbles. Then, taking the reins, she began to lead him across the narrow divide. Everything seemed to be going fine when, at the worst possible place, as if in a dream, Buck awoke to realize he was walking along a thin ridge with lots of open space on either side. White eyed, ears back, nostrils flared, the horse stopped dead in his tracks and reared his head back, nearly jerking an unprepared Elle off her feet and over the side. Scrambling to regain her balance, Elle tried to reassure the horse in the most soothing voice she could muster under the circumstances. Buck was not persuaded. He continued to struggle and with the lead wrapped securely around her hand she was unable to release it to get a better hold. The terrified animal had but one aim now and that was to reverse off that strip of concrete. She could see Buck was nearing the edge and if he fell he would take her with him.

Without warning from the corner of her eye Elle saw the dog shoot past. Too busy with her own efforts to calm Buck, she did not see what the dog was up to at the rear of the horse but could hear a low menacing growl and then a sharp bark. The horse stopped trying to retreat, hesitated for a heartbeat and then bolted straight toward Elle knocking her over the ramp's railing. There she momentary hung, partially suspended in air from the hand bound in the horse's lead, before being pulled back and slammed into the guard rail and then onto the surface of the ramp. The sudden increase of weight provided by her being temporarily airborne and her subsequent fall, abruptly pulled Buck's head sharply around bringing the animal to a complete halt. Now sprawled face down on the road, with an arm held aloft by the reins, Elle looked up to see Buck frozen, wide eyed with fear and the dog, tongue hanging out, dripping drool, looking at her with pure satisfactions.

Keeping a firm hold on the reins, Elle waited until she could get her breath back before pulling herself to her feet and dusting herself off.

"Bloody stupid animals. It's no wonder people preferred cars," she said, speaking to Buck as she checked to see if any of the packs had moved in all the recent exertions. "And as for you," looking at the dog, "I have no idea what it was you did, but thanks." The dog's tail went into complete overdrive as it came and sat by her. She started to touch the dog with her left hand but stopped, withdrew it, and then reached out with her right giving it a gentle scratch behind one of its ears and looked over at Buck to see how he was doing. A small trickle of blood ran down the back of one of Buck's hind legs where the dog must have nipped him. She managed a weak smile remembering how Buck had reacted. No wonder he had shot past her as if the hounds of hell were in hot pursuit. Nothing like that had ever happened to him before.

Having the wind knocked out of her, she needed the railing for support and so rested there while waiting for her breathing and heartbeat to return to normal. The near-death experience left her feeling sweaty, filthy and very annoyed at the persistence of the flies that buzzed about her head. There were going to be consequences tomorrow after being battered and bruised from head to foot. To increase the discomfort, the afternoon heat whelmed up from the tar seal and beat down from above making her feel like she was the winter solstice's chicken being roasted from the outside in. Buck stood as still as stone when she grabbed the reins and placed a foot in the improvised stirrup. She noticed her hand tremble a little as she heaved herself up and onto the sack of grain just as a stone, dislodged by Buck, rolled to the edge and disappeared. It had been a very close run thing. With that she led them down the last leg of the ramp and onto the road below. The dog raced ahead, causing Elle to wonder how that animal could survive out here with all that hair.

Annoyed by flies that continued to buzz around her, Elle took another drink from the canteen. Sheltered under a bridge in the middle of a non-existent creek, she could hear both the dog and the horses noisily finishing the water she had given them. It was a relief to get out from under the sun for a few minutes. The glare and the haze made it difficult to see the road up ahead clearly. A hundred metres or so it looked like another road led off from the one she was on. The best guess was that road would lead to the spring, somewhere just over the rise she could see in the distance. "If I was them, I would be sitting on that rise waiting for me." Elle said to herself as she took one last swallow. Putting away the horse's canvas bags and the iron pot she had used for the dog, she climbed back on Buck. Not wanting to make the same mistake as the man in the barn, Elle ran her hand along the seam of the Kill Joy. Upon sealing she could feel the vest attempt to conform to her body like a second skin and it amused her knowing that its struggle to fit that thin frame of hers would end in failure. The vest did have one major drawback, which was probably why the man had his open. As wonderful as the material was, it did make the Dry just that bit warmer.

Leaving the creek bed and moving into the open Elle felt relatively safe, figuring even Noah would find it extremely difficult to hit a moving target at more than five hundred metres, but, as an added precaution, she leaned as far forward as she could. Within the last five hundred metres of the rise, she slid off the sack of grain and into a prepared harness that hung on Buck's side. With Belle alongside forming a defensive box, she kept watch on the rise to see if there were any hint that anyone was there waiting for her. Soon she was at the top of the rise and looking down at a small forest oasis.

Alissa was much larger than The Maiden, maybe thirty to forty acres. After being so long in the homochromous wastelands, the shock of so much green foliage made it impossible to take it all in.

Chapter Twelve
Where there is water, there is life.

To avoid another surprise like the one at the homestead, still in the harness along Buck's side, Elle circled the entire perimeter of the spring twice. There were plenty of clues that an extensive local wildlife population lived in and around the spring, and that a week or two earlier a party of about twelve riders had stopped, stayed less than a day and then left. No signs of any wagons. Whether the riders were headed toward the rest stop to join that mob, or had been with them but were now headed elsewhere, she could not tell. The winds had obligingly removed that bit of information. She was sure of one thing; they knew each other. You just didn't have a large number of people roaming the same area of wasteland ignorant of one another. Assured that this time she was truly alone, Elle retraced her steps back to where she'd seen a cabin tucked into a hillside with an adjoining shed. Just as Nicole had described, it was only a stone's throw from the spring and the creek that flowed from it.

Strange that places like this, during the Before Times, weren't considered that special. Elle thought otherwise. Despite the obvious disregard shown by the previous visitors, she felt it would be a form of sacrilege to ride straight in without showing some hesitation and respect. She slid off Buck and led the animals out of the glare of the wastelands into the shade of Alissa's Spring. Immediately she could feel the difference, just as she had at The Maiden. The air felt softer, cooler and, when taken into the lungs, wetter. The taste was so sweet she wanted to smack her lips. Here, the absence of harsh light allowed her eyes to open wide and drink in colour. The moistness of the earth, the grass and the leaf litter removed the hard clatter of the horses' tread. This was what the world had once felt and smelt like. Even the dog's normal effervescence was curtailed. With its tail down, softly whining, it hugged close to Elle, almost tripping her as they turned toward the cabin. At any other time the dog would have received a sharp rebuke, but a raised voice here would have been out of place and somehow unacceptable. Too bad the earlier guests had not shared Elle's reverence. They'd left a mess, smaller but similar to the rest stop. Fortunately, time and nature would take care of some of it and she would see to the rest.

The spring was not a cloistered, untouched oasis, and it had not escaped the inferno. The fire had been here. Like the rest of the land she had ridden through since the pavilion, this place too had been devastated. The fire would have left nothing but ash and a few smouldering tree stumps upon its departure. Yet, because of the spring, the oasis had recovered; the fire-scarred stumps were surrounded by a new copse of trees. A sudden revelation came to Elle; the cabin had to have been built after the fires and, judging by its current weathered condition, that would have been several decades ago. There would have been little in the way of millable timber for many kilometres around. Someone had gone to a considerable amount of effort to find and transport the materials from which the cabin was built. A book, a clay bowl, a welded join, or in this case, a cabin, contain within them the signature of their creator. That is the inescapable essence of being 'handmade'. Noticing the attention to detail and the style of the joinery, she had a good idea of the identity of at least one of the carpenters.

The exhausted horses had been through a punishing ordeal. Once again relieved of their packs, brushed and washed clean and watered, the horses were hobbled a comfortable distance from the spring and creek and left to forage on the abundant succulent grasses surrounding the marsh. Just as tired as the horses, Elle delayed her personal grooming; there was a more urgent task. She took the dog and busied herself with setting as many snares as she found animal 'runs' coming in from the wastelands to the spring. Even an untrained eye could read the signs that there was a plentiful supply of game present. By the time the pair had walked the entire circuit twenty-two traps had been laid and set. With luck, maybe even as early as this evening, fresh meat would be roasting on a spit. If not, by tomorrow morning surely there would be something worthy of her efforts, a thought worth savouring. The dog had no idea what this strange human was doing or why, but was eager to find out. So, as each trap was carefully put in place, the dog came over and gave it a personal inspection before running off to see what this mad, hairless, two legged creature would do next.

Back at the cabin, Elle did a quick clean and then stored everything inside before locating two canvas buckets and the bag containing her toilet kit. She disrobed. Leaving the dog, which seemed bent on finding whatever it was that lived under the porch of the cabin, she picked up an assortment of weaponry and headed for the creek. She had decided, despite the rules governing wounds, that when she sat down this afternoon to eat, she would do so clean. This spring shared several similarities with The Maiden, but there were a few differences. For one, the Maiden was more park-like and its spring flowed from, over and through nearly continuous sandstone. At Alissa's the rock was broken; here and there a boulder protruded from rich loamy soil. The spring had no well-defined boundaries but rather rose up to form a pool surrounded by marsh filled with reeds and other water loving plants. For another, The Maiden had a good stand of trees and grass but little else in the way of plant life. The richness of the well-watered earth at Alissa led to a profusion of different kinds of plants including an abundance of wild flowers, the likes of which Elle had never seen before. Another difference. The Maiden was located in a depression, a kind of natural hollow surrounded by hills. Here, except for a few raised mounds along one side, the land was flat. The oasis had blurred edges that ultimately became the wastelands. The real difference, though, was one particular insect. A creature on the brink of extinction before the coming of the Dry, honey bees thrived at Alissa's, just as they did on the Farm.

At the creek Elle scooped up a bucket full of water and, as was the custom, moved away to wash. She found an idyllic place. A flat stone, just big enough for her to stand on, rose like an island in a sea of green. She raised one of the buckets over her head and poured. The shock brought a gasp from her lips and a shiver of delight as its coolness cascaded down her body raising goosebumps all over. It was delectable. The soap her mother had made did not lather but it did get you clean. After a few minutes of enthusiastic scrubbing, avoiding the nicely mending wound over her heart as well as the one on her leg, Elle poured the second bucket to rinse off; she was now ready for a dip in the spring's pool. The mud oozed between her toes and then up to her ankles as she pushed her way through the undergrowth and reeds toward open water. She had chosen this spot because of a willow tree trunk that curved and twisted along and above the pool: a good dry place to keep her weapons within reach while she swam. Elle eased into the crisp clear water until it reached her chin. She could feel the heat, the dust and the dryness melt away. This was unadulterated luxury.

She was just about to plunge her head beneath the water when she was alerted to a movement rushing toward her at considerable speed. Before she could react, a white and black blur launched itself into the air with a loud bark that was quickly followed by a big splash. This immediately informed her that the dog was not afraid of water. It had also neglected to wash before joining her.

That last item was something she would have to correct in the future. Right now, however, a swim with a dog was not what Elle had in mind. Trying to ward off an animal that wants to climb on you while you try to stay afloat is not only difficult, but very distracting. Nonetheless, Elle could not suppress real pleasure in its company. Few humans prosper alone, and for a child this is particularly true. An adult in similar circumstances might have continued to worry about being pursued and the consequences of a lapse of alertness, but even in a well-trained child such as Elle, the mind does not always perform so mechanically. It strays. Fortunately for the occasional inattentive rabbit, the sky is sometimes empty of hawks flying overhead.

Leaving the pool, Elle sought out one of the larger boulders in amongst the trees and climbed up to rest. She had to fend off the dog, which joined her on the rock and then attempted to demonstrate the need to sit in her lap even though there was more than enough room for the two of them. Elle did not play much for a girl of almost fourteen. Discounting the day with the Traders, the time just spent in the water having the dog retrieve the same thrown stick over and over and over again was one of the few times that she could remember laughing at the antics of an animal. The dog never seemed to grow tired of swimming out to bring back that stick, but Elle did. She arrived on the boulder dripping wet but the air, even in the presence of the spring, was hungry for moisture and eagerly absorbed each droplet on her skin, in her hair and from the puddles that had formed in the stone's hollows.

She watched the puddles disappear with some amusement. In a matter of minutes, she, the dog and the rock were dry. The pool's surface had returned to its former tranquil self. All the ripples, as well as all the squeals and barks of joy had just faded away. If not for the images in her memory, nearly all the evidence of the past hour was gone, as if it had not happened. Elle found herself wondering if the same thing would happen regarding this voyage to the mountain. Whether she lived or died, what evidence would there be of her having existed at all? Is life nothing more than a single thread upon which one's memories are strung? And what about all those people in the terminal? Calling such a thing a Cleansing was a monstrous distortion of her language and yet so chillingly apt.

Dried, rested, and with the obligatory rifle slung in the crook of her arm, Elle and the dog went for a walk to see if she could locate the graves Nicole had asked her to visit. They were supposed to be in line with the cabin and the pool, but she hadn't seen anything that looked like markers indicating the presence of a grave. Retracing her steps back toward the cabin, she passed on the far side of the rock she had climbed earlier. Something looked out of place. Near the base of the rock, instead of continuing its slope as it did on the other side, its surface looked unnatural, as though it had been cleaved. Closer inspection revealed this to be true. An area just 500 mm square had been altered. The Dry had ensured that Elle had plenty of experience in the preparation of grave stones. Therefore it was not hard to recognize that someone had put in a good deal of effort into its construction. She touched the relative smoothness of its surface and to trace with a finger the letters engraved on it. "Alissa." "Nina."

It was dark outside and the sky was again ablaze with starlight. The two in the cabin, stretched out on the floor with stomachs slightly distended in satisfaction, watched the last of the embers in the fireplace wink out. The day had been filled with good luck. There had been no unexpected arrivals. The horses had fed well around the marsh and now were resting in the shed. The graves had been located and cleared and respect had been given. Not one but three rabbits and an animal that she had never seen before had found their ways into the snares. Wild greens had been harvested; roots had been dug up and had added immeasurably to the lusciousness of the meal. She and the dog had eaten their fill. For Elle, the meal, while not unrivalled, had certainly been memorable. From the dog's perspective, it had never been so contented. Up to the moment of being freed from the sack, life for the dog had been tenuous at times, terrifying at others. True, it did not understand this strange creature or where it was heading, not that it mattered, and everything about this female was outside its previous experience. For example, instead of lying contented and comfortable, letting sleep find her, the girl would frequently get up, go out and walk about a bit, before returning to the cabin. The dog felt duty bound to tag along. The girl never seem to find what it was she was looking for, and the evening breeze brought nothing to the dog's nose that hinted of danger or was worthy of any further activity.

The sleep had not been long enough. The dreams, having come and gone, left her restless and strangely discontented. Still feeling tired and in need of much more sleep, preferably undisturbed by those dreams of hers, Elle started preparing to leave. She would not spend the night here as she dearly wanted to. To stay was an invitation to push her current run of luck too far. It was time to go. According to the map there remained only one more source of water between here and the mountains. That source, Empty Cup, was three days ride, four if she did not travel at least some of the distance at night. Three additional days ride further west and the map's detail ended. From then on it was empty, uncharted territory and best to be avoided as far as the Traders were concerned. Nicole had said that, going by the maps of the Before Times, add another day and Elle would be standing at the base of the mountains. The added day was only an estimate because, not only had it been many years since any Trader had gone more than two day's ride west of the spring, those who had had never been heard of again. Although the map did show a couple of places that might have water, there was no guarantee. Mentally adding two more days as a margin of safety, Elle planned for a round trip lasting up to ten days. Not counting her requirements and the dog's, the minimum needs of the three horses would be nearly five hundred litres, which was a lot of weight. That was why everything not absolutely essential would be left behind, even the coveted stove, and she would be walking once again, at least for the first few days. They could further conserve the need for water if they travelled mostly at night and what passed for the cool part of the day. Something out there might kill her, as it apparently had all those others, but should she die, it was not going be from thirst. As to her treasures, she could only hope that they would be there upon her return. But all that lay in the future. Right now she had to make her way to Empty Cup and, as recent events had shown, a lot could happen between now and then.

Further north and south of her present position, the Traders' map did show other sources of water, but they were well off the Great Central Highway. Even if they had been marginally closer, the ruggedness of the terrain would make the journey more difficult, requiring additional time to navigate, and time was becoming even more precious. She folded and rolled the map carefully before tucking it back into its protective cylinder. As if needing a physical action to emphasize that she'd done musing, Elle slapped her knee with a hand and got up. After leaving Empty Cup, if it became evident that there was not going to be enough water or provisions to make it to the mountains and back, the dog would be the first to be killed and then Ted and then Buck. But she would do everything in her power to see that they all got back alive. Noah would not have it any other way. Right now, pushing such thoughts from her mind, it was time to finish breaking camp.

An hour later, with the moon on the rise, Elle, the horses and the dog marched past the stone marking the burial place of Alissa and Nina. She couldn't see the memorial but she knew it was there within the dark shadows of the rock. She'd kept her promise. Two fairy rings of wild flowers had been placed below the names. Only three hours remained before the sun rose. Under the waning moonlight the road ahead looked clear and open, so she wanted to cover as much distance as possible before morning. Over the last few days all of them had been surviving with little rest and even less sleep. It would be nice to find someplace safe. Being exhausted made you careless and slow to act, not a good combination. But until then she'd push onward.

The dog, having raced ahead on an urgent mission known only to it, left Elle with her thoughts which inexplicably turned to Nic's harmonica still tucked away in her right breast pocket. The left pocket contained one of the books she'd taken from the homestead. She had amused herself reading from it from time to time. It was a volume of *Pithy Quotes for Angry Women* from people not only long dead but for the most part unknown to her. Its episodic style with accompanying quotes did not require prolonged and intense concentration. Elle could pick it up, read a paragraph or two, and then set it aside without consequences towards its continuity, a good trait in a book when time and opportunity were in limited supply. The other book she was reading was science fiction, *Invasion of the Body Snatchers*. It amused her but she couldn't quite grasp the reasons behind why the protagonists were so terrified of being possessed by an alien life form. She'd ask her mother when she got back what the fuss was about because she must be missing some vital subtext of the story that would explain their fear. The emotions, customs and beliefs of the Before Times often seemed to Elle not only mysterious and unwarranted but, at times, damn right unfathomable. For example, why have separate facilities for men, women and women with a child when emptying your bowels and bladder? Made no sense to her no matter how many times her mother tried to explain such seemingly arbitrary social taboos.

With not enough moonlight to read, Elle pulled the harmonica out and began to pick out a few notes. She could recall in detail the tunes Nic had played and the songs that she and Noah would sing when out in the wastelands. The sounds that began to flow from the harmonica certainly were an improvement over her first efforts. One could almost recognize a tune rising in volume covering what it lacked in skill. It helped that she had good dexterity and, like most of the family, a good ear. They all could carry a tune, enjoyed singing and found pleasure in this simple pursuit. This was especially true of her mother and Noah, who would sometimes sing a duet with Elle and the rest of the family as their appreciative audience.

Cloaked in near darkness, the landscape along the route from the spring back to the highway took on a more sinister appearance than it had during the previous day when it was washed in sunlight. But as the tune struggled to take shape, the music made it, if only momentarily, less dire, less bleak. Music, even when played badly, always gave Elle's lagging spirits a lift. She had felt this on many occasions with her family or, as she had recently discovered, with the Traders. Elle had once asked her mother about the way some music made her feel. Her mother's reply was that every child spends nine months listening to their mother's heart beat and every breath they took. It is the first rhythm any of us hears, so maybe that is why music sometimes has such a powerful effect upon us. Maybe we are recalling that time.

Perhaps it was coming so close to being killed in the barn, or maybe it was the time she'd spent with the Traders at The Maiden, or the graves or maybe discovering a Cleansing, or maybe it was all or none of them; perhaps it was due to the dreams that were becoming more frequent and more intense. Whatever the reason, Elle felt she was undergoing some kind of change. The Dry was all there was to her world, that and her family. Unlike her grandfather who sometimes grew moody and withdrawn over what had been lost, she hadn't. Now, she wondered how she could have been so unmoved by the stark contrast between places where water was available and those places where it was not. Yesterday, the last rays of the fading light had revealed the devastation all along the road leading to Alissa. Without having to see it, she knew that in every direction, for as far as you could go, it continued unabated, ubiquitous in its uniform desolation. The only exceptions were in the presence of water. Only there, in those ever diminishing locations, lost in the millions of square kilometres of the wastelands, did you find evidence of what it had been like in the Before Time. Out there, away from the springs and the wells, the only life that was in abundance was the ever-present swarms of opportunistic flying insects that relentlessly pursued any animal, human or otherwise, for the smallest suggestion of being rewarded with a gift of moisture.

Elle played and rode on, watching the occasional flash of black upon white as the dog freewheeled far up ahead. In a week or so she would be at the mountains, the end of her journey. Sometime around then she would turn fourteen. Deep in her subconscious, a mental cog fell into place. Elle stopped playing the harmonica and bolted upright. Why didn't the families at the homestead move to Alissa? Never mind who built the cabin, why wasn't the spring occupied?

Chapter Thirteen
Death is life's constant companion.

Finished eating, Elle put the pot on the floor for the dog and reached up to take the photo off the mantel. Ever since Alissa, having it where she could see it had become a kind of comforting ritual. The ritual's origin began while rummaging in the pack for an item needed for the preparation of the eagerly awaited rabbit stew. She'd removed the photo and positioned it out of harm's way on the mantel above the fire. There it had remained until it was time to pack up. Now, each time they stopped to make camp or wait out the heat of the midday, out came the photo. Sometimes she'd find herself tracing the outline of the young girl just as Nicole had. There was familiarity, as if she'd seen that girl before. But that was nonsense. Elle never forgot a face, never. And yet, there was no denying she was drawn to the photo, the girl's face, the mother's hand resting upon her shoulder, their smiles. Family? The mirror had brutally informed Elle that the two of them shared nothing but their gender. There were tens of thousands to pick from throughout the wastelands so why keep this particular photo? Maybe it was because of the interest shown by Nicole, or maybe it was nothing more than to keep her company, make her less lonely.

The photo was returned to its place of safety on the shelf. The highway, in spite of its inherent dangers; the occasional landslide, fallen bridge, collapsed overpass, a well-hidden assailant, had been a good choice. So much so they had the luxury of being able to extend the midday break until the sun had lost a little of its sting. With what was left of the day and following the moon tonight, there was an even chance she'd be eating breakfast at Empty Cup. For the first time since leaving the Maiden, Elle was feeling a sense of joy and of accomplishment. In keeping with this tranquil mood and wishing to momentarily postpone the necessary chores of cleaning up and readying the animals, Elle employed an age-old delaying technique used by all literate people; she opened a book. *Pithy Quotes from Angry Women* had less than twenty pages to go before it was finished and, as every reader knows, to be so near the end was all the excuse needed. She removed the marker that held her place.

Yesterday afternoon they had sought refuge from the heat in the ruins of a huge enclosed mall. Not much of its former glory remained; anything deemed to be valuable had disappeared long ago. Still, there was the odd chance the rampaging hordes might not have been completely thorough. While the horses rested, ever the optimist, with rifle in hand, Elle had wandered about to see what there was to see. Poking in amongst a pile of rubbish in one of the stores she came across a mound of bright metal rectangles about half the size of her palm. Surprisingly heavy, they were blank on one side; the other had a gothic styled letter of the alphabet embossed in enamel. Having no idea what they could have been used for, she picked up a few only to discard them before coming across one bearing a large green capital letter '€'. This was the marker she removed from the book to read: *'So many men, so few bullets'*, Anonymous. She stopped, closed the book and returned it to her pocket. An unfortunate quote in the circumstances. The good mood evaporated, leaving behind the familiar melancholy. Like many of the quotes, she failed to understand why anyone would have thought them amusing. Cruel, mean perhaps, but not funny. Why did the Before Times' people seem to treat the taking of a life with such casual disregard?

Situated on a sharp rise, with nearly half of it projecting out from the hill, sat a house that overlooked the highway below. There were only two ways to enter the house. The limited access provided ideal protection from the sun and intruders. The horses had been settled in the garage, while Elle and the dog had taken up residence in what had been a very large living room. The roof overhead was still intact, but, like the house with the swimming pool, most of the front wall was gone. Other than that particular shortcoming, the room was ideal with ample shade, a fireplace and an uninterrupted view of the Grand Central Highway. The dog, who had been content to lie beside Elle with a moderately full tummy, suddenly leapt to its feet, eyes fixed ahead, hairs bristling along the ridge of the back, emitting a deep rumbling growl between bared teeth.

Elle placed a hand on the dog's shoulder, ordered it to be quiet and slowly picked up the rifle. The dog seemed to have sensed something out there that it had taken exception to. Sadly, her attention for a considerable time had been focused elsewhere. Caring for the horses, fixing and sharing a hot meal, trying to read without success had all distracted her. She looked down at the highway trying to recall if anything appeared out of place. Directly in front of the house, just on the verge on the far side of the road, there was a black smudge. She didn't recall seeing it before but it could be just a pile of previously unnoticed debris. There was no shortage of such piles in the wastelands. Not for the first time, Elle wished she had thought to bring a pair of field glasses.

Then, from the corner of her eye, a flicker of movement. Turning her head to the left, she saw a man with a rifle dart out from behind a burnt-out truck, run across the median strip and disappear behind another vehicle on this side of the road. The increased intensity of its growl meant the dog also saw him.

They had company.

Thankful for the warning, Elle gave the dog a reassuring pat and a scratch behind an ear. Because of it, Elle had been given a little more time than she might have had. She lifted herself a bit further off the floor in order to get a better view of the running man's hiding place and, as she did so, realized she'd made a terrible mistake. Too late. A flash of light and a hard blow to the chest sent Elle reeling backwards. On the leading edge of unconsciousness, Elle heard the crack from the rifle that shot her, then another and then one more. Just as she slipped into darkness she thought the last two sounded different, further away, muffled.

Sometimes a hawk does find an inattentive rabbit.

Dazed, pain in every breath, her eyes closed tight in order to concentrate, Elle forced herself awake. Everywhere hurt. Added to the battering received on the overpass, it felt as if someone had punched her in the chest, hard. She tried to sit up but was forced back down as pain radiated through the length of her body. Shot in the chest. Not survivable; if she wasn't dead by the time they got to her, she'd be dead when they left. She watched the cobwebs strung along the ceiling, touched by a breeze, quiver. Her hand slid under the vest expecting to find a blood-soaked shirt, a mortal wound. It was dry. She withdrew the hand and rotated it in front of her face. The hand was clean, well, as clean as days of not washing allowed. No blood, not a speck. With a chest wound, there would be blood, lots and lots of blood. Her hand unbuttoned the shirt and reached inside. Other than the dressing from the last time someone had tried to kill her and being tender to the touch, there was no evidence she'd been shot at all. But she had.

She was sure she'd been lying there only a minute or two at the most; otherwise her assassins would have come to finish what they'd started. Elle tried to sit again only to discover the dog draped across her legs, preventing her from doing so. It gave a soft whine as she pushed the reluctant animal off and rolled over, found her rifle, and started to rise up on one knee. Remembering that this was why she had been shot the first time, Elle dropped down and, ignoring the pain, crawled over to the very edge of the floor. How many times did she need to get shot before learning to keep her head down? The excessive adrenaline that flooded her blood stream was causing her heart to race and making it difficult to breathe. She closed her eyes and, as she had been taught, willed her heart and breathing to slow down, to relax, to quell the sense of fear that was beginning to bubble up. Calmness washed over her, bringing with it control. She drew in a deep breath before slowly letting it out and carefully focused her attention on the highway. The 'smudge' remained unchanged but there was no sign of the running man. She remembered the scope on the rifle she had taken from the farm cart back at the homestead. It was in the garage with the rest of the gear.

Staying as low as it was humanly possible, Elle squirmed backwards on her stomach until it was safe to stand, then began to run down the hallway to the garage. The dog was faster. It went first and then stopped a couple of metres in. Its tail washed back and forth in that slow unconcerned way that these animals have when they are in a comfortable place. Not wanting to be too trusting of a dog's tail, with the rifle at the ready, she cautiously followed. A single glance over at Belle confirmed everything was just as she had left it. Had anyone approached this side of the house, Belle wouldn't be standing quietly, half asleep, with her two companions. Relieved, her hand briefly touched the dog's head as she passed and then reached out to stroke

Belle's muzzle. Her spirit lifted a little at feeling the horse's warm breath on the back of her hand and inhaling the musky smell of dry hay. The barn and her family in the kitchen flashed in her mind. This was not the way it was supposed to be, but then few things were. She retrieved the rifle and went back to the living room.

Next to what remained of an outer wall, Elle lay on her back, just short of the edge of the living room floor that hung suspended three metres above the ground below. She unclipped the scope from its mount, rolled over onto her stomach and brought it to her eye. Its power and resolution was impressive and quickly resolved the mystery of the black smudge; a man lay beside a bipod mounted sniper's rifle. "That's one," she murmured. "Now for the other." She swept the area immediately in front of the house and over to where the running man had disappeared, but there was no sign of him. She turned to look at the dog. It kept making a muted half bark and half whine. Its eyes rolled up to meet hers for an instant, and then it turned its attention back to whatever it was watching. Hoping the dog would remain content with its near inaudible whine and not start barking, Elle went back to looking for the missing man. At first she saw nothing. Then, at the base of the slope leading to the house, half hidden by a tree trunk, she saw a man sprawled in that crumpled marionette look that the dead have. "He looks dead." She swung back to the 'smudge'. Either they were both very patiently waiting for her to reappear or they were truly dead. Puzzled, she shifted to another position that would allow her to see further in both directions. Maybe she'd get a glimpse of her benefactor.

A few minutes later, exasperated, she lowered the scope and rolled onto her back. There was nothing that seemed either out of place or even remotely suspicious, and yet there was someone out there. Those two hadn't just shot themselves. In the wastelands you had to be very careful not to assume too much. As thankful as she might be, whoever had shot these men need not be a friend.

Like the story Noah had told her concerning the action of a hunter and a wolf. A hunter, coming upon a nearly frozen bird, stuck the bird deep into a pile of fresh bear poo to warm up and then left. It worked and soon the bird started to sing with joy. The singing drew the attention of a passing wolf which promptly found the bird and ate it. The moral, as Noah was happy to relate, was that "Those who put you in the poo need not be your enemy and those that pull you out of the poo need not be your friend." He must have told her that story a couple of dozen times and it always ended with both of them laughing.

So, who then was the missing shooter; friend or foe? She again rolled over onto her stomach and, starting with the man at the base of the slope, began to examine the part of road she'd travelled just a little over an hour ago. At first everything was as she remembered; then, in the median, at the highest point of the road before it disappeared over the hump, there appeared to be another body.

Three dead men and no sign of the person or persons who had shot them. What should she do? To answer that question she needed a place and time to think. Elle crawled to the far back of the room that was in shadow and sat there. Wedged in the dark corner, she would be 'invisible' to anyone entering from the bright world outside, giving her the advantage for a few seconds while their eyes adjusted to gloom. She pulled the pistol from its holster and laid it close by her side. In this confined space the pistol would be easier to wield than a rifle. She pressed her forefingers against her temples. She could feel a headache coming on. There were three dead men out there. So how many shots had she heard before passing out, one, two or three? Unless they had somehow ended up killing each other, a highly unlikely scenario, somebody was out there, waiting. Waiting for what? Did they think she was dead and therefore saw no reason to waste time to come up and make sure? That didn't seem likely. People of the Dry didn't trust the living or the dead. They would check because it helped to avoid getting shot in the back. Friend or foe, in the wastelands the enemy of my enemy may still be my enemy...

Thoughts tumbled in her head, too much to think about, too many uncertainties. The onset of a headache and the persistent throb of pain emanating from her chest did not help. She stopped rubbing her temples and opened the vest. A finger poked through the webbing and wiggled. "So much for the wonders of Before Time technology." There was a corresponding hole in the shirt pocket and one in the front of the book. She removed the book and carefully turned each page until she reached the 'page saver'. The medallion had a neat bulge in its centre which nicely cradled the bullet's flattened remains. Elle wondered how much luck one person was permitted in a life time; surely she must be using someone else's as well. With the shirt unbuttoned she could see that blood was beginning to weep through the bandage. The way her chest hurt, it was a safe bet that the renewed bleeding was the result of bullet impact. She buttoned up the shirt, returned the book to its pocket and closed the vest. She was alive and uninjured. That was a good position to be in considering the other possibilities. And if she wanted to stay alive and uninjured, sitting waiting was unlikely to be of much help. The dog, pressing against her thigh, had stopped its whining. It didn't seem too worried. Maybe... She paused in thought; maybe I should get up off my tail, go out and have a look. After all, the answer to her questions would not be found inside this dilapidated house. The pistol was returned to its holster. With one rifle slung across her back and the other in her hand, she went to saddle Belle.

A grove of dead trees surrounded the house and the driveway and extended all the way down the slope, stopping just short of the service road where the man lay dead. In amongst this densely packed, tangled mixture of downed, leaning, and upright trees, an army of assassins could be lying in wait for her, or it could be as empty as a beggar's bowl. If they were there, once she'd made her presence known, she'd have no more than a second or two before they opened fire. Elle removed her hat and tossed it to the far side of the garage. No need to worry about the sun as much as a broad brim that might hinder her vision. She extended the stirrup on the right side six notches and mounted Belle. A series of soft mechanical clicks glided a cartridge into the rifle's chamber and a thumb slid the safety to off. Leaning forward to clear the beam over the garage's door, Elle dug her heels deep in the horse's flanks. The pair burst from the garage, cleared the low stone retaining wall and began to weave their way through the trees. The dog rushed to catch up.

As she neared the road and before she left the protection of the trees, Elle slid from the saddle onto Belle's side. With one hand gripping the saddle's horn, the reins tightly woven in her fingers, she brought the rifle up and over the saddle. For the second time in as many weeks Elle placed her life in Noah's training. Girl and horse cleared the protection of the trees and raced across the road in a wide sweeping arch. The idea was to come up behind where she thought any remaining shooters might be lying in wait. It was a gamble; for all she knew they could be at this very moment drawing a bead on her. But alone and in unfamiliar territory, there wasn't enough time nor options to carry out a more protracted engagement. One way or another it would end here.

As she neared the man that had been the black smudge, Elle, still holding onto the saddle's horn, removed her remaining boot from the stirrup and, taking long strides, started to run beside her horse. Near a large, over-turned, metal waste bin, about 20 metres behind the man, she let go, took three steps, before dropping to the ground in a roll that ended with her pressed against the bin's side, the rifle at her shoulder. The dust raised by Belle engulfed her, making it difficult to see for a couple of seconds, but as it cleared, Elle saw that the man was most certainly dead.

Like a lizard running atop hot sand, she scurried over on all fours for a closer look. The dog had taken a more direct route and now stood over the man. A low rumbling growl came from the animal as it stood there as if waiting for a signal from her to attack. She almost wanted to hug the dog, but feeling exposed, she instead used the dead man for cover and lay alongside his body. His finger, poised to fire, was still in the trigger housing, his cheek rested against the stock. If you ignored the neat round hole in his right temple and that half of the other side of his head was missing, you would have thought he had fallen asleep. With the addition of a camouflage cap, he was dressed much as the man she had killed in the barn and the one she'd found at the rest stop. This one, however, appeared much younger, maybe sixteen, certainly not yet twenty. He wore a Kill Joy vest. Lying there next to her killer, and wondering what to do next, a movement caught the corner of her eye. An arm was waving something – a battered old hat very much like the one she wore. Elle called Belle over, grabbed the horn of the saddle and swung up. Wheeling the horse around and keeping low, she headed for the rise in the road at a gallop, feeling pretty sure she knew who she would find there.

Noah put down his field glasses and rolled onto his back wincing with the sharp pain that shot up from his leg. The sun overhead forced him to close his eyes. He put his hat over his face. All he could think about was all that blue up there and that the bastard had missed. Elle was alive.

He had been trailing her for over two weeks, all the while cursing himself for being so preoccupied about returning to the Miner's Hat that he had completely missed all the signs that she was planning something. The fact that he had not been more suspicious worried him from the moment he had found out she was gone. The final clue should have been her meekly accepting her mother's edict that she was not allowed to accompany him. Elle was never meek about anything, quite the contrary. It was not in her character to calmly accept anyone's, even her mother's, verdict if it meant it went against something she wanted to do. Since the age of three she had never missed the opportunity to accompany him. By then she could ride Belle as well as kids four times her age. In those early days, the two were inseparable. Noah felt Elle would have slept in the stall more often than she did if her mother had not restricted her from doing so. That is why he should have known, the moment she wished him well, waving from the porch like a dutiful and compliant granddaughter, that she was up to something. Dutiful she might be, but compliance was not in her nature. In one way or another she would have finagled a way to ride alongside him and Chook for the first few kilometres or so.

Chapter Fourteen
To regret that which one cannot change is
futile, but it is what humans do.

At Miners Hat, dawn had found Noah and Chook
unloading the last of the remaining equipment. The
young man had no problem recognizing that his uncle
had not been in the best of moods since Spencer's
Graves. Luckily, being deaf spared him from the torrent
of hostile verbiage Noah lavished on even the most
trivial incident that could be interpreted as deliberately
thwarting their efforts to finish setting up camp. This
included getting the portable forge fired up, as it was the
first priority. Because it was too heavy to relocate
without risk onto the ground, the forge was left in the
wagon bay under a tarp that had been drawn across
makeshift supports to provide some relief from the sun.
Once that was done, Noah ordered his nephew to begin
the task of providing a continuous supply of fuel while
he attended to the forge's hearth using the coals from
their breakfast fire and what remained of the wood pile
collected earlier.

Noah worked the bellow with, perhaps, more
enthusiasm than was required. Instead of being rewarded
with the birth of fire, he found himself enveloped in a
cloud of ash. Not daring to show his amusement, Chook
was happy to leave his uncle wiping the soot from his
face while calling upon any god within hearing range to

punish the fool who had designed this monstrosity of a forge. From past experience Chook knew this monstrosity's maw not only consumed copious amount of wood, but that each piece needed to be cut and split to a given size and then stacked within arm's reach. Back on the Farm, he'd have the help of others and several days to gather the necessary fuel. Here, it would be just him.

A bucket of water stood off from the wagon in every direction of the compass. Even with the 'cage' mounted on top of the chimney, each squeeze of the bellows sent a few sparks shooting skyward. Fire, however unlikely in this barren landscape, was not a thing one ever took lightly. As the coals reached the required temperature Noah signed to Chook to stop and come over to help retrieve the windmill head. Not only was it heavy, with the blades measuring two metres across and the head assembly another metre, it was also very awkward for one person to manoeuvre and he did not relish the idea of dragging the smashed windmill over to the wagon by himself. The pair, one on each side, soon looked like a pair of crabs scurrying along with their burden. Side-stepping up to the wagon, they lowered one side to the ground while tilting the other up until it was securely propped against the wagon. Satisfied that it was not going to fall over, the pair set about taking it apart, a slow and repetitive task that took a good deal of effort. Even without rain, metal has a way of fusing. At least for the moment, whether it was the heat or the exhausting work that lay ahead, Noah was silent.

Noah was not a happy man. He had planned to camp at Spencer's Graves for the night, just as Elle's father had predicted, and had even gone so far as to have removed the saddle from Blue. But as he started to help Chook with the other horses, he stopped, buckle in hand. With a muttered 'damn', he looped the leather strap back through, found the hole, pressed the prong home. Tapping Chook on the shoulder, he signed that they weren't staying and for him to redo the harness. Without comment the boy did as he was told and, as soon as the horses had finished drinking, he threw the canvas buckets into the cart and climbed up on the wagon. His uncle was not a man one questioned. Whatever it was that had made him change his mind, Chook figured he'd find out if and when his uncle felt inclined to tell him.

Noah was irritated. At first he had thought that it was because he had tarried unnecessarily that morning and hence there was, perhaps, a subconscious urge to make up for the lost time. But that didn't feel right. True, he had not left first thing in the morning as he had initially planned. And true, if they travelled while the moon was up, technically, they would make up for the time lost. But it was equally true that the loss of a few hours here or there weren't going make any real difference to the repair. But like a maddening itch that lay just out of reach, there was a nagging suspicion he had failed to notice something important this morning. From past experience, until he'd figured out what it was, there was little chance of sleep tonight. An annoying tic in his personality would see to that. And since there was little benefit in spending the night watching the stars revolve overhead, once the moon was up, they might just as well continue on to Miner's Hat.

Once there, after helping Chook finish brushing down the two draft animals and store away the tack, Noah left him to set up camp and start a fire. The sun wouldn't be up for a few hours yet but the moonlight was bright enough to inspect the damaged windmill and the well head. There was just enough water remaining in the trough to catch and hold the moon's image. Noah knelt down and touched the water. The moon rippled. In a sudden fit of anger, he slapped at the water, shattering the moon's reflection and then sat watching it reassemble itself. "Why do you bother? In the end we'll all be dust anyway."

Angry at himself for allowing his irritation to surface, he got up and went over to the wagon, grabbed his bedroll and went to find a place near the well head to bed down. Even if the water was several dozen metres beneath the concrete slab, he liked be close to it. To be close to water was why he and Alissa had built the cabin where they did. They and the kids spent the evenings on the porch just watching the water flowing in the creek. There were other reasons the cabin had been rebuilt after the fires but he had no desire to revisit them. Such memories, over two decades old, still remained too painful.

His movements had attracted some of the cattle and sheep and, being curious, they began to congregate around him. The scene would have been comical and should have brought a wry smile to his sun battered face but for the continued niggling at the back of his mind. It simply refused to leave him in peace. With one of those longs sighs that come naturally to the old and to the frustrated young, Noah pushed himself erect. He was tired, and knowing the morning would come soon enough, he turned to his audience and informed them, "I'm going to fix something to eat and then I'm off to bed. I've done enough thinking for one day, so back up and give me some room." Noah pushed one hesitant cow aside and walked over to join Chook by the fire.

With a somewhat contented stomach – Chook might not the worst cook he'd ever experienced but he was pretty damn close – Noah lay down in the vain hope of getting some sleep. If he had a weakness, it was that he was not a man who thrived on ambiguity. He preferred rock hard certainty, up/down, in/out, yes/no, right/wrong, nice clean cuts. All his life he had relied on a kind of instinct, a sharpened sense of awareness and it had served him well. It enabled him to perceive when something was a bit skewed, the tiniest bit out of kilter. He could distinguish between being told the truth or a lie, just as he could tell if there was an ambush ahead in a featureless landscape. Now, that sensitivity seemed to have deserted him, denying much-needed sleep in the process. What was it he'd missed back at the Farm, and why was it so damn important?

It is one thing having to work in the heat of the day, but to be huddled around a forge was bordering on insanity. And yet, the one saving grace had been the foresight to bring the forge. Noah took another drink, swallowing a draft of salt along with the tepid water. He was exhausted and must have lost five kilos through sweat. Whatever it was that still tickled the back of his mind, he was just too fatigued to worry about it now. They had not stopped for the customary lunch break to avoid the noon day sun. It seemed foolish to allow the coals to cool only to have to fire the forge up again afterwards, so they thought it best to keep going until the job was done. The whole time they had to weave their way around the animals. Whether in anticipation of more water to drink, an affinity toward humans, or inbred curiosity, every animal bar Blue seemed have found a degree of pleasure in being as close to the men as was physically possible.

From the protective shade provided by the wagon's shadow, Noah watched Chook. The boy was at the top of the support strut using the last rays of a setting sun to secure the final set of mounting bolts. Once that was done, with luck, so would be the job. Then they'd find out if all the day's efforts were worth it. A wind-driven and free-spinning set of blades was one thing, pumping water was another. Of course it would be nice if the wind came up a bit more. He could not help but feel his age as he admired the boy's agility. Amazing how fast that boy had grown. A lot of power in those arms, thought Noah, and a lot of energy. He dearly loved his granddaughter and more than once wished they had her there as a much needed gofer but if he had to choose between her and one of the boys for a job like this, he'd have to pick one of the boys. Here intelligence was desirable but not a necessity; upper body strength was.

"Elle!" Noah bolted upright with the image of her standing on the porch watching them leave. "That little skink, as if butter wouldn't melt in her mouth." Just as he understood what it was that had been needling him, Chook began banging on a metal strut with his wrench. Noah looked up to see his grandnephew frantically pointing toward the horizon and signing that someone was fast approaching. All thoughts of exhaustion and Elle's subterfuge forgotten, Noah leapt to his feet to race around to the front of the wagon. Joined by Chook, who had literally flung himself from the scaffolding, they pulled their rifles free. Knowing they had a few minutes to prepare, Noah signed for Chook to go off to the right, find cover and wait. He grabbed his field glasses and starting running off to the left toward a rock formation.

Wedged between two massive boulders, Noah settled in, binoculars pressed against his eyes. The distortion caused by the heat made it difficult to see whether it was friend or foe. A couple more minutes would answer that question. From this distance it was just possible to make out a fine line of dust rising into the air, marking the path of the lone rider. Whoever it was, they were coming hard and fast. No one pushes a horse out here that way unless it's something so serious the rider is willing to risk both of their lives. He lowered the glasses to signal Chook that it was one rider. Chook signalled back that he understood. Noah again raised his field glasses to check the rider's progress and found himself smiling. Even at this distance Noah recognized Nora's riding style. Elle's mother rode low in the saddle and moved with grace few could match. Perhaps it was just a father's pride but there was no denying that that woman could ride. He signalled Chook the news and then both men ambled back to the wagon to await her arrival.

He felt himself relax as he whistled for Blue. That irritating mental itch that had been pestering him ever since he'd left the farm had disappeared. He was pretty sure he knew what Nora was going to tell him just as he thought he knew why Elle had not argued with her mother to go with them. That kid had had plans of her own. Any lingering doubts regarding Elle evaporated the moment he saw his daughter speeding toward them. Blue, who had removed himself as far as possible from the unseemly activity of the other animals, raised his head at Noah's whistle. At the second whistle Blue's leisurely stroll broke into a gallop. There would be no need for a third; Blue saw Noah with saddle and tack in hand waiting for him. By the time Nora sped into camp Blue was saddled and ready.

The dread Nora felt since awaking that morning to find Elle's letter had made her physically sick. Though it gave no indication as to why she had gone or where, it did not need to. Elle's mother knew exactly where her daughter was going and some of the dangers she was to face. She also knew if Elle was not found and brought back well before she reached the mountains, like all

251

those before, she'd die. This was as certain to her as what needed to be done. Nora went to look for her husband.

Jacob immediately wanted to go in pursuit. Although Nora agreed, she inserted a few caveats. From his perspective, the women of this family seemed to share the trait of speaking to the men folk as if they were five year olds. "Jacob, you are to take the west road out of the valley. Go straight to Lone Willow. If you see no sign that she's been there, you immediately turn back because she's taken one of the other routes. I am betting on the southern. If you see signs, wait for Noah at the spring. I'll go to Miner's Hat." Jacob was about to add a few caveats of his own when his wife leaned into him, resting her head upon his shoulder. "I love you, Jacob. Be careful. Don't do anything foolish, because I don't want to raise this child alone."

After second of confusion before he understood what she'd just said, Jacob put his arms around his wife, pulling her closer. "Not to diminish my importance, love, but Elle is perfectly capable of caring for herself or haven't you noticed?"

Nora stepped back from his arms, smiled weakly at her husband and then took his hand and placed it on her stomach. "You be careful, Jacob."

To see her father's figure, already standing by a saddled Blue, greeting her approach with a wave of his hat, Nora felt an immediate sense of relief. Noah knew because Noah always knew. As she entered the fringe of

252

the camp Nora pulled back on the reins, slowing her horse to a walk. The animal was bathed in sweat. Its sides heaved from the efforts demanded of it since they had left the farm that morning. She dismounted. Noah signed to Chook to take care of the horse. Signing a 'Thank you' to the boy, she walked over to Noah. Like her horse, she was covered in sweat and dust. She tried desperately to keep her tone flat, unemotional, so as not to convey the distress she felt within, but despite her determination, her voice quivered.

"Dad, Dad, Elle's gone."

Noah nodded. And for the first time in many years, as if she were a child, he enfolded his daughter within his arms, drawing her close to him.

Her voice, muffled against his chest, "It was that damned conversation at breakfast yesterday. She's going to the mountains. Dad, she doesn't have the slightest idea of the dangers."

Noah stroked his daughter's hair, trying to soothe the fears he knew were raging inside her. "I'm sorry honey, I should have known. The moment she didn't argue with you about riding out with us to Miner's Hat, I should have known." Pushing her back gently so as to look into his daughter's eyes, he continued, "But you're wrong about your daughter. She knows the dangers. Just as you and your sister did at her age; she'll know what needs to be done. Remember honey, just as you did, she's trying to save her family."

Nora turned her face up to search his, startled that he would bring up that which was still painful for them both and seldom talked about. Twenty-five years. Then the tears came. Between gulps for air and uncontrollable sobs, she struggled with all the emotions inside her. "Dad, I'm so scared and I'm pregnant. You've got to find her and bring her back home."

Yesterday's outburst now made sense to Noah, but the information did produce a few problems of its own. Once he had figured out that Elle would sneak off and head for the mountains, his mind had listed the various options open to him and the merits of each. He was sure, with a bit of luck, he'd be able to intercept her before she got into any real danger. There hadn't been any sighting of Scavengers for years, certainly since he and others had performed their own Cleansing thirteen years ago. And there had not been any sighting of roving gangs for years. What he had not thrown into the mix was that his youngest daughter was pregnant. Since the pandemic, women found becoming pregnant extremely difficult and far too often did not go to full-term. After asking her how long and being told three months, Noah found his feelings moving from being surprised to understanding. His daughter, as with most women of the Dry, had had a number of miscarriages before Elle. With Elle, they had nearly lost them both several times during that first year. As with his wife, he knew he should have been there. He also knew that it had been impossible.

He would leave immediately, using what daylight there was left to his advantage. Chook was instructed to stay behind to finish up, making sure the pump was working. If his aunt's horse had recovered sufficiently by tomorrow, they were to return to the farm. He was to take it slow for the sake of the horse and for Nora. Neither could afford a mishap brought on by any unnecessary effort to hurry. If the pump failed, he and his aunt would have to assess the severity of the problem and take what corrective action they deemed best.

Mounted and ready to go, Noah reassured his daughter once more that Elle would return to her safe and sound in both mind and body. Making sure everything was secure and not likely to fly free, Noah dug his heels into Blue's flanks. "Come on boy; let's not keep Elle waiting."

This horse was born for moments like these. With yesterday forgotten, Blue was soon streaking across the land, gobbling up the distance. Noah could not help himself, knowing that they would pay for it later; sometimes there is just an unquenchable need to let it rip. Taking the hat from his head, leaning as far forward as his large frame would permit, Elle's grandfather fanned Blue's backside urging him to go even faster. Blue needed no encouragement. Like a pair of kids who had spent too long being good, they raced along, Noah shouting at the top of his lungs, flapping his arms, fanning his hat at the pure joy of the exhilarating experience. The last few days of built-up tension flowed from him to dissipate in the vast emptiness of the wastelands. For Blue it was the culmination of ten million years of evolutionary perfection and five thousand years of association. If a horse could love its rider, Blue loved this man. Nearly fourteen years ago they had been warriors and, as hard and as difficult as those times might have been for both man and beast, when Blue dreamed, he dreamed of those times.

Later, when the initial rush of adrenaline had subsided, Noah alternated between walking and riding through the night, arriving while the farm was still dark. In the light of a lantern, and with scant regard toward the amount of water used, he scrubbed every speck of dust and sweat from Blue's hide. It would be many weeks before this animal would again get this level of attention. Leaving him to drink his fill and eat, Noah went about gathering those items he'd need in the coming days before getting Red Bear. Red Bear was, until the wedding party returned, the last of the Farm's large work horses.

A little after sunrise, Noah heard the approach of a horse. With his rifle tucked in the crook of an arm, he waited by the barn door. Seeing that it was Jacob, he hoped there would be good news but one look at Elle's father's face told him there was none.

While the two men ate breakfast, the first meal for Noah since yesterday morning, Jacob filled him in on what he had seen, which wasn't much. There was no evidence that Elle had headed for Lone Willow. That did not mean much. Elle was experienced enough in the ways of the wastelands to ensure there would not be any tracks left of her passing. Even the horses' dung would be buried. Still there should have been something in and around the spring. The ground was too soft not to leave at least one print.

On the chance that Jacob was wrong and had missed a sign that Elle had gone that way, they talked over the merits of the three possible routes Elle could have taken. The main road was the easiest and quickest to travel. There were sources of water every day or two. It was also the route most familiar to her. She had travelled along that route to just short of where their valley road met up with the one of main western highways, maybe two weeks' distance. Elle had also travelled the northern route with him on many occasions. Before The Dry it had been very heavily populated; a couple of cities and dozens of fair sized towns were dotted along it. A good hunting ground, even now, for items needed for the farm. It did have two major drawbacks. One, there were few places where water could be found running clear. The second, it was dangerous, very dangerous. Being a good hunting ground, it drew all manner of souls. If Elle had gone north, there was a very good chance she'd never live to see the mountains. The southern route was physically the most daunting, largely empty, few roads, no cities, a couple of small towns and very rough country. In the Before Times it was called the Hundred Lakes District, an area mostly given up for recreation. Maybe it was because of the hundred lakes that the route remained relatively well watered and favoured by the Traders. Elle knew it fairly well up to the old homestead and, if he were an almost-fourteen year-old on a quest and being pursued, that's the route he'd take.

The two men finished eating and worked together to prepare for Noah's departure.

"Are you going to try to get some sleep before heading off?" inquired Jacob, strapping a spare coil of rope onto the back of the pack horse.

"Like to, but no. She already has a two day head start with two fresh horses. Blue has spent nearly two weeks on the move, so to save us both time and effort while minimising risk, I'll take the central road. It will also increase the probability of interception since ultimately the southern and central converge to ascend the pass through the mountains."

Jacob nodded. It was a better alternative than trying to follow her route. The best of circumstances would be if he could catch up with her at Honey Comb. As soon as he thought of the name Honey Comb he immediately corrected himself to Alissa.

The last item fixed to the pack horse was a long, large and very heavy leather wrap; his 'tool kit' as he sometimes called it. Grinning at his son-in-law's expression acknowledging what the wrap contained, Noah gave it a reassuring pat saying, "I never leave home without it."

Time was never Elle's friend; the hoped-for five days' grace had been cut to two.

Days later found the big man squatted beside Blue puzzling over what he saw on the ground. It certainly was not what Noah had expected. He had met up with Nicole and ended up staying longer than he had intended. His daughter confirmed that Elle had indeed taken the southern route and that she had met up with them, under very amusing circumstances, at The Maiden. According to Nicole, the kid was in good spirits and a credit to the family. Nathan's prediction had been proven correct; during Noah's short stay with the band of Traders, the story of his and Nic's capture had indeed been told and retold with everyone laughing uproariously at each retelling, to the boy's continued embarrassment. Noah would have loved to have been there when Elle led her captives down the hill and forced his daughter's band to sit on the ground. Yet here was an annoying anomaly, here were three sets of horse prints, not two, and one of a dog. Where had the dog and the extra horse come from? Looking at Blue, he said, "I guess we'll just have to wait a bit to find out, won't we?"

Covering the droppings with handfuls of dirt and clearing away the horses' tracks, Noah remounted Blue. Taking his watch from its place he looked at the picture inside as well as the phase of the moon that night. He slipped it back, gave Blue a gentle nudge, and the trio moved off down the road, noting that Elle, with a few mishaps, had continued covering her tracks well. If it had not been for the dog's droppings, it was entirely possible that Noah could have missed Elle's tracks that led him up to the restaurant. Seemed he had left a lesson out of her training. He had taught her about horses and the need to remove any evidence of their passing. Too bad he had neglected to inform her about the nefarious habits of dogs, who were less discreet.

Stepping over rubble and around fallen debris, Noah entered the restaurant to look at Elle's handiwork at making a camp. To the casual observer the place was a mess. It appeared that no one had been inside for years, certainly not three horses, a dog and a thirteen year old girl. He had to admit it, she was good. She might be his granddaughter and she might have been trained by him, but observing how she had applied that training, he couldn't help himself, he was impressed. The old restaurant had been a good choice. The fire and other evidence of her having been here had been covered or removed. Yet there was something that troubled him. The camp lacked the degree of casualness that he would have expected. Perhaps it was just his imagination but it looked more defensive than he thought was warranted. If this observation was correct, it had to have a connection with the presence of the additional horse and the dog.

The truth was if he had wanted to, even at her sustained pace, Noah could have caught up with his granddaughter. He suspected she had counted on him being absent from the farm for four or more days, just as it was likely that she had counted on her parents waiting for his return before doing anything. She had seriously underestimated them and this was, he felt, to a large degree, his doing. Since her first birthday, Elle had been his constant companion. While her mother and father and the rest of the family struggled to run the farm, it was Noah, with Elle in tow, who went out in the wastelands for days, even weeks at a time, hunting, exploring, salvaging. This relationship might have been detrimental to her parents' efforts to keep the farm viable but only marginally, and it was not as if their outward journeys did not have benefits for the family. The problem was that Elle, like every child born before her, had no real understanding of her parents' lives. From her perspective, her parents had no past. They were never children or even young; they were always the way they were now for they had no real history. This two dimensional view can become further exacerbated as a child approaches a certain age. Parents are no longer viewed as all-knowing and powerful, but as dull and unimaginative creatures. Because of this, Elle had seriously misjudged and underestimated what her parents were capable of. And that is why Elle was able to manufacture such an elaborate scenario that envisioned her parents as passive and, without meaning to be cruel, ineffectual, which would allow her the time she needed.

As it was, Noah was torn between the demands placed on him by his daughter to find Elle and bring her home safely, and what was best for Elle by allowing her to prove she was worthy of a life. What if he caught up with her? What then? Embarrassment – bringing her home like some foolish child on an impossible mission? He couldn't do that to her. As it had been with his children, a time came when a parent had to step back and let them go. He trusted Nora would remember that and understand. Sometimes, for a child to become an adult, they must risk what no parent could permit. But letting go did not mean he couldn't be lurking in the shadows. No parent or grandparent, for that matter, ever relinquished that right.

The dog's deposits told him she was perhaps six or seven hours ahead of him, maybe less. The camp told him he might not be the only one she did not want to find her. Noah pulled himself up into the saddle, gave a flick of the reins to urge Blue to a trot. For the time being he would not interfere. To be safe, however, he would close the gap between them. Besides, the spring was only a few more hours ahead. Thinking of Alissa brought back buried memories that contained a raft of mixed emotions, some good, some not so good.

The flowers of the fairy ring smelled sweet. A good choice, Alissa would have approved, he thought, returning the circle of flowers to the graves. He remembered watching Elle's mother show his granddaughter how to make them just as Nora had been taught by her mother. If only... he thought. That was what they had been doing the afternoon he had gone hunting. Since the whole family would be leaving the next day, his two young daughters and the young son of a Trader had spent the morning searching the meadow, gathering flowers to present to their mother as she sat on the porch. Each of them wanted a fairy ring to wear on the trip as it was a Traders' custom for children and women to wear them in the belief they would ensure a good and safe journey. Though they had been hard, sometimes dangerous, the years with the Traders had also been good ones. The kids had grown so fast he could not believe how soon they would old enough to leave. Do all parents feel the same, he wondered? Now that Alissa was pregnant and soon to give birth, they would return to the farm. Both the others had been born there so Alissa saw no reason to change the routine.

After separating from the Traders Noah and his young family had been travelling with, they rode the short distance to the Honey Comb with plans to stay a few days before proceeding to the farm. It was Alissa's idea and not just for the chance of perhaps finding a beehive to raid, always a treat. This was their place, where Noah had taken her camping right after they had married. The bridal bed, a gift from their Trader family, had been placed on the same spot she and Noah would later build the cabin. They had hauled timber and other 'found' items from miles around. He had no idea how many hours they'd spent stripping, renovating and stacking material along the route taken by the Traders' wagons so it could be picked up by them and delivered to the spring. Those were some of the best of times. It became a home away from home even for the most ardent free-footed Trader. In those days the Traders seldom missed the opportunity to stop and stay when in the vicinity. Even if they tended to treat the Honey Comb as a kind of semi-permanent base camp, in Alissa's eyes this was their place. They, along with friends and family, had built the cabin and shed. It had taken a good deal longer and been much harder than any of them had anticipated. By the time of its completion, Noah and Alissa had one child and another on the way.

The cabin's memories pressed in on Noah as he knelt by the fireplace. The ash in the hearth was still warm to the touch, which meant he was, at the most, only a couple hours behind Elle. Once out on the wastelands there was a good deal of open country ahead of him. Not wanting to be detected, he decided to stay a little longer. Of course, maybe he just wanted to tarry by the graves of his beloved wife and child. Leaving the horses, Noah walked over to the spring.

The memories of that day followed him. He had been just about to bring down a pronghorn buck, already fantasizing about the many ways Alissa's cooking skills could be employed, when he'd heard the gunfire. The rapid exchange was not the result of the kids hunting game or target shooting. As the startled buck bounded away, Noah swung the horse around and began to race back. Driving the horse as hard as he could, he knew from past experience that it was unlikely he would arrive in time, for such was the nature of these events. Most of the time it was a sudden flurry of violence and then it would be over.

The boy, the son of Traders, friends of the family, who had been planning to spend a few uneventful months with them on the farm, diverted the men by forfeiting his life. When the men rode into their camp, Noah's oldest daughter, Nicole, was inside the small building adjoining the cabin loading a few things into the cart for their departure. Nora, his younger daughter, in the company of her mother, was heading over to the spring with canvas buckets to fetch some water for that night's meal. The boy had found himself a cool and comfortable spot to read when he saw two men approaching the cabin with drawn weapons. He had left his weapon behind, a mistake that cost him dearly. Knowing the others would not see the men in time, he had jumped up and begun running toward the cabin, shouting as he went. One of the men turned in his saddle with a casual indifference, took aim, and shot the boy.

Nicole heard the shooting and, with her rifle at the ready, ran from the outbuilding in time to watch her friend fall to the ground. On seeing the man shoot the boy, without hesitation she raised her own rifle and fired, striking him full in the chest just as he was turning back around. The smile that was about to form turned instead to a look of surprise. As the dying man slipped from his saddle, the remaining rider started shooting at Nicole. In an attempt to gain some cover, she raced up onto the porch for the safety of the cabin. Before she could reach the door, the first bullet hit her. It struck her in the right side; the force slammed her against the wall. As she slid down the wall, leaving a bloody track, the second bullet struck, grazing her temple.

Thinking she was dead, the man turned his attention to Alissa and Nora. They were also trying to gain the cabin's perceived safety. Enraged by the death of his companion as well as this inconvenience, the second man urged his mount forward. As he came alongside Alissa, he reached down and seized her by the hair, wrenching her back hard against the horse. Maintaining a firm grip, he dismounted and struck the pregnant woman, driving her to the ground. There, as she lay encumbered by the unborn child, he proceeded to shout at her, delivering one kick after another to her prone body.

Nora, hearing her mother scream, stopped running toward the cabin and sprinted back. She attacked the man as any child might. Clutching his raised arm in her small hands, she bit down with all the fury and strength she could bring to bear. Both the pain and the unexpected intrusion further infuriated the man to the point that foam formed on his lips as he yelled and cursed, trying to dislodge her. The child remained firmly attached to his forearm with the tenacity of a pit bull, forcing him to fling down his rifle in order to free his other hand. Sensing the shift of his attention away from her, Alissa joined her daughter in the fray lashing out in desperation, causing as much harm as she could, drawing blood by raking his face with her nails. Struggling to ward off Alissa and pry Nora loose from his arm, the man bashed the child into unconsciousness, losing a chunk of his arm in the process. Then, holding Alissa again by her hair he drew his knife.

As he raised it to strike, his expression, distorted in anger, suddenly went blank; his muscles, rigid with strain, slackened; the knife, poised above Alissa's head, tumbled from his grasp. A small hole had appeared between his eyes and he slumped forward, pinning Alissa beneath him. In a haze, Nicole let the rifle slide from her hands as she watched her mother's efforts to extricate herself from beneath the dead man. She then slipped into unconsciousness, not knowing until later that her mother had gone into labour.

The memory of the scene that greeted Noah as he broke into the meadow rose up in his mind unblemished, as vivid as the stone that marked their graves. Two men and the boy lay in the clearing leading up to the cabin. Nicole, with a rifle by her side, sat propped up against the wall of the cabin, drenched in the blood that flowed from her wounds. At the foot of the stairs, Nora sat crying, cradling her mother's head in her lap. The child's left arm lying limp by her side was broken while the right kept stroking her mother's face.

The boy died during the night. Alissa, after giving birth, died along with their newborn daughter the following afternoon. Nicole's wounds, while painful, were not life threatening. They would heal leaving her with ugly scars, reminders on her body and in her thoughts. Nora's broken arm would also heal, but the child would not utter a recognizable word for the next three years. The family had just been unlucky, one of those random events that occur no matter the precautions one takes to avoid them. If those men had arrived just a day later, Noah and his family would have been well on their way home. If they had arrived earlier that morning, he would have still been there. If the boy had not left his rifle in the cabin. If only … If only… If only I had been there was a refrain that haunted him in spite of knowing that that was how life was, had always been, even before the coming of the Dry.

The distance was too far to take them home to the farm so Noah had buried his wife and newborn daughter beside the boulder leading up to the spring. He then dragged the dead men out onto the wastelands, leaving them there to rot unknown and unmourned. With his two children and the body of the boy in a hurriedly-made coffin, Noah caught up with the Traders. There they would stay for another two years before he and Nora returned to the farm. Nicole was given over to the Traders' care, a life for a life. Over the following years, he would return many times to work the stone's face.

Chapter Fifteen

The wisdom of any decision can only be judged in hindsight.

The tracks from Elle's horses leading from the spring indicated that she was not heading back the way she had come; rather it looked like she planned to intersect the main road further west. That being the case, Noah stayed on the paved road reasoning it would allow him to come up behind her, hopefully unobserved. Until necessity demanded, he would leave off any decision as to whether he should continue to follow or join her.

Concerned at being discovered by Elle's dog, Noah waited in the morning shadows, up-wind and well back, for her to exit the mall. After all the effort of trailing her, he didn't want to risk the dog exposing his presence. Every Trader family had dogs and from his experience it was foolish to underestimate their particular talents and skills. The dogs that had survived the last sixty years of turmoil were smart mongrels and tended be one-person animals. They could also be rather pugnacious if they felt a member of their 'family' was under any sort of threat.

The dog bounded out from the mall's loading bay in the back. It stood for a moment with its nose held high in order to catch any interesting smells. Apparently satisfied, it turned and started leaping about in excitement until Elle, leading two horses, rode out and down a ramp. This was the first time Noah had seen his granddaughter for three weeks. He sensed a change. Her carriage was different, less childlike, more sombre. Something had happened and he could not help feeling a little sad. He did not think the person up ahead of him would be requesting stories, seeking his lap or even his company. It was then he heard the melodic sounds of a harmonica.

As he watched Elle disappear up the road, he thought to himself that at this leisurely pace she wouldn't arrive at the Empty Cup spring until sometime tomorrow. He could continue following her as he had been or, better yet, he smiled, swing around and be waiting with a pot on the boil at the spring. Now that would be unexpected and hopefully a pleasant surprise. The more he thought of the scheme the better he liked it. He would enjoy the look on her face immensely. With some time to kill, ensuring Elle was well away before he left the main road for Empty Cup, Noah reached into his saddle bag. He hadn't had breakfast so he got himself something to eat while waiting.

Swallowing the last of his breakfast, he took a drink to help to wash the food down. With the bland taste lingering in his mouth, Noah warmed to the idea of skirting around Elle and meeting her at Empty Cup Spring. He was tired of this kind of tucker and the thought of cooking a proper meal with a huge kettle of bush tea for the two was just the ticket. He was getting too old for this rough living. Then, as he was about get up in preparation to follow Elle, he heard Blue suddenly snort and perked up his ears. Noah froze to listen as he slowly reached for the rifle leaning against the wall. A familiar sound, horses and the rumble of a wagon's iron rims riding over tarmac. Because of Elle's dog, luck was again running with him. Not wanting to be detected, he had set up camp within a building whose only access was through a single side entrance facing away from the road. Lost in its shadowy interior, through a fist-sized hole, Noah watched two men on horseback ride past followed by a large two-wheeled wagon with a single occupant. "Scavengers!" he hissed between clenched teeth. "Bloody Scavengers!" In the darkness, leaning with his back against the wall Noah felt hatred, a deep primal, unbridled hatred surge up within, and fear. Not for himself, for Elle. What could she have done to attract their interest? It could be, of course, nothing more than pure opportunistic bad luck, but he did not think so. Whatever it was, those men were definitely trailing her. In the Dry, never trust a coincidence for it will rear up and bite you in the butt.

To avoid alerting them of his presence, Noah remained absolutely still while waiting for the driver and wagon to roll well out of earshot. In the stifling heat of the enclosed room, he thought about the Scavengers. The coming of the Dry had eventually swept away a vast, interlocking and interdependent network of civilizations. Death, savagery, deprivation, degradation, he had seen it all. Yet, even though the magnitude of the destruction exceeded human comprehension, most of those who did survive retained, to various degrees, qualities of humanity. In Noah's experience no such qualities existed among the Scavengers. It was as if for some the Dry drained from them any semblance of grace. Their mode of dress, their behaviour, their near limitless indulgence toward cruelty set them apart. They brought a ferocity that eviscerated any area they inhabited. They didn't just kill; they butchered.

Twenty years into the Dry, there had been those who thought the worst that nature could fling at them had passed. There were signs that some areas were not just surviving but prospering. This was especially true of those communities dotted along the sea shores and the larger lakes. Everywhere people were digging wells, installing solar pumps, building desalination plants from which life-giving water flowed; nothing like the Before Times, that was certain, but it did prove they could adapt. They could adjust. They could manage. Life would remain hard but surely the worst was over. Then it came. It smashed into them with such a fury that even now it was only referred to only as the Sorrow. A pandemic of unprecedented ferocity, it shattered the last vestiges of government, of law, of order. Religious centres, sanctuaries, filled to overflowing. Not just the devout and the pious cried out for the nightmare to end and for the rains to return, but the nightmare remained and the rains never came. The disease raged back and forth across the country for over five years and then, as suddenly as it had appeared, it vanished. In its wake the stunned survivors awoke from this devastating cataclysm to find communities that had not been annihilated by the

Sorrow isolated, separated by fear and death. Then, as they struggled to recover, another plague descended upon them. This time it was a plague of man upon man – the Scavengers.

The effects of the pernicious visitations of the Scavengers and the Sorrows meant that even places with abundant water such as The Maiden and Alissa's remained unsettled and sometimes forgotten altogether. Theories abounded but none knew for certain the origins of the Sorrows. Those that might have were counted among the dead. What was known before the last links were severed with the rest of the world was that the disease's deadly effectiveness was universal. An imperviouscurtain was drawn across the world's community of nations. As to the Scavengers, the general belief was that they grew out of what had been a number of fanatical, religious doomsday cults. Noah did not fully subscribe to this belief. Perhaps there was a religious element, even the most depraved crave a sense of purpose, and certainly the Sorrow had its part to play, but the real culprit was the subsequent scarcity of women that heralded the arrival of the misogynistic Scavengers. The Dry and the Sorrow brought death to that poor gender in far, far greater numbers than they did to men. By the time the Sorrow's veil of wrath lifted, for every female there were three to four males. And yet the grief did not end. Many of the women who had found the means to survive were now infertile. To Noah, the Scavengers were what became of men without the anchor of a family. Wives, children, without them...

what was there to live for? Quickly and quietly Noah saddled Blue. He would leave the pack animal. However, just in case he did not return, he made sure she would be able to get out on her own. From one of the packs stacked against the far wall, he removed four padded leather 'boots' and carefully placed one on each of Blue's hooves. From the leather wrap he selected an assortment of weapons: two knives, two pistols, a short barrelled carbine with a silencer, a semiautomatic shotgun, ammunition. Finally Noah unzipped the end of the 'tool kit' and removed and assembled a rifle with a very long barrel. To it he fixed a large telescopic sight and a silencer. Securing the knives and pistols on his waist, the carbine and shotgun on Blue, Noah once more checked the hole in the wall. Nothing. He listened but heard nothing but his own breathing. They had passed on by. He grabbed the saddle's horn, placed a boot in the stirrup and swung up and into the saddle. The weapon was allowed to ease naturally into the crook of his right arm.

Ready, the pair left their concealment and edged from the shadows into the bright sunlight. From years of experience, Blue knew he was being readied for a 'hunt' and trembled slightly with excitement and expectation. Domesticity was not in his nature. This was.

Exiting the building, Noah turned Blue onto an adjoining service road that ran parallel to the main highway. By staying back and off to the side, using the available cover provided by numerous dilapidated buildings strung along the road, he stayed in contact with the three men. The Scavengers were so intent on their pursuit they failed to take precautions against the possibility that Elle might not be entirely on her own. This carelessness, this arrogance seemed to Noah to be uncharacteristic. Perhaps they had been following her for so long that it had become routine. "You can't escape, Blue, for everything is connected," whispered Noah into the horse's ear. Illustrating once again life's indifferent fickleness, that single decision three weeks previously to take the central road now allowed him to be the hunter and not the hunted. Had he chosen to follow Elle along the same route she'd taken these men could be trailing him as well.

Just before midday, from behind a crumbling cinder block wall, Noah sat and watched the men through the binoculars. They had come to a halt below a crest on his side of the road. The riders dismounted and tied their horses to the back of the wagon as the driver joined them. Whatever it was they were talking about it required a good deal of gesturing. They gestured toward the road in front of them. They gestured toward the road from whence they'd come. They gestured toward both sides of the road. Earlier that morning Elle had been more than an hour ahead of them. Since the men had not appeared to be in a hurry to catch up with her, Noah wondered if they had been waiting for her to stop to wait out the heat of the day. If she had, it was reasonable to believe these men were in the early stages of setting up an ambush.

The gesturing stopped. After reaching into the wagon to extract weapons, two of the men moved off to the far side of the road and down its embankment. Noah could see that one carried a rifle with what looked like a sniper-scope similar to his. The other carried a military style assault rifle. The third man climbed back into the wagon, took up the reins and headed back down the road about a hundred metres. There he turned again and began to traverse the road in the direction of where Noah now sat. Knowing if he remained he would soon be fully visible to the approaching Scavenger, he led Blue deeper into the ruins of the building. Though technically still in plain sight, the two of them would be almost invisible within the ruin's shadows. The brightness of the sun's reflection off the surrounding concrete and asphalt would see to that. There he waited to see what the man was up to. In a few minutes the wagon came to a halt under what remained of a petrol station's service roof. The driver leaned over to pick up a rifle from behind his seat before getting down to secure the horse. Once that was done, he walked out from under the shelter and, putting a hand above his eyes to shield them from the sun, stood looking up and down the highway. Noah raised the rifle when the Scavenger seemed to pause to look directly at where he and Blue had taken refuge. Should he show the least acknowledgement of their presence, Noah would kill him then and there, but this would not be his preference.

The moment slid slowly past. Noah's rifle, trained between the man's eyes, never wavered. Apparently satisfied, hoisting the rifle onto his shoulder, the driver began to walk back up to the ridge where he and the others had previously been. As the man neared the summit of the ridge, Noah began to wonder if he should have killed him the instant he had stepped down from the wagon. At least then there would have been only two to contend with. But that opportunity had passed. Hoping he would not later come to regret that decision, he mounted his horse and proceeded out the back of the building. If they were setting a trap for Elle, he had wasted valuable time. However Noah wanted to have a peek inside that wagon before he took any action against these men. Not that it would stop him killing all three. They were after all, Scavengers. With such men there was no room for humanitarian gestures or yielding the benefit of the doubt. Hesitation in dealing with a Scavenger got you killed.

Since the wagon would be clearly visible from the position taken by the driver just below the ridge, Noah circled around to come up at the rear of the station. Dismounted, he peered around the corner. Seeing that the driver was otherwise occupied, Noah ducked over and looked in to see that a large tattered canvas covered the wagon's contents.

He'd been witness to many horrors, starvation, mass suicides, the murder of whole communities, desperation and depravity in all its manifestations. Long ago he'd lost count of the number of people he'd killed or had seen die. Whatever the world might have been before the coming of the Dry, surely it must have been better than what it had become. Searching the wagon's boxes of supplies, canisters of water, fodder for the horses and weapons, Noah came upon the proof, if there was any needed, of the Scavengers' limitless evil. Preserved in a wooden salt box, along with other unidentified slabs of meat, were the upper torso and legs of a child. Noah closed the lid, re-covered the box with the canvas and returned to Blue. He had seen evidence of cannibalism before. In their desperation to survive it was not unknown for some to resort to the most basic of instincts. This was seldom the case with Scavengers. It was their hallmark. After all these years, he could not comprehend men such as these. Their wanton carnage and malignance was so voracious, so immoral, so ubiquitous, no one expected from them mercy and none was ever given.

The Dry, the Sorrow and the Scavengers had taken from him members of his family, his wife, his child and friends. He had an unshakable sense that he had failed to protect them, and the feeling never left him. He shoved aside these thoughts. They were distracting and he needed to concentrate, so he forced the anger down deep inside and held it there. These men had every intention of killing Elle, his beloved grandchild. Taking an extra clip for the rifle from the pack, he felt a tremble in his hand. Noah swore under his breath. "What is wrong with us?" Exasperated, unable to reconcile himself to man's inexhaustible destructiveness even as the world teetered on the verge of dying, he slipped the additional clip onto his belt and released the safety catch. His whole life revolved around the dead, the dying and his family's survival. "Tell me old friend," allowing the horse to nuzzle him, "will there ever come a time when this ends, or is this all that there will ever be?"

Making sure Blue would not follow him, he hurried along one of the side streets that would eventually bring him level with the driver of the wagon. What he wanted was a place that would provide enough elevation to allow him to see without being seen. Easing through the frame of a shattered doorway Noah crossed the room and climbed the stairs.

Through his binoculars, from an upstairs window, he could see the driver lying in a drainage ditch that ran through the median's centre. This was good, well chosen, he thought. The shooter could cover the open area in front of him while remaining relatively hidden. The position did have one major drawback. Lying as he was, the raised walls of the drain severely restricted his peripheral vision. To see over them, he'd have to lift himself up to such an extent he would become exposed. Either way, Noah could use this to his advantage. If the man stayed low, perhaps waiting for a signal, he'd be unable to see Noah closing in on him. Should he attempt to look over the drain's walls or behind him, he would become a clear target.

It was best to keep things simple. Sneaking up on the man in the culvert without being seen by him or his companions was not simple. He really should have killed him back at the wagon. The regret died in mid-thought when movement outside alerted him that something was going on down there. Noah returned the binoculars to his eyes. Another hundred metres further along the highway, off to the left, he saw the Scavenger with the assault rifle wave back to the wagoner. Hidden by the carriage of a burnt-out truck, Noah would not have seen him if he hadn't stood up to wave. The wagon driver waved back. The man behind the truck then turned and waved to what Noah could only guess would be the Scavenger with the sniper rifle somewhere further up the road.

The family luck was still with him. Had he killed the wagon driver earlier, there would have no one in the drain to wave. That would have alerted the other two that something was amiss. It was better this way where the advantage remained with him. Though he had no idea where the third man was, it was obvious to Noah that whatever their plan was it was about to go into play. Elle was in grave danger and he couldn't risk the time necessary to sneak up. He had delayed too long. Noah put the rifle to his shoulder, aimed and, in rapid succession, fired three times. There was no accompanying loud bang of an exploding cartridge, just a muffled whoosh with each pull of the trigger. The weapon was nearly a one of a kind. In the Before Times its production had been limited. Modern warfare, with the advent of pilot-less air drones and driverless mobile gun mounts, saw little point in manufacturing a weapon that cost as much as this one did. Its only advantage was that it was silent and fired a projectile that maintained a near flat trajectory for four kilometres.

Noah picked up the binoculars. Not bothering to check if the Scavenger in the drain was dead, he looked to see if the one behind the truck had been alerted. It appeared he hadn't, but as Noah prepared to kill him, he moved. All he could see now was the top of his head. Not wanting to risk missing him, and thereby alert the remaining Scavengers to his presence, Noah raced down the stairs and out the door. He'd lived a hard sixty-some years and, considering his size, it would be reasonable to think of him as being built for endurance not speed. This was not so. There were over hundred metres between him and the dead wagoner, and it was all uphill. Aware of his capabilities, he knew it would take less than thirty seconds, at a cost. Laden for battle Noah began to sprint up the road's incline. Within seconds, sweat poured from him, soaking his clothes, blurring his vision, stinging his eyes. He tried to clear the sweat from eyes with the back of his hand as he ran, to no avail. The wagoner's body was now less than forty metres away. He turned off the road and on to the median, running alongside the drain. His breathing remained steady and deep, the stride measured, but Noah was aware he was nearing his limit. Thirty years ago, even fifteen years, this rise would have been a doddle. Twenty metres to go; he could see the man's body wedged within the shallows of the drain.

Still running, he began to hunch down so as to stay below the ridge line when suddenly a portion of the ground beneath him gave way, hurling him forward onto the wagoner's back. A wave of blinding pain surged up his left leg, forcing a muted cry between clenched teeth. Fighting the need to cry out, Noah buried his face in the wagoner's back. The dead man's coat afforded a means to muffle the sound of his heavy breathing and the uncontrollable gasps at the pain. He waited for it to ebb a little before turning his head to survey the damage. Being big had its advantages. Lying face down on the back of a dead man, he could appreciate one of its disadvantages. So intent had he been to reach the ridge without being seen, he had failed to notice a grate that covered a drain pipe leading off and under the highway. Time and neglect had ensured it couldn't support the weight of a man as big as he was. Had he been a smaller man, or had he been walking, it might have held. Even then, if it had collapsed, he would have suffered little more than a skinned shin. A large running man carrying a thirty kilo pack, it seemed, was vulnerable. His boot pointed at an unlikely angle which meant his leg was broken. Luckily, if one could call it that, his momentum had pulled his leg free of the culvert. Had the leg been pinned, the pain of trying to extract it would have most certainly consumed him. As it was, the tiniest movement was agony, depleting his ability to concentrate.

He looked around and realized he was metres from where he needed to be and there was a sense of time flowing against him. Gathering his will to fortify against the pain, stifling an urge to cry out, Noah gradually dragged himself up to the ridge, sliding the rifle alongside him.

It seemed to take an incredibly long time to crawl a few metres. With one more pull, he could see the road as it stretched out before him. The effort left him momentarily drained so he lowered his head to rest, letting the pain subside before drawing the weapon up to his shoulder. Muttering under his breath, "Two to go," he looked through the scope and began to sweep the area to find them. The one with the assault rifle had moved and was now crouching near the rear of the truck. "That's one," as he swept the area further along the left hand side of the road. A prone figure came into view some fifty metres up from the 'truck' man. Smiling, "That's two." The attentions of both men were firmly focused on a house on the far side of the road about half way up a hill. Wincing at a stab of pain, he swung the rifle around and, using the scope, looked for himself. At first he saw nothing. If she was up there, Noah willed her to be smart enough to keep her head down and out of danger, at least for the next few minutes. He was just about swing both his attention and his rifle back to the prone figure when he saw her, for an instant, looking down onto the highway from the edge of the house. In that same instant, a shot was fired and Elle was gone from sight.

The shot's echo still lingered as Noah, thrusting aside the pain, brought the rifle to bear on the prone figure and fired. There was no drama in the man's death; no sound reverberated against the surrounding building; his head simply slumped to the ground, a cheek coming to rest against the stock of the rifle. Again using the scope, Noah found the one remaining Scavenger. No longer behind the truck, ignorant of his companion's demise and his own imminent death, he had started heading up the hill toward the house. The bullet struck him in the back near his left shoulder, knocking him face forward on the ground. Putting the rifle down just in front of him, Noah reached behind to retrieve the binoculars from the pack. Even that little movement sent a wave of pain shooting up his leg.

He had no knowledge of where they had come from nor who they were, neither did he care. Their deaths were meaningless and brought no satisfaction. They were two more nameless men. His granddaughter, she had a name. How was he going to tell her mother? How was he going to explain to her why he had been unable to save her? Noah lowered the binoculars and lowered his head into the fold of his arms, letting his age and the pain wash over him. He felt so very, very tired.

The crack of a rifle being fired brought Noah's head up. Seconds later he heard another and then another in rapid succession. It sounded as if a small war had just erupted below him. He snatched up the binoculars expecting anything other than what he saw.

Chapter Sixteen
I am left in the hands of a child.

Riding up the slope, Elle was elated. She had recognized the hat and the massive frame of her grandfather lying on the crest of the hill. However, as she approached, the elation gave way to concern when her grandfather did not rise to greet her. Instead of standing up and waving as she would have expected, he remained on his back, lifting only an arm in recognition, beckoning her on. Even before she dismounted, Elle could see the reason behind his languid response. Her grandfather's left leg lay at an impossible angle. She dropped to the ground, letting the reins fall, to run over to him. By his side, she took a weathered hand into hers.

Noah studied his granddaughter's face, letting a minute or more pass before he spoke. Squeezing her hand with his, he said, "Hi Elle, glad to see that bastard was a lousy shot."

Tears came as she leaned down to kiss a dirt-encrusted forehead and whisper, "He wasn't, Granddad." Drawing back, she opened her vest so that he could see the hole in the vest and shirt.

Just as she was about to explain that the origin of the blood collecting around the hole was not from a bullet, Noah exploded with a string of expletives and questions as he tried to sit up. It took all Elle's strength to hold him down as she quickly told him what had happened, including the fight in the barn.

"You were stabbed?"

"Yes, but it's no more than a scratch." As she finished she took the book from her shirt pocket and gave it to him. He face looked grey. Wiping his hand on his shirt, he reached up to take the book. Elle drew in a sharp breath when she saw that his hand was covered in blood.

Noticing her startled look, he said, "It's not mine." Pointing at the man in the drain, "It's his. I fell on him when I broke my leg." With the book in his hand, he thumbed through the pages, stopping where the bullet had struck the pendant. He touched the splayed bullet and pendant. Before handing the book back, a smile crept upon his face, followed by a forced chuckle. "You're one very lucky girl, child. If you hadn't been wearing that vest that bullet would have gone through the book, the pendant and you," said Noah as he handed it back to her. "By the way, have a read of the page where the bullet stopped and then look at who the author is."

Elle took the book from his hand and flipped through the book until she reached the pendant. Removing the pendant she read aloud, *"Always speak to a man as if he were a child, to do otherwise would only confuse him."*

"And does that remind you of anyone?" They both started laughing, forgetting for a moment what had just taken place here as they both recalled the many times she'd heard her father ask her mother not to speak to him as if he was a five year old.

"Yes..."

"Nasty habit the women of this family seem to have," said Noah.

Returning the book to her pocket, Elle said, "I know," and leaned over to apply another kiss to his forehead while giving him an affectionate pat. Smiling, she continued, "a very nasty habit. Now lie back and try not to move while I have a look at what you've done to yourself."

"And the author?" he asked. "Don't you recognize the name?"

Atticus, Nadia's tree! At the bottom of the main trunk there were the names of her great-great grandparents. "Yes, I do. How in the world....?" Her voice trailed off into stunned silence.

The dog, tired of being left out, tried to insert itself between Elle and Noah only to be pushed away.

"And who is your new friend and does it have a name?" asked her grandfather as he beckoned the grieving and dejected dog, rewarding it with a stroke along its side.

Three men lay dead, one only a couple of metres away. Her grandfather lay with a broken leg struggling not to show the pain. Elle sat in the dusty gravel at her grandfather's side with bullet hole in her breast pocket. Her face became expressionless, lost in thought. Then, as if coming out of a deep stupor her face re-animated. Feeling really pleased, she said, in what she thought was a reasonable response to his question, "Her name is... Mutt."

Now it was Noah's turn to have his face go blank. Her answer was too much for him. In spite of the ensuing pain, a huge reservoir of tension suddenly burst from its confinement. He began to roar with laughter and, once started, he completely lost control. Tears rolled down his cheeks. He gasped for breath. His arms flailed helplessly about in the air. His whole body shook in convulsion. Because of the pain in his leg, he tried desperately to bring it under control but every time he looked at Elle's increasingly befuddled expression it set him off again.

For her part, Elle, immobilized and confused, could only sit looking on with unadulterated bemusement. This certainly did not appear to be a joke she could participate in.

After his laughter finally subsided enough for him to gain some control, still holding her hand, Noah told Elle there were a few things that needed to be done. He listed what he wanted her to do in order of importance. Elle listened, nodding her head when she understood, asking a question when she did not. When he had finished and before she left to begin her various tasks, Elle erected a small 'tent' to protect his face from sun. He watched her ride off, thinking how much she reminded him of his wife. Lying on his back and unable to move without experiencing excruciating pain, he thought about the enormity of their predicament. There were no doctors now. No hospitals. No emergency number to call or ambulances to respond. All that had disappeared years ago. If he wanted to avoid dying here, they would have to attend to his leg and get him mobile. Until then his survival rested on the shoulders of a not quite fourteen-year-old girl.

There was little else to do other than to stare at the cloudless sky that bordered the little tent and listen to the drone of insects' delight in finding the Scavenger's body in the culvert. He was never a man who enjoyed prolonged periods of inactivity, let alone being incapacitated, and hearing a single shot shortly after she rode off didn't help matters. His first impulse was to call out but he thought it better to wait. As the time went by, lying there, he started to worry something might have happened to her. Another Scavenger other than the three he'd seen perhaps. He was just about to try to roll over to get his weapon when he heard the unmistakable rumbling sounds of a wagon coming up the road. Minutes later the sound of the wagon was accompanied by a hail from Elle. Stretching his neck as far as was comfortable, he saw her sitting in the wagon trailing a string of horses, including the intransigent Blue and his pack horse. He watched as she jumped down and walked over to him.

Kneeling by his side, she avoided answering his first question. Instead, she said, "I buried the little girl in a field next to where you had camped. I threw away most of their bedding and extra clothing except for a couple pair of boots and some blankets… Couldn't see being overzealous. I've also got all my stuff and yours loaded into the wagon. We now have a wagon, a dog and eight horses, a machine gun, nine rifles, five handguns, an assortment of knives, four long green boxes that looked like they have never been opened, several boxes of ammo, food and water for us and the horses and these," handing him a metal container. "I've also found the type of boards you said we needed. And oh yeah, we also have two more armoured vests, although it didn't seem to do them much good. So what's next?" Her grandfather did not respond. "Granddad?"

Noah did not answer but instead undid the clips and lifted the lid of one of the boxes. Inside were six cylinders in two rows and what looked like a pistol, although its muzzle was completely out of proportion to any she had seen. In a voice devoid of emotion, Noah asked, "Read me what is on the other boxes." Elle leaned over and read out a stream of what seemed to her meaningless numbers, letters and words. "And the boxes have never been opened?" he inquired in the same flat tone of voice.

"Don't seem to have been 'cause the wire seal is still attached," she said.

With difficulty Noah raised himself into a sitting position. "Elle, unhitch the horses and get them away from the wagon. We don't want a fidgety or spooked horse to try to take off while we are in the middle of setting my leg. When you're done get my first aid kit. It's in the saddle bag. Set it over by the wheel." Elle nodded as she stood up and then headed over to the horses. Noah began to scoot himself backwards, toward the rear wheel of the wagon.

She returned and tried to help, but after several failed attempts, was resigned to the fact that she was a hindrance. It was not because she was frail; that she was not. He was just too big. After another incidence of causing him to wince with pain, they agreed that it would perhaps be better if she let him do it himself. But it wasn't easy for her to stand passively aside. Each time she saw him tremble from the exertion and the pain, she would again attempt to help only to be waved away. Sweat ran down his forehead and along his nose to drip into his beard. Elle became mesmerized watching each drop of sweat form at the tip of his nose before falling away. Dust, disturbed by Noah's scuffling, collected within the crags of his face. With each push, air gushed from his mouth, sounding like the efforts of a steam train on an incline. His face grimaced, all focused on minimizing the pain and getting to the wagon. At last he was able to lean back against the wheel. His shoulders sagged with the exhaustion that rushed over him. Elle offered an old, battered, water-filled thermos which he quickly emptied. Setting the container down, it toppled over and began to roll away. Instinctively he reached out to stop it, only the pain that shot up his leg flung him back against the wagon wheel. Drawing a deep breath, he waited for the pain to subside before turning to watch Elle retrieve the container and put it in a safe spot. The irony of having his granddaughter rescue him did not go unrecognized.

Broken bones were a recognized occupational hazard of the Dry. Although this would be the first time she had actually set a broken bone, Elle knew pretty much what was required. The difference this time – there were no adults around to help. Setting a bone, especially a leg bone in a man the size of her grandfather, would normally require the strength of two grown men. All Noah had was a 45kg granddaughter. After driving the stake into the ground to a depth that satisfied her grandfather, Elle laid out all the stuff she'd need: the wooden slats, a blanket, rope and the leather straps. The last thing needed before she began was a length of soft leather which she folded over several times before handing it to her grandfather.

As he took the leather, he enclosed her hand in his. Neither spoke for a moment.

Finally Elle leaned over and gave him a kiss on the forehead. Strands of hair fell across her face and she pushed them back behind an ear. Seeing him watch her, she smiled. "It's been a while since I had a haircut."

He returned her smile and then placed the folded rawhide between his teeth and bit down as he reached back with each hand to grab a spoke. Bracing himself for what was to come, he nodded to Elle to proceed. With a tinge of regret at ruining a perfectly good boot and pants, Elle cut along the seam of the pant leg and then rolled it up far enough so it would be out of her way later. She then did the same with the boot, cutting along its inner seam so that she could remove it without having to pull it off. The problem, from Elle's perspective, was not that the boot or the pants could not be repaired. Living in a time of such scarcity, it just felt like vandalism. A short snort was all Elle heard as she tilted the foot back to remove his heel from the boot. Once the boot was off, she examined the leg to be sure that the skin was intact and reasonably clean. Other than wastelands dust, some bruising and a small cut on the shin, everything seemed ok. She opened the first aid kit and, using grain alcohol, she cleaned the leg. The Farm had opiates for pain they traded from their gypsy friends but neither of them, in their haste to leave, had thought to bring any with them. Noah would have to endure the setting of his leg without their benefit. There was, however, an alternative. When she'd finished cleaning the leg as best she could, Elle, making sure there was already ample supply of water in the cup to dilute its potency, added a generous portion of the alcohol before handing it back to him. He sipped Jacob's very strong home brew, "good for both external and internal uses". When he'd finished, she picked up the rope.

Elle was not strong enough to pull the leg so that the bones could align. This was where the rope and stake came into play. The first step was to make a 'loop' about four metres long. Then, after winding a strip of soft leather around the ankle to provide some protection, she secured one end to the ankle using a knot called the timber hitch. If it could keep a log straight while being pulled by a horse, she reasoned, it could be used to set her grandfather's leg. To ensure that the knot would not slip, she gave it a small tug which elicited a muffled grunt from Noah. Ignoring, as best she could, the pain she was causing, she hurriedly placed the far end of the loop round the peg, leaving enough slack that a portion of the loop rested on the ground, and then tied it off. Happy with her handiwork, she put a stick between the two lengths of rope halfway between the peg and Noah's foot. She was ready.

In the open and without protection, the midday heat bore down on them both. Even without a breeze, the sweat seeping from every pore of their bodies did not linger long on their skin. It quickly evaporated in the dry air leaving the insects scrambling for their share. Elle looked at her grandfather as he braced himself for what was to come, and waited. When he again nodded, she started to turn the stick. The first few turns took up the slack in the rope. Elle paused when she heard the first gasp from her grandfather.

From between clenched teeth came an exasperated demand. "Go on. Don't stop. Keep going."

Elle began to turn the stick again. As she did the rope tightened, lifting the leg slowly from the ground. Keeping her attention on the tightening of the rope and leg, Elle heard Noah straining not to cry out, forcing his teeth deep into the leather thong as he took in air with great gulps, letting it out as a deep throated growl. Again and again, with each turn of the stick, Noah's muscles strained as his hands grasped the spokes ever tighter to aid a determination to not call out "Enough!"

Half a turn more and Elle watched the foot rotate into the desired position and the leg now appeared straight. Securing the stick so it would not unwind, Elle moved next to the leg and with both hands felt for the bone. Her hands could feel both breaks and it was clear that Noah had been fortunate. The breaks were clean. Trying not to be distracted by the sound of distress from her grandfather, Elle, manipulated the two sets of bones into their proper alignment as gently as she could manage. She kept her hand around as much of the leg as her small hand could cover so the bones would not drift apart. She reached down and picked up the piece of blanket she had placed there earlier and slowly wrapped it around the leg. Working as fast as she dared, she secured the blanket with two strands of rawhide. This was followed by the six slats. This too was hard to do on her own. What she needed was someone to hold them in place while she ran the rawhide cord around them. After several attempts, much to her frustration and a sense of her grandfather's increasing impatience, Elle ran a pair of slip knots around the leg to hold the slats temporarily in place. Once that was done and she could see that they remained where she wanted them, she began to coil the remaining rawhide up the length of the lower leg. Every few turns she would stop and slip a finger beneath the cord to check it for tightness. Too tight and it could cut off the flow of blood to the leg, not tight enough and the bones in the leg would not remain aligned.

As she finished, kneeling in the dust, Elle was just about to sit back onto her heels to admire her handiwork when the air was suddenly ripped apart by a flood of the most inflamed profanity that she had ever heard articulated by her grandfather or anyone else. The last lines were forever etched into her memory and the subject of many an evening's tale. "Girl, if you don't get off your skinny little ass and untie that rope, I will get up from here and personally skin you alive."

Startled by his outburst, Elle turned to look at her grandfather. She noticed how drawn his face looked and could see, though he also looked tired from the ordeal, his smile had returned. She got up and went over to the rope and, with infinite care, gingerly lowered his leg until it again rested on the ground.

Attempting to stand, Elle discovered how stiff she had become. As she rubbed the back of her neck, it seemed to her that every muscle in her body had become fixed in place and was now reluctant to move. She'd been so focused she'd not realized how tense and cramped she'd become. To work out the stiffness, Elle raised her arms over her head and then, without bending her knees, reached down to touch her boots with her fingertips. Straightening back up, she then moved from side to side bending at her waist, striving to get some feeling back into her muscles. Rolling her shoulders she recalled watching her grandfather dismount after a day in the saddle and she suspected this was how he must have felt. If the opportunity had presented itself, she would have gladly found a place out of the sun, lain down and slept.

"What in the hell are you doing, girl?" Her grandfather's rebuke for the second time made her jump, snapping her out of a momentary distraction.

"I'm stiff and stuffed," said Elle, grinning at her grandfather as she walked over to the wagon to draw water for them both from the Scavenger's barrow.

Taking the offered cup, Noah looked up at her. "I'll need some help getting in the wagon," he said as he took a drink. "Bloody hell!" He spat the water out. "This stuff is foul."

"Yeah, it is," said Elle, looking into her cup as if expecting to find the source of the rankness. "And there's lots of it." She tipped the rest of her cup into a bowl for the dog and then filled several canvas bags for the horses before filling their cups from her own supply. Crouching by Noah they watched the animals drink every last drop on offer. "It may taste like something died in it but they don't seem to mind," said Elle.

"Perhaps they have less discriminating tastes," said Noah as he put the now empty cup on the ground and, using the spokes of the wheel, attempted to lift himself up. Noticing Elle watching him he said, "Well don't just stand there watching them drink, girl. Give me a hand into the wagon. We need to find some shade and I need to have a look in one of those boxes. Also, just so you know that I've noticed, I want to hear how you ended up with an extra horse and a dog."

Elle thought about her grandfather and the difference between her mother and dad when either one of them was sick or injured. Didn't take him long to start ordering her around.

The floor of the wagon was too cluttered to afford room for Noah, so Elle busied herself clearing a place for his considerable bulk.

Once that was done, and after a great deal of laughter, grimacing, grunting and expletives and with Elle's help, Noah finally sat in the wagon with his back resting against the green boxes that had been stacked to one side. Shuffling his backside a bit to find a position that was comfortable and eased the pain in his leg, he took time to glance at the sun's position. "It's getting late, Elle, and I don't know about you, but I'm getting hungry."

Under the overhang of the abandoned petrol station, Noah tossed a piece of his food to the dog, licked his fingers and began to brush off the last remnants of the meal on a strip of cloth hung around his neck. "Elle! I strongly suggest you had better not let your folks know how well you can cook."

Grinning, Elle could feel her face begin to flush. It was good to be in the company of her grandfather again. She didn't look up, keeping her eyes fixed on the plate in her lap, and did nothing to prevent the dog moving over to finish what she had left. She hesitatingly asked, "Are you going to take me home?"

"No, Elle, I'm not. I should; I promised your mother I would, but I'm not." Gesturing toward the four green boxes visible in the wagon, "Those things in the wagon change everything. If I hadn't busted my leg, I would send you to catch Nicole to deliver a message before going home. As it is, it looks like you, a cripple, and that bottomless gut of a dog have to find out what the Scavengers are up to. Who knows, our presence here might mean we have come in the nick of time to save the world."

Elle was not sure how to take that last remark. If he was kidding there was no accompanying smile to indicate it.

Chapter Seventeen
Friendship, family – what else is there of value?

Noah's hands gently worked the reins, guiding the horse around the worst of the pockmarked and rutted mountain highway. The horse was capable of picking its own route, but the animal was not always mindful that the man in the wagon did not want to feel every jarring imperfection. His injured leg, elevated and propped up, rested along the full length of the wagon's driver's seat. This meant he had to sit almost sideways. Not only was this position uncomfortable for such a big man, it made the task of applying the brake with his good leg somewhat difficult. And, like having a sore throat makes you aware of just you how often you need to swallow, the twinge that shot up his leg was an excellent reminder of how often the brake was needed. Fortunately the intensity of the pain had subsided to more of a dull, throbbing ache, so a twinge now and again was tolerable. However, each time he failed to evade one of the numerous potholes or piles of debris that littered the way, a sharp surge of pain refocused his attention on the road ahead.

Off in the distance, Elle and her horse were but a single dot on the rim of the skyline. Watching them, he mulled over the numerous reasons why they should turn back. Each one was sensible, rational and, and above all, practical and yet, they would continue westward. Their world was dying and not just because of the continuing drought. Since the Sorrow there were fewer births. A family with three children was almost unheard of and cause enough for any family so blessed to rejoice at their good fortune. Death, on the other hand, continued unabated, a constant companion that came in a myriad of ways. Not the least of these had been the Scavengers. Because of them, away from the fortified communities clinging to the large northern lakes, the eastern seaboard and southern gulf, there were only a few scattered settlements and the roaming bands of Traders that linked them. And the dying was not confined to humans. The hardiest of wildlife that had at first flourished when the land was vacated by mankind, eventually succumbed as the Dry bit ever deeper into the landscape. The remnants, like their human counterparts, now huddled near the diminishing areas where water could be found. And if that wasn't enough, there was the dust, the malevolent gift of the Dry. Dust covered everything. It covered you as you were born and when you died. It rose up to greet you in the morning, and waited for you at day's end. A dust so fine it found means to ease itself into the smallest and tightest of places. It crept into and upon every surface, nick, crack and fissure. It formed lines in the folds of your skin, around your eyes and mouth. It bordered and confined every rivulet of sweat. You took it into your lungs with each breath causing some to die of the 'miner's cough'. It clung to your skin, your clothing. It settled on the food you ate, the water you drank. It followed you and ran before you. The dust was devouring the earth, rendering it sterile.

He would not be returning Elle home. There was a tightening in his chest from knowing he would not be able to keep the promise he'd made to Nora to bring Elle home safely. Elle knew nothing of the world before the rains stopped. He did, or he thought he did. Perhaps they were not memories at all but only dreams that had taken on the guise of memories. After all can one really trust the memories of a child? Rivers, forest, wild life, vibrant cities, who was there left to verify or refute that they were not but dreams? And when he died? What would happen then to all those memories? One thing he did recognise as a dream, a false hope, was the idea that they were safe on the Farm. That they had survived the hard times before and would do so again. None knew better than Noah that this was simply wishful thinking. Though he knew his daughter might never forgive him, they would not return to the Farm just yet.

Accepting that he'd been wrong, that the last of the Scavengers hadn't been killed, what had they been up to for the past thirteen or more years? There had not been a single sighting or incident that could have been attributed to them and he, of all people, would have known if there had been. Even if some of them had managed to survive, to escape, where had they gone? And, if it wasn't Scavengers, who was it collecting the petrol and fuel rods? Whoever they were, you could bet they weren't going to use it to cruise a city's empty streets. As to the shoulder-mounted rockets found in the wagon, unlike the flares, this was serious hardware. The kind you'd need if you wanted to start a war. And if those men they had killed weren't Scavengers, but just a bunch of men who, for reasons known only to themselves, wanted to dress like them, that didn't change anything. He would still need to know what it was they were up to and, even if he could convince himself that Elle could make it back to the Farm alone, the truth was, he needed her help because he could not do this by himself.

He had been only a boy when he saw the last major effort to find out what the secret was that the mountain held. A great army moved through their valley heading west. There was hope that they would somehow be able to undo that which had been done. Standing by the bus in front of his mother, he had been pulled tightly against her with an encircling arm. He remembered that her body trembled as if cold.

Some said the army numbered a million or more. What are such numbers to a child? To him, the army looked like a living carpet of ants as it moved along the road through the valley. It took weeks for all of them to pass with their trucks, tanks and armoured carriers. Then, suddenly, one day they and their noise were gone. Peace. The ensuing silence sat upon the land like a funeral shroud. Later, the pitiful remains of that army returned. Clothed in their collective madness, fear and despair, they streamed past the farm in a torrent. Locust-like, they paused only long enough to strip the land bare before fleeing again ever eastward. And what they could not eat nor use nor carry, they would often destroy, killing any and all who had the misfortune of being in their line of flight.

A wheel dipped into a pothole, thrusting Noah back into the present with a surge of pain. "Bloody hell!" was his sole response. Quickly ensuring there were no further 'surprises' awaiting him in the form of another pothole, he saw that while he had been lost in his daydream Elle was returning at a unhurried lope. A good gait, he thought, a pleasure for the rider and not too strenuous for the horse. In a few minutes she was close enough for him to see that she looked pleased with herself, smiling from ear to ear. It was not difficult to be fooled into thinking that this tall, thin as a rail, smiling bundle of raw youthful energy coming toward him, was as she seemed. But, as he very well knew, despite the smile, the warmth, once in a while you'd glimpse something into those eyes that gave even him a degree of discomfort. As she swung her horse around to sidle up next to the wagon, there, for an instant, it was, a vacancy framed within a face consumed with sadness. Then it was gone; Elle was once again full of smiles, eyes all bright and shining.

The dog arrived a minute later and, exhausted, leaped into the back. It had had enough, for the moment. Panting heavily, it looked for both water and shade. Not finding any of the first, it secured the second by flopping down under Noah's seat.

Elle, still grinning, streaked with dirt and gleaming with sweat, said, "Once over that little rise the road is in better condition. We should be able to make good time.

Farther on, maybe another five kilometres, there is a much higher rise, so I could not see what lies beyond."

Noah glanced at the lengthening shadows cast along the road's edge. There were just a couple of hours of day left and the moon wouldn't rise until nearly daybreak, even then it would be but just a sliver. If his memory had not become addled, they would reach Empty Cup sometime later in the night, if they decided to travel by the light of the stars. It was not without risk even if he had been uninjured and not driving a heavily laden wagon across unfamiliar ground, but under the circumstances, it was the best option. The tightness in his chest remained.

"I want to make it to Empty Cup tonight and to do that I'll need to know what lies beyond that other rise. So give that poor dog of yours a drink and, as soon as Belle cools a bit, do the same for her, because as soon as they're finished, I want you to ride out again. Go as far as you can, but be sure to get back well before dark." He paused before adding, "And, if you can, find me a pole about 50 mm thick and two metres long. Now, climb up here and give me a hug, 'cause I'll need to get as many of them as I can for when we get back your mother is going to kill us both."

Her grin slid into a giggle as she did as her grandfather requested, moving from the horse to the wagon with the grace of drifting smoke. They held each other tightly for a long time.

She knew where he did not that she should have died this morning, not once but twice. The man by the car had not been dead. When she'd looked at him through the scope both hands had been clearly visible, but not when she rode up. The right arm was now tucked underneath him. So she did not dismount but waited, silently watching the sand just in front of his face. It moved ever so slightly. The image of the interior of the terminal flashed across her mind as she raised the pistol and fired. When she rolled him on to his back, she saw that he had a semiautomatic pistol in his hand. No mercy asked for, none given. A little later, she buried the remaining meat she'd taken from the homestead, the meat she'd been feeding to the dog, next to the butchered body of the child. Whether it was human or not didn't matter. There are times when it's best not to know the answer.

Another lurch of the wagon startled the pair, bringing a flush of embarrassment to them both and a shot of pain from Noah's leg. Physical sentiment in these hard times, even when death was frequent, was rarely expressed. Why this should be so, neither of them understood. Like so many things in Elle's world, it just was. She removed herself from her grandfather's enclosing arms as he brought the wagon to a halt so that she'd be able to give the animals a much needed drink.

While she waited for them to finish she looked down the road. Out there was a whole lot of unknown. One mistake, one miscalculation was all it would take. She turned her attention to their new acquisitions. Unlike the horses from the Farm and now the dog, she had no emotional ties to these animals. Should the need arise, to survive, they would be killed and eaten. Although she'd eaten horse meat before, there was an undeniable prejudice against doing so. Horses, unlike any other animal of the Dry, were special. They were a necessity. Without them no one could traverse this bleak landscape. Still... she left the thought unfinished, listening to the only audible sounds – the slurping of horses as they sucked their respective buckets dry and the melodious humming emanating from the ever present insects. Thousands of the winged opportunists ebbed and flowed about everyone's head. They, just like every other creature living in the wastelands, pursued with a suicidal persistence any chance to secure a morsel of food or a droplet of water. The unenthusiastic deterrent of an intermittent wave of a hand or the swish of a tail gave no relief or satisfaction.

As she placed the buckets back in the wagon and secured the water barrel, she desperately wanted to ask her grandfather what he had meant by 'to save the world', but did not for fear he'd change his mind and return home.

"Then, maybe I shouldn't hang around here any longer." A flick of the reins, pressed heels against the horse's flanks and she was off. The dog, perking its ears at the sound of the horse's departure, fearing it was about to be left behind, leaped from the wagon in pursuit. Considering the events of the last two weeks, Elle wonder if the more appropriate question might be 'Is this a world worth saving?' Soon she and the dog had disappeared over the rise.

***

Tired but pleased with the distance covered, she flopped bonelessly to the ground. From her perch, the desolate land rolled out before her toward the yet unseen western mountains. Considering the terrain she had ridden through, from what she could see staring into the glare of the setting sun, the road ahead was all that Noah in his delicate condition would want. It was getting late. She'd have to be heading back soon but not just yet. For a few minutes more she would continue to take advantage of the shade the roof of the veranda offered. Except for the ubiquitous smashed windows, and the generic looting of the interior's furnishing and fixtures, this 'hill top diner with a view' was surprisingly unscathed. The benefit of no fires, she thought as she read the menu. It amused her that the menu was decked out with pictures of smiling men and women on horseback, an assortment of farm animals that were also smiling and the various meals on offer, presumably from the body parts of these same farm animals. She had seen similar menus before. Different illustrations of course, but the meals, despite their different names, looked much the same. This one read "Old Time Full Breakfast", "Steer and Beer", "Farm-hand meatloaf with Salad Bar", "Kiddie Meals for those Hungry Hunters". She stopped reading from the faded, plastic laminated menu and tossed it back to where she had found it. All that food, all those people, all that noise, what must it have been like back then when places like this were filled with people?

Except for a speck high in the sky, the solitary cry of some animal off in the distance and the insects that forever hovered about her head, there wasn't much evidence of life. Added to that dreary assessment, the cruel blue of the sky, the grey ash of dead trees and the dung brown of the earth were the only colours on offer. A long sigh escaped her lips as she absentmindedly stroked the dog that had come over to lie against her leg. Picking up a twig with her free hand, she started to poke the ground in front of her, making little holes in the dirt. Here, on this veranda, the deafness of silence invaded her thoughts. Sometimes a strong sense of longing inexplicably rose up within her, invariably accompanied by an acute awareness of profound loneliness. A loneliness not born out of want of company, but that spirit-depleting loneliness that came from the wasteland's dearth of life. Up here and at times like this Elle felt the living world, like some dried up old piece of fruit, was shrivelling around her. She was the youngest in her family and could end up outliving all those she knew and loved. Although that was unlikely as, according to her dreams, she was to drown in a silvery sea sometime soon. Which one was her future or was there yet another path for her?

At the end of the twig a movement caught her eye. "What have we here then?" An ant was making its way up the stick. She brought the stick up to have a closer look at this intrepid adventurer. "Ah, a *Linepithema humile*, we've got you fellows at the Farm." At the Farm, in the wastelands, in the abandoned towns and cities, all along the coasts and lakes, anywhere a person cared to look they would eventually find *Linepithema humile*. In the realm of ants, this species was ubiquitous. Allegedly it was introduced to this continent well over a century ago and, if Elle's book on ants was correct, this ant on the stick belonged to a single mega colony that stretched all around the world. No other ant species, once separated from the colony of their birth, could expect to be welcomed 'home' as the *Linepithema humile* was. Elle delicately put the stick back to where she had picked it up. Whether her Before Time book was correct or not, she liked the idea that that ant was a part of one very big family that would continue uninterrupted for countless centuries. Even the idea of them being all 'sisters' seemed appropriate. After all they had proven to be very resourceful and adaptive creatures. Elle thought of Nicole, her mother and the aunts on the Farm. They were certainly in a better position than her species was at the moment. Elle reached into saddle pack to retrieve the photo of the young girl by the river. One long look and then the photo was returned to its place. It was time to head back to re-join Noah.

***

Shortly after re-joining her grandfather, Elle was back in the saddle riding in the dark with Noah following close behind. If she ignored the increased likelihood of being shot out of the saddle, the hooded 'tail lamp' worked like a charm as it swung back and forth at the end of the pole that protruded over Belle's rump.

Watching the lamp's hypnotic sway a few metres in front of the wagon, Noah was resigned that they weren't going to break any land speed records. Being confined to the wagon as they groped their way toward the Empty Cup had left him in a solemn and contemplative mood. With the possible reintroduction of the Scavengers every aspect of Elle's life was about to alter. They were not like any other danger she had faced and he needed her to understand this. Out here in the wastelands there were just the two of them, and one of the two was a cripple. She had neither the support nor the safety of the Farm and the rest of the family. If they should encounter a Scavenger under any circumstance, what must happen had to be instinctive and brutal. Not counting the man in the barn, twice before she had demonstrated her ability to kill in self-defence and he was sure she was just as capable if it came to defending the life of another. The question was could she kill without provocation? When it came to dealing with the likes of Scavengers there could be no other option. How do you instruct someone in the art of cold calculated murder as the Scavengers had taught him?

Only the closest of his earlier companions knew what had taken place after he found the remains of their burnt-out bus, the bodies of his mother, brother, sister and several of their friends. Only those closest to him in those earlier times understood that there are circumstances when a person is compelled to do things that are reprehensible by some standards, even unforgivable. For weeks Noah tracked the men responsible and when he found them, he killed them. The sentry was the first to die, quietly and quickly. He then proceeded to kill the others while they slept beneath a moonless sky. One by one, he held a hand over their mouths while he drove a knife into their hearts. Once they were dead, he gathered their bodies and all their belongings onto a pyre he had built and then set it alight. He watched it burn all though the night until nothing but ash remained. This he then scattered. The murder of those men was done without anger, remorse or pity. Years later, angry at a fox as it ran off with one of the Farm's chickens, Elle had missed what should have been a clear and easy shot. His only comment to her was to say that, "Anger makes one impatient and imprudent. It tends to spoil a person's concentration which can lead to all manner of dissatisfaction."

Noah sensed a change in Elle, he did not yet know what she'd seen at the terminal or that she'd killed the third Scavenger without compulsion or remorse. Anger, she'd learn, did make one impatient and imprudent.

Absorbed in thought and unaware that Elle had stopped caused a momentary confusion for all concerned including the horses as Noah nearly drove into Belle's backside.

Turning around in her saddle Elle spoke in a raised whisper. "Isn't the lamp working?"

"It's working fine, so long as you don't stop every time you feel the need, and why are we whispering?" Noah replied in an exaggeratedly mocking low voice. Besides the weak light of the lamp, the only other source of light was the broad band of stars that slowly rotated overhead. Moon rise, what there would be of it, was still more than an hour away.

Elle felt a little piqued at his mocking. As it was in Alissa, here in the dark and the stillness, it felt inappropriate to speak in a normal voice. So she said nothing. Instead, she swung around to come along side.

Noah could not see Elle's face in the moonlight but he knew her well enough. "Have something on your mind, Elle?" he asked.

"Granddad?"

"Yes Elle."

Silence and then, "How close have you been to the mountains?"

"Close enough," he said. "Now can we get a move on? I still would like to get to Empty Cup some time tonight."

Chapter Eighteen
All desire peace, but only if it is on their terms.

Locking her knees to keep her leg straight, the woman leaned back into the saddle as the horse, with its haunches nearly dragging the ground, stiff-leggedly negotiated its way down the steep soft slope bordering the gully. The birds had shown her the way, black specks lazily circling high in the sky, effortlessly riding the updrafts from the wastelands below. This many of these opportunistic feeders usually indicated that an unfortunate animal somewhere below, dead or dying, awaited their attention. She hoped it would be nothing more than that as she turned her horse to investigate. Still several metres from the gully's edge, she heard the vociferous squabbling of many, many birds.

Traders accepted that things seldom go to plan. Sixty plus years since the coming of the Dry had taught them that the world was indifferent to their wishes and so they had come to expect a number of inconveniences and setbacks, no matter how simple the task might appear. Mishaps happen in the wastelands; things go wrong – an injury, a broken axle, an unforeseeable diversion and death. Countering this indifference made them a very resourceful people. The family's failure to arrive at the designated rendezvous at the appointed time was therefore not of immediate concern. A delay of two or three weeks, though not common, was certainly not unexpected. After all, the wasteland was big and it was empty. Even so, what possible catastrophe could overcome thirteen wily and experienced Traders with three wagons? However, as a precaution, towards the end of the second week, the woman and other riders had been sent out to find them.

On the ninth day she had.

The woman was no longer of child bearing age. If she had been, custom would have forbidden her from endangering herself unduly. The coming of the Dry had been most unkind toward women, the pandemic and the conflicts that followed even more so. She was lucky both of her children had been born alive and remained so. The father of these children had not been so fortunate. Stemming from an infection in a small scratch, a 'nothing' in the Before Times, he had died from septicaemia, blood poisoning. The man she now shared her wagon with was among the riders selected to find the missing family. So it was not unexpected that he was the first to arrive upon hearing the rifle shots.

Surrounded by the dead and dying birds, the figure looked up at her husband high on the same ridge from which she had descended into this carnage just minutes before. Her face was filled with grief and despair. Racked with convulsive sobs, she tried to stem the flow of her tears with the back of her hand as she sat fumbling with another magazine in an attempt to reload her rifle. Even from this height he could discern that ravages wrought upon them was not solely because of these birds or any other four legged carnivore. Eleven bodies lay stripped and mutilated in the unnamed gully. The impact of seeing them this way had caused his wife to act in uncharacteristic rage. She shot the feeding birds until the magazine was empty, killing far too many. Their extended bellies and the thin air of the Dry made taking flight impossible.They were easy targets, just as the dead Traders must have been for those who murdered them.

He made his way down to her.

Without a word he took the rifle and the magazine from his wife's hands and then drew her tightly against him. What else could he do? The Traders were one very large family. Hardship had welded them into a seamless fraternity that stretched all the way to the eastern coast. The death of one was known by all. The murder of so many...? Drawn by the sounds of rifle fire and hovering birds, other riders began to arrive but stayed up on the ridge allowing the couple below their time. Their turn would come soon enough. For a people who lived so interwoven, the need for privacy was understood and respected. Inside the arching canvas of a wagon is a very small and intimate world.

More time passed before the pair turned to signal the rest to come down. There was a good deal to be done and they would need all their help. As she was the oldest woman among them, the men fell easily under her directions. The bodies could wait a bit more. First it was vital to ensure their own families were kept safe. The youngest rider was sent back to camp to alert and inform the group. The best tracker among them was sent on an outward spiralling route to ensure those in the gully were left undisturbed and did not become victims themselves. He was also told to determine the direction these butchers had come from and where they were headed. For the remainder, setting aside the grisly task of burying their friends and loved ones, it was critical to find out what had happened here and who was responsible.

Trying to ignore the smell from the rotting corpses, the flurry of feeding insects and their own need to retch, the Traders moved cautiously in and around the killing area. Traders could read the blood-soaked sand as easily as if the events had been transcribed by a dying hand. There were few spent cartridges, far too valuable an item to be left behind. This was not the case with other evidence, which was plentiful. Numerous impressions of those who had done the killing were left undisturbed along the gully floor and up on its ridges. This was not the work of a murderous gang bent on robbery. The evidence indicated the ambush was not serendipitous but had been well planned and well executed. No, it was no gang who might want to remain anonymous. There was arrogance here, an overt challenge to anyone who came upon this because these murderers had made no visible efforts to conceal or disguise any aspect of what they had done. On the ridge gully a dozen or so had lain in wait for the family to pass below. So brutal was the onslaught, the family was unlikely to have been able to return fire. Once it was over, the killers had climbed down to inspect their handiwork and also to ensure none were left alive. The bodies were then dragged into a line along the far wall of the gully. Blood marked the existence of thirteen yet only the remains of eleven were present. Two of the children were missing. The savagery of hungry teeth and beaks could not obliterate what had befallen those whose bodies remained. They had been butchered in the same efficient manner as their dead horses. There were no signs of the wagons. Riders had mounted them and continued down the gully, travelling south. At the mouth of the gully the Traders' wagons were joined by five others. The total number of mounted men numbered about twenty. All this was there to read. One unanswered question remained, why hadn't they been more circumspect? Surely they must have known, once the family had been found, there would be a host of Traders in pursuit. Was there something they had overlooked? Did these murderers want to be pursued and, if so, for what purpose? The sand could not answer those questions. One question the sands could reveal, however, was that the end of the nightmares they had all hoped for did not occur thirteen years ago. The Scavengers still lived.

Traumatised, the younger men rode in silence, their hoods pulled as far forward as the garments would allow in an attempt to block out this new world into which they had been suddenly thrust. They were Traders and as such were neither naive nor unaccustomed to violence or death. The Dry ensured this. Stories of the Before Times and the aftermath were fused into the very marrow of their bones. From the first sip of their mother's milk they learned of the importance of family and friendship. The

318

sight they had left behind would forever haunt them. The questions of how lives could be taken so brutally and then the victims carved up like cattle would remain unanswerable. The older members understood what these young people were feeling, so said nothing. What could be said that could resolve the turmoil that now existed within each of them? Not all of life's scars are carried upon your skin. So let their parents, wives, lovers attend to them. Let them be enfolded by arms, pressed against warm bodies. Let them be softly stroked by caring hands, reassured by gentle whispers of affection. Let time pass. These boys, these young men were but children when it was thought the last of the Scavengers had been run to ground and slaughtered to the man. And yet here the Scavengers were again, inviting, even daring, the Traders to come after them.

A momentary panic seized Nic when he saw in the distance that the campsite was deserted. The rifle sprang into his hands as automatically as a flinch from a raised fist. He was about to dismount to take cover when a lone figure perched upon the trunk of a fallen tree began to wave to him. His sense of relief attempted to counter the injected adrenalin but failed to halt a slight tremble in his hands and the clenching of his teeth. He stood up in the saddle and returned the wave. Can't be all that bad, he thought, or they wouldn't have left that kid behind. But it was. It was very bad. While the rest of the families had relocated the wagons to a more defensible position, one of the younger boys had been left with two fresh horses, water and food to wait until Nic returned from hunting. He listened to the younger boy as he flung his saddle and personal belongings on to one of provided horses. Other than the location and that approximately six weeks earlier a family of Traders had been ambushed, there wasn't much in the way of additional information. They didn't even know if the two missing children were still alive. What they did know was that the party was made up of approximately thirty mounted riders accompanied by several heavily loaded wagons. For the Traders there was little doubt who the perpetrators were; the killings had all the signature of Scavengers. The note to Nic in his mother's clear hand was as simple as it was direct.

'Dear Son
Head for Empty Cup and find Noah! It is imperative that he is given this letter.
If there are no signs of him having been there, do what you think is best.
Stay safe
Mom.

Nic never cease to be impressed by his mother. The wastelands might be big but there were few places where there was water. If they weren't already making their way back to the Farm, going to Empty Cup would indeed be his best chance in intercepting them. Telling the boy to tell his parents and brother that he loved them, he rode away.

In the thick underbrush Nic lay comfortably concealed; his rifle trained on the fire's dying embers. There was not a part of his body that did not ache. Having ridden for three days and nights with little sleep and less to eat, Nic had dismounted on the far edge of the spring. Traders sometimes left a message for others of their kind in the form of a coded language, rocks placed in a pattern or quipu, a bundle of woven horse hair cord with a series of knots along each thread. He'd found nothing. There was no denying his disappointment. Although he had known it was unrealistic, he'd harboured hope they'd be here. And if not, then signs that they had been.

That didn't mean that there weren't signs of previous occupations. There were plenty, all indicating that Empty Cup had hosted many visitors, but none were Traders. He was far too young to have participated in the last of the Scavenger conflicts so he had no experience to draw upon to tell him who these visitors were. Yet there was a lingering rancid odour that hung in the air reminiscent of rotting garbage. With the horses contented to just rest in the shade, he looked for evidence that would tell him who they were. Hearths, old fires and bits of food scraps were always a reliable source of information. Nic peeled back the layers of each hearth with a stick, closely examining its contents. Each held its own little secrets. In the failing light, satisfied he had gleaned as much as he could, he selected the one furthest from the spring for his own use.

The horses were in worse shape than he was. After freeing the poor creatures from their collective burdens, he brushed them down as they drank and ate. When he'd finished, the pair wandered off to languish in the shade provided by a small grove of trees. He had not eaten since yesterday evening and could feel his stomach rumbling in protest. Except for the two remaining disks of pan bread, nothing was left of the food prepared by his family. So, if he wanted something to eat, he'd have to cook it.

Later, in spite of it being a little crunchy, a result of his impatience in not letting it simmer long enough, Nic gobbled down his porridge as fast as he could shovel it in to fill that gaping hole in his stomach.

This was his first visit to the spring and, like every spring; its configuration was unique unto itself. Here the water bubbled up from the earth filling the spring's 'cup', a deep depression, from below before spilling over the 'lip' onto the surrounding smooth rock surface and disappearing into the encroaching vegetation. He preferred the lushness of The Maiden yet the 'cup's' simple symmetry struck a cord that The Maiden did not. Like every spring he'd ever seen, the Empty Cup and its immediate surroundings stood in sharp contrast to the world where its water did not reach.

New growth on the parts of plants where a horse might graze and the decomposition of some of the items strung about suggested no one had been here in over a month. It was possible that his mother was wrong and that Noah or Elle had taken a different route. Being so tired it was hard to stay focused, and he decided that tomorrow would be soon enough to worry about what to do next. The crackle of the fire merged with the sounds of horses which, having rested a bit, busily shuffled from one scraggily edible patch of fodder to another. Thinking of the horses, he wondered where to secure them for the night. If they had visitors he didn't want to go stumbling around in the dark trying to find a hobbled mount. The best solution was to tie the animals close to where he planned to sleep, but not too close. An episode of once being stepped on while asleep was fresh enough in his memory that he saw no benefit in it being repeated.

There was also the need to avoid in being 'surprised' while he slept. The remedy was to prepare a little subterfuge. Adding a few more small logs to the fire, arranging the bedding so it looked like someone was sleeping there and erasing any evidence of his whereabouts should do the trick. The sun was just setting when all that was deemed necessary was finished. Perfect timing, he thought as he crawled into his hiding nook with the every intention of sleeping so lightly as to be wakened by the smallest of disturbances. Such are the plans of both mice and men. The sun's last rays had not yet dissolved into darkness when the soft rhythmic sounds of sleep could be heard if one was but to listen.

The moment he felt the cool barrel of a rifle prod the exposed skin of his neck Nic came instantly awake. His mother's face and those of his family flooded into his mind as he awaited death.

"Wakey, wakey, time to rise and shine sleepyhead," came a familiar whispered voice near his ear.

He recognized Elle's mocking tone. "Bloody hell, not again!"

As he rolled over onto his back to be greeted by the vague outline of her face a millimetre from his, she continued, "Are you rested enough to give me a hand with Noah?"

Minutes later the clearing was cluttered with all the gear, the cart and the restlessly milling horses. The fire had been revived. Elle, with Nic in attendance, prepared the meal. The dog sat next to Noah, who, with his back against a pack, read aloud the contents of his daughter's letter. This was done with some difficulty, the fire being the only source of light. Coupled with the wish not to be in the path of the drifting smoke, the dog and Noah's bulk, there just wasn't that much room for the cook and her assistant to manoeuvre.

Finished reading, Noah tucked the letter inside the pocket of his shirt before calling his grandson away from his duties. As Elle continued preparation of the meal without her assistant, Nic shared what information he had, which wasn't much. When he was done they all talked, each filling in the blanks of their respective adventures over the last three weeks. Nic listened intently to Noah and Elle's encounter with the Scavengers and could not help but feel an increased admiration toward his cousin. He had grown up hearing stories about his grandfather in the wastelands. However, Elle's miraculous escapes from certain death, not once but twice, were somehow more relevant, more personal. Although there was every opportunity to do so, Elle again did not mention the terminal or the man she'd shot in the back.

The talk began to trail off as their attention was increasingly drawn to the aroma that seeped from under the cooking pot's lid. The dog sat right up against Elle, watching intently as its strange friend lifted the lid to add a few more herbs before giving the bubbling, brothy mass a few final stirs. Nic and Noah moved to a more comfortable distance from the fire and sat there with nearly the same rapt anticipation as the dog. As the cooking smells wafted over them, the boy, noting that the porridge was not resting at all well in his stomach, did not feel it necessary to inform the new arrivals he had already eaten. Food for this family, regardless of the bleakness of any tomorrow, was central to their wellbeing. A confirming sip followed by a sharp rap on the pot's edge with the spoon signalled the conclusion of Elle's culinary efforts. Dinner, late as it was, was ready. Two bowls thrust forward and a yelp from the dog signified the gallery was ready as well.

The boy spun the end of his mother's pan bread around the bowl's rim absorbing the last remnants of the rabbit stew. Still hungry, knowing there could have been seconds, his love of dogs had been severely tested. Seeing the animal at Elle's feet licking the pot clean was almost too hard to bear. Elle and Noah passed their similarly cleaned bowls and cutlery over to Nic signifying the end of the meal. He was on kitchen duties as Elle had cooked and Noah was temporarily immobilized. As Nic removed himself from the fire's ring of light, Noah called out, reminding him that, since he had had his sleep, he could take first watch.

Suppressing a giggle Elle helped her grandfather to his feet and together they walked and hobbled over to their bedrolls in the undergrowth.

Trying to lie down presented a series of problems for the big man. Using Elle for support, Noah began to lower himself down. The laws of physics however insured that at some point Elle, as a counter weight, would be overwhelmed by the bulk of her grandfather. The landing was abrupt for them both as Elle toppled over, spilling the pair onto the hard and unforgiving ground. Their previous giggles erupted into laughter as the two untangled themselves while trying not to cause Noah additional pain. That done, the old man's backside now found the rubble under his bedroll uncomfortable and it took considerable effort on his part to eject the many offending objects. Satisfied at last, Noah rolled on his back and stared up through the bushes at the night sky. All those stars... He let the thought trail off. He turned his head toward Elle and saw that she was doing the same.

"Does it go on forever Granddad?" asked Elle.

"Nothing goes on forever, but it sometimes feels that way."

"Yeah, I know what you mean."

They both yawned. It was very late and they desperately needed to sleep, the horses needed to rest and dawn would come soon enough. Even though he would have preferred to spend tomorrow in pursuit of the spring's last visitors, he could see that even Blue, all-conquering Blue, needed a day off. Nic came over to wish them a good night before taking up his post.

The sky was silver white. The stars swept by her as if caught by a powerful current. She was engulfed in a noise that neither rose nor fell but droned on and on as it was absorbed into her every pore. She couldn't breathe, her lungs only sucked in the silver-white sky and its stars. She was drowning. Far off, her name was being called, over and over again, louder each time until her head breached the clinging sky to take in a breath. Elle became conscious of the strong musky odour of her grandfather as he held her, caressing her hair.

"There, there, it's all right, you're safe now. It was but a dream, nothing but a dream."

Elle started to cry. It had seemed so real. Nic had heard Elle's scream and came running back to the camp. Seeing the look on the young boy's face as he knelt beside them, so full of concern, brought a smile of greeting to her own. She drew in another breath. The dream, the most powerful yet, clung to her still.

"Now that we are all awake, what was that all about?" asked her grandfather. Before she could answer, Noah told the hovering boy at his shoulder, "Go and make us all a cup of tea." Turning his attention back to Elle, he asked, "Now tell me what that ruckus was all about and speak loud enough so Nic won't feel the need to come back over to listen before the tea is ready."

The dog whined, uncertain as to the source of its strange friend's distress, circling around the pair trying to intervene.

The black and battered tea pot had been left buried in the coals so it would not take long to bring it to boil. The bush tea was as bitter as it was hot. In between sips Elle, for the first time, told of her dreams and how they were becoming stronger, more real. The two listened.

Nic, at first, seemed only mildly interested. Being a boy of barely fifteen, how could it have been otherwise? That changed when he realized his grandfather seemed riveted, stopping her again and again with probing questions, requesting more information and details of her dreams. Both children began to sense that for Noah these dreams were far more than Elle's imaginative nightmare. Nic knew his grandfather's life held many secrets, but it was Elle who wondered if Noah also dreamed of whispering silvery seas and misty skies filled with swirling stars. She wanted to say something to him but did not. The sun was up and the thinnest sliver of a moon could just be seen peeking above the horizon. Nic went back to finish his watch and Elle and Noah put down their empty cups and lay down to see if they could catch a bit more sleep.

It was late in the morning. There was the tiniest flicker of life in last night's fire in the form of a single, wafer thin ribbon of smoke from a very small ember. With care and dedication, it was soon coaxed into a full bodied flame by the judicious addition of a few small pieces of wood. Elle had taken the last watch but Nic soon reappeared complaining he was hungry and that he'd take over if she would cook up something for him to eat. The Dry, the Sorrow, the Scavengers, the very end of a whole civilization hadn't changed the sad but true fact: men and boys have pretty much remained unchanged. If there was a woman or girl around, they'd ask her to cook up something.

Though the pickings were rather dismal, the stomping of horses and humans had not kept thirsty animals from the spring. In the snares were two bush rats and one ground squirrel. Not enough for even one person, let alone three, but with a little grain boosted with some salted meat it would have to do.

Suddenly Elle heard her grandfather call her.

"In a minute," she called back, letting the pieces of fresh meat drop from her fingers into the camp oven before giving the concoction a quick stir. She started to clean up the mess from her preparation but saw that there was nothing left to clean up; the dog had seen to that. It was a bit unnerving for Elle as she watched the dog slurp in a rat's tail. Dusting off a few specks of flour, she went over to see what Noah wanted.

Without something to hold onto or lean against, Noah was having difficulty sitting up. Big men, even ones as fit as her grandfather, find suspending their upper body in such a position fatiguing to an aging back.

"Sit down girl; we need to talk." She did as instructed. "Elle, as you know, your grandfather is a sceptic bordering on cynic. I do not believe we are here for a purpose and I certainly do not believe in divine providence. So how am I supposed to deal with you?" Elle was not quite sure how to answer that. Noah produced the photo of the family and placed it on the ground between them. "I saw it sitting by your pack. Nicole said you had something I would want to see and I am guessing this is it. Where did you find it?"

Elle, feeling very uneasy at the tone of his voice, told him about her stay in the house on a hill. When she'd finished he asked, "Do you know who these people are?"

"No," said Elle, her discomfort increasing. "I don't."

Just as Nicole had done, his finger traced the girl's outline and he had the same kind of longing expression. "Do you still have the book?" She did, it never left her breast pocket. She removed it and placed it in his outstretched hand. Noah, after removing the medallion, laid them both next to the photo. "The ring and knife?" he said, extending his hand again. This was not a request. She said nothing. Taking the ring from around her neck and the knife from her waist, she handed them to her grandfather who then placed them in line with the other items.

"What do you think the odds are of us finding my father's ring and knife?"

Elle wasn't sure how to respond so again remained silent while trying to understand what lay behind his questions.

"Then, consider that you have also found a book written by my grandmother, your great-great-grandmother, long before either of us was born, from a world that no longer exists. That same book, along with a vest that shouldn't have been anywhere near the homestead and a cheap metal medallion you found and just happened to use as a means of keeping your place, stopped a bullet designed to punch through twelve millimetres of steel. That bullet should have killed you." He stopped to clear his throat and then asked. "Do you remember what was on the page where the bullet stopped?"

"Of course." She closed her eyes and, as if reading from the book, "Always speak to a man as if he were a child, to do otherwise will only confuse him."

"And on the opposing page?" requested her grandfather.

Again she closed her eyes and recited, "*A woman gives life; men take it.*" When she finished she opened her eyes and watched Noah place the book on the ground.

"Why did the bullet stop there? Why not one page more or less? Personally, I cannot think of a more apt description of a Scavenger's motivation, for it was a Scavenger that put that bullet there and the hole in your chest. So what are we dealing with here, Elle? Is it more than a series of blind chances, unrelated coincidences or something else? Again he traced the outline of the young girl with his finger tip. "When exactly does a set of random unconnected events stop being random and unconnected?"

He went quiet and then, in a voice she had never heard from him before, he said, "I do miss her."

Very hesitantly Elle asked, "Who is she?"

His voice was barely audible when he answered. "This is my wife when she was your age, the mother of Nora and Nicole – your grandmother. Six years after it was taken, she was the only one left of her family. The rest were taken by the Sorrow." He paused. "I was never there when she needed me most."

Elle could feel her grandfather was drifting away from her. His eyes seemed to be unfocused as if he was in dreamtime. He'd not been in the barn. If he had been, Elle would not have had to fight for her life.

He let out a long sigh and then said, "So what do we have here? The photo on its own would have been more than interesting. But it seems it is only one link in this highly improbably chain of coincidences. There is also a knife, a ring, a book, a bullet, a medallion, a vest, each having played a part in keeping you alive. I am at a loss of what to say or think about eight coincidences."

Elle did a quick count in her head. "Eight?" she asked. "There are only seven."

"Ah, but there is an eighth – your dreams of the mountains. Mountains you've never seen, crowned by silvery mist. A mist you, by all rights, should know nothing about."

Noah had never envisioned he'd be one day telling this story to his granddaughter. Taking in a deep breath, he continued. "I've been to the mountains, or to be more precise, to Sweetwater, a town three to four days ride west of here. From it we had an uninterrupted view of the mountains. Maybe we could have gone closer but all of us felt this was as close as we dared go."

Elle saw that he did not want to dredge up these memories. "Why was that?" she asked.

"I really don't know, fear perhaps. After all, none of us had ever seen anything like it before or since. It was just as you described; the peaks were hidden in a shroud of silver mist, and at night it was as though the mountains were covered in shimmering stars." This time the pause was much longer. And then he asked, "Elle what made you want to go to the mountains?"

Avoiding looking at her grandfather, Elle provided an answer that she hoped would not provoke further inquiry. "Mom said all the men had failed. I am not a man."

Noah would have laughed if it had not been for the seriousness he saw in her face. He knew she was not telling him the whole truth but instead of challenging her he pulled her close. "Honey, thousands of women have tried as well. There were women in that last great effort, not nearly as many as men perhaps, but they were there nevertheless, and they died or went mad just as the men did."

Elle pulled back to look straight into Noah's eyes. Keeping her voice low and without a trace of a tremor, she said, "Then why didn't you take me home?"

"Well, for one thing, with all that you've been through, I thought you had earned the right."

He was reluctantly about to add that there was possibly another reason, when they were interrupted by aggressive growling and barking from the dog mingled with an equally vigorous protest from Nic.

"I wasn't going to take it you stupid dog. I just wanted to see if it was done." The dog was not buying it. Standing between the boy and the pot, it continued to threaten him. "Elle!" Nic called out in frustration, "Will you come here and get your dog before I have to shoot it."

The relief on her grandfather's face did not go unnoticed as he released her so she could rescue Nic from the dog. She jumped up and ran over to separate the warring factions. She had not fully answered Noah regarding her reason for going to the mountains. Noah always had secrets which he kept to himself. Now she did as well, and perhaps because of that she was no longer completely comfortable in his company. In addition, there was something troubling him and that made her uneasy. She preferred to think that he was unflappable, rock hard, immortal and certain. Perhaps it had something to with photo or her dreams. Whatever it was, she was sure that it was more than just the possible return of the Scavengers.

The revelation to Elle that he had been close enough to the mountains to see them was just the smallest portion of a much bigger story. The story of his visit to Sweetwater had been intentionally left incomplete for he had no wish to tell her more. Elle would find out soon enough that people's morals, even those of good intentions, are often flexible. Good people can do bad things and find the means to justify them. There was no way, to his knowledge, that he could successfully explain to Elle how hunting the remnants of the Scavengers had become a pleasurable murderous sport.

Back then, the plan had been to follow the road until they'd reached Sweetwater. If the town was empty of Scavengers, they'd make camp, care for the horses, cook a hot meal and then spend the night. The following morning, taking a different route, they'd head back East.

Hardened by the Dry, the wastelands and years of conflict, they were not prepared for what awaited them as they crossed that boundary. Sickened by what they saw, what it meant, they rode without stopping or speaking until they reached the town's most western edge. There they stopped. This was as far west as any of them had ever been and in front of them, filling the horizon, were the fabled mountains. At first they had thought the peaks were covered in fog, not unlike what he'd seen in photos of mountains in the Before Times. However, one of the men with him, a friend, disagreed. "That's not mist. That's the mountain's Guardians." Tilting his head back toward town, he continued, "And if we don't want to take up permanent residence here, I think we should turn around and go." If he had meant to be funny, no one laughed. Whether his companion was correct or not didn't matter at the time. From their perspective, not one of them felt a desire to go further and test that theory. Spending only the time necessary to feed and water the horses, they soon returned the way they had come. They'd seen enough. Not even a Scavenger would be crazy enough to come here. This was not a place to linger or to satisfy a curiosity.

After all this time, the memory of that day stayed with him.

The day was declared a day of rest by Noah but it would have been a mistake to have taken it literally. Noah and Elle slept until they were called to lunch. Afterwards, Elle and Nic were given their orders for the afternoon. Everything was to be opened and spread out and cleaned. Everything, that is, but those four green boxes; they were set away from the camp under a tarp, hopefully out of harm's way. When the two had lifted the first of them out of the cart, Noah's descriptive narrative left them little doubt what would likely happen should they drop one. By way of illustration he crushed a small clod of dirt between thumb and forefinger, allowing the breeze to carry away the remaining dust.

The heat finally drove them to cover. They had worked non-stop for several hours in the hottest part of the day and now all they wanted do was lie in the shade and sleep. However, that pleasure would have to wait, for Noah had other plans. He'd been preparing an early dinner, a task made more difficult by being encumbered with a leg in a splint. In order to avoid tipping over into the cooking pot, his legs were splayed at right angles to one another, which put certain parts of his anatomy uncomfortably close to the fire. Handicapped as he was,

Noah had decades of experience with living rough and was determined not to let the matter of a broken leg prevent him from doing his share. Unfortunately the range of food possibilities had been reduced to beans and salted ham hock. Not to be daunted, in the camp oven there was a surprise of sorts waiting for them: fresh damper bread to pour the beans over. Telling the kids what he had waiting for them did not elicit the level of keenness he had anticipated. No cook handles indifference well, let alone insults or suggestions of what he could do with his beans. "That's all right," he replied. "I have a few more things for you both to look after. And the one who eats the most does the least." Nobody turned their nose up at his culinary offering with impunity.

The dog, with its head on the chest of Elle's prone figure, allowed its ears to perk up. Food in the offing was serious business to this animal but, if Elle, content to lie in the cooler shadows, did not rise instantly to her feet, nor would it. Loyalty always comes at a cost.

Despite their earlier disparaging remarks, Nic and Elle were ravenous and filled their bowls to near overflowing before retreating with Noah and the dog to the cooler shadows around the spring. What followed in the shadows was an experience every human is well acquainted with. Compared to the dog, whose aggression toward food was accompanied by near complete silence, humans make a substantial range of noises when eating. Along with conversation, there was slurping, burping and pleasurable grunts. Which, from the dog's perspective, was one more puzzle in the ever increasing series of unanswered mysteries surrounding its new pack. Further confusion for the animal occurred when Elle, bending over to help her grandfather to his feet, farted loudly. The two males roared with laughter while Elle tried in vain to shift the blame. This only extended the laugher to the extent that Elle let go of her grandfather who then proceeded to fall heavily on the ground. Instead of showing any sign of concern, all three fell into a period of helplessness, laughing until tears ran down their cheeks. The dog sulked off seeking its own solace. Once again the antics of these creatures were beyond its comprehension.

The rest of the afternoon had been profitable even if it had not been all that restful. This was the last leg of Elle's journey. In three days, four at the most, she would be at the mountains. Noah had seen to it that they had checked and rechecked everything. From his bedroll he had supervised the packing, making sure all would be ready for tomorrow's departure. He had made the two children pay special attention to their weapons. If either of them were to get themselves killed it would not be because of a faulty weapon or lack of preparation, he informed them.

Elle was working on her own for the moment while Nic and Noah were over by the spring, deep in conversation. Since they would be leaving Empty Cup just before dawn, her grandfather was ensuring Nic understood exactly what was expected of him. In addition to writing lengthy letters to both of his daughters, Noah was also going over what both he and

Elle had seen and done to date. Nic was to tell only that which he had been told. In so far as it was possible, he was not to leave anything out. He was to resist any impulse to embellish. He was to repeat as closely as his memory would allow, word for word, what he was being told. In Noah's words, "They must know what we know." In the wastelands, telling the truth was a matter of life and death.

Elle acknowledged that her Grandfather had a penchant for accuracy, but recently she found it was not always possible to separate what was true from what was false, what should be kept and what should be set aside, what should be said and what should be withheld. "What are the odds..." had been revolving around and around inside her head. What are the odds? Twice she should have died, her heart pierced by the hand of a Scavenger, but a book and the ring had intervened. She was still alive. The festering wound over her heart told her that much. Was this because she was supposed to die elsewhere? Was that true? And the dreams – what of them? True or false? Her head ached, far too much for a not yet fourteen-year-old to carry. A melancholy born from a sense of betrayal briefly engulfed her at the thought of her mother on the veranda waiting for Noah to bring her back home.

Absorbed within her own thoughts, Elle's hands busied themselves disassembling, cleaning and reassembling the Scavenger's sniper rifle. The weapon had to be all of fifty or more years old. It might have even been made in the Before Times. Despite its obvious age and the fact that much of the original blueing was faded or worn away, it was evident that its previous owners had lavished a good deal of time on its care and maintenance. A precision weapon, it possessed, in the same way a viper does, a lethal beauty in its simple symmetry. As she wiped the excess oil from around the bolt and trigger, she idly wondered how many different people had owned it, what had happened to them and how many lives it had taken. Its last owner had used it to kill her and had died for doing so. Not that she actually thought that she was dead but that was the only way she could explain this feeling she had. Looking at the rifle, she felt that as long as it remained in her possession, her death, if only temporarily, was somehow commuted. The sound of her name being called stopped any further introspection.

Despite the custom of not being allowed to enter a source with an open wound, especially one showing sign of infection, Elle, with Noah's consent, spent the next hour frolicking in the cool waters of the spring with Nic. The bruising was clearly visible as was the knife wound. It covered an area about the size of the palm of her hand and went from light reddish-green around its edges to a deep indigo near its centre where it turned bright red. Upon seeing the bruising and being impressed by its size and colour, Nic instinctively reached out to touch it, only to have Elle slap his hand away. This resulted in Nic pushing his cousin's head under the water. A fight of sorts ensued which, among other things, tested each other's aquatic battle skills. Nic was bigger, stronger and trained by the Traders in hand to hand combat, but Elle was fast, blindingly fast, and incredibly agile and she had been trained by Noah.

Every time Nic thought he had her, she'd slip out from his grasp, and slide away. She was conserving her strength, waiting for him to tire, before closing in for the 'kill'. The boy never stood a chance. Try as he might to corner Elle so that he could physically overpower her through pure brute force, she'd just laugh at his failed attempt as she darted away. After Nic finally conceded defeat, like two pups spying a sleeping cat, they turned their attention to the prone figure of their grandfather. They were just about to douse him with the water they had collected in their cupped hands when he suddenly rolled over sending a wall of water their way from a pot he had hidden by his side. They might be younger, but he was smarter. They had to content themselves with taunts and intermittent sprays of water in his direction, which delighted them and Noah immensely.

Moments like this triggered his memories of all those former times, as a child with parents, as a parent with his children. Now, with a broken leg, all he could do was watch the pair. When Elle was wrestling with Nic in the pool he saw an expression on her face that was rarely seen among the people of the Dry; the complete abandonment of care. He could also see that they made a good team, each offsetting the weakness of the other. While a young woman might have some degree of choice when picking a mate for life, young men did not. His wife had been raised by his family after being left an orphan. Elle and Nic were cousins by custom and necessity, not by blood.

Childhood, if you're privileged to have one, does not last long in the wastelands. If she had the time, it was possible Nic would not simply remain a friend. For even now their relationship was changing; it was already different from the one she had with her other cousins. They were family, but Nic was that and more. Though the thought that any time soon they all could be dead never strayed far from the mind, for now at least, she could enjoy the pleasure of being in his company. And with that somewhat morbid thought, Noah felt he'd not live to see Elle marry or have a family of her own. Death came far too often and in many forms in the Dry. Though each life might have its own unique path to follow, it shared the same ending as all the others. His father, mother, sister and brother, all murdered. All those he had travelled with in his youth were dead. His friend from all those years ago in Sweetwater, the one who gave the mist on the mountains a name, died a month later from a snake bite. His wife died giving birth to their child. Life had not been any easier for his daughters. Elle was Nora's only living child and Nathan was Nicole's. Nic, removed from the womb of his dying mother, was given to Nicole who had lost a child a few days earlier. A life for a life, if one is lucky.

None of the Traders knew who Nic's mother was or the whereabouts of her people. She was just another of those anonymous people left alone to die. Although by the time of Nic's birth such tragedies had become less frequent, it was not because of any change in the wastelands' cruel indifference. Rather the Dry had depopulated the nation's interior to such an extent that there just weren't enough humans left for such tragic events to occur with any regularity. Leaving out the occasional deadly scrimmages between the various groups settled along the shores of sea and lakes, this thinness of population did have its benefits for it permitted a kind of suspension of hostilities to descend on the remaining people of the Dry, a temporary hiatus.

All that would change now that the Scavengers had returned. The few settlements that had managed to survive throughout these waterless lands would again be threatened with extinction. Even the larger populations might find themselves under threat from a reinvigorated insurgence of Scavengers. At just the thought of the Scavengers, for such was his hatred, Noah could feel the bile rise in his throat and the muscles tense along his shoulders. He would sacrifice everything to once more ride against them and to rid the world of such vermin. It had long ago ceased to be a matter of survival for him to hunt them; it was an occupation. He would not be content until they were exterminated and even then there could be no release for him.

The discomfort Elle had been feeling had not left but rather had been confined to the deepest recesses of her mind for the time being. Not since The Maiden had she felt as rested, pleased and clean. She was tired but it was the kind of tiredness that allowed one to ease into sleep and such a sleep she was looking very much forward to. Except for her turn at watch, Elle had an entire moonless night reserved for it.

It was growing dark and although they had had Noah's early dinner, everyone was again hungry. It was Nic's turn to cook, a rather unknown factor; the evening meal had all the potential of being an occasion. The draw of water had once again been a lure for some of the wildlife living near and within the spring and the snares had yielded three rabbits and two very large rats. Their good fortune did not stop there. The dog, perhaps feeling a little piqued at being ignored by Elle, had wandered off while the two children played in the 'cup', only to return demonstrating its value to the rest of the pack. It had bagged a plump ground grouse.

Noah was almost beside himself with delight upon seeing the bird dangling from Mutt's mouth. It had been nearly a year since he'd sunk his teeth into one of these delicious delicacies. Of course, had he had the time, he would have hung it up for a couple of days to let it 'cure'. That was not going to happen. The bird, along with the rats and rabbit, was on tonight's menu. He would be doing the plucking and gutting of this beauty, far too valuable a treasure to risk to the hands of an inexperienced boy. And it certainly was not going into some innocuous stew either. This worthy bird was going to be rotisseried.

Not fully trusting her cousin's culinary skills, and under Noah's watchful gaze, Elle worked alongside Nic preparing their last real meal together. Tomorrow's breakfast would be tea and damper bread. Because the three had decided to consolidate the remaining provisions before redistributing them, tonight was to be a feast of sorts.

Leaning against the wheel of the wagon, their grandfather waxed lyrically on the merits of the ancient feast of the winter solstice. "Though none of us here has been caught in the smallest of a rain shower, let alone in the grip of a long cold snowbound winter, there was a time when such things prevailed. If a family judged badly or had a poor harvest they would face hunger, even starvation and death and not just for themselves. Oh no, for all their beasts and fowl as well. The winters had no mercy for the fickle, the careless or even the unlucky."

The kids loved this. Books were wonderful, though not as wonderful as a story being told by someone like Noah. Elle knew his skills. For Nic this was perhaps his first encounter, so she was keenly interested in watching the expression on her cousin's face as the story unfolded.

"On the shortest day, each family would walk among their family members. They would judge the health of each of their animals. They would gauge how much feed and provisions were left to last them till spring. They would even calculate what family member had become a burden." Noah, as he said the word 'burden', looked straight at the boy. "Especially one who is not attending to my bird properly." Nic missed it, but Elle caught the wink. As the tale continued Nic became captivated by Noah's story and his attention drifted away to the point that Elle found herself continually poking her cousin to bring him back to the tasks at hand. Finally it was easier to just let him sit and listen while she did the job on her own.

Listening to the story while she worked, Elle positioned the camp oven so that the fat from the fowl fell into the simmering stew below. She fed the fire, moved the coals around, rotated the bird skewered by a stick, removed a toasted unleavened bread from the stone slab to be replaced by dough for another. To make it a feast to remember, she used everything that could be spared. The seasonings, the salt, the dried vegetables, as well as some of the edible wild plants, freshly picked, were all used.

Mutt's tail made slow swishing arcs in the dry soil, as the dog, filled with anticipation, sat upright and alert beside Elle. Regardless of how its fellow pack members viewed the coming meal, it was certainly going to remember this feast.

All this took place as the man talked and the boy listened. Elle was beginning to understand what all women of the Dry know; the world might have changed but men and boys have not, nor the role of women. They were still the keepers of the hearth.

Elle, knowing by the shift in tone of his voice that the climax was fast approaching, braced herself.

"As the last bone was gnawed clean, as the last morsel of food was eaten, the leader of the clan, sensing his loyal followers were not yet fully satiated nor fortified for the hard winter months ahead and knowing there was still one among them that was expendable, thrust his knife into his heart." Noah, pronouncing the word 'heart' with a loud roar, simultaneously struck Nic in the chest. The boy let out a terrified screech as he toppled over backward onto the ground. The dog, startled at the apparent attack so near her mistress, lunged at Noah. She was halted in mid-flight by Elle's quick reflexes, grabbing it by the scruff of the neck. Noah, seeing the lunging dog from the corner of his eye, flung up both arms to protect his exposed face only to fall over sideways. A silence followed briefly before the air was ripped apart by their laughter.

The meal was over and it had met, even exceeded, expectations. Nic and Elle had agreed beforehand to gift their portion of the grouse to Noah. So attentive had he been to the proper preparation and subsequent roasting of the bird, to do otherwise would have bordered on cruelty.

The dog did not share the cousins' altruism and became, if it is possible for a dog to do so, miffed as it watched Noah devour its bird. Elle's offer of Noah's share of rat, rabbit and other tasty titbits from her bowl did eventually win the dog over, but it kept a wary eye on the old man for the rest of the meal just in case. Sensing he might have somehow crossed the line of propriety, by way of making amends, Noah had kept a few pieces and the 'parson's nose' aside to mollify the dog. In this he was successful, allowing the four to sit around the dying fire feeling content.

Elle pulled Nic's harmonica from her pocket to hand to it to her cousin. Nic shook his head as he pulled one from his own pocket, suggesting they perform a duet. She declined. "You play, we'll clean."

He nodded and began to blow. There was just enough light remaining to get water on the boil for tea and to clean up from the meal while being entertained by Nic. That boy could play. Elle once again swore that, no matter how long it took, she would learn to play like that before she died. Later the two went off to have one last dip in the spring.

They drew straws. Nic ended up 'winning' the first watch, then it was Noah and finally Elle. She had hours of uninterrupted sleep to look forward to. On her back she looked up at the night sky, watching the brief life of a meteorite as it streaked across the heaven, then she fell asleep.

The dream came. She stood on the embankment of what once had been the beach of a large lake. Far off on the other side she watched the silver sky, like thick mist anchored to the mountains, reaching upward, extending as far as she could see. It shimmered and undulated like an unrolled bolt of cloth caught in a breeze. Then, imperceptibly, the mist began to contract from the heavens. As it oozed down the mountainsides gathering speed, the silvery sheen darkened into an *impermeable* black. Soon it filled the old dry lake basin as it rushed toward her, striking with such force she was knocked down and submerged beneath its relentless waves. It flowed into her lungs, filling her with its whispers.

This time when she woke, although she had thought she had screamed, Nic remained asleep and the dog seem undisturbed. She wanted to lie back down and try to fall asleep again but it was out of the question. Not only was she filled with adrenalin, one look at the stars told her it was nearing time for her to relieve Noah anyway. She might as well get up.

Chapter Nineteen
A person's bias will always distort their judgement.

In the wasteland, sunrises do not linger modestly below the horizon. There are no fluffy pink clouds to herald their approach. There is no softness to them at all, nor gentleness. They come with a suddenness that jars the senses and the ensuing long shadows have no blurred edges. Lines between light and dark are always as crisp as a knife blade. The sun rose to blind the eye, as Elle bore witness. She had the last watch and so had been sitting there listening to Nic and her grandfather fumbling around in the dark. Soon her grandfather would call her to a hastily prepared breakfast designed to fill an empty stomach and nourish a hungry body, but it would be a spiritless concoction of leftover bread and porridge. Till then, with the dog's head in her lap, she would continue sitting cocooned within the shadowed hollow of a mound of rocks. There was an indefinable comfort in its companionship as the dog seldom left Elle's side. Minutes later Nic called that breakfast was ready.

Time to say farewell. Goodbyes were not casual among the Traders or Elle's family. The uncertainties of the Dry and wastelands would not permit it. Elle solemnly handed the bloodstained Trader's cloak to Nic before pushing back his cowl and leaning forward to press her nose against his, drawing in his breath as he did with hers. Noah watched them from the wagon and then pulled out his massive timepiece. In a single cycle of the moon his granddaughter's life had irrevocably changed. He had been witness to this change as she rode from the mall and he saw it now. This was not a child saying goodbye, but not yet a woman. Where does the child go when they start to become an adult? He wondered, recalling such moments from his past.

"You are worth a life, Elle," said Nic.

"As are you," replied Elle, "and don't you dare damage that stove." The boy smiled at her but it left Elle puzzled. When she said they'd meet again soon, Nic, seemingly on the verge of tears, only nodded, as he gently squeezed her hand in farewell. He turned to mount his horse.

Nic had done what had been asked of him, now it was equally important he returned. His family would need to be informed of what he had learned and that one of the missing children had been most likely found. They, in turn, would tell all the others. This would be done by the means of one of the Traders' jealously guarded secrets, their possession of shortwave radios from the Before Times. Before Nic knew of the killings, every Trader family within range that could be contacted was. By the time he had arrived at Empty Cup, the news of the murders had reached even those Traders along the coasts and the great lakes. Similarly, within days of his return, every Trader would know what he had learned here. Already more than a hundred wagons were converging on the Great Central Highway. Many more would soon follow. This time the Traders meant to finish what had been thought to be finished thirteen years ago. As to the cloak, it would be returned to the family. Each cloak was handmade and would have a personal signature woven into the material telling who made it and for whom. The dog let out a soft whine as Nic rode off leading all but four of the horses. Elle's reassuring hand stroked the animal's head.

"I know Mutt, I'll miss him as well." Although Noah had said she would go to the mountains, with Nic's arrival and the news of the murders, things had changed. Elle found herself trying to come to terms with her grandfather's decisions. Why had he sent Nic home and not her? Knowing what was at stake, she would have gone without protest. He was older and stronger. He was also, if the obvious needed to be stated, a male and therefore, in the Traders' tradition, more expendable than a female, especially a young female. She waited with the dog for a few more minutes before mounting Belle.

Nic had a long ride ahead of him. Noah, concerned for his grandson's safe return, had instructed him to head due east to reduce the chance of running into Scavengers. He was to stay on that course for the first day before turning toward the Trader's designated rendezvous. His grandfather had given him all that could be spared in the way of horses, weapons and provisions, including one of the green boxes. The Traders would be interested in the reasons behind this particular acquisition of the Scavengers.

Mounted with the Scavenger's rifle in the crook of her arm and dressed in her Trader's cloak, Elle joined Noah to begin their pursuit of those who had camped at Empty Cup. The re-emergence of the Scavengers altered far more than Elle's private quest to reach the mountains. It was now a matter of survival for all of them.

Noah was adamant that the Scavengers were preparing something truly major and were confident enough in their enterprise to provoke a confrontation with the Traders, the very same people who fourteen years earlier had attempted to annihilate them. Whatever it was they were planning, it required the efforts of a large body of men using a sizeable number of wagons over many months to achieve the single purpose of collecting every drop of fuel and fuel-cell they could find within an area of a hundred kilometres or more. In the form of those long green boxes, there was evidence they had also been acquiring a lethal arsenal from the Before Times. And Noah knew of a place where such weapons could be found in vast quantities. What he needed was to confirm his suspicion and, in doing so, live long enough to communicate that information to the Traders. As he explained to Nic, he did not think the group that camped at Empty Cup were the same ones that ambushed the Traders. They had been there about the same time as the killings took place. Taking into account Elle's information from the rest stop, he believed there were at least three separate parties, maybe more. And if he was guessing correctly, they were all returning to the town of Sweetwater.

The wagon lurched forward throwing Noah back against the seat as it fell in behind Belle.

"Bloody hell, easy there," Noah chided the horse as he adjusted himself into a more comfortable position on the hard wooden plank. "Have you forgotten you've got a wounded man up here?" He was not looking forward to another week perched in a wagon like a bird on a wire and it wasn't solely because of a broken leg. Noah was impatient. The pain was still annoying but the swelling had gone down enough that he had had the kids rebind the support. As long as he put no weight on it, he could hobble around with a crutch he'd fashioned from a tree branch. While the grandkids busied themselves readying the wagon they had watched their grandfather, not without some difficulty, manage to mount and dismount Blue. This was only made possible because Blue had been trained to kneel on command. Seeing him swing his bad leg over the saddle, Elle could not resist commenting to Nic that it was a wonder Blue was able to get back up with all that weight. Noah knew that it was time consuming and not without risk, but it did ensure that if the need arose he would not be confined to the wagon. Poor Blue, fully saddled, would have to be satisfied with being tied to the back of the wagon along with the other horse.

The terrain northeast of Empty Cup was the start of a far more broken landscape than Elle had travelled through before. The area in the Before Times had been home to several rivers. Fed from the runoff of the once immense snow fields that entombed the mountain tops, they bore through the lower foothills in their youth, gouging out deep ravines before maturing into broad, meandering rivers of a mellower disposition. However, even then there had not been much of a forest, save for a few scattered pines, and little in the way of grasslands. Rain had never been a frequent visitor, yet the hot dry weather, broad vistas, soaring pinnacles and plunging gorges had been a popular destination for the nation's older and more affluent population. The region's sparseness and lack of a dense habitation had allowed it to escape the more destructive fires.

Elle stood up in the stirrups to scan this dry, empty, fractured land. She was getting hungry and wanted dearly to get out of the sun for a few hours. From what she could see, that was not a likely option. Nothing in any direction looked remotely like offering them a respite from either the heat or sun. There was a hill not far off that would be a good place to check if they were on their own. She took a drink of water and then removed her hat to wipe her face with a moistened cloth. The Trader's cloak had its advantages but she'd found the cowl restricted her peripheral view, so it rested in folds on her shoulders, having been replaced by her new hat.

Though the trail was over a month old and frequently obliterated by the vagaries of wind and time, there had been no storms, so the tracks left by the heavy freight wagons made following the Empty Cup Scavengers easy. At least they got to sleep at night as the moon, thin as a razor's edge, set less than an hour after the sun. There was no desire to ride over this rough country in darkness. It was hard enough in the daylight. They stayed with the Scavengers' trail until it intersected a feeder road that led off toward the highway, the same highway they had been on before turning off to Empty Cup.

Noah suspected that the Scavengers would stay on the sealed roads, if possible, as the wagons would fare better on hard and unobstructed surfaces. His idea was not to follow directly behind them. Instead they'd ride well off any beaten path, avoiding roads, skirting around built-up areas and any other place that had seen earlier habitation. This would help enable the pair to avoid detection if the Scavengers did stay on the paved roads or if there were stragglers or an unknown party coming along one of the other roads.

As a further precaution, they kept half a kilometre between them. In the event of stumbling on the Scavengers or an ambush, by being separated as they were, one of them might have a chance. He did not elaborate on the likely results for the lead person if they had to deal with as many as twenty fully armed Scavengers. His advice, while grinning at her concern, was, "Just don't go down easy."

She didn't see the humour. Twisting in the saddle to look back at the dark smudge in the distance that was Noah, the dog and the wagon, she thought, I won't have much of a chance with a hole punched through my skull. And I don't think he'll have much of a chance either.

Elle urged her horse forward and rode up to just below the crest of the hill and dismounted. Keeping low she crept up to peer over the hill at a whole lot of nothing. The main highway she judged would have to be about five kilometres north of her. She rolled over onto her back, deciding to wait for Noah, at least then there would be a bit of shade under the wagon's canvas top while they ate. You have to question the sanity of anyone who would choose to live in a place like this in the Before Times, she thought. I would have lived by the sea next to a river and with two large swimming pools, one for the outside and one for the inside.

The old Before Time map was open on Noah's lap but it was difficult to keep it flat as little gusts of wind wanted to fold it over. "We are here," pointing at a spot on the map with his finger. "This is the road they took and it will link up with Great Central Highway here and, if I am right, this is where they all are heading." His finger moved over the map to point at a dot with the name Sweetwater Springs next to it. "Brilliant." Noah had to admit there were sound logical and logistical reasons for choosing Sweetwater. There was water. A spring, for which the town was named, was located alongside the Great Central Highway in the park at the town's centre. A major highway and several minor roads fed into the town before continuing on through the mountains. It was also isolated. Since the coming of the Dry, few ventured this far west and of those that did most never returned to talk about what they'd seen. Despite his one and only visit, Noah, as well as the

Traders, made a point of avoiding this area lest they too join the other unfortunate travellers. So the questions were how the Scavengers had survived when others had not, and how long had they been here? Of course, the bigger question, from their perspective, was what would the pair of them do once they got there and found the town full of Scavengers? For that question, Noah was still working on the answer.

The land around them was as featureless as a piece of dirt could get. Not a dead tree or overhanging rock anywhere to be seen. In such a landscape, there was no place to hide. So, on the theory they wouldn't be spotted by anyone venturing out from Sweetwater, they'd chosen to stop just below the crest of a hill. The four horses huddled under the awning that Elle had extended from the side of the wagon. It didn't provide much cover from the blistering sun overhead, but it was better than nothing. The two, listening to the sound of the horses slurping the last of the water from the buckets, ate their meal in silence. The sun seemed particularly ferocious, but that was more of an illusion than fact. Sweat beaded on their foreheads before rolling down their cheeks or running off the tip of their noses. Their garments were drenched with sweat and the vests that the two wore beneath their cloaks only added to their discomfort. The coming of the Dry had brought equilibrium to the previous complexity of weather. Though the tilt of the planet did afford a degree of seasonal relief for those in the higher latitudes, each day's weather, broken occasionally by a sand storm, remained interminably similar. The worst of the storms could flay the flesh from man or beast unlucky enough to be caught in the open and unprotected.

Elle felt the tug of drowsiness. They were two days out from Empty Cup and in ever-present danger of encountering a Scavenger. Neither had gotten their quota of sleep since, even at night, one of them had to remain alert. Succumbing to the pleasure of sleep could extend to a permanent state.

Noah nudged Elle as she nodded off once more. "You'll be more comfortable lying down. I'll take first watch and wake you in an hour or so." Elle did not feel the need to protest at such a generous offer and allowed herself the luxury of sliding down onto the top of the green boxes.

A scream startled the horses and the dog and only the strong enveloping arms of her grandfather had been able to stop the child from flinging herself out of the wagon in an attempt to flee the terror that now gripped her. She clawed at the restraints, struggling to free herself. *The dead were so many. The shrivelled faces with their empty eyes sockets staring sightlessly at the sun, lips pulled into humourless grins. All around her they lay, the countless minions stretching in all directions.*

"Shhh, it's all right honey, shhh, shhh." Several minutes passed before Elle became aware of being held and that it was Noah's deep voice issuing the sounds of reassurance.

A few more minutes passed before Noah felt it was safe to let her go. "Let's risk getting killed, I'll build us a fire and make us a cup of coffee. Nothing can be that bad, love, that a good cup of coffee can't help."

Noah knew as soon as the word 'killed' came out of his mouth it had been a mistake, but Elle had regained enough control to allow it to pass. "Sorry love," was all he could find to say as he crawled out of the wagon to prepare a small fire. The fact was Noah had not had a 'good' cup of coffee in forty years. Coffee was one more of the many items no longer available. Fortunately the Traders had found a substitute of sorts but even it was used rather sparingly, and only on auspicious occasions, due to its scarcity.

Elle clung to the hot cup as if she was frozen with cold. Her eyes remained unfocused, her thoughts a world away. Noah sipped his drink and waited.

Without looking up or changing expression Elle said, "You've killed a lot of people." This was not a question so he did not answer. He again sipped from his cup waiting to see if more was to follow and where it might lead. "There are thousands of bodies not far from here." This too was not a question. Noah knew this to be true but again said nothing. He feared he was about to be forced to go into a room he had hoped to never visit again. Elle look up at her grandfather with those eyes of hers. "What happened?" This was not a request.

The tone left Noah visibly shaken and he almost averted his eyes from her stare. "They all died. An entire army."

Few living knew the details of Noah's darker side. Those that did were his companions, adults, fellow conspirators, seasoned and hard, accustomed to the savagery they saw and what they had done. This was a child. "Some say over a million men and women lay out there."

"When?" she asked.

"When I was about five, fifty-five plus years ago now, I stood with my mother as we watched them pass our bus heading westward. By the time I rode out this far, they had been dead well over twenty years."

"How?" She could have been asking him what it was he had had for lunch such was the lack of emotion showing on Elle's face and in her voice.

"That I don't know. Whatever it was, it appeared to be able to kill instantaneously and without leaving a mark. Most died where they stood, although there were some who seemed to have had time to turn in an attempt to flee."

"Did you enjoy killing the men you hunted?"

He could not answer this question even if he wanted too. How could he? There are deeds even people of good heart do to survive and protect those they love. They do things that are cruel, malicious and unforgivable in a gentler time. And when it is done, these same good hearted people strive to bury, to lock away and forget what they had done. Noah drained the cup and was about to refuse any further questions when Elle spilled the dregs from her cup onto the fire and stood up. With the side sweep of her boot she covered its smouldering embers, then extending her hand she helped him stand.

"I know why you didn't take me home."

Not another word of explanation came from Elle as she helped him back up onto the seat, harnessed the fresh horse to the wagon, folded the awning and cleared the camp site. Mounted, she just nodded to Noah and rode off, expecting him to follow.

That evening they camped in a shallow depression that was deep enough to afford them a degree of anonymity and protection in the otherwise naked landscape. Elle had not spoken to him beyond the occasional grunt. When he settled next to her to take his turn at watch he tried once more to talk to her but Elle would have none of it. Every attempt was politely but firmly rebuffed.

Later, in the darkness, Noah heard small whimpers from Elle that mingled with those of the dog as they both struggled with their respective dreams. What he wanted to do was to go over, comfort her and banish the nightmares as he had done when she was little. Fearing that that time had passed, he sat in the dark and did nothing, allowing himself to be lulled into a kind of mental numbness. Not since the death of his wife had Noah felt so inadequate and so full of guilt.

With the vague detachment that comes from too little sleep, he watched a thin, pale streak of light cross the sky near the horizon, then another, then another. The streaks of light shattered, becoming stars that haloed the setting moon, whose pale grey light transformed the landscape into a stage where the stars danced and a breeze sang in harmony. Noah came fully alert. His dream state vanished. This was definitely wrong. Stars don't dance around the moon and the wind does not sing to it.

Elle's breathing changed; she was awake and, with the dog, was soon moving stealthily toward her grandfather. Instinctively, sliding into a shadow next to him, she became small and still. They were not alone. Off to their right and closing was something moving in their direction. He looked over the perimeter of the depression into the night yet detected nothing but the moon, the stars that ringed it and their song. The rifle leaped to his shoulder of its own volition and fired into the moon's heart. The night exploded into a billion points of light, like a scattering of fireflies. Then it was gone leaving the moon silhouetted against a mantle of fixed stars.

Her rifle at the ready, Elle stood by her grandfather as they both stared at the moon until it slid out of sight over the brow of a hill. The dog growled, its hackles raised. It too had witnessed the dazzling light display.

"Now that was impressive," said Elle as she stood on her tiptoes to better survey the terrain in front of them. "They looked a lot more inviting out there than they usually do in my dreams."

Noah was sure his mouth dropped open as he tried to come to terms with what had just taken place, his granddaughter's apparent casualness, the word 'they' and that she was speaking to him again.

"Come on old man, we have to get going. With you blasting away like that, any Scavengers here about will surely have heard it." She was right of course. Anyone within several kilometres would have heard that shot and come to investigate. It would be best to put as much distance as they could between themselves and this place.

After the incident with the 'fireflies' and the subsequent rifle shot, they broke camp in an orderly but hurried fashion. Elle took the lead, turning due north. When you are surrounded by friends and family, when you are busy doing the thousand and one things that need to be done, the world is full of noise. The twittering of a bird, the rustle of clothing against skin, the muted sounds of hoofs treading on sand are lost amongst this wider din. This is not true when one prefers silence; the footfalls of their horses thundered and reverberated endlessly off every surface. The wagon, to Noah's disgruntlement, seemed more raucous than usual as it banged, clanked and clunked its way in the darkness. He might as well be letting off those flares back in the wagon, he thought. Their only hope was that any Scavengers about were deaf, mute and barely ambulatory. Otherwise, with all the noise they seemed to be making, they didn't have a chance. Once again Noah found himself cursing the circumstances leading to his confinement to the wagon. "You're a bloody idiot."

In a few hours, even at the ponderous, plodding pace of the wagon along this rock strewn, high desert floor, they'd covered enough distance to safely seek a site to spend the rest of the night. Noah was certain they must have crossed or were very near the boundary of the killing fields, but they'd have to stumble over a bunch of bodies or wait until sunrise to know for sure. And that was still several hours away. Their current trek meant they were heading slightly away from the mountains and were therefore, perhaps, a day's ride from Sweetwater. The further away they were from there the less likely they were to stumble upon a nest of Scavengers. What they wanted was to find some kind of shelter that would hide them from both the sun and uninvited attention, made all the more difficult considering they had four horses and a cart in the middle of a rather flat featureless desert landscape. Then Elle came upon the wall. A solid stone wall that went off in both directions as far as her limited vision in the dark could see. Not only that, there seemed to be a kind of pebbled apron along its base some two metres wide. She waited for Noah to catch up.

She could hear her grandfather chuckle as he examined the wall. He then hobbled over to her atop of Belle to whisper, "I am not sure, Elle, but I think it could be a gated community. There are dozens of them dotted throughout this area."

"What's a gated community and why the wall?" she whispered back.

"Well, I know it sounds odd, but there were those who felt safer behind walls like these, even when in the middle of nowhere. If it is one, all we've got to do is follow the wall and we'll come to a gate and the road that leads into it."

"What's inside?" asked Elle, trying very hard to understand why anyone in the Before Times would want to live behind a wall.

"Could be a few houses or a whole village; won't know until we get inside. Either way, if the Scavengers aren't there, we'll have our place to stay for the rest of the night and tomorrow."

If the distance they travelled along the wall to reach a gate was any indication of its size, it was a village, a very large village. Once at the gate another problem arose – how to get in. The road leading into the community and the gate itself were jammed with an assortment of vehicles. It was impossible to tell how many there were in the light provided by the stars, certainly more than a few dozen.

Leaving Noah to try to thread his way through the maze of cars and trucks, Elle rode away from the gate to find how far back these vehicles went. She returned in time to hear the closing description of the apparent impasse emitted in her grandfather's deep reservoir of particularly colourful language.

Trying without total success to get his voice down, he explained to an amused granddaughter as she came alongside the wagon. "I can't find a way through. There's not enough bloody space for a horse to pass through let alone a wagon. What in the hell were they thinking?" As soon as those words left his mouth Noah knew why these vehicles were there and there was no need to look inside them either. He knew what it was they'd likely find. In a more solemn tone he said, "Elle, I think we had better find another way in. Continue around the wall and I'll follow as soon as I can get myself untangled." It was too dark for him to see her depart but he could hear the horse's footfalls fade into the distance. "This is not going to be good," muttered Noah to himself as he worked the horse around enough for the wagon to clear the metal carnage. "She's not going to want to stay here."

Quietly muttering to himself he said, "This is what it's like being blind. What I really need is to light a lamp, but that is out of the question." Any light out here would be one sure way to alert people he would prefer to keep ignorant of their presence.

Finding that the second gate was blocked as well, the two sat in the wagon going over their options. Noah told her of his suspicions about what they might find and suggested they should perhaps move well away from the compound.

Elle thanked him for his concern but declined, pointing out the obvious. They were tired, as were the horses. It was hard work stumbling around in the dark unable to see where you were going. Better to stay put until dawn than attempt to find another place. "Let the dead mind the dead, I'm tired." she told him.

That decided, the horse that was hitched to the wagon was released from its harness and given food and water. Should the unlikely occur and unwanted guests arrive unexpectedly, Belle remained saddled and bridled as did Blue. The idea of Noah with his broken leg trying to mount Blue in the dark passed without comment.

Other than leaving him stranded in the wagon or on foot, it was the better option under the circumstance.

With Blue tied alongside, Noah opted to sleep in the wagon along with a carefully selected array of weapons ranged around him. Elle took up a defensive position in what would prove to be a ditch a short distance from the wall. Settled, the pair waited for dawn and all that it might bring.

The squeak from the wagon's leaf springs followed by the softest of grunts woke Elle from another restless, dream-filled sleep. Huddled up against the side of the ditch, the dog cupped in the hollow formed by her foetal position, Elle listened to her grandfather trying unsuccessfully to silently extricate himself from the wagon. It had not been a good night. How can a thirteen-year-old be this stiff? she thought to herself. And why didn't I learn from my lesson at Red Rim? Elle rolled onto her back before opening her eyes, fixing her vision firmly skyward. The dog stayed as close as it could to her side. Both knew what lay with them in the ditch and Elle had no wish as yet to acknowledge their presence. The dog's whimpers suggested she was not alone in this.

The eastern sky washed in a pale grey blue touched the cusp of dawn. "Same old, same old," observed Elle to no one in particular, lying there watching the bluing of the sky overhead. A series of muffled clicks informed her that Noah was going through his routine of securing his weapons.

Try as he might, getting out of the wagon without making noise was out of the question. The obstinate leg banged into every obstacle it could find. He had wanted to get over to Elle before she woke but that was proving unlikely. Scooting on his bottom with his legs jutting out in front, Noah worked his way to the rear of the wagon and then out. It was as he had thought. On the one good leg he swivelled around to retrieve the rifle and shotgun, tucking the pistol into his belt. He checked to ensure their chambers were clear before putting back the shotgun and shouldering the rifle, an old habit that had served him well. The last thing he wanted was to end up shooting himself in the other leg. He again turned and looked around him. The wall, blocking the sunrise, cast a dark shadow across the wagon and up to the leading edge of the ditch and within the shadow lay the fruit of a nation. No wonder he had been unable to find a way in last night. The gate was wedged closed by the concertinaed remains of dozens of civilian and military vehicles that stretched for a hundred metres down the road. Nothing but pure, undiluted fear could have driven these people down a road to their death to what was effectively a dead end. Fifty-five years ago this had been a place of carnage as one vehicle, at speed, ploughed into another and in turn was ploughed into. Those who had not died upon impact or been severely injured must have got out to continue their flight only to be cut down along with hundreds of others all along the wall and in the ditch. There was no doubt in Noah's mind that this scene would be replicated at the other gate. He limped over to the back of a large military truck that had avoided the pile up only to slam into and demolish a sizeable portion of the wall. All that remained of its former occupants were bones, skulls and the tattered vestiges of uniforms lying in a heap in the cab. They would have never stood a chance at the speed the truck must have been going. Military vehicles did not have seat belts or airbags, deemed too dangerous in combat. The irony was not lost on him.

Noah was about to open the cab door for a better look inside when a voice called out. "Take a look at the petrol tank." Looking down at the tank, he immediately understood what she meant – the familiar sight of evaporated fuel droplets in the dirt below a punched hole in the truck's fuel tank.

Coming to stand by her grandfather, Elle continued, "Bet you won't find any weapons either and the fuel-cells will be gone as well."

Startled by her matter-of-fact tone, Noah turned to stare at her. "And why do you say that?"

"Stands to reason, if they're going to go through the trouble of getting every trace of fuel they can find, like before they will take the fuel-cells and weapons."

Noah once again felt that he was standing with his mouth open in what could only be called amazement. Roughening her hair with his hand he said, "You're beginning to scare me kid."

Elle was not amused and ran her fingers in an attempt to smooth out her hair. "I found a way in."

Chapter Twenty

Fear drives reason from even the best of us.

It was a village. If the remains of the sign was any indication of its contents, somewhere in the enclosure were an 18 hole golf course, three restaurants and several cafés , a medical clinic, cinemas, a fashionable shopping centre, a social centre, a gym and two swimming pools, to name a few of its amenities. They'd found their way in through the east gate. There were far fewer vehicles on the road at this end of the village and what there were all pointed east. Like the others, they had been incapacitated in one way or another, like ramming into a tree or another car or into a house. The fear must have been palpable, thought Noah, because many of the vehicles, like the ones at the west gate, contained the dead.

Elle moved off the road toward one of the houses. Nothing in her previous experience had prepared her for the sight of the neat rows of pale sandstone houses with red tiled roofs that were strung like coloured beads along wide, gently curved streets. The trees were dead, the grass lawns and lush gardens were long gone, but with a little imagination it wasn't too hard to see what it must have looked like in the Before Times. Considering the years of neglect the houses were largely undamaged, or at least the eastern portion was. Leaving Belle, Elle and the dog inspected one house after another while Noah kept watch from the wagon. Around the tenth house her expression migrated from a keen interest to one of mild disappointment, akin to finding that the tooth fairy is your mom.

Catching up to the wagon, Elle looked at her grandfather pensively.

"Well, did you find anything interesting?" he asked.

She told him, aside from seeing a lot of animal signs, both big and little, and not counting the skeletal remains at the bottom of a birdcage, there were no bodies in any of the houses or even signs that there had been. The remark was delivered so flatly Noah turned to look squarely at Elle to see if she was jesting. He drew a blank.

"Anything else?"

She went on to explain in that same flat tone that she thought the houses had been initially ransacked long ago by people taking only stuff they could easily carry. "I am thinking food since the pantries are pretty much bare. There were, however, definite signs that someone had recently done a more thorough job." She paused as if considering something more pressing, forcing Noah to say with a degree of impatience, "And?"

Her reply was delivered in a tone bordering on indifference. "Your friends have been here and not just for petrol." There was a heavy emphasis on 'your'. He let it pass. She went on explain that there were numerous 'clean' areas surrounded by thick layers of dust. It appeared someone, years after the first search, had been more methodical in what they took.

They continued heading toward the '19th Hole House and Restaurant', a large building fronting what could have only been a golf course at one time. Ignoring the occasional metal pole sticking out of the ground, the golf course was now indistinguishable from the surrounding desert.

"You know, they're all the same," said Elle.

"What are?" asked Noah.

"They're all the same," she repeated. "Every house is the same, even the stuff inside. It's all the same. Why would anyone want to live in a house that looks the same as everyone else's? How would they even know which one was theirs?"

Once again Noah felt the need to check his granddaughter's expression in an attempt to glean a better understanding of what was going on in that head of hers. Her face seemed deeply concerned. It was a trivial thing to him and yet there was she was brooding over the fact that a bunch of old people from out east wanted to come to the middle of the desert to live behind a wall in identical boxes filled with bric-a-brac. The thought of them huddled out here, protected by their wealth, brought out a petty vindictiveness in him. He could be bigoted in certain respects concerning wealth and privilege; a gift from his itinerant parents perhaps. As far as he was concerned, they'd got what they deserved.

"I have no idea why anyone would want to live like this," replied Noah. How could he, wandering as he did, the first twenty years in a bus and, after that, quite a few more years in a horse-drawn wagon. And yet, he and they did share the same fate. Death had smashed its way into both of their worlds taking from them all they thought was secure and safe.

Affixed to the fence next to the entrance that led to the golf club, a large, faded but still legible billboard showed the pictorial layout of the entire village. If their own imaginations failed to capture its former glory, the billboard left them impressed by the village's size and collection of amenities. From the mundane to the extravagant, every possible desire and whim of the inhabitants seemed to have been accommodated. The outside of the 'Club' shared the same general architectural motif as the houses, only it was bigger, grander, more lavish. Before the coming of the Dry it must have displayed a truly tacky opulence, thought Noah as he stood bordered by the large twin doors of the foyer's entrance.

"Built with the old and enfeebled in mind," he observed as he took hold of Elle's hand. "No steps, straight from the street, ramp up the curve and into the building."

She was silent.

"Having lots of money is no guarantee of having good taste," he muttered to no one in particular as he, accompanied by his crutch's tapping echoes, limped through the double doors and into the Club's foyer. Stopping at the fountain that dominated the room's centre, he waited for Elle who followed leading the horse and wagon.

The clippity-clop of horse's hooves and the expletive "Bloody hell!" announced Elle's return to his side. Her mouth fell agape. There was a bejewelled chandelier overhead and an enormous picture window across the foyer overlooking what must have been a pond with its obligatory marble nymphs and the beleaguered golf course beyond. In all her fossicking with her grandfather, she had never seen anything even approaching this.

"But why isn't it all smashed up?" was the first question both asked themselves.

Noah looked over at his granddaughter again, forgetting she did not share his memories. To her, this was a museum of a long dead and nearly forgotten race of human kind. "I suspect, after the army's demise, no one was left and those like me stayed away because they did not want to share their fate."

"And the Scavengers?" she asked in a tone he found vaguely unsettling as it implied that he was no longer privy to her thoughts.

"I don't know, other than that I am sure they've been here." He was just about to say something more when, without a word, she left him standing there to retrieve the other horses.

Once the packs and saddles had been removed and the unvarying routine of caring for the horses had been completed, the pair left the horses to their water and meal. Both were near the end of their reserves. They were tired from lack of sleep, and hungry, but there were a couple more hours before the customary mid-day break. As strange as it might seem, an adherence to routine made living in this indifferent wasteland possible. It gave the semblance of order where there often was none.

With weapons casually slung on their shoulders and sleep and lunch deferred, they decided to explore the rest of the 'Club'. Sun and heat cause damage, as those who lived in the Dry can testify, but in the desert hundred year old dwellings from the Before Times still remained and probably would exist long after he and Elle were gone. Water, fire and the hand of man were the true destructive forces of the wastelands. Remove them and a building such as the 'Club' could be held suspended in time. The preservation of the interior was remarkable. Aside from the thick blanket of dust that covered every surface and the evidence of some pilfering, the rooms appeared as if the previous occupants had just left.

Finding the plate glass window and the chandelier undamaged was just the beginning. Noah, taking the role of 'guide to antiquities', attempted to explain the functions of the various rooms and the objects found in them.

For Elle it was an odyssey into an unknown world. The bar was of particular interest. Miraculously, it was much as it had been. Whoever had seen to the removal of all traces of alcohol had been relatively restrained. Except for a few items strewn about and a few shards of glass on the floor, it was left unmolested. Wine glasses hung in their cradles; racks and stacks of bar paraphernalia were neatly stored away; the big bar mirrors, save for one, were unbroken. Trying not to be too obvious, Elle sneaked a peek at herself in one.

She almost jumped when Noah asked her, "See anyone you know?"

Her first impulse was to respond by saying "Not really". Instead, she gave a weak grin and said nothing.

The dust that lay on the wooden barroom floor had been disturbed by hundreds of small prints of scurrying animals. Mingled among them were human footprints, reminding them they were not alone. There had been others interested in this room, but judging by the thickness of the dust layered over the footprints, it had been more than a year since their last visit. Elle was very appreciative of their restraint, having only seen man's destructive impulse previously. Spooked by their presence, a small, dark furred figure shot from under a table. Scooting across the floor, the animal headed for the safety of its hole in the baseboard on the far side of the room. Ever the opportunist, the dog leaped in pursuit nailing the poor animal just millimetres from home and safety.

"And sometimes there are hawks in the sky," murmured Elle under her breath as she watched the dog devour its prize. "Life is always about hawks and rabbits."

The restaurant reminded her of the dining room back at the farm – if there were ghosts in the Clubhouse this was where they'd live. Tables were set for a meal that would never be served. Along a wall caked in dust stood a row of stainless steel, self-serve food warmers on what would have been pressed white linen. In each one were the crusted remnants of a meal never eaten. Like the bar, Elle had only ever seen the scattered and broken debris of such places. Here was the Before Times in situ.

"What do you think happened here?" asked Elle as her finger traced a line through the dust on a plate revealing the white porcelain beneath.

"It looks like they expected to eat." Noah was over by the buffet table lifting up the lids to probe the dried contents of a food warmer with the point of a steel swizzle stick he had picked up in the bar. "Well, we might not know for sure what it was, but I think I know when. They were preparing for lunch." Intrigued, Elle walked over to the table to peer into the warmer. "See, my guess is that there would have been slices of meat in this one and over here," raising the lid on another warmer, "slices of what I think was cheese. But most important," pointing under one of the warming trays, "no pot for the flame. This stuff was served cold. A lunch, not a dinner menu." Noah replaced the lid. "However, the big question is who was here before us and, if it was the Scavengers, as you have already pointed out, why didn't they trash the place? After all, it is one of their many endearing traits."

A short tour of the pro-shop and a failed attempt by Noah to explain the objective of the game was enough for Elle to conclude that golf was too strange a sport to be taken seriously. When Noah tried to demonstrate how to hit the ball the results were decidedly unimpressive from his granddaughter's point of view, having to duck as the golf club flew over her head and into a previously undamaged display case. Again, other than the now shattered display case, the shop was almost pristine as far as sports items were concerned. What were missing were hats, clothes and 'street' shoes. Not a single one of these remained on their respective racks and shelves. Seeing this, Noah looked over at Elle who was busy try to fathom the purpose of the tennis racket she was holding.

"Elle, when you were going through those houses did you see any clothes lying around?"

She stopped amusing herself by trying to balance the racket on her chin, pausing to remember. "No, but I didn't look into any of the closets or drawers."

"Curious! Let's go upstairs and have a look and then we'll head for the kitchen to do lunch."

The entire upstairs comprised of about three dozen suites. Judging from their size and furnishing, Noah suspected they were reserved for visiting VIP guests and the like, not for general use. Elle selected to stay in the first she inspected. The three rooms that made up the suite were enormous, but that was not what captured Elle's discerning eye. Despite the shredded curtains and the musky smell of nearly six decades of dust, one look at the bed and the choice was made. This bed did not sit in the room, it possessed it. It was the room. The monster was clearly four times the size of hers and, even if it was as old as her grandfather, it had not been slept in for years. Her poor single lumpy excuse of a mattress at home was as old as her grandfather. In point of fact it had been his bed when, as a child, his family visited. How many times it had been 'restored' was unknown but all such attempts had failed. It conformed to no known human form and defied Elle's best efforts to make it comfortable. Here was a real bed and an opportunity not to be missed.

Noah's choice was the corner suite, which was more strategically located, overlooking as it did both the driveway entrance and the golf course. He returned to the suite Elle had chosen to find both her and the dog sprawled on the bed with a thick cloud of dust suspended in the air around them. "Come on you two, I don't know about you but I am getting hungry," said Noah.

The last of the rooms to be explored was the Club's kitchen. The pair was greeted by a sea of stainless steel from floor to ceiling. Like the rest of the building, it too had not been vandalized. Except for the fact that not a single pot, kettle, fry pan or piece of cutlery remained, it seemed as if it was waiting for someone to return – this time the cooks. Given a wipe, the ample counter space provided not only a relatively clean surface to prepare meals but was an excellent place to lay out their gear. Better yet, the mysterious, massive brick edifice dominating a corner was found to be a wood fired oven. The discovery greatly increased the prospects of a hot meal. That it had been used solely for the purpose of baking pizzas left Elle once again marvelling at the extravagance of the Before Times.

But the real find for the day had to be what the dog found lost and forgotten under one of the workbenches; a hermetically sealed can of real coffee. Pursued by the dog, it rolled out from the counter coming to stop against Noah's boot. From that moment on, the dog's life of luxury was assured. While Elle went out to collect wood for a fire, Noah set about preparing lunch and his first cup of coffee in many, many years.

Lunch completed, the threesome walked out into the lobby where the horses and the wagon remained to head upstairs to their respective bedrooms. The lobby was as good as any barn once the entrance doors had been closed. Although Elle felt it was sacrilege to leave the mess made by the animals unattended, Noah was dismissive. "Don't worry, old girl," was his reply, ignoring the stench emanating from the steaming yellow-brown dung. "Between the flies and heat, in a month it'll be dust and you won't be able to distinguish it from the dust already here."

Elle, looking at the mess, said in that flat tone she seemed to have adopted, "Same with us. Everything is waiting its turn to become dust. Still, wouldn't it be nice to leave it as we found it? If not, we're no better than the Scavengers."

Being compared, even in jest, to a Scavenger removed any amusement from him. He knew then that he'd have to help clean the floor before they left or be forever viewed as just another wastelands' vandal. No grandfather of any value could stand the thought of his grandchildren having a diminished opinion of him.

The nap, the bed, the room, there were many advantages to living in a place this well-appointed Elle informed her grandfather as she waited for him to make his way down the stairs. Noah chuckled at the remark and agreed that there were indeed a lot of advantages.

Elle informed him that she was going to have a look at the western half of the compound on her own. She was curious as to the whereabouts of the original inhabitants. There didn't seem to be anyone else other than the soldiers in and around the military vehicles wedged at the main gate. Had they all simply disappeared?

Noah agreed because he wanted her to check on a few things for him while she was out and about. As she went to get Belle, he retraced his footsteps back to the Club House to fix himself another cup of coffee, find a comfortable chair, take it outside and sit down to wait for her return. In a high back captain's chair taken from the head of the dining room table and with both legs propped up on a low stool similarly liberated, Noah sat in the shade provided by the wide veranda with a mug in his hand and a rifle across his lap. Through his binoculars he watched Elle and the dog navigate their way through the wreckage at the western gates. Taking the binoculars down and resting them on his lap, he took a sip of coffee, made a face and then took another sip. The taste was divine, although his memory was not to be trusted. A little fresh cream from the Farm and a half spoon of sugar would not go amiss either. How coffee should taste after sixty years in a room that had never been below thirty five degree Celsius could be a matter of debate for anyone other than Noah. Amazing what a bite to eat, a short kip and a six-decade-old cup of coffee could do to refresh a soul. He raised the binoculars again but couldn't find her this time. Looking down into his cup, Noah realized he had to be more judicious if he wanted this coffee to last. This was his third cup and it was almost gone.

Astride Belle, Elle ambled up the driveway an hour later. At the centre of the golf course she'd found a small lake fed, she suspected, by a spring somewhere in its depths. The presence of water explained why there was so much wildlife running around. Other than expressing regret that she wished there was time to lay a few traps, she felt her afternoon foray had proven successful. She had been told what to look for and she was now able to supply the answers. In every house she visited, she had found women's clothing scattered about, but the men's, including shoes, was gone. Not knowing what the original contents of the houses might have been, it did seem to her that other items had been taken as well. No alcohol was found, no firearms anywhere, no canned food and, as he had suspected, no tools of any kind. She had looked into the back of every truck. They were all empty. Considering that the army was supposed to number over a million, where were the supplies? Many of those trucks would have been laden with all manner of goods for the campaign. If they had been, Elle informed him, they were long gone. She had managed to find something that might be of interest. She handed him a badly weathered and nearly disintegrated piece of plastic. Knowing how many he eaten as a kid, he recognized immediately that it was the cover from a RTE, a Ready to Eat meal pack.

"That's it?" he queried.

"Yep, that's it," said Elle.

Looking at the plastic he shook his head, and asked, "What are they up to?"

Stranger still was the arc of death as Elle described it. Except for a couple of bodies found in a wrecked car, there were none in any of the houses or other vehicles on the eastern side of the complex. It was a different story once you crossed that invisible boundary. There were hundreds of bodies, bodies in the trucks, the cars, the vans, the houses, on the streets. As if they had been watching something, many of those found in the houses seemed to have been standing either at a window or on their front steps.

In a near whisper Noah said, "Silver clouds striking them; they died where they stood." Elle stopped in mid-sentence looking a little ill at ease. He grasped her hands in to his. "Silver clouds, silver seas, your dreams, Elle. The Guardians, the mist, they're your silver clouds. That was what the man who hung himself in the barn was describing. What we saw in Sweetwater and all along the highway happened here as well. That's why this place sits like a ghost town. Seeing the terrified remnants of an army tearing through their streets, people dropping dead where they stood, any survivors would have abandoned everything as they fled. The village would have stood empty in minutes. I've got to get out some maps."

The leather roll was opened to its full length on the main countertop so that every weapon could be removed, cleaned, checked and loaded before being returned to its allotted place. Elle working opposite him was, on a smaller scale, doing the same. Several maps from the Before Times were spread out on one of the other benches. It was clear to Noah that he had almost made a fatal error of judgement and, if it hadn't been for Elle, they could have easily ridden to their deaths. Sweetwater was not a day's ride away as he had assumed, nor was it west of here. The town was just over those low-lying hills, not more than four hours north-west from the village. Elle had guessed correctly about the arc. They were literally camped on the boundary that once had separated the living from the dead.

From here on out, the road leading to and through that town had been a scene of unmitigated horror that still haunted him. It would be impossible for them to count the number of dead or comprehend their fear before dying. Tanks, artillery, armoured troop carriers, huge supply trucks surrounded by their dead crews brought silent testimony to the speed at which death had come. Twisted metal wreckage of helicopters and what must have been fighter planes littered the landscape along the battle line, each housed in its own blackened, burnt circle. The dead and their machinery of war occupied a corridor that was twenty-five to fifty kilometres deep and four hundred kilometres wide. Nothing trapped within that cauldron had survived.

Those that had somehow managed to escape that day's carnage fled forever eastward.

Since that time, of those who ventured inside the killing zone very few ever came out. This only added to the myths that already encompassed the mountains. He and his friends had not died, nor had the man found hanging in the barn, although the same could not be said for his companions. But, for reasons unknown, the Scavengers had somehow found a means to live within the boundary unmolested. That was why no one had seen them for all these years. Who would have thought to look there, amongst all this death, but a Scavenger?

"They didn't destroy the village because they plan to live here."

The bolt of the light machine gun slid home. He then gave it a quick wipe with a cloth before returning the weapon to its allotted place in the leather roll. He pulled his watch out; the hour was getting late and he and Elle had to go and clean up the muck the horses had left in the lobby. The one thing he was sure of; if he had his way, the Scavengers' plans for expansion were never going to come to fruition.

Chapter Twenty-One

We do not fear death as much as dying.

Being insular provided a degree of protection from the effects of a life filled with violence, death and loss. Accustomed to living his life at a measured distance from even those he loved, Noah had found the last few days disorienting. He was struggling to come to terms with the changes in Elle. Her dreams had played a part, as did encountering the Scavengers. He turned for a moment in an attempt to reappraise the girl who lay beside him with binoculars pressed against her eyes as she studied the town that sprawled below. He returned his attention to the town. Even without the field glasses the changes were clearly noticeable since his last visit. The town was not just occupied; it was invigorated, a hive humming with activity as people moved purposefully along its streets. The pale washed-out blue had been fused with a blackened pall that drifted above the settlement and, like the fog in a seaside village, seeped into the open spaces, filling the alleys, streets and town centre with its dark malaise. The air had an almost metallic sheen and the large quantities of burning coal explained the dense sooty haze, thought Noah.

"They're using a lot of coal to make that much of a mess in the air. So where did they get it, and what are they using it for?" He wiped sweat from the inside of his hat with his handkerchief. The heat on the ridge was stifling. "I think we can safely rule out the need to keep warm." The scene below was not unfamiliar; he'd seen just such a sky before, in the bigger towns. The Dry had ushered in certain behavioural adjustments. The disintegration of central authority and the absence of the ready availability of oil forced communities to employ a range of alternative energy sources. Other than wood, that alternative was coal, which was still relatively easy to procure in any number of places. You just needed a lot of muscle. "Forges and furnaces!" The realization of what this meant stunned him. He'd thought they had nothing in common with his kind. Scavengers, as the name implied, were eaters of carrion. They did not make things, they did not build, they did not toil. They lived off the efforts of others. Now, here they were, right in his backyard, doing something that required forges, furnaces and the energy to drive them. In the stillness, in spite of the withering heat of late morning, sweat pooling in the hollow of his lower back, he felt a chill pass up his spine.

Their vantage point was the crown of one of the hills bordering the town's southern fringe. With only Blue and Belle, they had arrived last night just as the moon set – perfect timing. In the event that they suddenly found themselves in a fire-fight, they did not want to be encumbered by the wagon. The wagon and the two other horses were several kilometres back under an awning stretched over an old river bed.

The rising sun revealed that they had chosen a plateau that was as littered with the refuse of war as the floor below. Vehicles of various types, tattered tents, caravan command centres, observation stations and their macabre interiors bore testament to the suddenness of death's rampage on this barren knoll. Being able to choose the ridge should not have been an option for them. There should have been a sentinel or, at the very least, recent signs of there being one. What signs there were had succumbed to the capricious nature of time, silt and sand. No one had camped on this summit for years. This could mean the Scavengers had become uncommonly careless – an unlikely scenario – or that they'd lived here so long undisturbed they'd become secure to the point of complacency. And why not? Much the same thing had happened at the Farm. Even if they had had the manpower, it had been years since they felt the need to stand vigil. The last encounter in which it was thought the remaining Scavengers had been decimated – pity about the ugly fact that they hadn't – would have brought a measure of safety to those who remained. The events being played out below certainly altered everything.

Just then Elle handed the binoculars to Noah with directions to look where the town ended and the lake's old shoreline had been. "There is a row of five poles placed at equal distance from each other. Tell me what you see."

The binoculars swung left, coming to rest on the last pole in the row. At this distance the mind could come up with an array of imaginative possibilities, but Noah had seen this before and knew its significance. A slumped figure was tied to it. The same was true of the other poles. Of course the distance made it impossible to tell their gender, but from his experience this particular form of death was reserved for men.

Elle listened to his explanation and then asked, "And why would they do that?"

Without removing the binoculars from his eyes Noah said, "It's what they do to their own kind. If they don't just shoot them full of holes, they stake them out in the wastelands and leave them, and believe me when I tell you, for a Scavenger, both those forms of death are merciful."

"And those things to their right and down toward the road leading out of town?" asked Elle.

Noah turned the binoculars to the right and down as instructed and let out an expletive. There on the side of the road on the town's most western verge, pointing toward the mountains, sat five massive battle tanks and twice as many armoured troop carriers parked in a line, side by side. Like ants, upwards of thirty men crawled over them performing all manner of tasks.

"Where did they get the expertise to even move them?" was the first thing that flashed into his mind. Like most people of his time, both he and Elle were accustomed to coaxing into life the neglected engine and machinery of the Before Times. Elle could strip and rebuild an old flywheel diesel motor without supervision. Anything that required a computer to operate, however, was out of the question. Out of the remaining main centres, it had been decades since Noah had seen anything work that relied on electronics. But the sophistication built into military hardware, including the ubiquitous trucks, relied on computers. Every function within those battle tanks was controlled by computers. It was just not possible the Scavengers had the specialized skills, let alone the manuals or required parts, to bring into operation a piece of equipment that had been sitting in these wastelands for fifty years or more.

A belch of black smoke and the faint roar of an engine revealed just how wrong his reasoning had been. They obviously did have the expertise and that was one very ugly fact. So startled was he by this depressing revelation he almost overlooked the bulbous modifications attached to the rear of each tank and armoured personnel carrier. What looked like large cylinders lying on their sides had been fixed into cradle frames. Before Noah could comment on this curious adaptation he was redirected by Elle.

"Now look to your right again, maybe three hundred metres or more, to the building next to a petrol station."

He swung the glasses to his right. Black, oily looking smoke rose from several steel chimneys jutting from the roof of a massive warehouse. Through large doors that opened onto the street more ant men toiled in the heat. Not only were there freight wagons similar to the ones used by the Traders, there were several trucks as well. All along the building's street front, there were also row upon row of fuel drums, stacked three high. As he watched, another drum was rolled out of the building on to what appeared to be an improvised loading bay.

"I think we need to know what's going on in that building, don't you? Tonight, I'll go and check it out. You stay up here with the dog and keep watch." Before he could offer an objection, she continued by saying, "I don't think we'll be able to kill them all, but we should be able to at least give them a moment's pause. The Traders can finish off what we missed."

Noah looked at Elle with what amounted to trepidation. "What?"

Responding to his surprised look, "Did you really think I wouldn't figure out why you didn't take me home? Whatever your original motives were, they changed the moment the Scavengers showed up and you found out I had been stabbed by one of them." She opened her shirt and pulled the bandage down. Oozing pus, a number of red lines radiated from the swollen wound. Replacing the bandage and closing up the shirt, she said, "You saw the red lines and so did Nic, yet neither of you said anything. I know it could be septicaemia but you said sometimes their knives were coated with a poison."

Her grandfather wanted to say something, anything, to stop what his granddaughter would say next but he was paralysed.

Staring at him with those ancient eyes of hers, she asked, "The only question then is how long do I have to live? My guess is that since you knew I was going to die anyway, why send me home when I would more useful here? Isn't that what you said in the letter you gave to Nic?"

With that she took the binoculars back and turned to watch the shimmering silvery mist. The glare from the sun reflecting off the mist made her eyes water. No dancing stars. To see them, Elle suspected she'd have to wait till dark.

Noah again tried to speak to his granddaughter. He felt a strong need to reply, to explain, to give some word of comfort, but the initiative was lost.

Elle returned the field glasses to their protective case and then began to scoot back, dropping below the ridge. The dog and Noah followed. Sitting in the dirt with the rifle across her lap and the dog panting at her side, Elle waited for her grandfather to adjust his leg into a comfortable position before speaking. Suspecting what was coming, Noah was resigned. After all, had he not trained her?

With a malevolent grin, she said, "Ok, Granddad, if we are going to be martyrs, what's the plan?"

It was all he could do not to cry. She was right of course. The poison had no known antidote. The Scavengers had taken so much from him and now they were about to take his granddaughter. There were perhaps six hundred men down there. Even with complete surprise, they'd be lucky to kill fifty of them. But fifty was better than nothing and the disruption it would cause would be tremendous.

Time to go. The moon hung low in the night's sky as they moved out from their camp in the valley to return to the spot on the ridge. The food was a lump in his stomach and he'd not been able to sleep. The day's heat still clung to them, but once away from the depression surrounding their camp in the river bed the breeze from the mountains would find them, making their evening outing more agreeable. Sweetwater was an hour's ride north and, except for the immediate vicinity, boulder-strewn and laced with gullies, the approach to the town would be open and level. There was little in the way of obstruction. Noah was mounted on Blue. The leg was bothersome but with little accompanying pain. However, with the leg hanging razor straight and not in the stirrup, riding was awkward and he wasn't sure what would happen if Blue made a sudden and unexpected move. Elle, dressed in the clothes given to her by the Traders, rode Belle. Both wore their Trader's cloaks. The wagon, considered too cumbersome, too noisy, and too visible, had been left behind with the remaining supplies. Unsure of what the night would bring, the other two horses had been loaded with water, provisions for two days and every weapon and box of ammunition the pair possessed, which included the three green crates. Ready, leading one of the pack horses, Noah edged Blue carefully out and away from the dry river bed. Elle followed, trailing the other pack horse. Later, clear of the clutter and out in the open, Elle came alongside and reached out to touch her grandfather's arm. It was too dark even with the aid of the light from the moon for Noah to see her expression clearly but he got the impression she was smiling.

"What are you smiling at?" he asked. He could feel rather than see her smile widen.

"Oh, I guess it's because I can't think of any other place I'd rather be."

He returned her smile. After what had taken place on the ridge, the remark was not what he had expected and it did not ease the guilt.

Ever since they'd left the ridge to return to the camp to get something to eat and a bit of sleep before the night's foray, he had wanted to explain his motivations, but all the thoughts in his head concerning the various reasons were in conflict. Despite the wound being inflicted by a Scavenger's knife and the likely consequences of such a wound, Elle should have been the one to return with the information, not Nic. It was against all their customs to endanger a young female regardless. At first it had been his pride at what she'd accomplished thus far, and he had wanted to see her reach the mountains. After the ambush? It was not easy coming to terms with your own folly. Nothing he did would bring back or compensate for the loss of those he loved who had died at the hands of Scavengers. He was old, he felt old, and in the zeitgeist of this time, should have been dead long ago. Save for his family, his death would not matter much – but hers? Angry and impotent, he acknowledged that what he had done could not be undone.

Aided by the last rays of moonlight and with the dog's head in his lap, once again Noah sat on the ridge overlooking Sweetwater, keeping watch and waiting impatiently for Elle's return. Except for a few buildings and random pools of light, the majority of the town was cloaked in the ash grey radiance of the moon. Somewhere down there a shadow, more mist than flesh, looked for answers. Elle was as capable as anyone in the craft of surviving the Dry and had proven this on several occasions during the last four weeks. Youth, skill and two good legs were good to have, but they were not enough. She lacked the experience of facing a real enemy, stone cold killers. Back at the camp he had attempted to drive the point home that if confronted, any hesitation on her part could be fatal. The Traders, the family, his companions had paid dearly to acquire this understanding and the result was that his hatred was visceral and unalterable.

Absentmindedly, Noah reached down to rub his thigh as if the action itself could somehow hasten the mending of his broken leg. Being stuck up here, barely mobile, caring for the horses and dog was wrong, so very wrong. A bitter taste crept onto his tongue. It was not supposed to be like this. He should have been down there. He should be the one creeping around watching his enemy from the dark corners of their camp. He should be the one discovering their secrets. From what he had already seen, there was no denying the magnitude of the Scavengers' endeavours and he wanted to be the one who had a closer look, not some thirteen-year-old kid, even if it was Elle.

In spite of his hatred, Noah could not help but marvel at what the Scavengers had apparently achieved.

For some unfathomable reason, perhaps even before their last major defeat thirteen years ago, the Scavengers had poured a tremendous amount of time, effort and resources into this project and what really irked him was that they had done so in complete secrecy. This should have been impossible in the face of his and the Traders' potential opposition. No longer was it a matter of killing a few Scavengers with the probability of being killed himself. The priority had shifted away from his personal vendetta.

But why battle tanks and armoured troop carriers? It seemed to him a poor offensive choice considering the sheer volume of effort that went into getting these machines up and running, not to mention their on-going maintenance. Other than being impressive beasts and potentially having huge shock value the first time they showed up, even with five hundred sun-struck Scavengers in support, who were they planning to fight? Traders would just scatter and then pick them off one at a time. And any town or city of notable size was nearly two thousand kilometres away. Not counting the fuel they would consume, these machines weren't designed to travel anywhere near that distance. The tracks would probably fall off the tanks before doing five hundred. As a defensive weapons they were even less effective. It just did not make sense. He stared out into the darkness and wondered how his granddaughter was doing down there.

In the years that preceded the coming of the Dry, rumours had circulated about a special project located somewhere in Western Mountains, and not just from the paranoid conspiracy fringe theorists. Too many noted scientists had simply walked away from too many universities and research institutes not to be noticed. For those who survived the Dry, the Sorrow, the starvation, the deprivation, and the Scavengers, all that was left was myth. The old rumours and theories had been interwoven into such an elaborate tapestry that fact and fiction were inseparable. Noah was never a man comfortable with conspiratorial speculation, myth or fireside stories to frighten children. He was drawn toward the cold embrace of facts and facts alone. And the facts were telling him that something sinister, whether by design or misfortune, had been created here. The dead around him were proof enough.

Thinking of the Guardians, he shifted his attention to their illuminated glow as they coiled and arched in a never-ending waltz among the mountain peaks. As far as he could tell, their deadly dance had not changed since he and his companions had watched them all those years ago from the very spot where the dead men were tethered.

Uncomfortable lying on his side, Noah rocked himself back up into a sitting position. Here, in amongst this wreckage, there must have been some who understood what had taken place behind those granite walls. If they did, was the information enough to save them? From childhood, he'd been told that there was a family connection with the mountains. The folklore said it was his grandmother's twin sister, Scout, a viral specialist, who had worked in those very mountains. And she must have known its secrets because it was Scout who told her sister to convert everything they could to gold, to buy a place for the family with '...a spring, in the middle of nowhere'. It was also Scout who had made and then sent the knife and ring to Atticus just before the start of the Dry. How much of this family folklore was true he did not know as there was no one living that could confirm the story. The thought that any of his kin had played a part in this nightmare made his skin crawl. Surely, if this was indeed the origin of the Dry, it could not have been their intention. Something had to have gone horribly wrong. The presence of the Guardians was a testament to that, and their destruction had been seen as the salvation of humankind. Why else would the authorities have repeatedly assailed those formidable peaks?

In the silence on the ridge he heard an almost undetectable whisper.

"They've no intention of heading east. They think they've found the means to succeed where all others have failed."

"Bloody Hell, they're heading to the mountains." Startled at speaking out loud he had a strange desire to put a hand over his mouth. It was all so clear, and so like the Scavengers; an assault on the mountains had to be it. The Scavengers must somehow have duped themselves into believing that, with these implements of war, they could gain access to the mountains. And the attempt would take place very soon. Why else would they risk revealing their presence and exposing their sanctuary by murdering a family of Traders, of all people? The answer was simple. They wouldn't unless they were sure there would be no timely retaliation or that if there were, it would be irrelevant. Noah had always assumed the Scavengers were stark raving mad, but never suicidal. Whatever rewards they expected to find in the mountains had to far exceed the risk of provoking a visit by an avenging army of Traders and their allies. Had they considered another possibility, one potentially more devastating? What if the assault provoked the Guardians? The dead that surrounded Noah were evidence, if evidence was needed, of what ill-conceived actions could initiate. They might not only succeed in getting themselves killed. The Traders would be only a few days away. That was a terrifying thought and one he would have to relate to Elle on her return.

Chapter Twenty-Two
Like rust, evil never sleeps.

Totally unaware of her grandfather's sudden insight, Elle was trying to come to terms with a problem of her own. What is it about Scavengers and hygiene? she thought, trying to pick her way through the squalor while wondering if they even possessed a sense of smell. The town seemed to vary from garbage dump to cesspit. The thick stench of diesel, waste and rubbish saturated the air to the extent that it liquefied into bitter droplets on her tongue and clung to her clothing. It had been easier for her to locate the sentries guarding the entrance to the town by their rank odour than by sight in the setting moon's dim light. Not that either had been necessary. The sentries talked and stomped about with such disregard she could have driven the wagon through the camp and not been heard over the din. Even so, remembering how close she had already come to dying by their hands, Elle understood any cockiness on her part would be potentially lethal. The Scavengers might be slovenly and careless, but it would be a foolish person who did not regard them as deadly. Therefore, even though she found no one guarding the building she had come to investigate, she did not take it for granted that they were not there somewhere.

There were lights coming from inside as well as voices and the definitive low throbbing hum of heavy machinery. Elle slid through a side door and sat, crouched within the borders of a shadow, to get her bearings. The cavernous interior, washed in white light, smelled of warm oil and exhaust fumes. This was not the first time she had seen electric lights, but they had been nothing like these. Elle felt a degree of awe and admiration at the extravagance. The lights provided by the windmill and PE cell on the Farm were there if needed, but the feeble glows her father had been able to extract paled in comparison to just one of the many sources of light strung along the ceiling. They must have a huge generator to be able to do this, she thought, looking up to follow the electrical cables. And I'll bet it's tucked somewhere in here with all this other stuff. The place is certainly big enough.

Small knots of men, in the laconic motion of routine, appeared to be working at various tasks all over the ground floor. The Dry had severely reduced the technical intricacy of the Before Times but it had not been obliterated as demonstrated by this building filled with the wizardry of pipes, suspended walkways and cranes, metal tanks, cables, dials and gauges. As with the electric lights overhead, they were not so unfamiliar that she was unable to guess or recognize what she saw, but this scale and complexity was new. This included the object that filled a sizeable space by the far wall, although it did take a couple of minutes before she was able to identify it. Bloody hell, she thought, it's a refinery. They're making fuel. And judging by the number of drums stored along the wall where she now hid and the ones outside, they had been for some time. Nearer to the entrance, cradled in spheres of light, men operated machine tools resembling the ones her dad had in the barn, only these were very much bigger. Thinking of her dad for the first time in days, and his love of tools, brought a wry smile. Without a doubt he'd give his right arm for a tool shed similar to this one, especially the metal lathes. The thought of all that electricity and the tools it could power would have given her dad's heart palpitations.

Staying well within the shadows and concealed by the numerous boxes and crates stacked throughout the building, she took the opportunity, when it presented itself, to inspect their contents. As at the homestead, most of the boxes seemed to be filled with miscellaneous stuff looted from all over the place. Books were mixed in with shoes, eye glasses with PSims, cooking pots with women's clothes.

In the midst of her inspection, a party of men came in through the large front doors and crossed over to stand so close that, had they wished, they could have reached out and touched her. But they were so intent on retrieving something that they never noticed the girl wedged in the corner or the rifle levelled at them. Loading several boxes from the stack onto a hand cart, the men headed back outside. A slow shallow breath left her lips. She'd escaped detection. She'd been told that people, left to their own devices, see only that which they expect to see. Though it was counter-intuitive and against all her instincts, remaining stock-still in a dark corner as she'd been taught, she really had been 'invisible' while in plain view. She wondered how many times Noah had relied on this simple trick to escape death. She waited a few more minutes before resuming her search of the building.

The overhead power cables led to a large makeshift shed in the corner at the far end of the refinery, making it a good candidate for the generator housing. It would be worth a peek. Not wanting to risk being spotted trying to cross any open area, lit or otherwise, she moved along the wall until she reached the refinery. There were so many pipes and dark places it was easy for her to reach the other side of the building and slip into the 'shed'.

Once she had seen enough, Elle pulled her hood forward and joined the darkness outside. Noah's prejudice against the Scavengers would make it hard for him to believe all this. The moon was long gone but the stars told her she'd spent more time in there than she had intended. Moving swiftly along the building's exterior toward another cluster of lights, she observed that there was a good deal more to explore before heading back. Judging from the building's contents they had concentrated nearly everything of value there. The generator, the refinery, the machine shop, general stores, repair depot, boxes and boxes of plunder, everything one could hope for but for one thing; no munitions store. That had to be elsewhere and there would be no point in coming all this way without finding it. She sped past a row of buildings toward a cluster of lights half a kilometre away. There was no need to stop to peer inside as the choking smoke that drifted down from the chimneys was enough to tell her where some of the forges and furnaces were. However, curiosity got the better of her. The deafening noise from the last of buildings was unavoidable so she edged over to have a look. Fortunately glass was missing from one of the window frames otherwise it would have been impossible to see through the thick coating of grime. Without a doubt, Noah would be amazed if he saw this, she thought to herself as she watched a team of men labouring away. They had not only the largest forge she had ever seen but a massive steam engine as well. This was not quite the activity she had expected of the parasitic band of ruthless marauders. These people made the achievements back on the farm seem primitive. It certainly could come close to rivalling anything she'd heard about along the coastal cities.

Gone were the previous days of gloom; Elle was ecstatic. The light of the early morning sun spilled into the valley. Between mouthfuls of what passed for breakfast and brushing off an ever hopeful dog, Elle eagerly started to tell Noah's the highlights of last night's visit. She described the large building's varied contents, exalting in the details. "They had everything there. Dad would faint at the thought of getting his hands on some of that stuff. The generator alone was beyond anything I've seen. It was huge – big enough to supply pretty much the whole town." Her eyes were bright with excitement.

Noah did not feel inclined to join in his granddaughter's high spirits. Even if her admiration of their technology was well founded, he had been to the east coast 'towns' and had been equally impressed with the technological efforts. Yet this was not the east coast with its interlocking infrastructure and the shared resources of half a million people. This had been created in the back of beyond by a handful of social outcasts.

Elle continued. "Now toward its rear," pointing beyond the building that housed the refinery and generator, "do you see a row of buildings banged against one another and a whole lot of smoke coming from their chimneys?"

"Yes."

"Each one has either a forge or a furnace of some sort. In the last one they were heating big sheets of metal. You can see the coal pile behind. Now go more to the right 'till you see a yellow building." The field glasses focused on the yellow structure. Two men and what had to be a child had opened a small entrance door and gone in. "It's filled from floor to ceiling with provisions, mostly with stuff similar to what you described, but there were boots, uniforms and a whole bunch of other stuff like that. They could feed and dress thousands." Suppressing the urge to physically grab the binoculars to hurry him along, she instead directed him to look at the buildings surrounding the town square. "You should see a six storey brick building sandwiched between two shorter buildings, one of which is white." Elle waited until her grandfather confirmed that he had located it. "That has women and kids in it, as did the buildings on both sides. It was easy to see inside because the lights were on in each of the downstairs rooms. Maybe it's their families."

Noah took down the binoculars to look at his adventurer. "Have you any idea how many?"

Elle shook her head before taking the glasses from Noah to sweep the town below. "I don't but it was very late. Most of them would probably have been asleep somewhere else in the building but I did see five women sitting in a room facing the street with two kids asleep on the floor. They didn't look very happy."

Noah had his interpretation of the scene. He did not think this was the time to attempt to explain the habits of men and women or the likely probability that these women were captives, so he let it pass without comment.

Unable to stifle a big yawn as it forced its way out, she stopped talking. She looked tired, and Noah once again had to remind himself that she was, physically at least, still a child and it was way past his granddaughter's bed time. Neither had had any sleep since yesterday. The sortie into the Scavenger's camp had consumed most of the night, allowing her just enough time to return before sunrise. All that time in the enemy's camp and, in so far as he could tell from their elevated perch, the current inhabitants of Sweetwater were none the wiser. This was a good thing considering that she might well have to go in again. The next time she might have to head in just after dark and people would still be up and moving about. There could then be the off-chance she'd hear them discussing what they were up to or at least find the building he knew had to exist. They had not found any weapons in any of the vehicles so they had to be stored someplace down there. The relatives of those rockets had to be there as well. There was no need to discuss it now but he considered it imperative that they locate the Scavengers' munitions and, if possible, destroy them. Right now there was little advantage in staying where they were. In a few hours the mid-day sun would be baking rocks around them.

He nudged Elle in the ribs, signalling her it was time to go, return to camp and unload their long-suffering animals.

Chapter Twenty-Three
The choices we make define our lives.

Sleep was again difficult for Elle. She was aware that she had not actually screamed or bolted upright disturbing all concerned as she had done before; nevertheless, she awoke in Noah's arms, hearing his cooing and the dog's distressed whine. Her head burrowed deeper into his embrace, breathing in the smells that were her grandfather. She waited for the adrenaline to ebb away. The dream had begun as the others but then dissolved into a fearsome storm. *Lightning pierced a leaden sky. Driven by brutal winds, rain painfully pelted her exposed skin. She clung to slick clay walls as the rage of the river reached up to claw at her legs in its attempt to drag her into its churning maw.* Powerful and terrifying like its predecessors, this dream like the others came not from Elle's experience. There was no shared resonance. Its contents were as foreign to her as nearly all aspects of the Before Times. Try as she might to explain the terror, she could not, for through her dreams she had truly experienced the fury of rain, wind and lightning of a Before Time storm. Beneath Noah's arm, her gaze fell upon the sheltering walls of the wadi, the old river bed, and comprehension, a clarity, came into her consciousness. A child of the Dry, she recognized that their camp lay confined within a river's artery, an artery that had once been filled with the water from the melting snows of those mountains. She held the vision of a barely contained, wild river rushing through this land. It helped to counter the dream's sense of isolation and alienation. It provided her tenure in two worlds.

They ate but there was little conversation. Nearing its first quarter, the moon hung low in the evening sky looking as if it reflected the light of a setting sun. The end of another day, the beginning of another night; wake, sleep; eat, defecate; be born, live, die – cycles within cycles.

Noah watched his granddaughter mechanically spoon the stew into her mouth, chew, swallow. Quite a difference from the girl this morning, so pleased with her abilities, animated with her stalking prowess, now sitting there expressionless, dulled. She had struggled all day with the desire to sleep a dreamless sleep but it had evaded her. Each time, from its depths she fled toward wakefulness, the residue of death clinging to her like a bitter aftertaste. The thin trail of smoke from the small cooking fire, spiraling upward to be whisked away by a feeble breeze, did not go unnoticed by either of them.

Noah shifted his backside, moving his weight from one cheek to the other in a futile attempt to find some comfort, a task he was sure was in vain as long the one leg remained encased between barrel stays. Besides trying to avoid his rear end becoming numb, there was another problem looming; water and provisions. While not dangerously low, two days from now the shortage would necessitate a tactical retreat. It was never prudent to allow options to narrow unnecessarily; the wasteland did not bluff. In five days' time they would be out of water and food. The nearest reliable water was back at Empty Cup – not a lot of room for error. Food? That was a bit more difficult to resolve. No matter how good you thought you were at this game of survival, the Dry always had the odds in its favour.

An alternative was to re-supply from the current residents of Sweetwater. The water was likely to be somewhat tainted by the Scavengers' unhygienic habits but there were ways they could deal with that. The food might be unsavoury but it was reasonable to think the fodder for the horses would be acceptable. The trick was to take without it being noticed.

Of course to actually implement this alternative presented a second problem. Tired people make mistakes and people feeling the inevitability of their own demise become careless. Across the dying fire Noah had seen the look many times before. Etched into his granddaughter's face was a resignation at her fate.

Feeling both tired and lost, Elle slowly raised her eyes, those incredible eyes, to meet his. A smile eased itself onto her face as she reached down to grab a handful of kindling to toss on the fire. "Granddad, what I need, if you feel like sharing, is a cup of your coffee before we go."

Noah was only too glad to comply. He believed that there was nothing in this world that a good cup of coffee could not set right. Right now they both needed one. During its preparation, it did not go unnoticed by him that the wound over her heart was painful but he let it be. Whether it was septicaemia or poison from the Scavenger knife, the likely results would be the same. Minutes later, cups in hand, they watched the sun slide over the mountains illuminating its celestial companion.

The breeze coming from the mountains made the night air softer. It also brought with it the muffled voices of men. This reminded them both that the night was young and people were about. The distant laughter of what sounded like a child was unexpected as was that of a woman calling out to someone, perhaps the laughing child. These sounds did not belong here. One more bit of evidence that this was not a typical Scavenger's camp with its grunts, belches and farts. Unless on the menu or for temporary creature comfort, women had never been part of any Scavengers' entourage before and if that was indeed a mother calling to her child, such a thing was without precedent. Noah shifted uneasily in his saddle. Mounted on Blue in the darkness, he watched and listened for signs that their presence in the village had been in any way detected.
***

Curious, he thought, the town is dotted with islands of light save for the spring. He wondered why that was. The disturbed water seemed to flick darts of moonlight in his direction. He could hear the soft slap of a cup as Elle dipped it into the spring and the gurgling of its content being poured into the waiting canister. Under the moon's influence he could make out her ghostly apparition as it bent ever so slightly over the pool, then straightened to ladle another cupful of water into the canister that sat on the stone cistern surrounding the spring. He had already drunk his fill, one small pleasure, as had Blue. At least the water, renowned for its sweetness, had not been adulterated by the presence of the Scavengers' unsavoury habits. The closing of the canister's lid signalled that the task of retrieving water had been successfully concluded. All they had to do now was sneak into the stores and, without being observed by a town full of Scavengers, load the horses with enough provisions to see them through another week. After the last canister was bound next to its brothers, Elle swung up onto Belle as gracefully as a bird alighting upon a twig.

Dirt and salt, the residue from evaporated sweat, made Elle's clothes feel scratchy. She longed for a swim; even a quick rinse would be sublime. The luxury of a wash in one of the streams leading off from Sweetwater spring would almost be worth the risk to life and limb. The better part of the night had been used lugging bags and boxes from the warehouse to the waiting horses as Noah kept watch. The building was a treasure-trove, a cornucopia. It was pitch black as the moon had set an hour ago leaving them to fumble in the dark from one shadowy edge of light to another. The lack of light outside the building had not deterred Elle from the task of replenishing their dwindling supplies with the zeal of an accomplished thief. The Scavengers had kindly left the lights on inside.

Noah had cautioned his young protégée to leave the impression nothing had been taken. Nice idea, but difficult to implement considering the quantity they'd planned to take. She started by selecting items located at the end of a stack or toward the back and when this was not convenient, she rearranged. This meant the work was not only prolonged but arduous, requiring her to climb over, under and around piles of inventory to procure the selected items, which in turn, meant a good deal of reorganizing. Even so, with the last crate secured to Belle, she went back to see if her efforts had hidden the theft. "The longer we can avoid detection, the longer we retain the advantage..." she murmured. Standing just inside the entrance, she surveyed her handiwork. "Hard to tell what it will look like in the light of day, but if you're not expecting someone to sneak in and steal stuff, it just might go unnoticed."

Tomorrow was her birthday; she would be fourteen. Even that seemed too far into the future. She closed the door, wincing at the audible click of the latch, before checking that nothing they's taken was likely to fall or shift when they made their way out of Sweetwater. She gave Belle an affectionate rub on her muzzle and then slipped a small pack onto her back. Adjusting the straps so it would ride high on her shoulders, she signed 'OK', stepping back to let them pass. Noah slipped into the folds of darkness trailing the heavily laden horses behind him. Everything they would need for the coming days had been found. They'd even been fortunate enough to find a sack of grain, like the one in the cart at the homestead, sitting on a pallet outside the warehouse, as if waiting for someone like them to come along and carry it away. Which they had.

She watched Noah and the horses disappear down the street. In seconds, except for the soft footfalls of the retreating horses, they disappeared into the dark. The leather boots covering the hooves of the horses worked well, even on tarmac. They had entered along one of the many side streets leading into the town from its residential fringe and would exit the same way.

Departing, he'd whispered on their apparent success: "You see what you want to see..." She waited until satisfied that he had retired without detection. A glance at the night sky told her she had plenty of time. Although time might not be her friend, the darkness was.

There were compelling reasons, other than curiosity, to find the whereabouts of the Scavengers' arsenal. In addition to pristine rockets and functioning battle tanks, Noah had wondered what other surprises lay in wait for them. "Find it and get out," he had instructed her. "We've pushed our family luck just about as far as it is going to go." Judging by how easy it had been to prowl about the Scavengers' camp for two nights running without being challenged, they'd developed a monumental confidence in their seclusion. It was proving hard to reconcile the people of Sweetwater with the men who were once the scourge of her world and who had tried to kill her twice. Here, unlike the Farm, they fought the Dry and seemed on the verge of winning. Having seen all that they had while in Sweetwater, she'd still bet that, if given the chance, Noah would gladly slit the throat of each and every person living here, be it man, woman or child. But could she do the same, even after having seen the results of a Cleansing?

Distracted in an attempt to remove a bit of grit from her eye with the hem of her shirt, Elle stepped around the corner and collided with the small figure of a child crouched against the wall of the building. Automatically the knife flashed into her hand to strike. The upturned smiling face could have been angelic if not for the filth. There was a bruise on her cheek, her teeth showed signs of decay and the clothes were worn, tattered and the colour of the earth she stood upon. At first the giggling child did not notice the blade poised millimetres from her throat nor the hardness in Elle's eyes, so proceeded to place a finger to her lips.

"Shhh, or they'll find me."

Light from a nearby lamp glinted off the blade and her words trailed away. She looked at the blade and then at Elle. The child did not cry out, attempt to run or turn her face away. She did not even look frightened but resigned, as if this had always been her fate, to die at the hands of another. Looking up into Elle's eyes she closed her own and waited.

Elle knew she'd have to kill the girl or forfeit her own life and Noah's. Instead the knife returned to its sheath.

She turned and fled, leaving the child unharmed. Elle ran blindly westward, past the startled guards by the tanks and into the open wastelands. She ran, stumbled, picked herself up and started to run again. Ignoring the shouts and the shots that tried to find her in the dark, she ran away from the town, until she could run no further. In the middle of the dead lake's basin, trembling with fatigue, overwhelmed by exhaustion, she stood alone in the darkness gasping for breath, labouring to fill her oxygen-starved lungs. Then, without the least interest in where she might be or what danger lurked, she sank. As if drowning, she sank to the bottom of a waterless lake until she came to rest on the soft white sand. Hunched over, her head millimetres from the ground, Elle wept. Tears came, followed by sobs that wracked the young girl's slender body. Snot, mingled with sweat, ran from her nose but she did not trouble to wipe it away.

Later, as her breathing gradually subsided, she sat and clutched her knees, drawing them to her breast, and grieved. Her wailing slid into a mewing, a whimpering and like some terrified animal she, despite the pain of her festering wound, curled into a tight ball and began to rock back and forth. Besieged by the cumulative weeks of fear, dread and uncertainty, the Cleansing and the sounds of flies hovering about the dead man in the barn, this child of the Dry, of the wastelands, crumbled. Fully aware of what could have, perhaps should have, taken place, Elle could not rid herself of the child's upturned face, its acceptance of death. It did not matter whether her eyes were open or closed; the image remained fixed before her. Fused within the dreams of the silvery sea, the near death of a child, the torso packed in salt, her own mortality, Elle retreated to the only place left –

within. The rocking slowed to a stop. Tightly curled, as if in her mother's womb, Elle lay on her side in the sand and slept.

Chapter Twenty-Four

Pandora's gift to humankind was payment for Prometheus' treachery.

Before Noah reached the town's residential edge he became aware that something had seriously altered the night's sombre tranquillity, disturbing the Scavengers' camp and causing a tremendous uproar. Lights sprang into life where there had been darkness. Shots were fired. A flare, like the ones he had found in the Scavengers' wagon, burst overhead. Men began to shout to one another. A siren began to wail. Something had set them off and there was a strong probability Elle was at its centre. Noah stifled his first impulse. Rushing back was not likely to help, especially if in doing so he only achieved getting himself killed. He dug his heels into Blue's flanks, urging his mount forward. Encumbered by the night's pilfering, he needed to get out and clear of Sweetwater. Only then, free of the other horses, would he be able to consider what options were available.

Unfortunately there was no moon. The ride back to the wadi was going to be difficult enough without rushing. Even as he wove his way through the empty cluttered suburban streets the earlier sounds of confusion and disarray had started to morph into a general sense of deliberate purpose. From years of experience in such matters Noah understood exactly what was underway.

After their initial confusion, the Scavengers were getting themselves organized.

At the end of the cul-de-sac facing the wastelands beyond, he stopped for a moment to reconnoitre. Here, alone within these crumbling ruins of former domesticity, there was a degree of anonymity. Luckily this would not change once he left the protection of the building and started climbing up to the ridge. Any of the aroused citizenry of Sweetwater, looking this way unaided by the light of a moon, would be unable to see either him or the horses. The one moment they could be seen would be that brief period when they would breach the ridge and be silhouetted against the night sky, but it was a risk he'd take. There just wasn't enough time for a more circuitous route. Right now, he reasoned, they were still trying to find out what was going on. That would not last much longer and nor would the night. He'd heard no more shots. That's good or very, very bad. No more shots could mean they had no real idea of the source of the disturbance. It could very well be nothing more than an overreaction by a spooked guard and have nothing to do with Elle. He had seen it before during the wars following the Sorrow. An unusual noise, an unanticipated occurrence, a movement caught from the corner of an eye could and did send even veterans running after phantoms. On the other hand, she could be either wounded or dead.

In matters of survival he could seem to act with cold indifference, doing what was necessary. Even so, this was his granddaughter, a child worthy of a life, even if that life was his own. Noah consoled himself that all the fuss back there did not necessarily mean they knew about Elle or himself. Not an inherently optimistic man, he saw no reason to assume all was well either and gave Blue a further nudge to hurry him along as he began to pick his way up the slope. To be captured alive by such men as the Scavengers was literally a fate worse than death.

Being careful with his leg, Noah slid from Blue as soon as he crossed the hill's brow. The events unfolding below had not as yet crystallized enough for him to determine what it was that had stirred them up or what their response would be. He watched lanterns as they moved through the streets of Sweetwater. They were too directed and not random enough to give the impression of a search, which meant they'd either found Elle or they were never looking for her in the first place. This should have brought some comfort but it did not. Uncertainty never sat easily upon him.

Back at their camp the horses were quickly and unceremoniously stripped of their pilfered acquisitions. Those things judged necessary for the coming days, as well as the all-important weapons, were redistributed between the two pack horses. Blue would only carry food and water for them both for one day. The rest, despite what they may have cost in time and effort, were discarded. He didn't even attempt to retrieve a canister of RTE's he dropped. They were left where they fell. The inconvenience of his leg reinforced how he had become dependent upon Elle. Without her, even with his strength, hefting the green box into place was awkward and consumed time he could ill afford to waste. There was a feeling of urgency as the last item was hurriedly strapped into place. The poor pack animals were loaded with as much food, water and other supplies as they could carry. It was unlikely he'd be returning to the wagon as he had an alternative place in mind. Everything was done and ready to go but Belle.

Humans are plagued by a host of fears and doubts. To appease them, even a man such as Noah, they plot their life's course to circumvent them if they can, confronting them only if they must. They arm themselves with beliefs, routine, habits and talismans in an attempt to bring some control, some order to nature's fickle indifference. Thus Noah wasted precious time attending to Belle's preparation as if the very act itself would alter Elle's fate. Against all logic, he felt that if he failed to adhere to this ritual it would expose his granddaughter to harm. Meticulously, the saddle was lifted and placed on the horse's back, followed by the saddle bags, rope and axe. Next the weapons, each secured into its rightful place. As was the custom, water for Elle and her mount, with enough food for two days were also safely secured into place. He hobbled around the horse, checking and rechecking. His hands never left the animal, gently stroking, calming her with word and touch. It is doubtful whether he, or anyone, could explain this need, but in ritual lay what it meant to be human. By the force of our will we cannot only control the flow of events but reel back time itself if necessary. He tucked the strap from the cinch into the loops and then allowed his head to rest on the hollow of the saddle. Leather is a living thing. When he'd given this saddle to his granddaughter it was brand new, sandy brown in colour. For nearly thirteen years, the sweat of a thousand rides, the oils rubbed into it by a caring hand had stained its surface to a rich mahogany. He straightened up, bracing himself for the task at hand.

He then remembered the dog. There was no whining. Cursing himself, he looked under the wagon. No dog. It was gone and it did not take an expert to see the animal had chewed through the rope. Bloody animal, he thought to himself. Where it had escaped to was anyone's guess and he did not have the time to look for it. The animal would have to fend for itself because he had to get moving.

Noah pulled himself up onto Blue. Though the distance was not far, there was an area where, had it not been moonless, they could have been seen by inhabitants of Sweetwater, silhouetted against the night's sky. Unfortunately the darkness would not last long. Soon the sun would breach the horizon. Before then he would be ready for another day in the wastelands. With a cursory look to see if the stupid mutt was lurking around, he started his descent westward.

The previous day, through force of a long-held habit, Noah had looked for an alternative to their current position should the hilltop prove untenable. In the unlikely event their presence in town was discovered, this bit of a peak might not be the first place they would search, but it would near the top of any list. What was needed was a most unlikely place, somewhere way down the list of probabilities, a place so near the bottom it could be justifiably ignored. He reasoned, if they did search, the Scavengers would expect an interloper to emerge from any direction but west – so the graveyard of a million soldiers would be such a place and the deeper, the better. With the aid of the binoculars he had mentally selected a possibility several kilometres west, parallel to the mountain highway. There, in a collection of rocky pinnacles and fractured outcrops, appeared to be a desirable nook, suitable cover to hide, to fight, and less than fifty metres from the southern side of a road that skirted a Before Time's lake, a lake that had once covered a substantial area in front of the of the town forcing the road to make a wide sweeping detour around its southern shore.

Halfway to their observation camp, lights, voices and activity seemed to be consolidating on the western side of town off to his right. Judging by the volume of noise drifting his way, a sizeable body of people had gathered there. Although it was too dark, too far away to be sure, Noah guessed it was coming from where the tanks were parked. This predawn gathering was a marked departure from the two previous mornings they had observed. Never one comfortable with coincidences, Noah guessed the gathering was in response to either their incursion in the warehouse or to Elle. He did not like either prospect. However, for the moment there was nothing he could do. With the false dawn softening the eastern sky Noah concentrated on selecting a route up the pebble-strewn slope leading to the pinnacles. The loose gravel endangered the heavily laden horses' balance with every step. As much as the situation demanded prudence, with the object of his efforts near and the sun fast encroaching, threatening to expose him, he was caught between the need to hurry and caution. This was neither the time nor the place for a mishap.

Concentrating on getting his charges hidden from the sun, he was not prepared for the roar of powerful engines springing into life. The noise shattered the serenity, drowning the distant hum of human activity and startling the horses, especially the two pack animals. "What the bloody hell was that?" growled Noah as he struggled to bring the animals under control before they did themselves harm. Directing his full attention to the skittish pack horses, Noah dropped Belle's reins. She'd follow him without the lead. The other two were another problem altogether. Given better circumstances and time, he would have preferred to dismount and soothe the frightened animals. He possessed neither for soon the rising sun would remove the night's protection, exposing them on this rocky rise to the enemy. Instead, securing their reins around the saddle horn and, using the brute strength of his horse, Noah drove Blue forward. The panicked horses were forced to follow.

The early roars soon subsided, diminishing to a dull throb. Moving in the greying light as briskly as he dared, Noah knew perfectly well what that noise was. The noise of powerful engines, while rare, was occasionally heard on the roads between the cities. The traders also had a number of large hybrid trucks used when time was most critical. After all the years the Scavengers had been labouring away here in Sweetwater, it looked to him as if their efforts were about to reach fruition. Perhaps this day all their secrets would be revealed. Excitement and anticipation mingled with his sense of loss – Belle's empty saddle was a tacit reminder of the cost of this personal quarrel. Again, even with the likelihood of Elle dying soon after, he should have returned home with her. He should not have permitted his vendetta to interfere with his daughter's request. He should not have broken a promise. The consolation that he might be in position to usurp a great threat posed by the re-emergence of the Scavengers would become a rather moot point if the only result was that he and Elle failed to return home.

What is the point of saving the world if you and those you love are not in it? What if the Scavengers' ambitions were thwarted and they were driven back into obscurity? What if he and Elle miraculously lived through this to return to the Farm? Would the Farm be any less isolated? Would it somehow miraculously recover, becoming the green fertile land it once was? Would humankind become anything more than pathetic remnants huddled in ever dwindling numbers? If another sixty years passed under these skies of interminable blue and life-robbing heat without a single drop of rain did it matter what happened here? When does the anger of one's youth become the bitter rage of an old man?

These and similar thoughts assaulted Noah. There was a time when he had sought the isolation of the wasteland and the comfort it brought. The loss of his parents, siblings, wife, child, friends drove him from the company of others lest they too, in his presence, succumb to the Dry's malevolence. Back then, at the conclusion of the Scavenger wars, he'd returned home to the Farm but had no intention of staying. He'd intended to drop off the horse his daughter had given him for Elle, have a meal, a bath and then ride off again. That had been the plan. Then there was a hand, so small that it could only grasp a single finger of his; a child, once placed upon Belle, exploding in pure delight and giggles; those eyes that even then looked so deep into his. What is a man but a part of a whole? So he'd stayed. And now Belle, with the empty saddle mocking him, followed Blue inside the pinnacles.

The last wooden peg was hammered, with persistence, into a small fissure in the rock surface. The sun was just above the eastern horizon and already Noah was soaked with sweat from the exertion of preparing the canopy while coping with a broken leg. Without its protection, these crevices of fractured earth would be Dante's hell tenfold, an inferno that could exceed fifty degrees Celcius by mid-afternoon. Even with all the water one could drink, without shade, this refuge would become unbearable. The lanyards fixed to the tarp's eyelets and looped over the hooks hung waiting for Noah's attention. With each of them pulled in turn before being tied off, the broad canvas rose into place.

The morning light filtered through the multi-coloured cloth created a soft vibrant range of different hues that quivered all around the enclosure as each breath of a breeze disturbed its surface. Noah took a long draft of water, held it in his mouth before swallowing, as he gazed up to admire his handiwork. "Not bad for a cripple."

One of the benefits of the Dry now worked in his favour; there was no aerial surveillance, no aeroplanes or drones of any kind to grace the sky this far west. If there had been, this colourful addition to the wasteland would have been impossible to miss. The erected shelter was rather large, considering the circumstances, and garish, a reminder of earlier times with his gypsy parents, but it lightened his heart. He and Elle had acquired this awning of many colours from Nic, spoils during their redistribution at Empty Cup. With it, barring discovery, he and the horses could sit among these crags, crevasses and shattered rocks all day without much discomfort.

By the time the sun had fully risen, everything that could be done had been done. Each of his weapons had been placed within easy reach. The long-barrelled rifle leaned against the wall, charged and loaded. The green crate had been opened and the contents removed and made ready. The family luck held for all this had been done within range of the Scavengers gathered less than four kilometres away. Situated on a slight rise, if a spring had existed within its confinement, this spot would have been ideal as it gave its inhabitants an undisputed 360 degree view. He watched the coming and goings underway in Sweetwater, but purposely avoided looking at the mountains' companions, as if the mere act would bring them down. He had seen enough to know what they could do to him if they so chose. For those soldiers whose skeletal remains he had unceremoniously removed upon arrival, this place must have seemed a sanctuary from the carnage taking place around them. It was not. The harbingers of death had found them cringing in terror within these walls and sucked the life from them. It might well happen again.

He looked out across this forgotten battlefield. Evidence of the massacre stretched before the mountains in both directions from his camp till it became lost between earth and sky. A million soldiers and their war material took up a lot of room. Only the old lake basin lay cleared of the events of that awful day. And now, so it would seem, where a million failed, a few hundred Scavengers were hopeful of success, and he had a prime position to watch if he wanted, interfere if he wished.

For the time being, brushing away the young scorpion that had wandered too close to his arm, all he had to do was wait to see why the Scavengers saw fit to start the motors of their tanks. He shifted his gaze toward Sweetwater. The binoculars clearly made out the bulk of those massive war machines. As he scanned the area there was a glimmer of hope he'd see Elle, having been delayed, working her way toward him. Seeing nothing, he looked back toward the summit of their previous camp, again in the hope he'd catch a glimpse of a descending figure be it her or the dog. Once more – nothing.

It had been a long tense night. Noah was thinking about having a bit to eat and maybe even a nap when the sudden distant gunning of powerful engines alerted him that the show might be about to begin. The binoculars focused on the five behemoths, tiny specks poised on the horizon. In line, they lunged forward, soon followed by a bevy of smaller vehicles. Noah was bewitched by the sight. It was as if he was witnessing the beginning of some heroic event as he watched them spill out of Sweetwater and straight down the road. The smaller vehicles, the armoured troop carriers, picked up speed and began to come from behind to take up positions along the flanks of the tanks. He could readily understand how inspirational a sight it must have been when such a frontal assault numbered in the thousands. For a man of the horse, it was terrifying as well as magnificent. Great plumes of dust rose, creating huge rooster tails behind the oncoming formation. Not since the southern wars, some forty years ago, had Noah seen anything resembling this. Faster than any horse he had ever ridden, they would cover the distance and pass his position in less than five minutes.

Noah put the binoculars down and heaved the portable rocket onto his shoulder. Whether he would actually intervene by firing on them was a decision he had not as yet made. However, should they veer off to the right as he suspected they might do before reaching his position it would leave him ineffective. In either case, there would be a few minutes yet. A deadly chill suddenly gripped him, as if an arctic breeze had somehow crept into his lair and travelled up his spine. Barely perceptible, another sound had joined the din of the engines and the clanking of steel treads. In the Before Times, it would have been likened to the sound of wind moving through the leaves of a forest; the hum of honey bees working a field of flowers or the drone of human voices far, far away. Here, in the Dry, in this graveyard, it was the harbinger of death. Noah lowered the handheld rocket and absentmindedly leaned it against the wall of earth where he stood. Picking up the field glasses he turned to focus on the peaks of the mountains.

The luminous silvery mist had begun to condense, briefly becoming an undulating ribbon caught by a powerful wind. Even as he watched, it appeared to swell and thicken, darkening into a deeper, more ominously impenetrable, grey body that draped itself along the mountain peaks. Noah stood transfixed, mesmerised. The Scavengers' intrusion, it seemed, had woken the mountains' Guardians or perhaps they had never been asleep, just waiting. The mist was rapidly undergoing a transformation right before his eyes. He wondered if this was what those men, whose corpses littered the landscape, had seen before they died. The previously faint twinkling points of pixie lights were fusing into long throbbing streaks of red, green, blue. The colours' brightness intensified all along its surface and began to throb as if driven by a beating heart. Tight bundles of light broke away only to explode like fireworks of the Before Times. He had seen that before, it was his 'fireflies'.

The activity of the Guardians certainly did not appear hesitant or sluggish. The speed at which the cloud was responding to the threat of the approaching Scavengers was astonishing. Within seconds a bulge formed along its side, opposite the oncoming Scavengers. Perhaps a hundred metres or more wide, it quickly enlarged into an inflamed distended boil. Then, as if under tremendous pressure, the huge amorphous mass spilled lahar-like down the face of the mountain. Lines of pulsating colours poured into the breach and raced along its length to converge on the leading edge. So dense were these lines of flashing colours becoming, it seemed as though the front of the torrent had been set ablaze. Noah imagined such a force, for it gave all the appearance of an avalanche, would have displaced great quantities of rocks. Not so. Though it gave the impression of mass, it acted more like a weightless vapour for all the damage it did, gliding like he would imagine a Before Time fog. But this fog was not silent – there was the noise. The cicada-like noise he'd heard had greatly increased, strengthening from the previous barely audible intrusion to a thunderous volume challenging that of the Scavenger's combined mechanized force.

The hairs on the back of his neck rose. His mouth dried. For the first time in memory Noah felt the taste of fear. "Bloody hell, what have they done?"

He shifted his attention back to the oncoming Scavengers. If they had noticed the events now occurring on the mountains, it did not alter their headlong charge. Though partly obscured in billowing dust, they were close enough now to be observed through the binoculars in detail. Each of the lightly armoured troop carriers had several men stationed on top and dressed in what had to be biological/chemical clothing, enclosed hood and all, manning what appeared to be some sort of short barrelled cannon. The battle tanks had similarly dressed men sitting on either side of the cylinder manning the same short barrelled cannon. However, they were facing back pointing their 'cannon' to the rear of the formation. Odd, thought Noah. He had never seen anything like it and was completely at a loss as to their purpose. He found himself asking himself, considering what awaited them, why have men dressed like that sitting exposed on the outside? What were they expecting to achieve? More to the point, in the heat of the Dry, how could anyone remain suited up like that for long? Just sitting in the shade as he was now, sweat pouring from every pore on his body, he could not help but think what must it be like inside one of those suits. They had to be just this side of insane. But then again, they were Scavengers.

Feeling vaguely voyeuristic, safely tucked away within the protective pinnacles, Noah switched his attention again to the mountains. The leading edge of the 'mist' had lifted up from the rocky surface bending into an 'S' shaped curve that extended out from the mountain. As it did so, it began to flatten and broaden, not unlike the spreading hood of a viper. There was lightning; each brilliantly coloured flash illuminated the head's interior, turning it momentarily translucent. It was an awesome sight as the form continued its plunge downward with its head extending out and over the plains. The head was at least five hundred metres wide now and so dense that its shadow could be seen racing along below.

Every nerve in his body urged him to leave. Like those before him, if he wanted to live, now was the time to go. No foraging, no lingering, no packing – mount Blue and flee.

He would not. He could not. Noah was imprisoned by his loyalty. The very thought of abandoning his granddaughter paralysed him, rooting him in place. Until he knew she was out of harm's way or dead he could not act to save his life. In every sense of the word, he literally was unable to entertain thoughts of his escape, his survival. A fatal flaw? If so, then he shared this flaw with generations of his kind. Whether it be family or friend, for Noah it was simple; where you stand, so shall I. This remained true even if he had no idea where Elle was at the moment.

In the briefest time, the hooded viper – he could not see it as anything else but a serpent – gained the valley floor and in doing so slowly raised its head further as if preparing to strike the approaching Scavengers. He half expected to see fangs. Coloured flashes dashed along the entire length of its body. Noah was starting to realise he had greatly erred. The event now unfolding before him was not as he had imagined. Here was something he had never considered. This thing was not, as he had assumed, a mindless, senseless creation. This apparition was driven by an intelligence that could modify and adapt to the changes in its surrounding circumstances.

His world's last great attempt to penetrate this mountainous fortress had been a military enterprise that comprised over a million men and women and had occupied both the land and air. Its battlefront had extended over two hundred kilometres on either side of Sweetwater and more than fifty kilometres in depth. Its destruction had not been piecemeal. Except for those units stationed farther back from the mountains, the army had died en masse. It had been obliterated in one all-encompassing, unrelenting onslaught. Was this about to happen now as the Guardians faced this latest human threat? Its effort was controlled, concentrated and deliberate. This hooded spectre had only expanded enough to meet the formation of the oncoming Scavengers. It knew.

The formation sped past Noah's position. He could have easily killed several of the exposed men and still had time to target one of the tanks with the rocket. He did neither. At the moment Noah was uncertain just who the real enemy was. He was surprised by an admiration for what these intrepid foes of his had achieved in Sweetwater. To maintain such precision at speed while navigating around the numerous obstacles strewn along their path illustrated remarkable discipline, a discipline he would have previously thought was beyond their capabilities. From his experience, their tactics had been more primordial: rip, slash and bludgeon. What he was witnessing would have taken many long hours of practice and a great quantity of fuel to reach that level of proficiency. Proficiency, from his perspective should always be admired, even when found in your enemy. So he had a half-formed hope they'd succeed. Of course, in the event that they were successful... the thought hung there, uncompleted. The irony was not lost on him that he too had employed the same methods of rip, slash and bludgeon when he thought it had been necessary. Right now, he acknowledged that the opportunity to participate in inflicting damage was momentarily lost. Until he knew Elle's whereabouts, he was reluctant to risk his life needlessly. Pending a change in circumstance, Noah would be a passive observer. One thing he was certain of was that once he found Elle and made her safe, the Scavengers would again have reason to fear him.

Two hundred metres further on there was a long gentle rise of the land that led from the road and onto the lake bed. There the formation turned and, having gained access to the lake bed, headed in a more northerly direction. If he had had any lingering doubts that this was a wild directionless charge by the Scavengers, such a deliberate and well-orchestrated movement removed them. The Scavengers had an objective in mind. Extending their present line of travel to the base of the mountains, he could detect nothing of note with his binoculars. Yet there had to be something there, even if he could not see it. He'd have to wait to see what unfolded. Deadly persistent the Scavengers were, stupid they were not. Noah trained his sights back on the Guardians. The viper slithered further out into the old lake, shifting its position to compensate for the Scavengers' change of direction.

Noah lowered the field glasses to stare at the receding dust cloud. What rabbit could they possibly hope to pull out of a hat to prevent sharing the fate of those whose remains were strewn the length and breadth of these plains? He lifted the binoculars back to his eyes. On the flats, clear of obstacles, the vehicles picked up speed, hurling themselves toward the arched viper's head. It would not be long now, mused Noah. He then recognized that he had been holding his breath. About to allow a smile at his fascination, Noah sharply inhaled instead. From the dust and the lines of rippling heat, a mirage, a lone spindly figure, emerged from behind a derelict cruise boat. The binoculars fell from his hands to shatter on the stone floor. The rocket launcher was wrenched from its resting place.

Cursing his awkwardness and the loss of his prized field glasses, Noah cut through the reins of the two pack horses, acknowledging that he might not be coming back. He knew they were unlikely to wander until hunger or thirst drove them elsewhere. Grabbing Blue's reins, he slammed the rifle into its scabbard and slung another on his back. The launcher was precariously balanced on the front of his saddle as he heaved himself up. He then manoeuvred Blue alongside Belle and, reached down to grab her lead. Fortunately, neither animal had been relieved of either water or provisions. With a glance around to ensure he had what would be needed, for it was unlikely he would return, Noah edged Blue out of the pinnacles by a flick of the reins.

The violence of Blue's surge forward nearly toppled him as they sprang out of the enclosure. With total disregard, they plunged down the embankment and across the road and then down onto the lake bed. Noah leaned forward in the saddle, shouting encouragement, urging Blue to even greater efforts, as he flicked the reins' ends back and forth across the horse's neck. The distance wasn't great, less than four kilometres, but there was no time left. Fully aware that he could not arrive before the collision between the Scavengers and Guardians, minutes away, he needed to try.

Chapter Twenty-Five

Where you stand, so shall I, though the gates of hell open before us.

Others were also disturbed by the distant roar of fuel powered engines and the corresponding rustling of leaves. The night sky had not yet relinquished the darkness to the rising sun when Elle, troubled by the far off rumbling, tried to wake. Deep in a kind of waking dream, she struggled to distinguish between the two. Even when she finally succeeded, it was only a partial victory. Groggy, disoriented and covered in dust-encrusted sweat, she was finding it very hard to focus her thoughts. For one thing, it was unbearably hot. Slowly she became conscious enough to recognize at least one possible source of her discomfort. The dog had found her and curved itself within the hollow of her body to join her in sleep. During colder times this would have been welcomed, even encouraged, an endearing act much sought after by its human companion. In the Dry such an act was less welcome. It was like wearing a fleece-lined coat. Elle did not act upon her impulse to shove the dog away from her. The nightmares had not yet dispersed, were too fresh. Instead, she gave the dog an approving scratch behind its ears, while easing herself back to allow the stirring of a morning breeze to pass between them.

It took several minutes to realize her flight from Sweetwater had ended in the middle of the lake bed. It was a mostly empty place. Except for the occasional boat or two and a surprising number of crumpled aircraft, it was free of military hardware and human remains. During the war, if extinction could be called war, there had been a dying but swampy lake here, a major impediment to a mechanized army. The lake was long gone. Other than the dog, Elle's only company was dust devils that momentarily appeared only to dissolve as the puff of wind lost interest. The front of her clothes was covered in dog hair and wringing wet. The feeble breezes that stirred up dust devils had a comforting effect on her skin as the moisture evaporated.

In a continued state of thick- headedness, Elle stared up at the mountains. At this distance she could see the effects of the war on the mountain. Countless numbers of craters pockmarked much of its surface, some so massive she wondered how anything had survived such punishment. And yet they must have. The sun, reflected from the shimmering mist, enhanced the impression of a living, silvery sea, her living sea. Richer and more densely packed than the night sky, billions of stars twinkled within. She got the feeling that the mountain's lofty residents appeared somehow more bulky than she remembered from the day before. Of course it was possible that she was confusing the dream with reality. Still… She switched her attention to the rising sun. Her mother had told her that she was born just as the first rays of morning had pierced the windows of the bedroom.

Turning her attention back to the dog to give it a rough rub along its neck, she told it, "Today I am fourteen." The dog reacted to the attention only to have its muzzle gently pushed aside as it attempted to give that fourteen-year-old face a lick. She smiled at her companion as she remembered the first time. "You almost got me again." She gave the dog another rub while breathing out a long soft sigh. There seemed so much left undone. She wondered if her mother would ever know what had happened to her. The dreams last night were explicit; on this day, absurd as it sounded sitting in the middle of a dead lake, she was to die by drowning. There should have been fear in that realization; instead there was a feeling of incompleteness. Fourteen years was not nearly long enough, but that was all the time she was going to have. The sea, the Guardians, would come down to claim her. Like a river following its course, this was her path. She was required to be here. Her hand moved to touch the ring that hung around her neck. The ring felt unnaturally warm. Almost – her thoughts paused at the notion – almost as if the warmth was coming from the ring itself. She let go of the ring but left it outside, resting on the shirt. The action elicited a tiny twinge, a reminder that, if the sea did not claim her, the Scavenger's knife wound would. It was becoming more painful. The fabric of the shirt that lay over the wound was stiff from the drying of small droplets, a mixture of pus and blood, which oozed between the stitches. Looking at up at the Guardians she said, "At least I won't die of septicaemia."

She was hungry and thirsty and suspected the dog was the same. Fortunately her backpack held a bit of food. Nothing flash, she had not expected to be in the middle of the lakebed, but it would take the edge off. The flask at her side would quickly remedy the thirst. She got up, removing the pack as she walked over to the nearest point of shade. The dog followed. Their destination was a relic of a more bountiful world. Attached to an anchor by a long link chain and left to rot, a flat-bottomed boat, maybe fifteen metres long, lay abandoned. Suspended along the whole of its length on both sides were the vestiges of its once colourful and festive flags, pennants and lights. The deck was a shambles of chairs, tables. Still tethered to the metal frame, tattered stripes of canopy that once protected the ship's clients from the sun and inclement weather flapped in the rising wind. Finding a good spot in its lee, they both sat down.

The canteen top took an unexpected amount of effort to remove. I must be getting weak, she thought. Taking a small sip, she held it in her mouth for a few seconds as was the custom before swallowing and then ran her tongue across her dry lips. The dog looked hopeful and since the canister was full, a liberal portion was poured into the cup and placed on the sand where it immediately vanished. From the pack Elle extracted a creation of Noah's consisting of bread dough, dried meat and any herbs or vegetables or anything that was handy at the time. Mixed and all rolled together, it was baked in the coals of the fire. Elle usually enjoyed her grandfather's culinary labours but often one needed stronger teeth and bigger jaw muscles than most humans possessed. As they had not benefited from their raid on the Scavenger's warehouse, this particular effort suffered from the lack of any seasoning but salt, and the only thing close to a vegetable was if the rabbit had eaten some. Still it was better than an empty stomach. The dog had no complaints at all. It was just happy to get something and wolfed down all that was on offer.

The wasteland was not normally a place for boats of any kind and under different circumstances Elle's curiosity would have gotten the better of her. However, impending death has a tendency of diluting your normal urges. She showed little interest, either in the boat or the mountain peaks. She took another bite of meal-bread followed by a sip of water to help wash it down. Cocooned in her thoughts, the nosiness that would usually have compelled her to climb aboard and explore was subdued. From her current perspective, what was the point? It was just another dilapidated relic decaying in the wastelands. Allowing herself a few more minutes of depression and misery, with eyes closed, Elle buried her head in the folds of her arms.

Finding the position only made her sweat more, with eyes still closed, she raised her head and leaned back letting it rest against the boat's peeling hull. Unable to fully extract herself from the previous night's dreams, caught between sleep and wakefulness, she opened her eyes and watched the mountain Guardians.

Their fabric had changed.

The dog edged closer as if seeking reassurance. She wondered if the dog sensed the presence of the area's macabre inventory, its ghostly inhabitants, or was there something else? In keeping with her sobriety Elle dismissed such thoughts out of hand. Save perhaps the density of the dead and the way they died, what was it that made this place different from other places she had ridden through where the dead lay where they fell? Was this place any different than the Cleansing? After all, the wastelands were awash with ghosts. Again she looked up at the mountains. Maybe this was the beginning. Perhaps the Guardians were waking and preparing to come for her.

She placed her hand on the dog's head. Was it about to share her fate? If so, they'd both come a long way to die. Not that it mattered much where you died, here or at home. "Small change", a term her grandfather had once said to her concerning a trivial matter. Small change when compared to the billions that had perished from the lack of water, at the hands of others and the Sorrow. Elle stroked the dog, allowing the dream's visions of her own death to not so much ebb away as become a thing of little importance. "We all die; it is only the place, the time and circumstances that change." In all that had come before, why should her death matter more than any other? She was indeed small change. She closed her eyes again. At least dying this way, out here, alone, was better than thinking such a death would include others she knew and cared about. The dreams had been clear – she died and she died alone. Well, technically not alone. She could feel the dog's heartbeat beneath her fingers.

Not only was that far away noise becoming irritating in its persistence, it was also becoming louder and uncomfortably near. Eyes squeezed tight, she concentrated in an attempt to overlook its intrusion, hoping by doing so it would desist. She might have been successful if the ground had not started to vibrate beneath her. The worried whine from the dog and the accompanying clanking and roar demolished any efforts on her part to stay absorbed in her own impending demise.

There had been no roaring, clanking and banging in her dreams, so if this was death, it was all wrong. She snatched up the rifle and loaded a round without thought; for Elle, it was as automatic as drawing breath. The boat's gunwales were too high for her to see over or easily climb so she scooted over to its bow. Dropping onto her stomach, she eased herself forward and peered around to see the source of the commotion. To her eternal shame, like a frightened little girl, she let out a high pitched scream. Completely alien and totally unexpected, the sight of the Scavengers' battle squadron bearing down on her position was too much even for Elle.

Terrified, she scampered back from the bow to huddle with the dog, expecting any second to be confronted and killed. The noise was deafening, numbing her ability to control her bodily functions. She wet herself. Sitting there pressed against the boat's hull, tightly grasping an equally frightened dog, Elle could only believe that she had been horribly wrong. This indeed was how she was going to die. This thought had the reverse effect from what she had expected. To die this way was acceptable, almost a relief. She had not killed the child; she would not drown in a silvery sea; and no one would ever know that she had been frightened enough to pee her pants. Elle huddled hard against the hull, grasping the dog tightly to her chest, waiting for the killers to come find her.

To her astonishment, the formation sped past without the slightest hesitation, completely uninterested in her whereabouts, leaving her choking on the dust from their wake and utterly mystified.

In zero visibility, Elle suddenly realized just how tightly she had been holding the dog. Much to its relief, she let go and then stood up. She brushed off as much dust as she could before reaching down to picked up her pack and sling it onto her shoulder. She retrieved the rifle from where it had been unceremoniously dropped in her haste to get away and checked that it was not damaged. Still attempting to rid her clothing of a few layers of dust, surrounded by clouds of twirling sand, Elle stepped out from behind the boat to stand in the middle of the tracks left by the retreating column. If they did not come for me… The thought died the moment she looked up at the mountains.

The sight that met her eyes was stupefying. Her dreams had suddenly been greatly exceeded by reality.

The Guardians were menacingly beautiful. Entranced, she watched the coloured pulses rapidly accelerate along the length of the enormous body, merging into multiple lines that beat in syncopated unison. The head, its coloured ringlets ablaze, throbbing in sympathy, reared back further and paused to hover above the approaching Scavengers. In that moment she stopped breathing as the world shifted into slow motion. Not unlike a leaf, the monstrous head seemed to drift down to embrace the assembled battle formation. As it approached ever closer the world suddenly returned to normal time and the sky erupted. Flares, ten, twenty, thirty or more, shot skyward, intercepting the descending Guardians before exploding. Fire abruptly enveloped much of the serpent's head as long fingers of liquid flame following the path of the flares arched upward, slicing through, dismembering the descending appendage. The monster dissolved amidst billowing clouds of oily black smoke and orange red heat, leaving fiery droplets to rain to earth. The men atop the vehicles swivelled their cannons back and forth, raking the air around and above, while the flame from the main guns followed the severed stump as it recoiled beyond the fire's reach.

The retreating Guardians melted into a darkening mass atop the mountains where all movement then ceased. No twinkling lights, no rippling ribbon; a stillness pervaded the whole of its formless body, as if considering its options. Yesterday's silvery mist sprinkled with dots of light congealed into an opaque mass, black as onyx. The Scavengers, however, pressed forward, either ignorant of the ominous alteration or so resolute the possible significance did not matter.

Elle felt an annoying distraction. Even through her shirt, the ring that hung from her neck was becoming uncomfortably warm. Without taking her eyes from the battle unfolding before her, she reached up to confirm this sensation with a touch. The moment her fingers touched the ring a signal passed from her to the summit. Like a river in flood suddenly released from its confining levees, a torrent, five kilometres wide and more than a hundred metres high, tore down the mountain toward the Scavengers, toward her. A wave of pain surged through her, almost driving Elle to her knees.

More flares shot up from each of the vehicles, exploding into the oncoming mass. The figures atop the vehicles, awkward in their suits, scrambled to swivel their weapons to meet the renewed onslaught, a descending wall of an impenetrable blackness. The moment it came into range the men compressed the triggers and once again plumes of smoke and flames slammed into the advancing cloud, presenting, it was hoped, an equally impenetrable wall of searing heat. The torrent and Scavengers collided within the conflagration. The inferno scythed through the front of the deluge, hollowing out a cavern two hundred metres wide at its base. The men played their plumes of fire upon the face of the flood, evaporating all that the flames could touch.

Where it could not, the flood passed unimpeded. It was as if the Scavengers had entered a tunnel and as the depth lengthened, the flood closed behind. They were enclosed, entombed as the black 'waters' surged up and over the formation. It appeared to Elle as if the entire battle formation been swallowed. Save for tinnitus like chirping sparrows in her ears, the howl of the fire and machines faded and then it was gone.

So engrossed was she in the convoy's death throes, neither the sound of the approaching horses nor the barking of the dog alerted Elle to Noah's arrival. It was only his quick reaction that prevented him being skewered by her knife when he touched his granddaughter's shoulder. She stared in disbelief at the man who stood there holding her by the wrist and shoulder. They both looked down at the knife blade, millimetres from its target. A half sob, half laugh was wrenched from Elle as the two collapsed into each other's arms, the surrounding conflict momentarily forgotten. Further yelps from the dog allowed them barely time to turn and face the oncoming wall. Neither noticed the intense glow that radiated from the stone in the ring and the handle of the knife. At the instant of inundation, all of them were enveloped within a cocoon the colour of an angry sea.

Chapter Twenty-Six
Most changes come without permission.

Elle sat up in agony. Down to cellular level it seemed her whole body was a citadel of suffering. She had a raging headache, so intense she could barely focus her eyes. She was thirsty; she couldn't remember ever being so thirsty. Her throat and tongue were swollen, so much so that each intake of breath felt like a rasp being drawn along their surfaces. She fumbled for her canteen with some difficulty. Her body was sluggish, unresponsive and reluctant to cooperate. Almost weeping in frustration, she finally managed to free it from her hip, and placed it in her lap. The hand, the fingers that twisted the screw top looked like dry, brittle parchment, an old woman's hand. The palm looked red, almost as if it had been scalded. She faintly remembered the handle of the knife feeling like metal left in the sun. Barely conscious, confused, she stared at the hands that held the canteen, suppressing the desperate urge to gratify this need for water. Years of training and experience did not relinquish its hold upon her. She hesitated, gained control before raising the flask to her lips and took the smallest of sips, just enough to moisten the interior of her mouth. Even then she held it and ever so slowly swallowed. A portion of the water, a single drop had formed and then fell from her lower lip to disappear in mid-flight. Another sip, then another, each like the one before, constrained. She sat in the dust and dirt, taking one small drink after another till the throbbing in her head became more bearable.

People of the wastelands are schooled in the art of survival. A healthy person, exposed and unprotected, can die from sunstroke in a matter of hours. The same is true with severe dehydration. The organs of the body simply shut down. Although she had never been this dehydrated, she knew the symptoms. She was dangerously close to irreversible damage. Once crossed, there was nothing anyone could do; she would die from organ failure. She needed a good deal of water, but it was vital to limit the initial intake to small amounts. "Saved the organs, but killed the patient." Elle took another small sip from the canteen and then looked around. Noah, the dog and the horses lay crumpled on the sand like puppets whose strings had been cut. For several minutes she didn't move or make any attempt to aid her grandfather. To be of any good to anyone, including herself, it was important she attend to her own recovery first. Being severely dehydrated, any exertion could make her pass out.

Careful of the tenuous hold she had on consciousness, Elle studied Noah. He was lying face down with his head turned toward her. She wanted to touch him but she was afraid that he might be dead. Just as she had done when she came upon the man lying on slope leading up to the house, she waited to see if the dust would be disturbed by an exhaled breath. This time, however, the breath dispersed across the earth's surface like a droplet of oil spreading on water. She cupped her hand in front of her mouth and exhaled. She drew in a deep breath and exhaled again and then again. Upon each exhaled breath a swirl of ethereal colour danced in the air before her. This was just too much to deal with at the moment. She dropped her hand and then placed a finger on Noah's neck – a pulse, weak but steady. At least he was alive. The bodies of the dog and the horses lay just beyond him. They too showed signs of life by the slight rise and fall of their chests. A number of minutes passed before she felt strong enough to turn him onto his back. Then there was the dog. It was lying so close to Noah she was fearful that he might end up rolling on top of the unconscious animal. She reached over and dragged the dog around Noah and out of the way. They had been through too much together for her to jeopardize its life.

Elle pulled her pack to put under Noah's head. At this point she had to stop and rest. She took another small sip, wishing she'd not been so liberal with the water earlier, and then tilted his head back, allowing a few drops to fall toward his lips. To her astonishment, each drop, as it left the canister's rim, vanished. Not sure what to make of what she had seen she lowered the canteen to his lips. This time the water did not vanish. He swallowed. She undid the pack and took out a small fold of cloth, soaked it with water before placing part of it into his mouth. To her joy, like a newborn, her grandfather started sucking on the cloth. She again soaked the cloth before securing the lid back on the canteen. He remained unconscious but at least his breathing seemed deeper, almost normal.

Satisfied she had done all she could for him at the moment, she crawled over to the inert horses to see if her grandfather had brought water. "Good old granddad," she said, patting one of several water containers. There was nothing she could do for the horses other than remove their burdens, which she did by undoing the cinches. Other than that, the horses would have to wait until Noah came around. The dog on the other hand she could help. She refilled her canteen from one canister and again watched in bewilderment as any stray droplet disappeared before it reached the sand. There was no puddle beneath the canister and there should have been. She hadn't been that careful. She took a long draft of the warm clear liquid and then deliberately tilted the flask to see what happened. None of the water reached the ground. As in the other instances, it vanished. Profoundly mystified, too much weirdness to be taken in at once, she turned her attention to the problem of the dog.

Fatigued by her efforts, she lay down next to the dog, held a water-soaked cloth to its mouth and squeezed. Over the next few minutes, using this method, she alternated between her grandfather and the dog until they both seemed to be responding to having something to drink. Her headache was subsiding, strength was returning as well as awareness. She took a deep breath, let it out slowly, ignoring the dancing colours, and looked up at the sky. There was no real sky or, at least, no washed out blue. No sun either. A jumble of remembered images tumbled into her consciousness: the black wall rushing toward her, the Scavengers and their war machines, Noah standing by her, the ring. The ring? She reached up to grasp the ring which was now cool to the touch. The stone was gone. Thinking perhaps that it might have just fallen out, Elle crawled slowly back over to search the area where they had been standing. She saw the knife lying half buried in the sand. It was minus its handle. The knife's beautifully formed grip was completely gone leaving nothing but its naked steel tang. What was going on here? Then, recalling the green mist and the sense of heat from the knife, she turned over her right hand and looked at the palm.

For the first time since regaining consciousness Elle began a careful survey of her surroundings, but feeling rather fragile, she did so while trying to move as little as possible. Nothing seemed normal – neither the sky, nor the sun or to be more precise, their absence. There was no breeze, nor was she being pestered by flying insects. Her skin was very dry, with no sweating. For that matter, where was the heat? Where was the ever-present heat? It was almost as if she was in a room of some kind although it was one with no clear walls or ceiling. Panic began to rise in her, but this was no time for hysterics; after all she was still alive, wasn't she? In her head she could hear her grandfather's voice. "Stay calm, everything has an explanation, even if you don't have a clue what it is." She picked up the handle-less knife, returned it to its scabbard and then looked over at Noah and the others. They were all still breathing, if ever so softly.

Elle stood up on wobbly legs that seemed uncertain that they could carry even her slender frame. A couple of hesitant steps brought her before the translucent wall that seemed to have enclosed them. Her hand rose up to touch it only to quickly withdraw her finger. The 'touch', like a pebble tossed into a pool, set off ever expanding ringlets of colour. Curious, she started to reach out again but this time the part of the wall in front of her extended a 'hand' and touched her. Startled, the touch was so unexpected, Elle stumbled back to fall onto her backside. That she was stunned at the unpredicted response was a gross understatement. Nevertheless she sat there for only a heartbeat or two and was about to get back up when the wall in front of her quivered. About a metre up the wall, as if from an invisible tap, poured a silvery stream that fell into an equally invisible receptacle. It was like watching a crystal goblet fill, only this goblet was moulded into the sprawled figure of a long legged, thin framed not-yet woman. It looked like mercury. Noah had once showed her a small beaker containing this mysterious liquid and by way of demonstrating its metallic fluidity, he poured it into another glass container. This 'liquid' had that same shimmering quality. As the process concluded, Elle found herself starring at an unblinking seated replica of herself. The ring, the boots, the creases and folds of her pants and shirt, down to the last detail, it was perfect. The voice in her head asked if it was all right to panic now.

Too taken aback to respond, Elle sat motionless, as did her replica. At first she thought maybe it was some kind of statue, until the replica blinked. When it blinked again she realized that she must have blinked as well. Elle raised her hand and placed it on her ring; the replica did the same, but unlike a reflection from a mirror. No delay at all. A real-time mime, thought Elle, reaching up to scratch her nose as did the replica.

"My name is Elle, what's yours?" asked Elle, giving her replica a wave as she spoke. In unison, the replica mouthed word for word and duplicated the wave exactly as well, but no sound issued from its 'lips'. Elle was puzzled; could the thing even hear? Appearing to speak was only its continued mimicry. It must have some means of 'seeing' since it had copied her every move. Thirsty, Elle pulled out her canteen and took a swallow. Her replica did likewise. Remembering the vanishing water, Elle tipped the canister enough to allow a small amount to trickle out. Not a single drop reached the sand. It vanished as it had done before. The silvery liquid from her twin's did the same.

Just as she would have with her cousin, Chook, Elle signed, "You're not easily fooled." Her replica mimicked every movement precisely. On impulse, she made the sign for water while allowing a few drops to spill from the canteen. Just as before, the droplets of water disappeared as they fell. She repeated the sign for water again while simultaneously tipping out one more drop of water. Her reflection copied each gesture and sign without flaw. Again and again Elle repeated the sign for water while allowing a few drops to escape the canteen's rim. Again and again the silvery figure echoed each movement in turn.

Elle was beginning to wonder if the creature had any intelligence at all, other than this display of mimicry. There was no telling how much time had passed as there were no visual indicators inside the dome, but she was faint from hunger and her head still ached. Sliding the canister back into its holster she got up to get some food and to check on Noah and the animals. Unexpectedly, she found that Noah was awake and sitting up with the dog's head in his lap. Its tail swished from side to side in greeting.

Anticipating her question, Noah smiling at the quizzical look on his granddaughter's face said, "A few minutes. Had to do something to stop the dog licking my face." Elle looked past her grandfather at the two horses. Following her glance, Noah nodded. "I think they're ok. I've been able to get some water down them but it will be a while yet before we'll know for sure. It will be better if they can roll over on to their chests." Examining the shrivelled skin on his arm, "At least one of the mysteries might be solved; how to murder an entire army." By way of demonstration he pinched a piece of skin on his forearm and then let go. The flap stayed. "No plasticity. When they rolled over us they somehow were able to suck fluid from our bodies. Any more than they did and we would have joined the army." He nodded in the direction of the convoys. "I suspect the Scavengers didn't fare any better so, as soon as we feel up to it, it might be a good idea for us to go and check."

Elle was astonished by Noah's miraculous display of self-control. As if being shrivelled nearly to death and confined within the interior of an invisible room with his granddaughter and her doppelganger was commonplace, not worthy of a mention.

Handing her a large chunk of meal-bread, he calmly inquired "So who's your friend?"

Elle looked over her shoulder at the figure which had not moved since her departure. "The Guardian, or rather a very small portion of it I suppose," she said before turning back to face him. She was taking another huge bite and about to continue her conversation despite having a mouth full of bread when she caught Noah pointing. Her 'friend' was quietly sitting just behind her, chewing. It even had a replica of the meal-bread in its hand. "Bit unnerving," signed Elle, noticing that her twin did the same. The dog, curious as ever, sniffed the silvery figure and, apparently unsatisfied with the information, squatted to pee on its foot before walking off to take a position beside Elle.

Noah suppressed any visible sign of his unease. Whatever this thing was, he was determined to show neither it nor Elle any sign of disquiet. None of this would get the better of him.

The figure took no notice of the animal's action, but Elle and Noah did. Not a drop of urine could be seen, either on the Elle image or on the sand. "Now that's spooky. I think that might be due to it being dehydrated," said Noah.

"Yes it is, but you haven't seen anything yet. Watch this." Elle demonstrated the disappearing water trick. He had watched this effect from across the dome. Up close, the action of Elle and the replica was even more impressive. She replaced the cap and moved past her image so the two were side on to Noah. Putting a hand behind her back hidden from view she signed "What is she doing?"

"Same as you," came her grandfather's signed reply.

In a spat of annoyance Elle said "This is getting me nowhere. It would certainly be a lot easier if I knew what it was thinking or if it thinks at all. For all I know I might as well be signing in front of a mirror. Noah, do you think it has any intelligence or emotions and if it does, what does it feel about us?"

Noah looked over at his granddaughter "I have no idea, girl, but watching them attack the Scavengers, I'm sure these Guardians possess intelligence in some form. As to them having emotions, I have no way of knowing."

Smirking at the thought, Elle responded wistfully, "Well you would have to admit it would be a handy talent if you could read someone's emotions. Sure would prevent any misunderstandings of another's intent."

Noah just smiled wryly. He would never want that particular talent. There were times when even he did not want to feel the emotions he carried. Too many ghosts.

Perhaps it was frustration or maybe just being tired, but when Elle attempted to take the top off the canteen for a drink, the canister slipped from her hand to fall with a muffled thud on the ground. Panicked at the thought of losing water, she instinctively stooped down to retrieve the container before much of its precious cargo was lost. This time the water that gurgled out onto the sand formed a small puddle before being absorbed by the dry, thirsty earth. Curious, thought Elle as she secured the top back on. The water didn't disappear. Nor had the image imitated her. It remained seated. On impulse, Elle removed the lid again and let the water spill out. Once again the water, unlike previously, didn't simply vanish. Dimples in the sand where the water had fallen were ringed by moisture. Elle signed 'water'. The silvery figure did nothing but sit there. Elle repeated the action of allowing a few drops of water to fall and was about to make the sign for water when the figure's 'hand' moved, making the sign for 'water'. Astonished by the replica's response, Elle replied by nodding 'yes' before recovering to make the sign for 'water'.

Grinning at her replica's apparent attempt to communicate, Elle was about call out to Noah when she was gripped by a rush of mind-numbing pain even more intense than before. It was so concentrated that it felt as if her brain had ignited. She cried out, pressing both hands hard against her skull. Reeling back under the assault, she collapsed to the ground convulsing. Struggling to stay conscious, her mind filled with emotions, raw and undiluted – bright, sharp-edged, penetrating emotions that collided and merged with her own as they tore at her thoughts. They fused with every memory, every refuge, every secret and private place. A flood of sensations surged and raged within her. Sixty years of emotional history coursed through her. Battered by the unfettered terror of millions as they died out here all around the lake bed, she was disintegrating, fragmenting into a billion tiny shards. All that was 'Elle' was eroding, dissolving and leaking away.

Just when she thought she could bear no more, a memory, a single slender tendril, her mother's voice, drifted into reach. She grasped this memory and pulled it toward her. With it came others, the warmth of her mother's skin, the smell of her breath. Just as one teased thread from a spinning wheel, she gathered memories, her father's laughter, his dry sense of humour, his comfort; he was a safe place for a child. Her first jump, her feeling of joy as Belle cleared the fence by the barn. The thrill of racing her grandfather and Blue across the wasteland, sitting among the Traders and the taste of their strange foods and the faces of the men whose lives she had taken, Nic's face; each precious memory and its accompanying emotions she gathered to herself. And from these memories, she remembered who and what she was. She remembered. The roar inside her head subsided to a whisper, the fury a sigh, and in the ensuing silence, she sensed the presence of others.

Lying inert in the dirt, Elle felt the disembodied emotions of others gently lapping at the fringes of her awareness. Oblivious to her physical surroundings, she listened, as if in an adjoining room, to this unintelligible ebb and flow of garbled 'voices'. Strange, alien and uninhibited emotions strove for her attention. Most seemed far away, like voices from across a field. A few, though, resonated closer at hand. All seemed confused, disoriented. Just as a person can concentrate on a single conversation while ignoring all the others in a crowded room, Elle strove to focus on one 'voice'. Like selecting from a bundle of thin strands of light, she traced a flow of emotions to its source, a whirling pool of colours. She felt herself mentally reach out to touch the pool. In an instant the pool galvanized, acknowledging her presence. The dog beside her yelped and almost overwhelmed her fragile state by its enthusiastic greeting. Dogs, as she was to later find with other animals, do not have the emotional complexity or subtle undertones of humans. They are disproportionably black and white with few greys, but they can be as penetrating. After her recent ordeal, it was rejuvenating to be immersed in such unqualified joy and thus very difficult to disengage. However, Elle was inexplicably drawn toward another strand of light.

It bore little resemblance to that of the dog. This time, there was no passivity, no waiting pool. Anger, anxiety, frustration, fear, grief, helplessness, loss and above all, a sense of rage raced toward her unfettered, to engulf and mingle with her own feelings. With such unrestricted access into the emotional being of another, it was unavoidable to fuse her soul with theirs. She became this old man, this private man. In an instant she recognized that it was her grandfather and that he too had identified his unwelcome intruder. Elle felt an emotional rigidity strike against this merciless invasion with such force it felt as if he had physically slapped her. Embarrassed, startled and gasping for breath Elle bolted upright and found herself staring into the equally embarrassed and startled face of her grandfather. Neither was sure of what to say for humans were never bred for such familiarity. Frightened, Elle instinctively did what she always did when the world became too terrifying a place, she leaned into the protective sanctuary of her grandfather's arms, shutting out the noise that seethed inside her head. Noah hesitated, but familiar habits are a strong force. He cuddled Elle, protecting her as he had always done.

Fourteen years is not long for someone to live, though for some it is all that they will have. She looked around her at the barely visible mist in the greying light of morning. The green tinged enclosure was gone. The 'fog' of the Guardians had dissipated enough for the fading night's sky to be seen overhead. The light of the rising sun, having travelled through the heat, the dust and the Guardians, all ablaze in glistening orange, sat on the horizon. Elle was uncertain how long she had slept but was certain that at least a day and a night had completely evaporated. Still in Noah's arms, with her head pressed against his chest, she tried to come to terms with the day's events and the continued din in her head. A momentary panic that they were out in the open, visible to anyone, quickly subsided when she realized they were still in the lee of the boat. It lay between them and Sweetwater, obscuring them from any curious eyes.

Though once again hungry and thirsty, she felt surprisingly alert, refreshed and in a good mood. This was in spite of being all too aware of her grandfather's early morning feelings as he awoke. Giving her a gentle push, he told her, "Get off me girl, I have to pee like old Blue." She did as well.

They each selected their own patch at the opposite ends of the boat to relieve themselves, all under the watchful eyes of their newly acquired mute companion and the dog. Sensing the presence of his granddaughter, Noah called over his shoulder for her to tone down her feeling of satisfaction.

"It was hard enough before this to get a bit of privacy. Now it's impossible."

Embarrassed, Elle knew exactly what he meant. There are emotions that one should never share and this was certainly one of them. She looked up at the bare peaks that towered above her. It seemed that the Guardians had elected not to return to their mountainous citadel but seemed content to fill the land around Noah and Elle as far as the eye could see.

Not sure what it had made of their toiletry, the two returned and sat down in front of the replica. As if he was a security blanket, Elle sat down beside Noah and pulled one of his arms tightly around her. As far as they could tell, the image had not moved during the night. The star-filled vessel sat in the sand, expressionless, with its vacant eyes staring at them. At first it was motionless, completely unanimated. Then, somewhat unexpectedly, a hand slowly rose up and made the sign for 'water'.

From its other 'hand' a canteen appeared from which 'water' flowed onto the ground forming an expanding puddle. Except for the rather unearthly, silvery, starry sheen, the mimicry was flawless. Elle reluctantly disentangled herself from her grandfather and with a great deal of trepidation and uncertainty, knelt in the sand before her image. Pointing at herself, Elle signed her name.

Chapter Twenty-Seven
Nothing made by humans can ever be truly alien.

With the dog and the doppelganger as company, the walk to and from the Scavengers' convoy hadn't taken long as there had been little reason to linger. Whether laid in a barn, propped against a tree, sprawled face down in the sand or shrivelled like old parchment as these men were, the dead look pretty much the same anywhere. On her return to the boat, her previous good mood had dissipated. Elle sat down with her rifle on her lap and watched Noah from across the fire as he stirred the contents of the pot with a piece of wood he'd pulled from the boat. Uninspired by the glutinous mass that lay within, he looked up with a cocked eyebrow.

"They're dead," was all she said.

Each felt the other's relief, although the sense of pleasure at the news that emanated from Noah was his alone.

In the shadow of the boat, the dry wood crackled in the fire and the pot's contents bubbled. The two sat there, encased in silence brought on by concentration. They were confused and in doubt as to what to do. It was clear that something had happened to them since their encounter with the Guardians. The continuous clamour of 'others' for recognition in their minds indicated that they were not alone in this predicament. With this new ability to sense emotions, their internal world was not only on display, it now contained mad, schizophrenic, ghostly apparitions that prowled the perimeter of their consciousness looking for a way in. Having already experienced a couple of episodes of mental volatility when unsolicited emotions entered, both were resolved to prevent it from occurring again.

And then there was the doppelganger – perhaps their only means of finding out what had happened to them. When the image made the sign for water and then imitated a previous action of Elle's by spilling a stream of silvery 'water' from its 'canteen', there was an anticipation they'd established the beginning of communication with this bizarre and alien life form. There was a sprig of hope. Since that seemingly auspicious start there had been nothing that could be interpreted as an intelligent response. Even the previous auto mimicry had ceased. The noises in their head had not.

Despondent over this fractured hope and irritated by the din in the background of her mind, Elle absent-mindedly tugged at her hair. It had always been kept bobbed like her cousins and its present length was becoming a nuisance, adding to her exasperation. Maybe after lunch she'd get Noah to lop some off. The thought of getting her hair shortened and then being able to plunge into a waiting pool of water to get clean sent a tingle of delight through her.

Noah looked up. "What was that all about?" he asked.

She blushed, alarmed at how even this small sense of pleasure could be felt by her grandfather. This intimacy was disturbing and annoying.

"I was thinking how nice it would be to have a bath," she said, still a little flushed.

Noah looked around him before responding. "Not much of a chance of that while we are out here." After looking into the pot, he continued, "I don't know why I am stirring this stuff. I don't think it's capable of burning."

Elle returned Noah's grin. What she wanted, what she needed even more than either a haircut or a bath, was a break. The previous two days had been gruelling, invasive and very discouraging. The tiniest surge of any form of emotion from either of them was picked up by the other.

Noah interrupted her thoughts by announcing that breakfast, such as it was, was ready.

Elle arched her back to relieve some of the tension as she watched the dog devour the remains of their meal. "Slow down Mutt, take a breath why don't you?" she said. In spite of a night's sleep, her body was stiff from crouching in the sand for hours on end in front of her silvery companion. The muscles in both hands and forearms ached from the effort, and her brain was clogged with nouns, verbs and adjectives. You can only get so far by pointing at and naming things, she thought. "How do you teach anyone about your world, your thoughts, your beliefs? How did I learn?" she asked.

Noah gave a snort and then said, "From the moment of your birth, Elle, from the moment of your birth, and you still have a very long way to go. It is sometimes hard to believe from what I have seen of it, but we are a forever-learning species, and that, my little girl, is what separates us from that dog and those horses. You will learn to walk upright and you will learn to speak. These and a million others are things we were born with the capacity to learn. The question you're really asking, though, is what is that thing of yours capable of learning?"

Until now, Elle had thought such things came automatically, if she thought about it at all. This sublime mystery that encoded everything she was, the way she lived, thought and spoke; all those unwritten laws that governed her, her family, the Traders and even the Scavengers – how does a person teach that which they themselves might not understand? There was the option of reaching out to the replica as she had done with the dog and Noah. Remembering her recent encounter with the voices of the dead, if Guardians were the source she did not feel any desire to go there again. "This is getting me nowhere," she said to her grandfather as she vented her aggravation on a small mound of sand by stomping it flat.

Noah, who had been lost in his thoughts, reached up and gently touched the ring suspended from his granddaughter's neck. "Elle, the Guardians had to have been created by those people in the mountains. While it is possible that, for some unfathomable reason, those people wanted the means to sense one another's emotions, the Guardians' purpose could never have been to bring a stop to the rains or to murder. No one except a Scavenger could possibly be that mad, so something most have gone very wrong. Aside from a few incidences in the past and the Scavengers in Sweetwater, everyone who ventured within fifty kilometres of those mountains has died, so why didn't we share the fate of those in the tanks?" Noah made a gesture in the air with his hand, indicating extreme frustration. "Remember what I was talking about at Empty Cup, all those coincidences? What would you think if I said the reason, or at least part of it, has to be attributed somehow to Scout, Atticus' sister. She was the one who sent the ring and the knife. Having them in your possession has to have been the key to your, and by association, my survival. The lock," indicating Elle's replica with the tilt of his head, "might very well be that creature of yours. So maybe, if you want an answer to all this, you shouldn't give up. As frustrating as it is, I suspect there is intelligence in it." He released the stoneless ring and, with a wink, said, "After all, it took more than three years before I could make any sense out of your burps, squeaks and jabber."

In spite of Noah's encouragement, it was impossible for her not to feel inadequate and out of her depth. Elle found herself missing home. Her grandfather, still hampered by the binding on his leg, hobbled over to the horses. She knew he was an immensely resourceful man who had taught her how to live in the wasteland, to understand the treacherous ways of the Dry and use that information to its best advantage. He, however, did not possess one of her mother's gifts, her enduring patience. Elle rubbed her temples with the tips of her fingers. This continuous emotional prattle that lapped at her consciousness was exhausting, intrusive and very distracting. From somewhere in the very depth of her mind came a memory. It wasn't real. This she knew because she'd been told her sister had died soon after being born.

Why did this thing look like her? She looked at the creature through the gaps between her fingers and again wondered if her persistence yesterday had had any effect whatsoever. Noah had to be right – some kind of intelligence had to reside in there, but how could she get at it? It was like trying to have a conversation with a fence post or one of her male cousins. She smiled at the thought. Relentlessly being jostled, interrupted and haunted by the emotions from people she could not see and did not know didn't help. Even when she slept, she found, they were there. These formless spirits were certainly unrelenting.

Elle needed to do something physical. Seeing Noah struggling, she went over to give him a hand with the horses. Over the last few days Belle had been terribly neglected and could do with a little attention. They both could.

Noah welcomed her company, but she could feel his sorrow. He was missing that old bond they once had. She looked across Belle at him with a whimsical smile.

"Sorry, Granddad," she said and then returned to brushing the horse.

Noah tried to smile back but couldn't, there was just too much noise in his head.

The horses were not recuperating as fast as Noah had expected and their continued lethargy was causing him concern. He and Elle moved around the horses, stroking them while gently encouraging them to drink. Since the two of them, as well as the dog, had pretty much recovered, Noah guessed that it was the horses' size that hindered them. Even after twenty-four hours, the effect of dehydration was still evident in the dryness of their mouths. This was especially true with Blue.

As she watched the animals drink, Elle's thoughts drifted to the irritating buzz inside her head. Chook had once tried to describe the tinnitus that plagued him, likening it to a continuous irritation that he had no way of clearly describing. He'd signed to her, "It's not so bad when you're busy, but try to read or sleep, and it bangs away at you." Elle suddenly got a clear image of her mother in the kitchen trying to prepare dinner while the rest of the family clamoured for her attention. She wondered if the emotional bedlam she was experiencing was what it felt like to be a mother and a wife. If so, she couldn't understand why any woman would voluntarily elect to be either.

Glancing over at her grandfather, she sensed that the horses were not the only ones having trouble. Physically he seemed fine, but it was obvious from the emotions that leaked from him that he was not coping well with their recent transformation. Enforced idleness only added to his growing irritation. He needed to do something, and anything would be better than his present occupation, sitting around watching her failed attempts to solicit a response from her eidetic image. Then, like one of the Scavenger's flares, a brightly coloured burst of emotion exploded in her head.

Anger; it came from grandfather. He grinned sheepishly at Elle, realizing that she had picked up his 'outburst'. He held up an empty water canister. "We've got to go tomorrow. We are running out of food and water for them and us. It's not safe staying out here with nothing between us and the Scavengers but a boat. We also have to find and warn the Traders. The Scavengers might think we've died." He looked over at the ash of their earlier fire. "If that's so, let's strive to keep it that way. No more fires and, as a further precaution, we'll leave well before sunrise."

Perhaps it was prudent for them to huddle here behind the boat, build no more fires and leave in the dark, thought Elle, but the fact was she'd seen no Scavengers venturing out from Sweetwater since the Guardians. It could mean, like themselves, the townspeople were recovering, because they weren't dead. The noise in her head told her that much. But something was amiss somewhere out there. Perhaps they were fearful of being attacked again or they had problems of their own to contend with. Whatever his concerns over the Scavengers were, they did not lie at the core of his outburst. Elle could feel him striving to suppress his emotions.

Noah sensed his granddaughter's gentle probe but he ignored it. The anger Elle had felt was not directed at her. "Noah, you're a damn fool." His pride and desire for revenge were responsible for them being here on the lakebed. They were also the reasons behind him breaking his leg. His granddaughter didn't need to apologize to him or anyone. She might have begun the quest, but he should have brought it to an end well before the ambush. Ten, twelve years ago he had been a different man. Since then he had indulged himself, living on the Farm, coming and going as it pleased him, living off a reputation of being a rustic and possibly dangerous loner. The fact was, he was old and worn out. The wastelands were no a place for such men and he, of all people, understood this. The thought of one last hoorah for himself and Blue had stroked his vanity. Even at the prospect of risking Elle's life, the appearance of the Scavengers had given him the pretext to regain the man he had once been. There was never a need for either of them to be here. At the very least, Elle should have returned in the place of Nic, regardless of the state of her wound. Consciousness of his granddaughter's concern and unease was bad enough, but the pity he felt coming from her was humiliating, making him want to lash out. Nothing could infuriate a prideful man more than to be exposed as a fool and he was not only a fool but an old one as well.

Fate did not determine his or Elle's lives. A fool he might be, but, as perceptive as his granddaughter was, there were more pressing problems than his bruised ego and the sickly horses that needed to be attended to. The continuous chatter in their heads meant they sensed the emotions of others and it was reasonable to assume that these same 'others' could sense them. What if these others were the Scavengers in Sweetwater? If they had survived the Guardians and then suffered the same fate as the two of them, it was certainly possible. Accepting the idea that Scavengers could rummage through his emotions repulsed him, almost making him ill. Of course, if they had been eradicated... There was no need to finish the thought.

He needed to know the whereabouts of the Traders. How close were they? Everything depended on whether or not they, too, had had an encounter with the Guardians and, if so, to what extent. Recalling how vulnerable he and Elle had been and the length of time it took to regain consciousness, he worried that, if the Scavengers were able to recover before the Traders, the results would be a massacre. A malevolent grin emerged. Should fortune favour the Traders he would happily participate in the Scavengers' annihilation.

Elle unintentionally shared all her grandfather's emotions: loathing, hatred, rage, resignation. She was repeatedly thrust into the depths of someone else's emotional world, an adult world. Sensing her distress, Noah strove to calm the storm within.

Blue shuddered. "Even the damn animals are in on this," thought Noah as he came around to stand in front of her. "It's not you who should apologize. I'm sorry Elle." He was. He was sorry for not taking her home, for dragging her into his personal vendetta and for not being the man she thought he was. A big, calloused hand came up and, as gentle as a feather, wiped away the tear that was forming on her cheek. "You're not a little girl any more, are you?" He then pressed his nose against her and drew in her breath. "You are truly worth a life," he said.

Elle threw her arms around him, nearly knocking him over, saying, "As are you."

Neither slept particularly well that night, so both were up and ready well before the appointed time. Chewing on something barely edible, he slid the big watch back into his pocket. The sun would be up in about two hours; it was time to get going. The horses were saddled, ready to depart. A slight shiver ran down the length of his spine. Surprisingly there was a distinct tingle in the air, an unaccustomed coolness. Noah came over and placed a hand on Elle's shoulder. "It's time for us to go. I have no idea what we are going to find out there. Whatever it is, we will deal with it." A wave of sorrow swept over him.

Elle put a hand on his. "I'm not going." Patting Belle, she said, "It will be weeks before either of these horses recover. You'll have to keep switching between them to get any distance from Sweetwater. So I'll stay here. I want to see, no, I need to see inside the mountain. I need to know why."

If there was such a thing as a person's soul, Noah could, in his mind, see Elle's. She did need to finish this. "What about your wound?"

She opened the shirt and pulled down the dressing. "It doesn't seem to have gotten any worse."

Torn between the need to find the Traders and Elle, Noah was about to say he couldn't leave her when she just said, "Go".

Knowing he'd lost the debate, he said, "I'll be back no later than tomorrow. You'll have enough food and water until then, especially if I take the dog."

The dog whined and moved out of his reach behind Elle. "Bloody hell, what kind of world have we stumbled into when a dog can read your mind?" He folded his arms around her and held her tight before stepping back. Both felt the emotional bond that bound them as no human before ever had. It was frightening. Again Noah tried to smile and again couldn't find it in himself to do so, but he would be damned if he'd give up the role of being the protective grandfather. "Well, if you are going off, leave markers so I can find you in a hurry if I have to. There might be additional supplies in those vehicles, but don't plan on it. If I am not back by the third day, assume the worst and do what you can to survive." He touched her heart. "If this doesn't kill you, promise me you'll go home." A small smile then did manage to find its way on his face. "And please don't eat the dog. I've grown fond of it."

As they had done the night before, Noah leaned over, pressing his nose against hers, drawing in her breath as she did his, repeating the timeworn words, "You are worth a life."

Lapsing back into silence, the ritual completed, they finished the horses' preparation and then, grabbing the reins, Noah mounted Belle and reluctantly headed out. He was travelling light. There was food, water and fodder at the pinnacles and back at the wagon, so he had taken nothing but a flask of water for himself and a canister for the horses.

It didn't matter if Elle's insistence on staying behind was not solely as she'd claimed. She suspected with this 'gift', he could read her motivations as easily as text in a book. For such a private man, she saw that this metamorphosis was much harder for him. It had to be claustrophobic having so many others crowding in, sifting through his innermost feelings, putting them on display for all and sundry to see. This had to be especially true if one of the many was his granddaughter. Maybe distance would provide him a respite, although that was unlikely since he intended to find out what had happened to the Scavengers and locate the Traders.

Chapter Twenty-Eight
I am my brother's keeper.

The fine dry sand crunched under the horses' hooves as they made their way across the lakebed toward the pinnacles. The night sky overhead was murky, as if the stars were being filtered through gossamer. "Guardians!" was his single comment, as if that was enough to explain that which he did not yet understand. It should be hotter than it felt, he thought. Somehow the Guardians, that haze that stretched out all around him in every direction, reduced one of the sun's more brutal attributes. It was cool, pleasantly cool, and not a single insect buzzed around him or the horses. Not a bad side effect. He was grateful that he and the horses were not being smothered by the heat or pestered by salt flies.

He stopped and got off to check the animals. Belle was faring better than his noble friend, Blue. "I think age is catching up with you, old fella." Feeling his tiredness, "I think old age is catching up with us both." As he reached over to give Blue a pat and a rub along his neck, Noah urged his trusted ally to make every effort to take care of himself for he was far too old and cantankerous a man to break in another horse.

Since leaving the Farm to find Elle things certainly had not gone the way he had thought they would. Disregarding everything up to the point of being swallowed by the Guardians, why they had not shared the fate of the Scavengers in the convoy nagged him. He thought about family folklore and his conversation with Elle on the subject of Scout being somehow connected with the Dry and the recent events. They should have died and yet they had not, although it had been a near thing. Had it not been for his granddaughter's quick recovery and intervention, he and the horses would not have made it. Perhaps they had been, somehow, deliberately spared. Nonsense! Such ruminations were not getting him any closer to the pinnacles. The horses remained dangerously dehydrated. He climbed back on Belle and started off again. Belle might make it another day, but he had to find shelter, food and lots of water soon if he was to save his old friend. He wondered about the horses he'd left behind.

If what had happened out on the lakebed also happened at the pinnacles? If so, there was no chance they would have survived, but for his own peace of mind he would have to check to make sure. The horses trudged up the loose sand of the embankment, their tracks and those of the Scavengers' still fresh in the disturbed earth. Had it only been a couple of days? He felt a 'ping' from Elle. She must have picked up on him. He had to watch it. This constant need to be aware of one's emotions rattled him – so much head noise. It was like 'listening', uninvited, to a private conversation. That he too being 'heard' never strayed far from his thoughts.

The pinnacles were not far when he stopped, just up a small rise. The bindings around his leg were loose with one end trailing along the ground. It would not do his leg any good if one of the horses stepped on it. Before dismounting, he looked over toward the east to see how much time he had before he would be visible. It would not be wise to be caught out in the open this close to his sanctuary. He lifted the broken leg carefully over the saddle horn and was surprised to find it didn't hurt as he did so. In fact, now that he thought about it, the leg had not given him any trouble since ... when? He sat down in the sand. The bindings that held the slats in place had not taken kindly all that hobbling back there at the boat. They needed to be completely rebound. He glanced over to where the lights of Sweetwater should have been but could see nothing in the dark, nor anything in the direction of the pinnacles. He suspected that what awaited him there would be unpleasant, not a place he would want to remain for any length of time.

Rebinding below his knee was easy but got progressively harder as he moved down the leg. Even with the leg bent, with the foot almost in his lap, trying to tie off just above the ankle was proving to be a bit of a struggle. It took him a couple of attempts before he was satisfied. Funny how relatively easy that was to do, and during the whole operation it didn't hurt. All the stumbling around, you'd think it should hurt, at least show a little discomfort. In the dust and sand he straightened his leg and again tried to remember the last time it had bothered him. Yesterday? His memory for once failed him. He just couldn't remember any discomfort. Had he even been limping? He had hopped around back at the boat he remembered, but out of pain or habit? He couldn't recall, and that was unlike him to let such a thing go unnoticed. Cautiously he undid and removed the binding that he had just tightened, admiring his handiwork as he did so. "Elle is not the only one with good hands."

Preparing for a stab of pain, Noah carefully pushed his bare heel against the ground. No pain. None whatsoever. He finished undoing the last of the bindings, removed the slats and the blanket. Keeping his leg as straight as possible and using one of the slats as a prop, he heaved himself up, striving to put as little weight on the leg as he could. Not an easy task for a man of his bulk. Upright, balanced – again no pain. He hesitantly put his foot down and took a step. The leg felt fine. No discomfort or pain at all. It didn't even feel stiff.

He stood there flummoxed. "How long ago did I break this bloody thing?" he muttered. "Certainly not long enough for it to heal to this extent and I should know," recalling the many broken bones he'd sustained in the course of his life. "What's the worst that can happen? Well, I could break it again." He gathered up the slats, the blanket and leather thongs, tucked them under his arm and, with the horses in tow, started to walk the rest of the way. He was sure, though he didn't know how, the miraculous and unlikely recovery of his leg was connected to events out on the lakebed and his aberrant ability to read emotions. He was also certain that the answer would not be found in the Sweetwater but somewhere across the lakebed, the objective of the Scavengers' doomed motorcade. The thought of the mountains made him wonder how his granddaughter was doing with her exploration.

An emotional burst from Elle, perhaps in response to his emotional astonishment over the leg, reminded Noah how much of his anonymity he'd lost. In the current circumstances it was not at all desirable, especially if it resulted in a whole village of demented Scavengers muscling in. Of course, there would be a few less Scavengers than there had been. From his knowledge of their carrying capacity, upwards of a hundred men could be rotting in those tin cans. But regardless of the number that perished, the remaining Scavengers were not the kind of people who would take kindly to anyone but their comrades emerging from that holocaust. The row of poles with their grisly ornaments strung near the highway leading out from town was a vivid, if disturbing, reminder of how they treated those with whom they were displeased.

The breeze from the pinnacles bore the sticky sweet odour of death, informing him that, as he had guessed, he was too late. For a man who had seen so much death and had contributed to it as well, he maintained an unexpectedly high degree of sympathy toward those whose misfortunes were not of their making. His explosive expletive was not just for the dead horses he knew he'd find but the awareness that this last emotional surge of his had alerted more than his granddaughter. He could feel their puzzlement and their attempts to identify him. With this reminder of his lost privacy, and still being in the open, he felt exposed and vulnerable, easy prey, something he needed to remedy as soon as possible.

The pinnacles and at least the physical anonymity they offered were a few metres away when a voice, unmistakably a woman's, informed Noah that it would serve his interests to halt and stand very still with both hands plainly visible. In the soft greying light, he complied.

"Now Trader, with all the care you can muster and with the assurance that I can shoot the eye out of a sparrow in flight, remove any item from your person that I would consider potentially harmful to my wellbeing."

Noah could not help smiling as he began the task of disarming. It was not only her phrasing that amused him but his stupidity. He had been so busy trying to block his emotional output, he had overlooked its inherent advantage. He too could sense emotions. If I only had, he thought, I probably wouldn't be standing here like this. The world of the Dry was full of the dead whose epitaph began with 'If only he had…'

"Now Trader, to reduce any need for you to do something foolish, drop your pants, keep them around your ankles and then walk slowly toward my voice while keeping those hands way up in the air. And wipe that silly smirk off your face before I change my mind and shoot you where you stand."

That final remark was the last straw for Noah. As he began dropping the weapons on the ground he could not hold it back any longer and burst out laughing. Her demand for him to stop only made it that much worse.

"Lady, you might as well shoot me now. I've had a hell of a time over the last few weeks, and the thought of being shot dead right here and now by an unknown woman is not all that discouraging. Besides, I'm not the kind of man to drop his pants in front of anyone I haven't been formally introduced to. All I ask is don't hit the horses and, if you don't mind, take care of them when I am gone." As he finished he thought he heard a stifled giggle coming from the pinnacles' interior.

Tired and frustrated by the constant bombardment of others, Noah closed his eyes; within the bundle of light, he looked for the tiny thread that shone the brightest and had the sweet taste of mirth. His lips began to curve into a smile of recognition as he followed the light to its source. The smile vanished. The impact for them both was instantaneous and brutal. This mind was not that of a young girl who, despite being born in the Dry, had been loved and protected. This mind was that of a woman who had experienced despair, cruelty and violence. The intensity of hate struck Noah as if it were a physical blow, causing him to stagger back. This was a hunter whose ferocity would match his. Yet, amidst all that pain and anger, he detected a spirit that had retained humanity, a mercy bolstered by a sense of humour.

A loud "Whoa!" came from behind the rocks. "Back off old man, NOW, or I swear I will shoot you dead where you stand."

Unless he made a threatening move, Noah knew this was not going to happen. He called out, "I am getting fed up with being bullied by a voice from behind a pile of rocks. We both know the state of each other's emotions. So if you don't mind, come out or let me come in. My horses need water."

A woman of about 45, of medium build and height, dressed in ill-fitting men's clothing, with a mass of unruly red hair streaked with grey protruding from beneath a large brimmed hat, appeared from between a pair of boulders that made up the pinnacles' western face. She carried a rifle in one hand, and in the other, one of his water canisters and a canvas bucket. Motioning to Noah to stay where he was, she put the canister and bucket on the ground and then backed away saying. "It stinks in there and I don't think your horses will be comfortable with the smell." She then indicated to Noah that he could retrieve both the water and the bucket.

In that first shock of golden light of a wasteland sunrise, Noah saw that she had a cautious smile and, save for a scar that ran the length of her cheek from her left ear to the tip of her chin, a once attractive face. She reached up to touch the scar. Conscious of his emotions being scrutinized by the woman, he was distracted when pouring the water in the bucket and nearly knocked it over as both horses edged closer to drink.

"They're a bit eager aren't they?" said the woman as she helped Noah by taking Belle's lead.

"They got knocked around a bit," Noah replied, declining to elaborate as he tried to dampen the anxiety her probing caused him. A flash of concern from Elle did not help. The woman nodded in agreement, saying nothing further nor giving any hint if she too had felt his granddaughter's interest. Things were certainly not going as he would have preferred; the old adage, 'from the frying pan'… seemed most apt. In his desperation to get away from his granddaughter's adolescent turmoil, he'd fallen victim to a woman whose own emotional fierceness threatened to engulf him.

Feeling, as well as seeing, his obvious stress, the woman tentatively reached out as if to touch him, causing Noah to instinctively shy away. "You're not handling this very well, are you?" she asked.

He moved the bucket over to Belle and refilled it. "No, not really," he said and wanted to say more but didn't trust himself. He didn't like being out in the open, in view of Sweetwater. "I don't want to be a nuisance, but I would rather not be standing out here like this. He glanced toward Sweetwater. "I have concerns that you might not be the only one with a rifle pointed at me."

She followed his gaze. She smiled, but it was a cruel smile, made all the more so by the scar that lifted the corner of her mouth abnormally high. The emotion that accompanied the smile was one of distilled hatred. "I don't think, at least for the moment, you'll be having any troubles from that quarter. They're much too busy with their own problems."

When he had headed out to return Elle to the Farm, life in the wastelands had been uncompromisingly hard but it was also understandable. Since leaving Empty Cup, all this had begun to change. There had been an increasing awareness that he was losing control of a tightly managed and disciplined way of life. Three days ago his granddaughter started to tread through his internal privacy with the grace of a bull and now there was this mental assault by a redheaded woman, who, it was very evident, had not bathed or changed her clothing in quite some time. Even more shocking; her hatred of the Scavengers seemed more visceral than his own.

He looked up from his watering task into a pair of the darkest, greenest eyes he had ever seen, so green they made her appear more feline than human. All he could think to say was, "Would you like a cup of coffee?" She smiled and asked if he was inviting her to join him for a drink. Nearly blushing at her unblinking stare, he paused before answering. "Yes."

Smiling even more broadly, she said, "Then I accept."

They collected the canister and bucket, each took a horse and started toward the pinnacles.

"How did you know I wouldn't have shot you the moment you stepped out from behind those rocks, unless, of course, you can read more than my emotions?"

She almost chuckled. "Trader, your emotions stand out like a beacon. I would have known the moment you did of your intentions. Besides, I had insurance. Even if you'd been able to kill me," she smiled as if she'd held some inner secret, "which is most unlikely, you would have died before I had hit the ground." She called out, "Come on out, Flea."

From behind a boulder came a little girl, no older than eight or nine, carrying a rifle as big as she was and dressed in clothing that was little more than an assortment of rags.

"Trader, meet some of my insurance – Flea, my daughter." Her emphasis on some words did not go unnoticed by Noah.

To his surprise there was only one carcass, poor old Buck, the horse taken by Elle from the farm. Ted was quietly standing toward the back and not looking very healthy. Seeing that one of the horses had survived gave Noah some joy, but the disappointment of losing Buck was evident to the woman.

"I'm sorry, we couldn't save them both. We tried," she said.

Noah knew this to be true. He looked around and seeing no other horses asked where their mounts were. When informed they had none, he was a little baffled. For Noah, to not to have access to a horse was almost unthinkable and he did not hesitate to inquire how they had got to the pinnacles. Did they walk? The woman told him that was exactly how they had got there. They were not Traders so this could only mean they were from Sweetwater but neither of these people were Scavengers either. That was one set of their emotions he could read with absolute certainty.

In order to make the pinnacles habitable they used the three horses to drag Buck's carcass to a spot a good distance away and downwind. He wished the poor animal could have been shown more dignity than being unceremoniously dumped. The only good experience during the whole ordeal was the continued absence of flies and their offspring, maggots. It reduced the unpleasantness of the task considerably. When it was completed, the child left the adults to their own devices and resumed caring for the horses by moving them deeper into the shade and lavishing them with water and fodder. The adults set about tidying the shelter.

Noah bent down to retrieve his binoculars. The woman looked over, aware of his sadness, and remarked that a lot of things, once damaged, are discarded. There was no need for her to elaborate. He understood all the meaning behind those words.

"True," he replied, tucking the broken field glasses into a pack with care. He could have added but didn't that sometimes it was through the fault of others or through one's own, but the real culprit was the fickleness of it all.

The woman uttered not a single comment regarding the items obviously pilfered from Sweetwater as she stacked the boxes into an orderly rectangle up against the back wall. Nor did she seem fazed at the remaining rocket-propelled grenade that he'd moved out of harm's way. Noah was both amused and comforted by the way the woman's curiosity appeared in his mind and how similar it was to Elle's. They both issued similar strong colours. Disturbing as it was to him to have a stranger touch his thoughts, read his intentions, he had to admit, if not for this ability, one of them could have been dead by now. That would have been a waste.

Later, sitting in front of the fire waiting for the water the boil, Noah couldn't hold back his inquisitiveness. "You haven't asked any questions as to who I am, why I'm here or what happened out there."

The head with its crown of red hair looked up with eyes now the colour of a brooding sea that locked onto Noah's face. "Oh, I know who you are and I suspect I know what brought you here to Sweetwater. As to what happened out there..." She let her graze drift out onto the lakebed before continuing. "They failed." That last statement had not been unexpected but he was taken aback by the venomous energy with which it was stated.

They returned their attention to watching the pot of water on the fire.

"Is the young girl that was with you still alive?" the woman asked. He had deliberately said nothing to indicate that he was not alone, that there was someone with him. His face remained impassive but the emotional surge betrayed him, prompting the woman to explain. "Your companion, while stealing from the warehouse," she inclined her head toward a stack of RTE's in the far corner, "ended up holding a knife at my daughter's throat. Flea has a good memory regarding near death experiences." The child turned the moment her name was mentioned but said nothing. "She could have killed her and the fact that she didn't is a good thing, don't you think? If she had, I would have killed you. A life for a life is it not? She continued staring toward the vanished lake. "Her running off across the dead lake like that disrupted a very carefully-laid timetable and upset a lot of very mean and unforgiving people. The last folks to do that ended up nailed to a post."

Noah waited for the redheaded woman to expand on her comment regarding the men 'nailed to a post' as he had a strong premonition that it was directly connected to the murdered Traders. Instead, she said, "The men, they're all dead." Her face remained noncommittal but her emotions betrayed a kind of savage fury mixed with joy. Noah's current mental fragility wanted to recoil at its intensity. "And it's a good thing for all concerned that they are," she finished.

He had his reasons for desiring their failure but could not understand hers. Questions were beginning to pile up but, before he could even begin, his attention was diverted by the fire hissing in protest as droplets of boiling water splashed out of the pot. He snatched the pot from the fire and deftly poured the water into his beloved battered coffee pot, inserted the strainer and set it aside to steep. Straightening up he had to ask. "Why do you want your own people dead?" Touching the scar on her cheek, the woman informed Noah that they were "…never my own."

Except for family, Noah was never comfortable with women; extremely awkward is how those who knew him would have put it. This one was no exception. He filled a cup, handed it to the woman and then waited. Hesitantly – it was scalding – she took a small drink, swallowed and then screwed up her face. "What is this stuff?"

"You don't like it?" asked Noah as he topped his cup up.

"Hard to say, after all, that was my first taste of coffee. Perhaps it takes a bit of getting used to. Some things are like that," she replied, taking another tentative sip, obviously trying not to offend.

He could feel that there many layers in that simple sentence and felt there was more she wanted to say but she was interrupted by a plaintive call from her daughter that she was hungry. Both adults looked over at the RTE's, fast food of the Dry.

When the meal, such as it was, was over, the fire was left to die and the refuse cleared away. To his disappointment he noticed that her coffee cup remained half full. Such a waste, he thought as he nestled the cup in the embers. A reheated cup was not as good the first but the thought of throwing it away was unacceptable.

The woman with the red hair had gone into another part of the pinnacles to be with her daughter. Over the course of the meal, they had talked. They exchanged names. Hers was Ruth. After telling him what had occurred in Sweetwater, they traded a good deal of peripheral, trivial information concerning their respective lives and histories but kept the darker times to themselves. He told her that the name of the girl who ran out onto the lakebed was Elle but refrained from mentioning that she was his granddaughter. Nor did he speak of any matters concerning the Farm or the rest of his family. By the same token he knew there were things in her life that remained restricted, private. The advantage of being able to read the emotions of another was the clarity it gave; it enabled a person to see the intent of another. Even so, he thought that it did not necessarily make life safer, only different. Nevertheless, it had been enjoyable, if guarded. It had been quite a while since he had actually been in the company of an adult who was not a member of his immediate family, longer still since that company was a woman. She was rough as a dried corncob and had a hardness not matched by any of the women in his family. Yet there was a keen mind that lived under that mass of red hair and a fierce will to survive, two things Noah valued in a person.

The coffee was just beginning to bubble around its edges when Noah rescued the cup from the fire. The two females had disappeared completely for private matters he suspected. He tried to take a sip but ended up blowing on it instead. A smile crept onto his sunburnt face. He blew on the coffee again and took an experimental sip, finding himself in an unusually good mood. With cup in hand, he meandered over to attend to Blue and Belle. The care rendered by the little girl even in that short time had improved their dispositions. They had been thoroughly brushed, curried and combed.

Blue gently nudged him as he put away the grooming kit. A bit of the sparkle had returned to the old boy's eyes, a good sign that he was becoming his indomitable self. He gave a contented snort as the hard brush went about removing several days of dirt and sweat from his hindquarters. Although Blue, in the short time he'd been here, seemed to have made a remarkable recovery from his ordeal, Noah did not want to risk riding him just yet. If she let him, he'd take Belle instead.

He put the cup on a piece of rock that jutted out and reached down to retrieve his saddle which he swung on to Belle. Getting on her with Elle's help out on the lakebed was one thing, but mounting her without Elle might be altogether different. Belle looked well enough to not only make it to their camp in the old wadi but to the village as well. He wanted to find if the Traders had made it this far and if they'd met the Guardians. In the event he ran into the Scavengers, he would deal with that when and if it happened. That was the plan anyway. The wagon and the items left in it were too hard to come by to be abandoned. At least the meeting with Ruth and her daughter had established one thing; the people of Sweetwater had suffered the same effects from being swallowed up by the Guardians as he and Elle. As for Blue, giving the horse a pat on his flank, he would just have to be content to tag along with a few light items strapped to his back.

Other than her apparent hatred for them, he did not know the full extent of Ruth's relationship with the Scavengers so was reluctant to discuss his plans with her. Especially in regard to the Traders or their whereabouts because she had been living in Sweetwater and in his eyes that alone made her untrustworthy. He moved between the horses adjusting the saddle and bridle on each of the animals. Regardless of what was said, he could ask if she had seen any Traders. The resulting flow of emotion would tell him what he wanted to know.

Of course that talent flowed both ways. Suddenly Noah felt an acute sense of alarm followed a few seconds later by Ruth and Flea bursting into where he was preparing the horses.

"We've got company," said Ruth.

Noah grabbed his rifle and placed a round in the chamber before he joined the pair who had positioned themselves against the rocks looking toward Sweetwater.

He could see nothing. "Where are they?" he demanded.

"They're just leaving the town," said Ruth.

"What do you mean 'just leaving'?"

Pointing at her head with her finger, "I can 'see' them here, just as I saw you and that girl."

The idea that she could sense Elle came as a revelation. "How do you know they're headed this way?" he asked.

"I really don't know," she said. "I just see them or at least their emotions as they are directed at me and Flea. I figure if they are doing that, they must be coming for us." She paused as if listening to something he couldn't hear and then said, "And you. No horses, they are on foot."

Noah asked her to elaborate on exactly what she meant. In reply she told him of her experiences.

Everyone with permission had stood along the western highway to watch the coming conflict. Between the heat haze, clouds of dust and smoke, those without binoculars had only the vaguest idea of what was happening. What could be seen with the unaided eye was the star-studded silvery mists solidifying, transforming the mountain's grey blue sides into an ominous black deluge. As was the Scavengers' custom, Ruth and Flea, along with rest of the women and children, were corralled off to one side. All were transfixed by the ferocity as great arched rivers of flame and clusters of flares plunged into the descending mass. Amid the yells, cheers and encouraging expletives, a stream of babbling commentary ranged along the line of observers. Years of unceasing labour to gain access to the mountains and all its secrets were only moments away from being achieved. None doubted that once armed with those secrets of the Before Times, the wrath of the Sorrow would be remembered with fondness. Not until some of the men with the field glasses started to turn and run did Ruth realize the previous elation had been woefully premature. Death was approaching.

The Scavengers' mechanical legion with its malevolent hope had been swallowed whole. All along the plains the obsidian torrent, having engulfed the convoy, flowed unimpeded toward them. Fear replaced exaltation. The men fled on horseback or on foot with no comprehension of what they had unleashed. Women, abandoned, encumbered by children, did nothing but huddle and wait. It was their eyes, not the men, who witnessed the burst of brilliant green that erupted at the point of contact with a marooned derelict pleasure craft. They were also the ones to witness, like the spread of a stain, the vast field of pitchblende mutate into a raging turbulent emerald sea that was rushing to consume them. Yet, when it struck there no feeling of force; it might as well have been a waft of smoke from a struggling fire.

The moment the men began to desert their forward position Ruth grabbed her daughter's hand and, dodging panicked horses and townspeople, ran. She had managed to keep them both alive through years of captivity and she was determined they weren't going to die because of the action of a bunch of dimwitted males. However, even Ruth could not outrun the town's inundation; everything that drew breath was rendered unconscious. For an hour or more, except for the shallow breathing of the living, the town of Sweetwater lay silent, completely still, with no wind, not even the sound of insects.

The children, along with the smaller animals such as dogs and chickens, were the first to regain consciousness and once recovered, they began to move among the adults rendering what assistance they could. Fortunately Flea and other older children recognized severe dehydration; everyone badly needed water, including themselves. If they hadn't started hurrying around dispensing the desperately needed life-giving liquid, many more would have died. As it was, the town sustained substantial losses – a quarter of the adults, mostly older males, a few children including a newborn, and over half the dry stock.

Ruth had woken with her head in Flea's lap. Looking up she was greeted with a smile on her daughter's dirty face and was about to tell her how beautiful she looked, when curls of colour issued from Flea's nose as she exhaled.

"What the?"

Her daughter laughed. "I know, funny isn't it? That's how I knew you were alive."

Weak, thirsty and with a cruel headache, Ruth asked for water and then drank until she started to cough.

Flea sat anxiously waiting until she stopped and said, "Mom, I've got to go help. You stay here and I'll be back soon." Then she was gone.

"Not bloody likely," Ruth thought, trying to get to her feet. The last thing she wanted was to be lying helpless in Sweetwater. But it took several attempts to get up. On wobbly legs that wanted nothing more than to collapse beneath her, Ruth found she was in the centre of town surrounded by a bedlam of people in even worse condition than herself. She was confused and disoriented in the midst of the noise of cries for water and help. A baby somewhere off to her left was screaming as if in terrible pain. She turned to walk in the direction of the cries but, in doing so, almost toppled over.

The cries persisted. By force of habit, driven by years of trying to protect the women and children from the endemic violence of Sweetwater, Ruth made her way to the terrified child, but she was too late.

Despite the disaster that had just befallen them, the men had begun to reassert their authority, irritably lashing out at anyone near them. As if they were responsible for this calamity, wrath was primarily directed toward any nearby woman. The women, for their part, relieved to find that their children seemed unaffected, took the blows without complaint for fear that doing so would only make it worse. This was not true for the mother and her infant; they had both been bludgeoned to death. The man responsible stood over them, still raining blows on their lifeless bodies. Ruth rushed at the man with every intention of ripping that smirking grin off his face.

This time she did not lose consciousness, although Ruth wished she had. The pain was unbearably intense, as if the top of her skull had been ripped open and scalding water poured in. Everyone, men, women, children, were screaming, clawing at their faces as if it would somehow relieve the torment.

Ruth went silent for a moment. Her eyes stared into the middle distance as if living through it all again. Noah watched a single tear make its way down the side of her cheek and then divert to follow the scar to the corner of her mouth. She made a sniffling noise before wiping the back of her hand across her nose. Taking a deep breath she began again.

The severity of the pain had seemed inexhaustible, sending people into convulsions. Ruth turned and began to move toward her daughter when she saw Flea running to intercept her, but she stumbled as wave after wave of demonic emotions slammed into her. Visions of unimaginable cruelty and the screams of thousands upon thousands of tormented souls crying out for release assaulted her. Crippled by the onslaught, she clung desperately to the thought of securing her daughter's safety. She watched helplessly as many of those around her descended into a kind of madness. Women mindlessly rocked backed and forth as they held their children to them. Men, as if possessed, raved, cursed, shouted obscenities at their phantoms. Some, wild-eyed and frothing at the mouth, began indescriminately killing. Others just stood there crying. Some turned their weapon upon themselves. The man who had bludgeoned the mother and her child stood over her daughter crouching in fear at his feet and drew his pistol and aimed it at her head. Ruth could do nothing to save her. The shot never came, the man just stood there pointing the weapon at Flea trying to pull the trigger. He couldn't. The next thing she knew the man's eyes rolled up and he fell to the ground; a spasm ran the length of his body and then he was still. The same thing was happening with other men. The killing had stopped. Even those who tried to kill themselves now found they could not.

Then it was gone. The pain was gone; the rage had subsided to muted whispers. Ruth found herself lying surrounded by the dead, the wounded and the terrified. Some were crying hysterically, others sat mumbling to themselves. People who recognized her asked for help but the unrelenting murmur that now rose and fell inside her head, making it impossible to think clearly, meant she was barely able to help herself. All she wanted to do was get Flea and escape. Knowing that even to try was punishable by death, Ruth nevertheless grabbed a couple of rifles. What supplies she could find she hurriedly stuffed into a couple of sacks. There was nothing the two of them could do for the others without losing their own lives. The Traders were coming and knowing what that meant, she was determined not to be there when they arrived.

They would leave by the same road taken by the convoy and head toward an isolated outcrop of stone. It would be a good place to wait while deciding what to do next. The lone rider they'd seen exiting the pile of rocks would have shared the same fate of the others out there. As far as the Scavengers were concerned, they had enough problems at present and would not be going to look for a pair of absconding females. Ruth and her daughter were ready but she needed to take care of some unfinished business. Walking over to the prone man who had tried to kill her daughter, Ruth raised the rifle and began to pull the trigger. She couldn't. Hard as she tried she just wasn't able to pull the trigger. Instead she threw up and nearly passed out. Never had she wanted to kill someone as much as she did that man and finding she couldn't made her weep.

On reaching the outcrop they couldn't believe their luck at finding an awning, food, water and two, albeit unconscious, horses. Despite all their efforts to revive them, by morning the big chestnut had died. The other, though listless, looked like it would be alright in a few days, which would give them a means to regain their freedom.

Rolling her eyes upward as if acknowledging the mockery of the gods, Ruth said, "And then you showed up." Noah listened but did not take his eyes off the approach to the pinnacles. Poking her head with her finger, "It never lets up. For three days they've been in our heads and we in theirs. It was bad enough living with them, but to feel their innermost emotional filth being spewed into your mind unsolicited is a living hell."

There was nothing in that statement Noah could take exception to as he was also finding it difficult to fend off the emotions emanating from her as she told of the events that had taken place in Sweetwater. There was so much helpless fury, which only added to his already full complement of demons and ghosts who, unlike hers, were without names. He placed both hands against his head, attempting to still the turmoil. Ruth reached up to him, pulled a hand free and held it. Faces distorted with terror darted about him as he frantically fought to shut them out. What was happening to him? With considerable effort, Noah fought back. Unable to push them from his mind, he found he could at least turn down the volume.

As if he had been holding his breath, he let a long sigh. "That was a bit rough." Ruth squeezed his hand and he in turn squeezed hers. Taking in a deep breath and letting it out again, he looked at the two of them. "What was that?"

Ruth just shrugged. "I don't think it's a good idea to fight it. It only seems to make it worse."

Trying to calm his distress by diverting his attention, she asked what he had been doing, sitting out there in the dirt earlier. When he explained about his leg, expecting them to be as perplexed as he was, they just nodded as if he'd confirmed a suspicion of theirs. Seeing that he had expected more than an affirming nod, Ruth said that it appeared the ability to read emotion was not the only 'gift' they'd been bequeathed. As if on cue, Flea grinned, showing two rows of not quite perfect teeth. "Two days ago they were rotting out of her mouth. And this…" She pointed to her scar, "it used to be thick, wide and purple."

Noah's hand went to his leg. Her eyes followed and then noticed the rifle in his hands.

"What do you think you're going to do with that?" she asked.

"What do you mean what am I going to do with it? You tell me a bunch of Scavengers are headed this way and you ask why I have a rifle in my hand?"

The woman with the green eyes projected a profound sadness toward him. "Noah, as much as you may want to, if you have been affected like the rest of us, it is unlikely that you'll be able to use that when they show up. It might even be dangerous for you if you should try."

Noah looked baffled as if he couldn't comprehend what was being said. "You could have shot me back there," he said.

Shaking her head, "Nope, I couldn't. Believe me, I've tried. Like I said about the man in Sweetwater, for all the things he had done to me and what he was about to do to Flea, if I couldn't kill him…then what chance do you have of killing anyone? The truth is, if you are infected as we have been, it's unlikely that either of us could have shot the other."

He was about to ask her to clarify what she meant by 'infected' when the kid spoke in a singsong voice.

"They're here."

Three figures were making their way along the road on foot toward the pinnacles. The one in the centre wore a Trader's cloak while those on either side wore the garb of the Scavenger. Noah brought his rifle up and took aim at the one on the far left.

"They've captured a Trader." Ruth tried to stop him but Noah pushed her violently away, warning her not to try that again. He repositioned himself and once more took aim at the Scavenger on the left, knowing that before that one hit the ground the other would be joining him. As he squeezed the trigger he could hear Ruth yelling at him but her voice seemed to be drifting away. A tidal wave of emotion slammed into him. A million shadowy voices cried out in his head. Noah felt a violent vertigo sweep over him. Disoriented, he became dizzy and began to sway upon his feet. Then, to his eternal mortification, his eyes rolled into the back of his head as he passed out.

The sun felt warm on his face as he and Blue came up the pathway to the cabin. Alissa, in a frilly white dress that was all lace, ribbons and bows beginning at her throat and ending just above her ankles, and heavy with child, stood on a porch smiling when she saw him coming. He had been out in the wastelands and was eager to be home and in her arms. A small bright red spot appeared on the dress below her waist and rapidly spread, covering her chest and stomach. She began to fall slowly to the ground. He tried to scream but no sound came out. He kicked and kicked but the horse refused to move. Then he was holding her, there was blood everywhere. It covered him and his wife. It flowed like a river from a wound he could not find.

The bus was still smouldering. His father, mother, brother, sister, friends, their bodies strewn like autumn leaves, looked at him with wide questioning eyes. He waded through their blood, a lake of blood to get to them but it was too deep and he could not swim. All the while they kept calling him, damning him.

A man, on his knees, begged for his life as had all those before him. Noah did not hear the shot that blew the man's brains out nor feel the recoil of the pistol. He watch the man slump to the ground as if he was made of treacle, bleeding from a thousand wounds that joined together to form a river that covered the earth until he stood alone surrounded by blood.

Out on the lakebed, the dead came alive. Among them he saw Elle. He called out her name but she took no notice. As he moved toward them they began to dissolve into stars, millions and millions of stars, they filled the skies and drifted over the land submerging all before it in their twinkling mist. He tried to run but could not. They came for him, he watched the stars became mouths, grinning mouths with pointed teeth. He screamed but without sound. The mouths laughed without sound. He could feel their touch, their cold, cold touch. They crawled into his mouth, his ears, his nose. They bored into his flesh. Always grinning with their silent laughter, they swam through his veins, heart and lungs. They filled his mind, replacing it piece by piece till he was no more and yet nothing had changed at all. He grinned and laughed in silence.

In the darkness he was drowning. He struggled beneath the waves of a silvery sea, fighting for breath. Suddenly he breached the surface and took in lungs full of air. Then, just as he began to sink back beneath the waves again, his feet touched bottom. There was the beach, just metres away. He could see Alissa calling to him, pleading with him. Then the darkness came again and from the darkness and the silence, a thread of light appeared, then another and another till the darkness was gone. A voice was calling his name, then another and another till the world was filled with voices calling to him to come home.

Chapter Twenty-Nine
Children pay for the sins of those who came before them.

Already Elle could see that the Guardian mist continued to dissipate and was now barely perceptible. She watched her grandfather leave, feeling the intensity of his sadness, and hoped he could sense her deep affection toward him. Sunrise was still a way off, but if she wanted to clear the lakebed unseen she would have to leave now. The dog moved under the hand that hung by her side. She gave it a pat and then asked, "Did you read my mind? Then why don't we do a little exploring and see what all the fuss was about. I'll bet it will be a bit more invigorating than spending another day in front of tar baby." The dog, feeling her excitement, vigorously thumped the ground with its tail. They had the whole day in front of them.

She let out a long, slow breath and watched the slightly illuminated wisps of colour from the turbulence; the tell-tale sign that, though the Guardians were becoming difficult to see, they were still very much present, within her and without. It is going to be hard to hide, even in the dark, if that happens every time you exhale, she thought. She looked up at the mountains framed by stars, real stars. For reasons of their own, the Guardians had elected not to return to their lofty peaks. Instead they appeared content to remain right here in the wasteland where she literally breathed them in and exhaled them out. Noah had told her last night that he thought it was because they were immersed in this living mist that they were able to sense emotions. The Guardians somehow acted as a kind of conduit connecting all those who resided within. The idea of being able to extricate himself from the Guardian's influence intrigued him, as did the prospect of regaining a bit of privacy. The possible rewards of silence would be well worth the effort to find out. Elle could only agree. The noise in her head this morning seemed to confirm that great multitudes, maybe many thousands, were swimming in this silvery sea. As she packed a few essentials for herself and the dog in the knapsack, it came to her; perhaps this meant that the Guardians were strung all along the mountain chain and, as before, as far eastward as the retirement village.

She slung the pack onto her back and picked up her rifle. "Never leave home without it," she quipped to herself. If her theory was true, Noah's fears concerning the inhabitants of Sweetwater were well founded. Elle signalled the dog, who came bounding over, full of excitement. The emotions of this animal, she realized, were uncomplicated and she wondered how the dog perceived her emotions. Was it all just white noise?

Last night Noah, considering the ramifications of this guardian's gift, had given Elle a wry grin and then asked, "How do you know you have changed when the very thing that keeps track of such changes has itself changed? How do you deal with the unknown if it remains unknown to you?" These questions, she thought, were unanswerable. What might be answerable, if she was able to get inside the mountain, was what the Scavengers had expected to find. Whatever it was, they must have thought it was worth dying for.

Weighed down by the improvised pack, she lumbered through the loose sand up towards the vehicles and their silent cargo. The expected strong smell of rotting corpses was strangely absent from the battle site. No doubt a tribute to the success of the technology that secured those entombed inside their vehicles from a hostile outside world. The same was true for those suited men whose lifeless bodies now lay either draped across their weapons or sprawled on the ground nearby. Fortunately for Elle's acute sense of smell, the Guardians' preferred method of killing seemed to reduce putrefaction to a minimum. When she was last here (was it yesterday?) there didn't appear to have been any punctures in their protective clothing, which meant the Guardians might have other ways of killing their intended victims besides desiccation. Noah will be interested in that, she thought. I think I had better wait until daylight and take a closer look at what happened here. There would be no need to peer inside the vehicles to see if any had survived. She knew they were all dead just as she knew of the living in and around Sweetwater and that the dog, though hungry, was happy running up ahead and Noah was having a spot of bother.

There was not long to wait. The greying of the eastern sky told her a new day was on its way and it should prove to be a very interesting one. She got up and, with the 'twin' and dog close behind, went over for a closer look at one of the tanks. Judging by their inflated suits, now like grotesquely shaped balloons, she could see that at least some putrefaction had taken place. The battle site surrounding the convoy left no doubt the Scavengers had not died alone. They had company to escort them to wherever the souls of the dead go. The evidence of the Guardians' sacrifice encircled the vehicles, littering the ground with their minute corpses for dozens of metres in every direction. In some places their charred remains were nearly half a metre deep. Each step sounded as if she was treading across fragments of glass and, although perhaps more brittle, it did remind her of the crumbled and blackened pumice she'd seen in books about volcanos. She reached up to scoop a handful from the fender of a troop carrier and brought it to her nose. It did not smell much, just the faint hint of carbon. Like a pestle, she pressed the point of a finger into the palm of her hand. The fine granules made a soft popping sound as they melted beneath the pressure leaving a dark graphite-like smudge. None the wiser as to their composition, she let the remaining ash spill from hand and then wiped what remain on her pants. Let the dead lie with the dead, she thought, as she and her shadowy companion skirted around the battle's perimeter to follow the dog, which had shot off up the old foreshore of the lake.

Minutes later, she stood in front of what looked like a large gash in the side of the mountain. This was definitely a way in and it was obvious something had made a mess of the entrance. You couldn't see the opening from the town and certainly not from the lakebed. An unpretentious rise on this side prevented that. Looking over her shoulder, she could imagine how the Scavengers had come to suspect such a hole existed. When she and Noah had been camped out on the ridge, if they'd known where to look, they would've seen the Scavengers' objective. She ran across the road with the dog and her image following close behind. This had to be the convoy's objective for here the outer walls of these facilities had most certainly been breached, but it would have been very long ago. The Scavengers had gotten so close.

Ducking to avoid a length of protruding twisted metal beam Elle made her way through the gaping hole in what had been a pair of massive steel doors. Her footsteps echoed off the walls and vaulted ceiling of a rubble-strewn, hanger-like enclosure. Just inside the doorway Elle slid a hand along a charred and blackened wall and inspected the soot covering her fingertips. Now relegated to a minor footnote of history, at the time whatever had slammed into those huge doors would have been far from trivial considering the devastation. The explosion had virtually disintegrated the steel doors with the resulting fireball plunging inside, incinerating all that it touched. Elle craned her neck upward as she attempted to gauge the size of the room. Incredible, she thought. All that expenditure of life and effort.

The furthest recesses were hidden in greying shadows, but there was enough light streaming through the opening for her to see that nothing appeared to have been disturbed since the war or, if you didn't count the shattered doors, longer. Was it possible that this place had been deserted since the coming of the Dry? It sure looked possible. She looked at the thick layers of dust that covered every surface with the sudden realization there were no tracks, not even from the ever-present insects. Not a single spider web, old or new, adorned the archways, the equipment or ceiling panels. There should have been thousands of creepy crawlies' tracks all through the dust. But there was not a one. The ubiquitous buzzing of the ever present flies were also absent. Ever since they'd seen the descending wave of Guardians, she had not seen or heard a single fly. Elle felt an unease realizing that the Guardians had within their capacity the means to sterilize the world. They could literally eliminate every living thing.

There were times that she'd thought her quest to reach the mountains would end somewhere out there in the wasteland. The village had been a wonderful experience but standing here, in the mountain's interior, was far beyond anything she could have imagined. The size of the room carved from living rock was enormous. She wished the rest of her family were here to share this with her. The colossal dimensions of this one chamber would astonish Noah and her dad for you could probably put the Farm house, the tree outside her window and the entire front yard in here and not feel crowded. If nothing else existed beyond those walls, this room would have been worth a visit.

Another 'prick' from her grandfather alerted Elle that he'd encountered a moderate surprise of some kind. She paused in her exploration to let the emotion settle. Her previous youthful naivety was lost. How could it be otherwise? Being exposed to Noah's internal world was traumatic enough but to host the most private emotions of perhaps hundreds of men and women, who had lived the most sullied of lives, had robbed her of any remaining innocence. This change was not a catastrophe, maybe because of her age but probably because of the kind of person she was. Unlike her grandfather who demanded absolute control over all aspects of his life, although unaware of the shift, she was already adapting. The ability to sense the emotions of another would soon be just another skill she could call on when required.

A quick look from an elevated position near the door showed that the inferno from the explosion had been limited to less than half the interior, leaving the remainder undisturbed. Like the village, it was a virtual time capsule of the Before Times. There was no doubt that the people who built this place thought and acted on a grand scale and knew nothing of austerity. The quality of material used on the interior's furnishing, the number of loading bays, trucks and assorted specialized vehicles left little doubt that a good deal of wealth and energy had been lavished upon what was essentially a place where things got picked up and dropped off. She could not help feeling insignificant. And yet, after peering into the cab of a mobile crane, Elle saw that their considerable wealth, power and scientific skills had not prevented their untimely demise. She moved gingerly across the floor disturbing as little as possible. This wasn't easy as the floor area was packed with vehicles and their drivers. By the time she had reached the far wall, she had seen more than fifty desiccated bodies that had been dead long before those doors had been vaporised. What she wanted now, most of all, was time to explore without being interrupted by the outside world.

She poked in corners, pulled open drawers and cabinets, inspected the contents of various offices and several vehicles and clambered up onto the stage-like loading bay, searching for what she did not know. And all the time she kept a running monologue with her hands for the benefit of her silent 'friend'. Whether or not the Guardian's representative beside her understood these visual ramblings, it gave no indication. The image no longer mimicked nor responded to her signing or conversation. Like the real tar baby, it just stood there, 'sayin' nothin'.

From the loading docks there was an unobstructed view all the way back to the entrance. Impressive as it was, this was not the 'main' entrance. That and the real treasures lay elsewhere. There were several doors along the back wall and a large pair up on the loading bay that looked promising. There was also what looked like a two lane service road running along the far perimeter. Any of them might lead her to where all the mountain's secrets and wealth lived.

But for the moment at least, this was the limit of her exploration. Any investigation into the inner sanctum would have to be put on hold until she secured a light of some kind. Other than at Sweetwater, the only ones she knew of were back in the wagon. Going there to retrieve one was not an option at the moment and not just because she was presently without a horse. The distance was not that great that it couldn't be made on foot, but the lake bed was where her grandfather would expect to find her on his return tomorrow. So that was where she would be. The Dry, as she rightly knew, brought with it the constant threat of death. He had left her on the western edge of the lake bed. Everything he did to make his way back would be predicated on the assumption that she was waiting for him as agreed.

Thinking of him brought his emotional state into sharp focus. She could feel his presence and he was not in a charitable mood. Noting what was apparently the logo of this installation was unlikely to improve it. Just how would he interpret the coming of the Dry, and the Guardians' hydrophilia, when he saw the figure of 'Aquarius', the water bearer of the Zodiac, encircled by the phrase, 'In the Public's Trust for the Public's Good'. It was etched on the glass of the offices and painted on their doors. It was on all the vehicles and the archway of the service road. Just reading the phrase out loud sent a chill up her spine and down her arms.

Standing in front of the large set of doors that led off the loading platform, she pulled one open but inside it was black as pitchblende. Frustrated at being denied the means to explore what was richer to her than a dozen Ali Baba's caves, she'd have to be content rummaging in the area framed by the sun's rays.

Elle turned to her entourage. "What I wouldn't do for a lamp right now."

The words were barely out of her mouth when her replica slowly began to phosphoresce, producing a soft yellow glow.

Elle's giggle gurgled up and exploded into laugher. "I'll be damned!" was all she could say as she pulled open the doors, pausing long enough to let the dog and her personal illumination go past before stepping through herself

The air was stale and tasted of dust. It was breathable but she'd have to be careful, although she'd no idea just how she'd manage that. There was no ventilation and there would be no warning of asphixiation by carbon monoxide poisoning. She'd just slump down and die in a coma-induced sleep. The light was pathetic, at best 5 watts she thought, but it did assist in navigating the hallways, avoiding bumping into walls and the occasional corpse. It also helped in finding the doors and their handles. The feeble light, however, was incapable of exposing the scale of this manmade subterranean world. Save for the echoes, she could not tell if the ceiling above her was just a metre away or thirty. Encased within the little circle of light, she found it impossible to appreciate the scale of the place nor was the light bright enough for her to read text smaller than a headline.

By the end of her first few hours of aimlessly wandering down innumerable hallways and inspecting various offices, her inability to see much in the dim light made her previous excitement wane. Elle turned her attention to finding a stairwell to another level. There had to be more to this place than hallways and offices.

At the end of a particularly long hallway stood a row of paired metal doors. She thought they might be elevators. Off to one side there was a single door with a large number one painted on it and the word 'exit' above it, which she assumed was a stairwell. She allowed her double to go first. A glance inside revealed stairs leading up and down. Elle swung the door open to let the dog through but it hesitated, reluctant to venture into what seemed a menacing black hole. Impatient at the dog's reluctance, Elle stepped into the stairwell herself, letting the door close behind her.

Distracted by a sudden stinging surge of revulsion from her grandfather, she failed to notice the body in the dim light and ended up sprawling across the floor, striking her head on a large metal container which momentarily knocked her unconscious.

Coming to, she heard the sound of the dog whining and scratching to be let in. Covered with decades of filth and with the taste of blood in her mouth, she pushed herself up into a sitting position and raised a hand to her head. The greenish yellow light gave the considerable amount of blood on her hand a decisively black appearance, as if she was bleeding ink. "Bloody hell

Granddad, what was that all about? You almost got me killed!"

As if it were something she had done all her life, Elle automatically reached out to Noah but felt only the smallest impression. Maybe he's too far away, she thought. Whatever the reason, she wrestled with a growing unease that things on the surface might not be going to plan. Her own plans were also for the moment in disarray. Raising her hand again to inspect the damage, her fingers felt a small cut high up on the forehead that was bleeding heavily. Other than the cut and a split lip, she didn't appear to have sustained any lasting damage. If she'd been a few millimetres more in the stairwell it could have been a different story entirely. This would be a very lonely place to die, she thought, opening the door to let the dog in. After dusting herself off as best she could while stopping the dog from licking the blood off her hand, she knelt down to take a closer look at this would-be assassin, the metal box.

A swipe of her hand removed enough grit to allow her to read the printing on its lid, 'Emergency First Aid'. She'd literally stumbled upon a cache of emergency supplies that was supposedly tucked out of harm's way. Elle, pushing the body out of her way, dragged the locker clear of the alcove where it had been stored. Opened, just as the lid had indicated, it was filled to the brim with an assortment of items relating to basic first aid. Smiling at the idea of its appropriateness, she hunted through its contents for a compression bandage. The gash was bleeding rather profusely, running into her eyes and down her face. Finding exactly what she was looking for, she ripped it free from its protective covering and secured it in place. Then, with a length of sterile cloth ripped from another plastic package, she set about wiping away the blood from her face and eyes. Head wounds seemed to bleed way out of proportion to the injury inflicted.

Satisfied that the bandage wouldn't come off any time soon, she began looking for anything else that might come in handy and stuffed the items in her knapsack and pockets. People of the Dry did not allow an opportunity to scavenge go by. One item of particular interest was a very large torch but sadly the batteries had erupted, corroding its interior to such an extent that even if she could find replacements, it was unlikely to work. That aside, patting her pockets after standing up, she was a bit more prepared for any other mishap that should befall her.

Just as she was about to close the lid, a clear plastic envelope attached to the underside of the lid attracted her attention. The contents were floor plans of the entire installation. With exaggerated care, Elle extracted and then unfolded the document, spreading it on the now closed lid of the locker. In the pale light offered by her companion and without the aid of a red 'You Are Here' sticker, it took a few minutes for her to find and orient herself. Once that was done, it did not take long to locate the one thing she wanted most, a major store room. The first one she found lay upstairs, close to the entrance. Too bad, she thought of the missed opportunity. "I must remember to check it on my way out," she told the dog who was trying to get around her for a better look at what the human was so interested in.

The level she was on, as she had already discovered from wandering around, was largely administrative offices and therefore not of immediate interest to her. Her finger dropped to the level below and skimmed over the various rooms until it came to rest on one with the title 'Main Supply Depot #3'. She glanced down at the lower right hand corner of the map for the 'key box' that contained the map's scale. This installation was really huge; nine levels that stretched nearly three kilometres in length and one in width. If she had traced the path correctly from the entrance to where she now knelt, #3 was about 500 metres from her present location. Better yet, she was kneeling in the stairwell that would take her there.

The door to the storeroom had been hermetically sealed and was difficult to get open. But when it opened, even in the limited light from her companion, the storeroom was a marvellous sight to behold, putting the Scavengers' warehouse to shame. This was not the spoil of petty thieves or the booty of wanton vandals. Depot #3 was pristine. Here, in this room, the plunder of scores of nations had been stored. No grubby, opportunistic, villainous hands here. There was food, tons of food, and bottled water, not as much of a critical item as she had first supposed since, for reasons she would soon come to understand, it flowed, if sometimes begrudgingly, from several of the taps she'd tried on level '1'. There were also rows upon rows of clothing, boots, shoes, blankets, sheets and towels. Pots and pans, cutlery, thick heavy white dishes, cups and bowls occupied a whole section. And there was the possibility for light, with racks of batteries, a range of various size torches and camping gas lanterns. There were even single and double burner cookers and hundreds of boxes containing fuel canisters for them and the lamps. Stacked up three metres or more were camping tents, still in their boxes with their faded illustration of a happy family of six. (Six? Four children. What riches.)

Elle could not help but wonder what in the world they actually expected to happen down here that would require camping equipment? Whatever the reason had been it had most certainly been lost in the Before Time. For right now, she was its sole beneficiary. She went back to the section with the batteries and torches. These people were looking ahead, she noted, taking down and opening a box containing 'flash' fuel-cell batteries. By the time she'd been born, this technology was long gone and, although she had never been in the presence of one that worked, she knew how to activate it. Grabbing a torch of the appropriate size, she took a flash fuel-cell out of the box, twisted the two sides a hundred and eighty degrees and then pushed them together. Satisfied that she'd done it correctly, she put it in the torch and flicked the switch, to be rewarded by a beam of light, beautiful light. The beam was powerful enough that she could see nearly to the end of the depot. Scanning the area immediately around her she said, "Now this is what I call a light."

Coming around the corner at the far end of a line of shelves, Elle stopped and looked with disbelief. Rapture. Heaped up to the ceiling was toilet paper, boxes and boxes of two-ply, ultra-soft white toilet paper. Elle pulled one down and tore open the plastic covering to feel the soft texture. What unimaginable luck. She would still have to squat to relieve herself in a bucket but at least next time she'd have toilet paper to wipe her bum. Along another row of shelves she stopped with a mixture of delight and surprise. "Noah is not going to believe this," she murmured, staring at whole shelves dedicated to coffee.

Enough wasting time. Elle quickly prepared several 'camp' lamps and stationed them around the depot. She requisitioned a large hand trolley from the back of the storeroom and loaded it to overflowing with anything that caught her eye, with special attention to the toilet paper. Satisfied that not one more item could be put in the trolley, she set out to find a place to sleep.

Since she came from the hand-me-down, vandalized world of the Dry, the choices confronting Elle were a tantalizing luxury. This place far exceeded what she had experienced in the walled village, for here she was the first person to visit in over half a century. Luckily there was no need to haul the booty far as she'd found a sizeable office on her way to the depot that was tailored to her requirements. Elle didn't read the name on the office door and a quick flick of her knife blade sent the plastic plate skittering down the hall. Once inside she propped the door open and placed one of the two lamps on a hutch that ran along the wall and the other on a desk on the far side of the room. Soon the office was ablaze with light.

A lot can be gauged of a person by the things they choose to surround themselves with. This person's taste in literature and science was in sympathy with her own. Art adorned the walls, the bookcases and desk. Blown glass, bronze sculptures, paintings, things she had never seen except in books or as smashed, broken and discarded fragments. And speaking of books, real books, an entire wall was dedicated to them. A brief perusal of the titles sent Elle into near ecstasy. The ravages of the wastelands had not been kind to such fragile things. Her eyes skimmed a couple of rows, reading a few of the titles before selecting one. Elle pulled it down from the shelf and opened it. The smell, that wonderful smell of an old book newly opened, was intoxicating. After glancing at the title and reading a few lines that caught her interest, she put it back and then slowly walked around the room inspecting each of the objects in turn, sensing once more the magnitude of the loss of the Before Times. "I think I would have liked this guy," she said, pausing before an oil painting that depicted two girls of about her own age reclining in a boat that sat in the middle of a small lake. Elle resisted the strongest urge to reach up and touch its surface. The girls, in floral summer dresses and wide brimmed straw hats, were asleep, an opened book resting on one's chest. She tasted a tear at the corner of her mouth. In the Before Times such a painting was already well out of fashion and would have been mocked by some as being overly sentimental. Had she known of this, she would still not have cared. The painting of the sleeping girls surrounded by water, more than anything else, made this her place.

The office had other advantages on offer besides the painting – its size and central location. There was an adjoining apartment with a large double bed, a compact kitchen and a bathroom. Water flowed thinly from the taps in the kitchen and washbasin. To her delight, the bathroom also had a working shower if you did not mind describing the pathetic stream that issued forth as a shower. There was no way of telling what her companion thought of all this, although it did seem to be uncommonly interested in the running water. With the doppelganger and dog trailing in her wake, she spent the next couple of hours removing dust and dirt and finding places for the things she had taken from her trips to the depot. Finally finished, she stood in the centre of the office to survey her work. Elle grinned as she remembered the countless times her mother had nagged her about the state of her room. The shock would kill her, she thought. Feeling all sweaty and covered in grime, she thought it was time to attend to her own personal hygiene. Even a child of the Dry had limits to the state of filth they were prepared to accommodate.

Unlike the light from her companion, the lamps gave off a harsh, unflattering, white light that reflected off the muted colours of the very well-appointed bathroom, giving the confined space a stark appearance. Elle barely noticed this as she stepped from the shower stall. With one towel casually draped across her shoulders, using another to dry her hair, she moved over to stand in front of the mirror over the sink.

The shower had been miserly, the soap had crumbled and the towel was stiff as canvas, but the experience bordered on divine. It had been wonderful. The girl that stared back at her did not seem to look any different than the one she had seen in the lakeside house or at the village. The same piercing eyes, dark skin, thin androgynous body topped by a mass of raven hair cut very short.

A small high pitched squeak escaped her lips. Her hands stopped their busy drying ritual as she leaned over the sink to get a closer look. Where was the gash on her forehead, the cut on her lip? They were gone. The hair, it was the same length as when she'd left the farm. She removed the towel, allowing it to drop to the floor, and twisted her body back and forth to see if anything else had changed. The ugly gash on her leg, the cut on her shin and the one festering wound over her heart were now just thin, fading, white lines. The bruising was gone as well. Other scars that she'd acquired through her numerous misadventures had completely disappeared.

"How do you know you've changed...?" Standing before both her reflected image and that of the guardian, a sudden flash of insight occurred to Elle as she hurriedly thought over the events of the last few days.

In one way or another, a number of minor miracles had occurred. An epiphany – she remembered casually wishing to be able to read the minds of others. She had also wanted the doppelganger to be able to sign 'water'. She'd been frustrated at being unable to explore the facility's interior due to the absence of light and had been discontented over the length of her hair. As to the disappearing scars, she didn't remembering wishing them away. Perhaps she had or maybe... At least she may have thought that she didn't want to die from the wound inflicted by the Scavenger's blade. She paused in mid-thought at another possible explanation – that their disappearance was related to something else altogether. Feeling decidedly ill-at-ease at the significance of this revelation, she reached up to touch her lengthened locks and then down to her heart and then the leg, probing the disappearing cut. "My friend you had better get control of your wishes before someone gets hurt."

She touched the ring around her neck and the knife on the sink. It appeared that not all wishes had been granted; the ring and handle of the knife remained incomplete. The doppelganger walked over to stand by her and to Elle's surprise the mirror revealed something unanticipated. Instead of an exact replication, the image in the mirror revealed a sort of pulsating nebulous cloud. Glancing back and forth from the mirror to her replica, Elle could not help but wonder, "what next?"

What was next was food. She was starving. Miracles, however impressive, do not fill a person's belly. The moment her thoughts drifted to the prospects of eating, the dog came over and stood by the pile of RTE's to wait.

"What's it going to be like hunting when every little creature can read your intentions from your emotion, eh?" All she received in turn from the dog was a desire that could only be interpreted as 'feed me, NOW'. Their thoughts are pretty direct, she thought, as she unpacked a twin burner stove and inserted a gas canister. Looking at the dog she said, "You're simple, you know that." The dog wagged its tail and licked its chops in anticipation.

Clean, fed and newly attired, Elle spread the map out onto the desk. With the wonders of a satisfied stomach and clean clothing, even the prospect that she might no longer be fully human did not have the significance one would have imagined.

Elle had given up the idea of signing as a means of communicating. In so far as she knew, this whatever-it-was seemed to possess little more intelligence than the dog and, since she spoke to the dog, she might as well speak to her image. It was a lot like speaking to herself.

Her hand slid across the map attempting to smooth out its years of being folded away. Excluding the main entrance and its grand foyer which appeared to be tucked away in a small cleft a short distance from the entrance she had used, the complex was divided into four areas of function: offices with living quarters; labs/work/machines shops; recreational, which seemed to cover kitchens, living, eating and sleeping facilities; and a huge area entitled 'Breeder Chamber'.

"Now that has got to be a place of interest," said Elle. "I bet this is the 'how' of their entire enterprise." Looking over at her replica, also newly attired down to the wrinkled folds of the shirt, she said, "But first, let's find out where the boss lived because if you want to know what the body is doing, talk to its head."

After following a circuitous route through the interlocking hallways and stairwells, Elle found the 'head'. Flanked by lesser executive offices, it was situated at the opposite end of a large open lobby. There was no mistaking the pompous significance of the marble statue of the 'Water Carrier' as a centrepiece of what would have been a fountain, nor the elaborate ornamentations, the embossed logos and their gilded titles and name plates. Here lived the rulers of this underground fortress. Like everything else she'd seen, it was built on a grand scale, designed to impress and intimidate. Each room was immaculate and well appointed. Similar in design to her own newly acquired 'home', the offices were bigger and their adjoining apartments were large suites. Even under thick layers of dust, there was no difficulty recognizing the presence that once denoted power and wealth. In the CEO's office there was a window, but without lights, it looked like a dark void. Had there been lights she would have looked down at what had been the heart and soul, the very essence of this place, the reason all these people were here. She would have been able to see the 'Breeding Chamber' two stories below with more gadgetry in one place than she had seen in her entire life. However, there was no need for lights; from the photos in the various offices she already knew what was down there. She thought of watching the look on her grandfather's face when he saw this place, if he saw this place. She'd not felt a strong presence for quite some time. The equipment and machinery would beguile him but all this opulence would be offensive for he truly was, at heart, as austere as a monk. Jacob with his love of machinery would be besotted.

If the mark of a man of power is the art they coveted, then the man who had sat at the head of the table in the conference room had been indeed powerful. Every wall and flat surface laboured under the weight of what had to have been his obsession. Unlike the figure in the hallway, Elle was certain these were not mere copies or reproductions. They were the real thing. Here, amidst all this treasure, her mother would have gone berserk. She'd have Elle's father hauling it all down to a waiting wagon, of that she had no doubt. As for the man most likely responsible for acquiring this collection, he, along with his colleagues, was dead. They lay in their respective crumbled heaps on the floor circling an oval table that was so big it would dwarf the one in their dining room.

"A least it seemed they had time to stand up before dying," mused Elle as she made herself comfortable in a cracked and crumbling chair. Sitting there she suddenly felt tired. She couldn't tell how long she been inside the mountain, but it seemed like it had been a long 'day'. By the time she had found her way back to her apartment and fixed something to eat, she was overdue for a bit of sleep.

Throughout the next 'day' Elle wandered aimlessly with the dog at her heels. Sometime while she slept, her doppelganger vanished. She awoke, turned on a lamp and, other than the dog at the foot of the bed, found herself alone in the room. A search of the apartment revealed no clue to its whereabouts or that, outside her imagination, it had ever existed. By the third sweep she was left with the conclusion that an ethereal being leaves no residue. Where such things went was as much a puzzlement as where it had come from in the first place. Strangely Elle found herself at a bit of a loss. So accustomed was she to having this silvery shadow accompany her and the dog, there was a sense of incompleteness. Silly she knew, but it did almost seem as if a part of her had gone. Slightly shaken, the plan of a return trip to the boardroom was put off. Instead, with a torch in one hand, floor plans tucked under an arm, food, water and additional flash batteries in the backpack, Elle went to find the 'Breeding Chamber' as well as to visit the labs and workshops that occupied the lowest level.

Yesterday's initial jubilation ebbed and flowed. Away from the offices, level 2 was crowded and 3 even more so. Like bundles of discarded refuse Elle came across hundreds of the former occupants in the stairwell, the hallways, workshops, personal accommodation, kitchens and dining halls. Some had died alone, others died in the company of colleagues. They died while at work, at play, at rest and asleep. Except in a few instances in the upper level there was virtually no sign of panic or flight. The majority died in ignorance, not even, it would seem, having the time to be surprised. With a torch held high lighting her way, she drifted for hours throughout the complex like some lost tormented ghostly aberration. Except for that one time at the homestead and perhaps the site of the Cleansing, Elle had always been successful at divorcing herself from the dead, an extremely necessary trait for those of the Dry. Ever since she had climbed through those shattered entrance doors this had started to change. Now, the seemingly most inconsequential of things had a powerful impact on her. It was not as if death and the mementos of the dead were unfamiliar. The wastelands were littered with such things. The difference here, much as in the village, was that everything was so pristine, so uncorrupted, so filled with interrupted possibilities.

A personal diary, a real personal diary, not a PSim, or linkbook, left open on a small desk, a gaily wrapped birthday present with a card from a friend left on a bed, a child's toy pinned to the wall along with a crayon drawing of the family, a photo of a smiling young man, perhaps her lover or husband clutched in the gnarled hand of a woman, and the newspapers, especially those that had been delivered on the last day of their lives. Some, still folded, lay as if waiting for their owners. How innocuous and ordinary everything looked. Inevitably drawn into the tragedy that had occurred here, that had brought forth the Dry, Elle was moved, often to tears, at the sheer naivety of these people. Was there no awareness of what was taking place, no sense of fear, guilt, doubt or dread? Was there ever a hesitation? If there was, not a hint was evident anywhere. How was it possible that so many people had been able to go about their daily lives seemingly so unconcerned? Could anyone be so indifferent or so driven that they were incapable of questioning what it was they were doing or were they so accustomed to a privileged existence the very idea it could end never entered their heads

People are not blank slates upon which anything can be written but that is not to say our companions do not leave their mark. Elle had been born and raised in a household of practical people. Art, literature, science were tools of practical people. Sitting in the spacious dining hall with the dead strewn around her, Elle read through a number of newspapers and magazines but found little of substance and nothing even hinting at the impending difficulties that were about to be unleashed. They were so vacuous, empty. How could anyone waste their time reading so much unimportant, trivial and sensationalized nonsense? Why would anyone subject themselves to reading articles and commentaries recounting the nation's recent murders, robberies, fraud or being alerted to some self-inflicted catastrophe that was occurring in one corner of the world or another? Why become embroiled in the lives of other people, people whose contribution seemed to be about how poorly they managed their life. What a waste.

The last chilling lines in a notebook she'd found made the contents of these newspaper seem all the more insignificant. Hidden away in this underground cocoon, people with their birthday presents, their lover's photos, their daily newspapers unread and waiting for them, had murdered her world. One of them had sat at their desk in a shared room and written, '*The nanopods are ready and will be released into the atmosphere tomorrow. If all goes as planned we will not just be able to predict the weather but manage it as well. And I will be able to tell my grandkids that I was here on that day.*

They were the first to die. They died quickly, cleanly, healthy and well-fed. They died surrounded by wealth and, in some instances, beauty.

Did any of them even once think of what it was they were actually doing?

A chill descended on her, a freezing of emotions. A person can become embittered by the careless inertia of others. These people, just going about doing their jobs, had unleashed a nightmare that consumed their world and hers. They'd stolen the rain and she dearly wanted it back. Showing the only sign of contempt she knew, Elle spat on the pages of the notebook in front of her and then hurled it against the wall shouting, though none but the dog could hear, "You should have not died so comfortably. You should have died writhing in unimaginable pain. You had no right to take the rain from us. Give me back the rain!"

Frightened by the outburst, the dog whined and sent out waves of fear. It was hungry and thirsty and saw no reason for this emotional eruption.

Agreeing with the dog she said, "Let's go and get something to eat. I've seen enough of this." About to take one of the newspapers with her, Elle suddenly threw it across the room as well.

The sound of the slamming door echoed and re-echoed along the hallway leading to Elle's chamber. A strong urge to hit something, to hurt something, boiled inside her. "Where are you granddad? Why aren't you here? How come it's so hard to feel you? You would know what to do. You would know what to say. Mom, Dad, I am so, so sorry." Head tilted, eyes squeezed shut, brow furrowed, fist clenched, Elle pushed her emotions out, trying to smash through any barrier that stopped her from touching Noah. He was alive, although he seemed so far from her she could barely feel him. Everything around her seemed to be more mist and mirrors than anything of substance.

Later, mechanically, a meal was prepared and eaten. The dog was given its portion but no rub of the head or scratch behind the ear. Elle was not in the mood. In an easy chair in a corner of the bedroom, absentmindedly sucking on the ring as if it was a pacifier, she was somewhat bemused that she was missing her double. Even with the company of the dog, it would be better if it was here as well.

In bed, asleep, she wept and dreamt of rain, gentle, soft, warm, life-giving rain. It fell upon her, wetting her face, mingling with the tears, soaking the earth. The sky overhead was dark, a blackness so intense and absolute, the mind saw light where there was none. The taste of salt was on her lips. She was awake; the heat of the sun must have woken her. As she sat up the boat rocked sending little waves off to the edge of the pond. The book fell into her lap. She picked it up but try as she might, she could read neither the title nor the author. She looked across at her sister who was asleep, her face all in shadows. She called to her but she did not stir. Then, since dreams are not governed by logic or physics, she sat at the head of the huge conference table with the faces of her eleven co-conspirators looking back at her. They waited for her to nod, giving the signal to begin a process that would be the making of history.

Elle's eyes flicked open. The room was not tar pit black as it should have been. A dim glow was emanating from her body, encircling her like an aura. Immobilized with fear, she lay there. The aura wavered and, as if a breeze had entered the room, drifted away in long flowing strands that coalesced into a slowly revolving vortex of swirling silver out of which her image emerged.

Chapter Thirty
You often find you need to share your chosen road.

The memory games she'd played with Noah out in the wastelands were proving to be very beneficial. As a means to entertain herself, Elle often did not bother to light a lamp as she moved through the corridors with the confidence of a blind person in their own home. In her mind lived a full scale three dimensional map of every place she had been and the means to get there. Time on the other hand was as elusive as ever. Not fond of keeping track of time, she never wore a watch. Having no sun to mark the passing of the day, no moon or stars to mark the passing of the night, when hungry she ate, when tired she slept.

In the light of several camp lamps strategically place about the room, this figure of a tall, thin, not-yet woman sitting in a high backed office chair seemed almost demure. Ten sleeps might not quite equate to ten days and for the last eight of these 'days', in between the eating and the sleeping, she was in the boardroom reading. The replica, in its interminable silence, remained at her side or within. A ball of light, much softer than that given off by the lamps, hovered just about her head. Finished with the file, she carefully closed the folder, ensuring that all its contents were secure, before putting it with the others. Fortunately, these people had been sticklers for detail and redundancy. There was a room on one of the lower floors that housed bank upon bank of computers. On nearly every desk was a display and a randomizer supposedly filled with their personal selected images. In nearly every desk's right hand top drawer sat a PSim of various sizes, from that of a large book to ones smaller than the palm of a hand. There were also PSims in their pockets or next to the bed or left, perhaps momentarily misplaced, in one corner of a room or another. And yet, among all this ephemeral technology, there were still books, files and photos. Strange, thought Elle, it appears that even here, there was a need to touch something that had a physical existence in the here and now. Although there were reasons to feel both, somewhere along the way her sense of rage and anger had dissipated. Despair and melancholy also eluded her. The scale of the betrayal was just too immense to be encompassed by the likes of her.

She eased herself up from the comfort of her chair, stepping over a desiccated body to retrieve several more folders from the file drawer and read the titles on each folder before returning two to the opened drawer. She placed the others, but one, on the boardroom table to her right before she sat down again to read. This had become an essential and invariable part of her 'daily' routine. Mimicking a swarm of flies in the wastelands the bubble of light hovered above her, following her every movement.

The morning following her dream Elle had been driven by a strong urge to return to the conference room adjoining the office of the CEO and, once there, it did not take long for her to understand why. Here, in this room, people had sat and talked of the need to control, to manage the world's essential and yet diminishing resources, especially water. Here in this room, the Dry and all its consequences were fashioned. Such arrogance, such duplicity, drove from her any sense of propriety. These people were evil, not the Scavengers' evil, but the evil born of ordinariness, of routine. What had given them the right, as they put it, 'to harvest the endless bounty of the seasons' by controlling the rain as if it were just another resource to be bought and sold? They wanted to 'manage' the rain. Under their control, it would not fall freely, dispensing its life-sustaining favours where it might, but rather be held in servitude, in *their* servitude, for eternity. Reading their intent, Elle found it difficult to draw in breath. She was not persuaded by the language of these people when alluding to 'the good of humankind', and it did not take an overly sceptical mind or even an educated one to taste their desire for power and the greed such motives breed. These people might not have wanted to kill us, but they did, was the only thought she could hold.

On the folders of interest, centred below the company's Aquarius logo, was printed in an unassuming type 'Water Management Project'. Below it, in brackets and in a smaller type, printed in blood red was the word 'Top Secret'. Her hand idly touched the ring's stone, black like onyx, taking it between thumb and forefinger twisting it back and forth, back and forth. It was comforting to have it and the knife made whole again. She had not seen it happen but guessed it had occurred at the same time as the doppelganger's reappearance. No longer a deep green, the items changed to meet her mood, which for some time now had slid from grey to black. Letting the ring go, she reached up and scratched an itchy spot in the middle of her head. The bubble of light bobbed out of her way. Ever since she had discovered the doppelganger could reside within her and be called upon at will, another talent had revealed itself. Being able to invoke a globe of light was stumbled upon while trying to see into a shadowed corner. Not quite a wish, more like a thought that took on a physical form.

She read a bit more and then looked up from the folder open on the table in front of her to once again survey the contents of the room. The huge conference table with the twelve high-back chairs dominated it. The irony of a collection of bottled water and an empty ice bucket as a centrepiece did not escape Elle's notice. Except for where she sat, eleven of the twelve chairs, eleven of the twelve identical reports ready to be read, eleven of the twelve empty glasses, eleven of the twelve leather-bound notebooks, eleven of the twelve pens, eleven blank displays and eleven of the twelve desiccated bodies were as she had found them. The twelve in this room must have held a great deal of power. Their voices, now mute, would have been listened to. Noah had once reached out with his knife to skewer the last bit of meat from a stew they had been sharing, citing his size, age and experience, explaining as he did so, "With very few exceptions, my little one, in the grand scheme of things, the possession of power, however small, is ultimately abused. It is the way of things, so do not assume you are immune from it, either as its perpetuator or its victim." And then with a smirk, he had popped the meaty morsel into his mouth.

Elle tossed the largely unread file onto the desk. "Well they certainly abused it here, Granddad. What were these people thinking?" The globe of light again quivered. Looking up she moaned, "Sorry, it's so hard not to allow a little irritation to leak out." She closed her eyes and steadied her breathing. The globe descended to hang above the papers and files that were neatly stacked in various piles.

The dog looked up, wagged its tail and sent a short burst of emotional concern.

Oops! thought Elle, having forgotten once again that the dog could pick up on emotions as well as she could. No wonder Granddad felt he had to get as far away from me as he could. Poor man. I must have seemed like a box of flapping birds in that carefully controlled world of his. A pat on the head, a scratch behind the ear and in less than a minute the dog's emotional output returned to its familiar 'white noise', a mental purr that Elle had come to recognize as its contented state. "I wish I could just let it go as you do. No problem so big that it can't be satisfied with a full stomach and an empty head."

Alone, without the physical presence of friend or family, the real problem was remaining sane. Between the constant background buzz in her head of the 'others', the lack of any strong contact with her grandfather and the knowledge of what had gone on in these facilities, Elle was finding it increasingly difficult to concentrate on the task at hand. She picked up the folder she'd just dropped on to the table and casually turned over one page after another. "But I would never have been as insane as these people," she muttered. "Not content to get themselves killed, they had to drag the rest of us along with them." Noah had been wrong. The Scavengers were not the only ones capable of such infamy that they would stop the rains. Elle was simply not capable of identifying with their motives. Had they no thoughts as to what might happen if things did not go according to plan? Did they even understand what water was? "And where is everybody? Why hasn't someone, anyone come here?"

The coming of the Dry ate into the soul of civilization. It unravelled its very fabric leaving nothing but the wasteland that gave no mercy to its dwindling inhabitants. To survive, one clung desperately to any remaining source of water and for those that did, they were always under threat of people like the Scavengers. She grimaced. Scavengers, another gift of the Dry and these people. When the rain stopped all other options collapsed, all other paths save one. Find and hold water at any cost. In that sense, within the confinement of the boardroom, Elle suddenly came to understand what she was, what the Traders, Noah and the rest of the family were. They too fought to possess water. They killed to stay alive, to survive. She had almost killed that little girl in Sweetwater and had tried to do the same to her grandfather on the lakebed. It was automatic, unthinking, and in that respect her acts were no different than those of the Scavengers, her appointed enemy. Or even these people.

The Scavengers were hated and feared by all those she loved and cared for, but in the context of the Dry they were at least comprehensible. Here, in this luxurious grotto, sitting among such wealth, knowing they wanted still more, these people were not. Their hubristic greed, their insufferable conceit made her again wish their deaths had been prolonged and filled with an infinity of pain.

The globe quivered, the dog whined. Elle took a very deep breath and then deliberately watched the muted paisley colours stream out from her exhaled breath.

Thinking of her grandfather and wondering if he was alright there came a shift of tone in the voices. Like a wolf raising its nose to sample the breeze, Elle stopped reading and lifted her head, closing her eyes to better 'listen'. A frown formed as she sensed her grandfather's grief. After days of near silence he had reappeared and although she did not sense he was in danger or in physical pain, his distress was nevertheless penetrating. In addition, the continuous clamour of the 'others' that she had successfully relegated to a mental dungeon, was no longer content to just nibble at her consciousness. They were demanding an audience. But the why eluded her. The invasion of her body had given her the ability to read the emotions of others; it did not make her clairvoyant.

Suddenly the dog sprang up from where it had been dozing as it too was aware that there a shift of some kind in the celestial ether of the world outside. Bathing Elle in reams of emotions, the animal sped out of the room and down the corridor. She barely acknowledged its emotional urgency, being fairly sure, as before, it would return soon with neither of them any the wiser. She saw no need to join the dog on its ventures. Once had been enough. She'd gone all the way to the entrance on the first level and found nothing that could possibly be of interest to either her or the dog. She did want company but she also wanted this place to herself for a bit longer and acknowledging that it was selfish did not diminish the desire to be left undisturbed.

Elle returned to her reading after radiating a string of emotional flavours to let Noah know she was safe and well while hoping he was the same. Emotions do not do questions, so adding a sense of mental disarray would have to do. This gift, if one considered it as such, had limitations. It did not come with either a sensitive range finder or a compass, nor could it tell her how many voices were out there, but it could differentiate. She had lived within Noah's heartbeat for nearly all her life and the days she'd spent with him on the lakebed, especially the sharing of breath, had unknowingly imprinted his emotional signature upon her. The entire time she'd been within these catacombs, from the barely audible mumble to the occasional roar, he was with her and she with him. He would let her know if she was needed. That she was sure of.

It was getting late or at least it felt that way to Elle. Satisfied with her day's efforts she stood up and twisted her body back and forth trying to lose some of the stiffness. Even if she were not wholly satisfied, she felt drained. The increasing emotional intensity was drawing her mind off onto other things. Elle sat back down, slid the files further along the desk's surface to make room for her feet. The world will be better off without us, she thought as she leaned back in her chair and glanced across the desk at the photo of her grandmother and her family. She kept it and its new companion with her everywhere she went. They had become a kind of totem, a means of linking her family at the farm and those members who had died long before her birth. The photo of her grandmother was now housed in a modest frame she had confiscated, as befitted her role as a survivor of these people's stupidity. The other was a serendipitous find, another piece of the jigsaw she was currently assembling.

There is a region of the mind that sets itself apart. It sits there and sees things and thinks about things that the rest of the mind does not seem to notice and, when it has finished mulling over what it saw or thought about, it alerts the rest of the mind to its findings. The dream that sent her scurrying back to the conference room also sent her to the bookshelf whose contents she had admired on her first day. There she pulled down the same book she had before. She had been unable to read its title and author in the dream. The opening sentence of the book's first chapter read, *'The universe and all that it contains abhors chaos. The atoms in a grain of sand and the atoms in a star organize themselves using the same laws of physics. Life, while adhering to these laws, organises itself through the laws of evolution. It is unavoidable. Even the most elementary of life's forms seek order right down to the molecule.'* The title of the book was *The Self Organisation of Viruses* and was written by Doctor Scout Evergreen.

Elle could be forgiven. A corpse dressed in a shirt and slacks, with short cropped hair and covered with sixty years of dust could be seen as gender neutral. The person in the chair was not a 'he' but a 'she'; Atticus's missing sister. She could only assume that her 'other' mind had seen the book upon her initial look but it had failed to register.

Elle returned the book and went out into the hallway. On hands and knees, it took several very frustrating and anxious minutes to find the plastic name plate that she had prised from the door. Sitting in decades of dust on the edge of the lamp's light she read the name that she already thought would be there, Dr. S. Evergreen. The suspicions of the family were confirmed. Scout had worked here and here she had died.

Elle regained her feet. There were several things that needed to be done before anything else. The body was carefully removed from the chair and wrapped in a thick cotton tarpaulin taken from the depot. It was then secured in a place where it would be safe and out of any possible future harm. Except for the photo, Elle returned all the other personal items she had removed from the desktop and put them back exactly where they had been. Elle's remarkable memory made sure of this. The photo, which she had previously avoided looking at, showed six smiling faces. She had seen this photo before in the family albums and knew all the names. With the three girls standing in front, Scout, tall like her sister, was sandwiched between Atticus and Zee and looked straight into the camera. This photo had to be over seventy years old. If circumstances permitted, Elle would ensure that Scout was returned home to the Farm and the family along with the contents of the room, for they did not belong here.

There was a great deal that Elle could not understand regarding the scientific contents of the files. She had no formal education despite the efforts of her parents and her grandfather. There were a lot of holes in her knowledge. In this case she suspected that even among the Traders there would be no-one qualified. In the Dry, especially for those who lived in the wastelands, such intellectual pursuits were an unaffordable luxury. Of course this did not mean that the Traders would not set about correcting this anomaly. They were that kind of people. Elle mentally corrected herself. She too was 'that kind' of people. It would take time but they would eventually pry all the secrets from these facilities including the PSims. She had replaced the batteries in the PSim found in Scout's apartment but, in spite of it apparently working, she could not get past the access code. But if the Scavengers could get a battle tank computer operating, then it was reasonable to assume the Traders could do something similar here.

Reaching into the vest of her waistcoat, Elle retrieved the harmonica. Like the rest of her totems; the photo, the book, secure in the other pocket, the sniper's rifle, it never left her possession. Soon the office and adjoining hallway were filled with the mournful sounds of a long ago melody bemoaning lost love and the general misfortune that life brings the living.

The science might be beyond her but the intentions of those who created the Guardians were not. Her mood darkened as did the music and the stone. She now knew what Guardians were and what they had been designed to do. In this the people here had achieved spectacularly. Intelligence had been bestowed on the microscopic synthetic life form they created. Once released, it did harvest any and all available water but most certainly not as intended. Funny how these people seemed to have gotten so caught up in their pursuit that even the most gifted among them forgot what every child knows. She wondered if they had been given the time before they died to remember they were more than 60% water. And, as Elle was coming to realize, water was not all that was harvested, they absorbed emotions as well. Any attempt on her part to probe her replica unleashed a torrent of terror, the same she had felt on the lakebed. It was as though the Guardians were the keepers of the souls of the dead. This could not have been their intention and nothing in her reading gave any indication that it was ever even considered. But what had Scout's intentions been?

If what happened to her was not intended by these people around the conference table, why did it happen? There were, she thought, two possibilities. Either it was the Guardians themselves, or else there was another player. While it was only a suspicion regarding the 'why', she needed to talk to Noah about Atticus's sister and she needed to read everything she could find here that Scout had written. Elle stopped playing the harmonica for a moment and, to reassure herself they were still there, touched the ring and its new stone before drifting down to the handle of the knife. They were. The stone and the knife handle had to be the key just as Noah thought, although the 'lock' was not just the replica but the Guardians themselves.

Noah had said that his grandmother and her sister were named after characters from a favourite book of their father's and that it had not been well received by either of them as they grew up. He remembered Atticus entertaining him with the stories about growing up as an identical twin. He especially enjoyed the ones about Scout and entertained Elle and family by retelling the 'adventures' of Elle's great-great-great-aunt. Scout, like her sister, was 'gifted', but, unlike her twin, was the personification of mischievousness. Atticus told Noah that she had lost count the number of schools and universities her sister had been asked to leave for one prank or another. Everyone wondered how she ever managed to stay out of jail let alone obtain a PhD in such a demanding field. Scout had made and then sent the ring and knife to her sister, so it seemed reasonable to Elle that they were 'designed' to 'interfere' with the Guardians. An intelligent life form? But if that were true, why send them to Atticus with no information regarding their purpose? Did she leave it all too late? By the time they reached Atticus the Dry was about to or had already started. You would think that if Scout knew what was about to happen, that it had all the hallmarks of a disaster in the making, she'd would have shown much more urgency than she did. It seemed all so haphazard, so wrong.

Whatever the answers to these questions might be, Elle felt she understood enough to explain why she and Noah hadn't shared the fate of those in the convoy. Scout had devised a means to alter the Guardians and shaped that means into the ring and the knife. For reasons that might forever remain unknown, she then sent them to Atticus, never knowing that more than sixty years would pass before her plan would be implemented.

She held Scout's PSim up and looked at the blank screen. "Maybe all the answers are in there, just waiting for someone shrewd enough to crack the code."

Until then, it was all speculation. But having said that, she wasn't convinced that being irrevocably contaminated by the Guardians was a part of Scout's strategy. No one was that smart. It was far too complex, with too many places for it to go wrong as the 60 year hiatus clearly illustrated. Elle did not need a PhD in chaos theory to understand that no one could plan that well and that far ahead. Yet something had happened out there. There was absolutely no doubt in Elle's mind that she and others had somehow fused with the Guardians. How else could you explain the way she could 'absorb' the doppelganger, or the way the globe of light could be 'encouraged' to emerge or that cuts and infected wounds could disappear. Surely that, as well as every exhaled breath, was a confirmation that these micro creatures now swam freely through her and everyone else so infected. Sixty years was a long time to leave something like the Guardians sitting alone up there on their mountains. What had happened on the lakebed could be partly explained if you accepted that they were not passive participants in Scout's grand plan.

The dog was returning for she could hear it scampering down the hall, engrossed in its excitement. The animal tore into the room and leaped into the air, bowling Elle over, imprisoning her within the arms of the chair. Seeing her at a disadvantage, the dog took the opportunity to give her a very moist, slobbery lick across the face before bounding off to sit well out of her reach, satisfied with itself and its achievement. Elle's only thought was that she was going to kill that dog one of these days. Ever since the dog had entered her life, she was forever picking herself up and wiping slobber off her face.

Again another sharp twinge came from her grandfather and the chorus. She collected the harmonica from where it had fallen and gathered up her other belongings. She had an abrupt reversal of an earlier determination. She had had enough of this nonsense, of not 'hearing' from Noah and being alone. After all had she not done everything she had set out to do and much, much more?

In an hour, pushing a heavily laden trolley along the service road, with the dog in the lead and her other self trailing behind, she was on her way out. Thinking about what she'd found and the Scavenger's convoy out there on the lakebed, Elle wondered as she exited from the main entrance, what was it they had expected to find after expending all that energy and time to gain access? Had they thought they would find the means to wield the Guardians as if they were some sort of weapon of mass destruction? If that had been their plan, unless she'd missed something while roaming around in that subterranean town, they would have come away very disappointed.

Chapter Thirty-One
The black swan is but the shadow of the white.

Pausing at the entrance, she took a deep breath. "How sweet the air is," she murmured. Except where the Guardians gathered above her, stars filled the heavens, the spiral arm of the Milky Way arched from horizon to horizon. Elle again took a deep breath, filling her lungs with the night air. With a wave of a hand, she extinguished the light that hovered just above the ground in front of her. No point in letting anyone knows of her presence. Old habits die hard. Surprisingly, the air felt cool on her skin, sending a delightful tingle up her arms. Comparing the stuffiness of her recent confinement in the mountain with the sweetness out here, people, she thought, could become accustomed to nearly anything. How could she have forgotten? And yet, while in there it had seemed... not proper or natural, but acceptable. That was the word. It was acceptable. She wondered if that was what happened to people, they just became accustomed to a way of doing things, an acceptable habit. "Never underestimate the power of inertia," her grandfather would remind her when she became obsessed with routine. "It requires neither reason nor intelligence."

A fire could be seen on the knoll. Someone was either very stupid or very confident. Either way, she was not prepared to take any unnecessary risks. She put down the two large bags she was carrying, unshouldered her pack and released the safety on the rifle. Closing her eyes, Elle let her mind follow a thread of light or two but found nothing that indicated an immediate threat. She went into her stalking slouch, prepared to give that careless person the fright of their lives, when the dog gave out a yelp and shot off toward the fire. Elle flung herself to the ground wanting dearly to shoot that dumb animal when a voice called out her name.

"Elle, it's me, Nic."

What followed was a great deal of screaming, laughing, hugging, plus general jumping up and down. In a rush of emotions, words gushed from them both creating a confusion of noise ensuring that neither understood what the other was saying, especially as the dog chimed in with its yelps and barks adding to the mayhem. Somehow, in the confusion of their mutual excitement, they leaned in to perform the Trader's greeting. Only this time Nic extended his lips ever so slightly allowing Elle to receive her first real kiss. The kiss was clumsy, inept and brief, bringing with it embarrassment and silence. There was every chance that they would have stood there a lot longer, rooted to the ground and afraid to look into each other's face, if Nic had not abruptly started babbling and pointing off in the dark.

Elle's replica 'walked' into the ring of light from the fire to stand beside her. Elle watched with considerable amusement her friend's reaction and his unintelligible attempts to utter a coherent sentence.

Finally, "What in the Scavengers' hell is that?" emerged.

"That," said Elle, smiling broadly and enjoying his astonishment immensely, "is a Guardian."

"Oh," he said and with that, stepped away from the fire's light to return with Belle, asking, "Can it ride then? Because we had better get going."

Giggling at his response she did the only thing she could do under the circumstances, she returned his kiss and then stood there awkwardly, finding it difficult to stop blushing. She could sense his emotional confusion as clearly as her own which only increased their mutual discomfort. As a means of distraction and to avoid looking at Nic, Elle directed her attention to her horse allowing him to retreat into the surrounding darkness to retrieve his mount.

Elle bent her head forward to rest against Belle's wide forehead and breathe in the animal's smell. A warm musky odour greeted her as did its emotional feeling toward her. A rush of memories flooded into her mind, prompting her to ask Nic if he had seen Noah.

If grief has a colour it must be a shade of black for that was how Elle sensed Nic's sadness and despair. "He is not doing too well, I'm afraid. We were pretty sure you were in the mountain because on several occasions we thought we heard a dog barking, but didn't know for sure. That's why Mom had me sitting out here for nearly a week, waiting for you to come out, if you were indeed in there."

"Then why didn't you just come in and check? You could easily have found me. It couldn't have been that hard."

Nic looked hurt. "We tried, Elle. We really did try."

They put out the fire and then started back up the slope to collect her gear from across the road. Nic told her that where he'd camped was about as close as anyone had been able to get. Any closer and they'd be set upon by the Guardian and rendered unconscious. What he did not tell her was that his attempt had almost cost him his life and if his mother had not insisted on securing a rope around his waist he'd be there still, face down on the tarmac. Nic pointed above the entrance. "See, they're still there. But why don't they try to stop us now?" he wondered aloud.

She glanced up and watched the soft starry mist sway as if moved by a breeze. "I don't know. Perhaps they thought they were doing me a favour," said Elle. Sadly, all her earlier joy and anticipation had evaporated. She grabbed her backpack with one hand and waved the other over her head. A brightly glowing sphere emerged from her palm which then took a position just in front of her, casting a light all around them.

Nic, who had been telling her of his hectic ride after leaving Empty Cup, fell silent.

Elle gave him a weak smile. She had been so proud the first time she did it, but now... She hefted the pack on to Belle and secured it behind the saddle before doing the same with the two carrying bags. In one were three vacuum-packed cans of coffee, a gift for Noah.

The replica easily kept pace with Belle, stride for stride, seemingly without effort. The image of Elle walking beside her was, of course, an illusion. The reflection in the mirror had revealed that what she saw, what anyone saw, was a kind of mental projection. As to why the Guardians took the time and energy to maintain the replica, Elle had no idea. What she did know was that instead of a girl walking across the lake bed and seemingly keeping up with a horse, there was a Guardian cloud. She reached out to her grandfather as she had done several times since Nic had told her that he was in some kind of coma. This time it was like viewing a battle raging far in the distance where one could not distinguish the combatants but sensed that no quarter was either asked for or given. She withdrew.

Nic told her what had happened to the Traders when the Guardians struck. They had been camped on a commanding rise just east of Sweetwater, straddling both sides of the main highway. A hundred wagons and some trucks, nearly a thousand people with more expected the following day. His mother had told him that there had not been a gathering like this in over thirteen years. Nic was with his brother and a friend in a forward position with a good view of the town and they were the ones who alerted the others that something was happening. Elle recalled the wall of blackness as it began to sweep over her and Noah and then the explosion of green. To Nic it first appeared as if a dark translucent stain was washing over the wastelands in front of them, rushing to cover everything before it. Then it started to change from a brooding black to a dark emerald green. Their camp was far enough away from Sweetwater that he and the others had had time to warn them. Several Traders were able to escape before it struck but turned back as they saw their friends and family inundated.

Nic, Nathan and their friend along with a few others woke to find nearly everyone else lying where they'd fallen. The first thing he noticed was how quiet it was, no camp noise, no one talking, no horses snorting or fidgeting about, no bird calls and no buzzing of insects. Except for a few people struggling to get to their feet, it looked as though nearly everyone else around him was dead. When he realized they weren't, only unconscious, he almost wept. They were so thirsty and weak they had to crawl when looking for their parents. Finding them alive...

Nic went silent prompting Elle to look across at him. There was enough light from the globe to see the glistening tear trails that had found their way down his cheek.

Fearing they'd be attacked at any moment by the Scavengers, they frantically scurried around the camp bringing water not only to people but to horses as well. Many had died – forty-nine men and women and nearly a quarter of their horses and most of their dogs. Then, when it seemed they were over the worst, they were struck again only this time few actually passed out. It might have been better if they had, considering the initial pain. She heard him snort as he stifled a laugh. It wasn't funny at the time but he was sure that in the retelling of the day – how everyone in the camp suddenly found themselves in the minds of others, it would bring a good deal of laugher a generation from now. Trader humour had its dark side.

Some started to cry. Most, however, were just very confused and it took a bit of effort by the likes of his mother and others to calm people down. A number of people started to keel over with their eyes rolled into the back of their heads. Some died, almost exclusively men, older men. Those who hadn't died woke within a day or two no worse for wear. A few, like their grandfather, remained in some kind of coma. Nicole was the one who figured out that all those affected had lived through the Sorrows and fought in the Scavenger wars. By the next day, the Traders knew that what had happened to them had also taken place in Sweetwater, only for the Scavengers it had been much, much worse.

Through a set of his parents' binoculars Nic had sat with Nathan to observe the carnage that was Sweetwater. The unattended fires that had destroyed several houses in a northern suburb were burning themselves out. They could see people milling around the town's centre as well as what had to be dead bodies. Some people just got up and wandered off. Some started to head towards the Traders just by following the road out and away from the mountains. When small groups made up of mostly women and their children staggered into camp it was decided to intercept the others, disarm them and load them onto wagons. The Traders took them to the camp's medical clinic. Many showed obvious signs of having been violently beaten. Some had even been shot. The Trader's consul had agreed it was time to intervene and help as much as possible. With as many good mounts as could be mustered, Nic and Nathan joined about a hundred Traders and rode into Sweetwater armed to the teeth, with the expectation of trouble. As was their custom when moving into danger, the party had fanned out as soon as they entered the town so as not to offer an easy target. They need not have bothered.

Like anyone who lived in the wastelands, Nic had seen a good deal of misfortune and the cruelty delivered by the human hand, but it did not prepare him for what he saw in Sweetwater. Here was humankind at its most depraved. The stench was the first thing you noticed, the absolute squalor. Corpses of animals and humans left to rot.

The younger Traders, those who had not taken part in the Scavenger Wars or were not present at the recent massacre, were unprepared. A young Scavenger of Nathan's age burst from one of the buildings brandishing an automatic weapon. His face was distorted in abject hatred. Nic could see him open and close his mouth as if he was shouting but no sound came out. A dozen rifles swung his way but neither the young man nor the Traders could find the means to pull the trigger. In fury and frustration the Scavenger dropped the rifle and pulled out a pistol placing it beneath his chin. Again he was unable to pull the trigger. Finally, with a look of hopeless despair he sank down onto the porch. The Traders, after an older woman among them volunteered to attend to the miserable creature, rode on into the centre of town.

Elle felt Nic's distress as he described the aftermath of the Guardians. More than two hundred bodies of men, women, and children littered the square with another fifty or so scattered throughout the town. Like a visitation from hell, people started coming out of the surrounding buildings, many showing signs of violence.

Nic brought his horse to a halt and turned to look at her. "Elle, how can people do things like that to each other?"

"Poor Nic, you have only scratched the surface of the depths to which we humans seem to be able to descend." She reached out, touching him with empathy and understanding in an attempt to sooth some of his shame and grief.

They rode up to where the poles, denuded of their grisly decorations, stood on the edge of town. Nic sensed Elle's uneasiness and guessed correctly that she had seen the men who had previously been tied to them. "They were some of the ones who attacked and killed our people. We took the bodies down and buried them," he said.

"And the others?" Elle asked.

Nic replied that he didn't know. He'd only been told that the attack was 'unauthorized' and that some of the men, by way of example, were executed. "Seems that the last thing they wanted was to alert outsiders to their presence in Sweetwater or their intentions. If not for old habits, in this they might have been successful."

Off the road Elle could just detect a lone figure standing in the derelict remains of a small structure. The sentry gave no challenge nor did Nic, other than a wave of his hand as a sign of recognition. As if he could indeed read her mind, Nic just said in passing that the girl went by the name of Samantha, a friend. Elle guessed that somehow Nic had been able to let the young Trader know they were no danger and to let them pass, a trick her week of isolation had not given her the opportunity to exploit.

A little further on, huddled within pools of light from the overhead street lamps, a large crowd gathered, blocking any further progress. Two figures were standing in the vanguard. Instantly she recognized her parents. Leaping from Belle, she flung herself into their outstretched arms. The emotion of their reunion was very personal but on display for all to witness. By now Elle's exploits were known to all the Traders and held in a deepest respect. She had done what had been thought impossible.

Nic held back. He had been told days earlier that Elle's parents were due to arrive soon. Having been given priority and allowed to ride in one of the trucks, it had taken less than a week. The people who had gathered around to welcome Elle suddenly parted, with considerable consternation, as the replica walked through the crowd to take its place beside Elle and the dog. The surprises just kept coming.

Nestled in their warmth without realizing that she was doing it, Elle gently touched her parents' minds.

They were startled for an instant then responded ever so cautiously and attentively to touch hers. She felt the warmth of their affection encircle her. If only she could purr.

Chapter Thirty-Two
Come friend, walk with me awhile.

Like the flicking of a switch, Noah was awake and to his astonishment was in a bed covered with several layers of sheets and blankets, yet he still felt chilled. The greying light spilled into the room from an open window directly across from the foot of the bed. A gentle breeze played with the tattered curtains. He was tired, exhausted. His mouth and throat were dry. The bedding was damp from his sweat. There was the sound of soft shallow breathing coming from someone to his left. He turned his toward its source to find his eldest, Nicole, folded as if she were a child, in a large overstuffed chair. She was asleep. Despite the hard years as a Trader, she looked surprisingly young, younger than he remembered.

Noah turned back to stare at the ceiling and listen to the muffled voices coming from outside the bedroom. From within his mind he traced a familiar line of light to its source.

"He's awake," cried a woman from somewhere in another part of the house. The next moment his bed was ringed with faces, voices and emotions. In amongst the bedlam that followed he learned that he had lain there for over a week. He also guessed, from dozens of partially completed sentences, that the world he was intensely a part of had irrevocably changed. Friends and family crowded around him wanting the opportunity to touch him, to press their noses against his, to share breath and be assured that he was indeed alive and well.

After each had their turn, Nicole shooed them from the room with instructions to dampen their emotions so he could rest. Then, with the commotion dying away, she leaned down and, after kissing him upon each eye, left the room closing the door behind her.

As the bubble of noise drifted out and away, Noah became aware there were still people in the room. They had not been among his initial well-wishers but instead stood quietly in a corner to wait. He did not need to turn his head and look at them as their individuals signatures were there for him to read. Elle and Ruth walked over and looked down. Like a mother, Ruth reached out and stroked his cheek.

"We almost lost you."

He knew that was true, it had been hard to come back from where he had been. He closed his eyes and found he could 'taste' the others, sensing their concern and finding a delight as they, in turn, reached out to 'touch' him. He did not want to sleep, there were so many questions he wanted to ask, and so he tried to open his eyes but could not. He reached out to Elle and was rewarded. He felt the emotions of the woman with the red hair wash over him. "She's OK. She's OK," he muttered as he drifted back to sleep.

The room was ablaze with the light from the midday sun pouring through the bedroom windows when Noah awoke.

"Feel like getting up and going out?" It was Ruth. Noah looked over at her. She smiled, knowing exactly what it was he was doing, and turned her head so that he could get a better look at the smooth cheek. "All gone," she said. "Now get up. You've been lying around long enough and there is something I want to show you."

He complied with the order and was pleasantly surprised. No weakness or dizziness. He felt great – hungry and strangely at peace.

While getting washed, dressed and fed, he listened to Ruth as she gave a cursory overview of what had happened to him. She described how he had suddenly crumpled to the ground. Then, with both of his eyes wide open, perhaps terrified at what they saw, he had started to convulse and scream. The arrival of Nic and two men from Sweetwater had been timely because Ruth and Flea on their own could not have effectively intervened and safely restrained a man of his size and strength. As it was, it took them several minutes and more than a few bruises all around to secure him. After tying him up, Ruth sent Nic back to Sweetwater for help. Nic went to get his Mom.

Upon her arrival, Nicole had wasted no time in seeing Noah transported to a house in the southern part of town that had remained unoccupied by a Scavenger. He had been there ever since.

"What happened to me?" he asked.

Ruth looked at him as a mother does to an errant male child and not a very bright one at that. "I tried to warn you. As you found out, it seems the Guardians do not take kindly to anyone trying to harm one of their own." She told him of another strange thing concerning a person's personal disposition. "The Guardians' gift seems to affect most adversely those who are inflexible with too much history and too much anger." Noah was certain that a twinkle came into her eye when she said the word 'inflexible'.

An hour and a bit later, according to his watch, Noah was outside waiting for Ruth to return with the horses. How often we fail to see the future by thinking it is the past revisited, he thought, trying to come to terms with the changes that had occurred within him. A minute later Ruth rode up from around the corner of the house on a big red mare, leading Blue. "What next?" exclaimed Noah. The fact that Blue could be led like a lamb by anyone but him was astounding enough. Seeing the old boy saddled and ready to go, in a strange way, injured his pride. Before, Blue had always taken exception to anyone attempting to saddle him.

Taking the saddle's horn into his left hand, Noah put his foot in the stirrup and swung up. Astride Blue, he waited for Ruth to come alongside. The way she stuffed her hair under a broad brimmed hat sporting a crow's feather amused him. Grinning from ear to ear, he detected that she had a secret that needed to get out.

Sharing his grin she looked at him and asked in that sing-song that only a mother would ever use, "Notice anything different about the place?"

Suspecting some kind of trick and knowing this was a game he was good at, Noah slowly turned around in the saddle until he had done a full 360. Except for the evidence of an expanding population and the attempts to remove the worst of the trash, giving the town a certain freshness, he saw nothing that should warrant her obvious delight. He checked again, still nothing untoward. Yet, the expression on Ruth's face and the heightened expectation he sensed from her made him look again. What am I missing? he thought. Ruth was near busting to tell him. In the way of providing a clue, she lifted her eyes skyward. Noah looked up.

Even though no one born during the Dry had ever observed one, there was no mistaking what was crowning the mountain tops. In what amounted to an astonished whisper Noah said, "Clouds! Bloody, bloody clouds."

The giggles could no longer be held back. "They started forming about three days ago about the same time as the others started showing up."

"Others?" asked Noah. "What do you mean by 'others'?"

As if speaking to a five year old she tried to explain. "As you know Traders are pouring into town from all over the country. What you don't know is that there are people who have been arriving from up and down the length of the mountain range. So far they are mostly settlers. Nicole suggested that Sweetwater was becoming a kind of pilgrimage destination.

"Knowing its recent history, that's a bit ironic, don't you think?" It was apparent he'd missed a great deal since his ignominious collapse and subsequent convalescence.

Over the following days, the cloud slowly turned from fluffy white to an ominous dark grey. There was anticipation that six decades of drought were about to end and every person in Sweetwater had gathered along the town's western boundary to be a witness. The children, including Elle's tribe – Flea, Samantha, the girl sentry, Chook, who had accompanied her parents, Nic and Tucker, a kid whose father had been a Scavenger – had raced their horses out onto the lakebed stopping just short of the old tourist boat. Everyone, from the very old to the very young, was eager to be the first to not only see rain but to get drenched in it. The air became sharp with a tingling edge and the wind dropped off completely. It was as if the whole world was holding its breath.

With her twin perched on the brow of the boat, Elle and the others milled around talking, telling jokes, and trying to predict what the rain would be like when it fell. The air ever so subtly began to change, becoming cool and crisp. The wind picked up and stirred small dust devils into life. Without instruction, the kids and the others on lake bed lined their horses up to face the mountains and waited.

What happened next is hotly debated by all who were there that day. According to Noah, who had the good fortune to not be on a horse at the time, a brilliant streak of lighting struck the mast on the boat producing a monstrous thunderclap followed by a tremendous torrent of rain. Terrified horses scattered in every direction, many without their riders. Elle, who had been casually sitting with one leg dangling down out of the stirrup and the other draped across the saddle talking with Samantha and Nic, found herself sprawled face down in the sand, which was fast becoming mud, with a broken arm.

That was how Noah found her, crying in the rain, all muddy and soaked. Her twin stood passively by, expressionless and as much an enigma as the first day. He didn't laugh though he might have wanted to, seeing how much she looked like a drowned cat. He just gently put her on Blue's back and took her to her mother who dried her off, cleaned her up, changed her clothes and put her to bed.

Elle soon drifted off into a deep sleep for two consecutive days. During those two days the bruises disappeared and the break mended, restored to new.

The adventure of the millennium, the return of the rains, had not worked out as Elle had envisioned. Such things seldom do. But she had survived, she had gone to the mountains and the rain had returned. The world was saved, right? The only thing left was for her and the people of Sweetwater to figure out what do with the Guardians' gift.

When she awoke her mother was by her bedside. She sat up.

Expecting her daughter to ask what had happened or what was it like when it rained, Nora was taken aback when Elle asked, "Mom, why does my name begin with 'E' and not 'N'?"

Nora smiled that smile only mothers have and said, "It is not as important now as it was then." When she saw that this was not going to placate her daughter, the smile became more wistful. Her hand went to her stomach and began to make those circular motions pregnant women often do. Elle watched Nora's hand as it gently stroked the extended belly and felt her leave the present to go elsewhere. The Guardian's gift could not read thoughts but Elle knew her mother was far, far away and not even conscious of what her hand was doing. The hand stopped and reached out to cup Elle's chin. "If this is so important for you then let us do it right. You get up and get dress. You've friends waiting. Tomorrow meet me at the eastern edge of town just before sunrise."

With the doppelganger tucked away within her, Elle stood in the middle of the Great Central Highway with Belle. She sensed her parents and Noah before she heard their horses approaching and could not help but feel a little disappointed that this was not going to be a mother to daughter conversation as she had expected. Then she became embarrassed knowing they had sensed her disappointment. This turned to surprise when her mother and Noah stopped while her father continued until he was beside her.

He dismounted and put his arm around her shoulders before saying, "Let's move a bit further on so as to get a better view of the sunrise." The hand on her shoulder was heavily calloused from years of physical toil. She could feel the bone-jarring strength in those fingers.

Her father was a gentle, quiet man who had stood back from both Noah and her mother, giving them all the room such personalities as theirs often needed. So it felt awkward and a little uncomfortable to be walking with him up the middle of the Great Central Highway without them. This was not at all what she had expected and she became frightened when she glimpsed his emotions. They were sad, so very, very sad. What was he about to tell her? Was she to learn, like Nic, she was a wasteland orphan and not their real child, that there was no twin, that it was all a misunderstanding on her part?

The sky was streaked with reds and pinks as the sunlight struck the clouds. Clouds made the sky so much more interesting, she thought. When Jacob cleared his throat and began to speak, she braced herself for the worst.

Almost in a whisper he said, "Your mother's mother died along with her new-born at sunrise. Your mother, after two miscarriages, one nearly full term, was terrified, fearing the worst when she was pregnant with you and your sister. Not a moment during those nine months did she let herself expect that either of you would be born alive. She went into labour in the middle of the night, giving birth to you both when it was still dark outside. Your sister was born first and named Nova. Thirty minutes later you were born and were immediately named Nellwyn. Your umbilical cord had barely been cut before..." her father began to choke up. The sun's rays made the tears forming at the corner of his eyes glisten. Elle rubbed the hand on her shoulder, at a loss as to what she could do to ease the emotion that poured from him. "Your sister died and I could do nothing to relieve your mother's grief. Bearing all that pain of losing a daughter she instructed me to take you to the window so that you could see the birth of a new day."

The sun was clearly visible on the horizon when her father stopped and turned to look Elle full in the face. "Such were the times, your mother did not expect for you to see the sun set, but you did. That evening with all the family present in the dining room, you were renamed Elle and it was inscribed upon Nadia's Wall." He then turned and both of them watched the sun until it cleared the hills beyond. "It seemed important at the time for your mother to change your name to Elle as the name Nellwyn meant bright companion. Your grandfather left the next morning."

"And the figure on the Wall standing next to me, is that my sister?" asked Elle.

Jacob looked surprised. "I don't know anything about that, Elle. You'll have to ask your mother. The Wall is not a male's domain."

Chapter Thirty-Three
Who checks the checker?

The cock's crow didn't wake Elle. It rarely did. She rolled over to look out the window letting it delay her a few minutes before getting up. The air smelled moist; rain before noon she predicted. There were drawbacks with what appeared to be the return of seasons. It got cold here at the base of the mountains. Reluctantly she pushed the covers back and stood up, feeling a shiver race across her body. The replica emerged and stood patiently waiting by Elle's side. After a year it still felt decisively creepy and would stop anyone in mid-sentence when it appeared in their presence. The silvery sheen had faded, leaving in its place the texture and colour of Elle. Although it still appeared to be 'dressed' identically to her, recently Elle had begun to notice small incremental changes in its wardrobe. A colour shade difference here, a style shift there, changes unnoticed by anyone not on intimate terms with her 'twin'. Elle had wanted to give her doppelganger a name befitting its mysterious origin, but because Flea referred to her as Aladdin's lamp, her friends started calling the doppelganger 'Jinni'. So Jinni it was.

A loud yawn escaped as she stretched, scratched and farted before walking into the bathroom to attend to her toiletry. A lot had happened since she'd left the mountain's interior. She still viewed the passage of time with suspicion since most of the changes had come without her consent and had nothing to do with the Guardians' gift. The reflection in the mirror revealed some of these un-requested changes. She was taller and her figure showed definite hints of being fuller, not so raw-boned, more feline. There was even a suggestion of hips and a bust which, for reasons she could not fully comprehend, seemed to affect the way she walked.

One of the things the mirror was unable to reflect had caused her more than a little irritation; she was now officially a woman. Having her mother here at the time shielded her some from the customary harassment by the Traders that such rites of passage attract. To make matters worse, once she found out, Flea started call her their in-house 'breeder'. Grudgingly Elle did admit, aside from its inherent inconveniences, the distinction of being a 'woman' had its benefits. It meant she was recognized as an adult by the community and as such, custom conferred numerous privileges. For one, she could choose where and with whom she lived. To be fair, the particular 'whom' the custom was alluding to was a long way off yet as far as she was concerned. This and a few other womanly duties she planned to largely avoid as long as she could.

Getting up from the porcelain toilet bowl and pulling the chain, Elle had to admit that indoor plumbing and toilet paper were the true marks of civilisation. The house was just far enough from town to have had a septic tank which had taken only a few days to repair and reconnect. It had been working now for about a month and it was far preferable to digging a hole, hovering over a bucket or going outside to use a long-drop. There was still no hot water and wouldn't be until she was able to acquire a 'wetback' for the fireplace or a boiler with a firebox. That sign of civilisation was still a way off. There just didn't seem to be enough time in the day to do all that needed to be done. Time, her old nemesis, was scarce. Maybe next year or the one after she'd find the time and means to install a wetback on the kitchen stove. After that, she could cook a meal and be rewarded with a hot shower or even a bath. At the moment she was content to have running water, though cold, flowing from both taps. The pleasure of water cascading over her body had lost none of its appeal. Goose bumps rose up on her arms as she washed in the spray of the cool morning shower.

With Ruth and Noah on their 'trip' and Chook's and her parents gone, Elle was feeling a little lonely. Since the Farm was the only place Nora would consent to give birth, all the adults had returned to the Farm several months ago, taking Scout's body with them. They were given a ride on one of the east bound truck-trains that now regularly travelled the full length of the Great Central Highway. Women had high status in the Trader's tradition; a pregnant woman, a mother, higher still. The fact that she was Noah's daughter and Elle's mother certainly didn't hurt. They were home with Ted and Susan in tow in a few days instead of weeks.

That was another thing that the mirror could not reveal. Elle had a sister, the first to be born of this new generation, and she was already causing her mother and the rest of the family a range of unexpected difficulties. An undisciplined Changeling was proving to be a handful. Thinking of her new sister, Elle wondered if Ruth would have her child at the Farm as all the women in her family did. Her family was strong on maintaining traditions. Along with her cousins' wives, her sister, Ruth and her unborn child would most certainly end up on Nadia's wall. It was a family ritual and like most family rituals it took on some of the hallmarks of a religious ceremony. For people who profess to be atheist and nonconformist, they certainly had a lot of rules to live by, and despite her high status and being an adult, she did not have immunity. She never did get around to asking her mother about the image of the girl standing next to her on the Wall. There are some things that need a degree of privacy. A recent letter informed her that Scout had finally had her date of death inscribed next to her image and had been buried next to her sister.

She returned to the bedroom, started to get dressed and was about to send a morning greeting to Noah and Ruth when she recalled that they would be unable to receive it. Noah had been right, once you were out of the Guardian's 'soup', the ability to send and receive emotions was, as he put it, grinning mischievously, amputated. She smiled, remembering how much fun the wedding had been. The idea that her curmudgeonly grandfather had gotten married last month was still rather unbelievable. To top it off, Ruth would present the Traders with a new member early next year. It was no surprise to anyone but perhaps Ruth that, when informed she was 'with child', Noah had insisted they had to get married. There was no other option. Noah and the Traders were sticklers for traditions. The presentation of the 'Family' wagon was particularly touching. Ruth became so emotional at its significance Noah had to lead her away to calm her down. As it was, even those few who were not familiar with the Traders' custom were tearful.

Much of Ruth's history was best forgotten. Her future, on the other hand, was another matter. Noah might be difficult man to live with at times and to understand but, as she knew, he was an easy man to love. He was also secretive. To make sure they had some time alone he'd kept their destination to themselves for obvious reasons. Traders were a roguish lot so there were some things that you could never trust them with – like where you were going after your wedding. Elle was pretty certain she knew where they were heading and not only because it was near their rendezvous. In spite of the Guardians' gift and his change in status as a married man, Noah was still a person whom the younger ones referred to as being from the 'Old Times', before the Guardians' intrusions, and thus too rigid to be able to take full advantage of the gift. Noah could never relax enough. Too much past, too many memories that required attending to. He would never learn to float.

The irony that Flea was to stay with her while the couple rode off and out of range from prying minds did not go unnoticed by either girl. Seemingly unaffected by the rooster's verbalization, Sam, Flea and the dog were still asleep in the bedroom next to hers.

Content in the knowledge that a recent amorous encounter with a rather energetic and ambitious Jack Russell had been successful, the traitor lay at Flea's feet. Samantha, occupying the bedroom across from hers, was a couple of months older than Elle and had also recently become a 'woman'. Never having had a female friend, Elle was at first hesitant to agree when Sam asked if she could share the house. In the months that followed, despite earlier reluctance, Elle, to her relief and bemusement, was finding that girls are not boys. They do, as quoted by the Mothers of the Traders, "...make life possible". Elle tried to stifle another yawn, but failed. She shot a jolt to wake the trio. It was going to be another busy day.

In the middle of the living room Elle stood for a moment before heading into the kitchen to see about rekindling the fire for breakfast. This room was her treasure trove. She had asked to keep the things from Scout's apartment. Permission was granted by the elders and her family. The books, including a signed copy of Atticus' *Pithy Quotes for Angry Women*, occupied one wall and part of another. The painting of the two girls on the lake and other works of art filled a third. The mantel over the fireplace held the framed photos of her family, five generations. The photo of Zee, Atticus, their three daughters and Scout that had been in the office, sat in the centre, the beginning of it all.

Elle studied the contents of the room marking each item in her memory. This was to be their last day in Sweetwater for several months and there was much to do before tomorrow's departure. This would be her third trip outward bound. The first had been to remove everything of value at the homestead and bring it back to Sweetwater. The only things of interest to her were a few of the books, which she kept to add to her library. The second was over the mountains and back, one week out, one back. Unlike the first time, just after the rains returned, the party was not greeted by complete and utter desolation every step of the way. No one, it appeared for reasons as yet unknown, had survived on that side. This time however, it was not as bleak, and the desolation was not so universal. Insects and a few animals had found their way over the mountains, and there were green shoots up and down the valleys. Elle still harboured the hope of one day reaching the coast and standing on a beach, swimming in the sea, eating a fish and seeing a whale breach the surface.

A sleepy, irritated moan from the bedroom gave Elle a mischievous delight. There were some merits in having a younger sister to taunt, although technically Flea was her aunt, a technicality she was determined to ignore. Sam was the quiet one. There would be no unnecessary noise from her part of the house.

Nic was up and moving. He always sent a warm 'Good morning' before heading over to her place. They nearly always had breakfast together since the rest of any day was sure to be hectic and unpredictable. Sometimes they did not get a chance to see each other again until the following morning, such was the work load on them all. There were sixty years of devastation and neglect to rectify and, with the discovery of the knowledge secured within the mountains, a sense of urgency permeated their ever-growing community.

The next 'Good morning' came from Chook and then Tucker. When his parents had accompanied Jacob and Nora, Chook had come with them and decided to stay. By the end of first month he could talk, although one could be forgiven in thinking that he was still mute as he was never much of a 'talker'. Silence suited him. He also came over most mornings on the pretext of sharing breakfast with her. This fooled no one. Chook might not say much but his emotions radiated like a beacon and his attempts to hide the obvious affection directed toward Sam only made him a vulnerable target for Flea. Tucker, on the other hand, was a good match against Flea's torment.

Everything in Elle's life was in flux; everything was in an accelerated state of change. She even had a Changeling sister. She nearly laughed out loud at the word 'Changeling' – everyone and everything ultimately gets named, defined and placed in a box. Who was the first to use the word Changeling was in dispute, but it was quickly adopted by the younger folk and once they started using it, everyone else followed. If it had been Elle's choice she would have gone with something more pertinent to the gift than Changeling, *Linepithema humil* for instance. "Granted", she had confessed to Nic, "it doesn't roll as easily off the tongue as Changeling, but don't you think it possesses a dignity that Changeling lacks?"

Her stomach rumbled in protest at being empty and she headed toward the kitchen. Whether you chose a name or, as in the case of the Scavengers, had it chosen for you, the desire to name, to differentiate, was an irrepressible human instinct. It was also an excellent instrument to promote violence against another. None knew this better than the survivors of the Scavenger wars. Finney's underlying premise in *The Body Snatchers* was wrong as far as Elle was concerned. The humans were the real threat, not the aliens. This had been vehemently illustrated recently. Without provocation, on a foraging expedition, a small group of Traders had been attacked up near the Great Lakes district. There was loss of life on both sides. Fortunately the moratorium on violence within their Changelings community did not extend to those on the outside when their intentions were not peaceful. A sad thing really, for the short-lived hope had been that if the Traders and Scavengers were compelled to fuse into one, then the conversion of humankind to something more peaceful was held as a possibility. That hope was proving to be barren. What worried Elle most was that being a Changeling might be no better than being human.

It was her grandfather, commenting on the attack, who said that, "The rains' return and Guardians' Gift will not and cannot change the simple fact that life, to sustain life, consumes life." This was not what she and others wanted to hear but Elle knew it was true – but possibly with one important caveat.

Within the Guardian 'soup' this sense of connectedness, of oneness, extended to other life forms. Animals could and did read your intentions and you, in turn, could and did read theirs. Try approaching a chicken when you were hungry or any other domestic animal designated to end up in the cooking pot. The Guardians' Gift did not prevent you or any other predator from killing another animal for food, but having their minds flooded with fear was having a disturbing effect on Sweetwater's meat-eating population.

The first drops of rain began to fall, splattering against the kitchen window, a good day to be inside. Checking the state of the fire in the stove, Elle knew she was not the person she had been. The Elle she really was had died that day on the lakebed, as had Noah and all the others who had merged with the Guardians. There were still people dying when they crossed the boundary. No one became a Changeling without 'paying the ferryman'. Her mantra, "How do you know you've changed...?" had become a common refrain for her. Elle looked over at her companion as Jinni peered at the thin threads of smoke rising from the small suggestion of a fire struggling to be rekindled. Jinni was, in her way, also changing and Elle wondered what price she would pay.

The wood range was the same one she had taken from the Homestead. Nic had not only been able to retrieve it from the Farm but had also managed to find a replacement for its missing leg. Elle was increasing finding it difficult to see herself without his presence. Strange, this adult thing.

The thousands of whispers of her community gently brushed against her. She smiled at the noise, knowing that the changes had not altered the constant negotiations involved in maintaining any relationship. It only made it public. With the tiniest of efforts, if she wished, she could 'visit' anyone of them, interrupting their current domestic interplay. She did not – it was a question of manners.

The flicker of flame was encouraged by being fed a few thin slivers of wood. Elle could feel their yawns as the two girls began reluctantly to wake up. In the few short months of cohabitation she had already forgotten what it was like to ever be alone in the way she had been before.

There was food left over from her birthday party last night in the town hall. The gang of three had liberated what they could carry and tucked into it the cooler they'd built under the kitchen floor. Lifting the lid, Elle was content that they had absconded with enough that even the dog would have a generous portion this morning. Elle and Sam had only managed to take a few nibbles; the rest had been skived off with by Flea. Even after living with her this past year, Elle was continually amazed at her sleight of hand. A skill that she most certainly had acquired while living in the company of Scavengers for most of her life. Back then such skills had kept her and her mother alive.

By the time the food was heated and put on the table, Chook, Nic and Tucker were already seated. Though they had ridden in the rain, none appeared too wet. Flea, yawning, sauntered in with the dog, followed closely by Sam.

With the meal finished and the dishes left to 'soak', a term employed by Flea meaning that she would get to them later, the eight retired to sit on the veranda. Four sat with their chairs pushed hard against the wall so as not to get wet and looked out into the drizzling rain. Flea, Sam and the dog sat on the steps leading down to the front yard. They did not mind getting wet. The mutt was still Elle's dog, but she suspected its loyalty became questionable when food, which Flea always seemed to have access to, was in the offering.

Puddles were forming in the hollows of the footprints leading to the house. Elle had chosen this place not just for its relative isolation and its unobscured view of the mountains, but for its full length, covered veranda. From there she had watched the wastelands burst into life. The scene of the returning grasses was intoxicating although she could have done without the flies. Whenever they were in the wastelands Noah would remind her when offering her a drink from his canteen, if hers was empty, that life was stubborn and persistent, saying, "Water is what makes life possible." However, there were very few flowers and that would remain true until the return of the insect pollinators, especially the honey bees.

Flea opened her hand, palm up. A butterfly with scarlet wings trimmed with iridescent purple settled there. Elle smiled at her antics. As she had surmised while still in the caves, Guardians had indeed been embedded within them. Forming a kind of symbiotic relationship, they coexisted beside and within each human cell. A butterfly living within a caterpillar or if you preferred a caterpillar living within a butterfly, that could be called upon to do some wondrous things. "Two living beings for the price of one," said a woman from the east coast, a non-Trader, who was currently working on unravelling the science behind the Guardians. "We are, in effect, a new species. After 30,000 years, humankind has a companion again." Then, as a kind of afterthought, the woman said, without a hint of humour, "And of course we know what happened to the Neanderthals when they encountered humans."

The young seedling she'd planted nodded and bobbed as the rain fell upon its leaves. It was a house-warming gift from Nic who had gone all the way to the Farm to retrieve the seed, and nurtured, it had sprouted. "In time", he had said, "it will help keep the sun off the veranda."

In time it may, she pondered, thinking how many times she'd sat beneath its outstretched bowers on her 'thinkin' log. Perhaps for my grandchildren.

She pushed herself up from her chair to announce the end of their morning leisure time. "Ok everyone. Sorry to break up this happy gathering but we have things to do. I, for one, still have to finish packing and," speaking to the girls, "so have you two." Damn, she thought, I'm barely fifteen and already sounding like my mother.

Tomorrow was a big day. Twenty-five teams, well over four hundred people, were heading out beyond the protection of the border. The rain might have pulled the world back from extinction but it did have its disadvantages. The Dry had left things of potential value to weather away ever so slowly. Water was far more insidious and aggressive. It found its way through damaged roofs, shattered windows and smashed doors, speeding the process of destruction and decay. There was now a race to retrieve as much of the knowledge of the Before Times as was possible and return it here to caves for safe keeping and study. They were also directed to collect seeds, seedlings and any wild or domestic life they could, including butterflies or queen bees, and to ensure their safe return.

The group that Elle was assigned to was expected to be gone for up to a year. They were instructed to head due north all the way to the Arctic seas in an attempt to find a long forgotten vault of seeds that had been collected from all around the world in the Before Times. According to the information found in the mountains, they were stored there in what had been frozen part of the northern continent, locked away in a field of perpetual ice. It was supposed to be a doomsday seed bank that the remnants of the human race could retrieve in the event of a global holocaust. The human race had forgotten about it.

Both for the Traders and those who were not accustomed to travelling for months on end, this was going to be an informative experience. Too bad about the fractious humans. It would have been nice to go out without the need to be armed and encased in a Kill Joy. Noah had warned that, indicating with a nod toward the lands to the east, "those out there are not going to take it kindly for an interloper such as yourself to come and take what little there is left." Even here, even now, within the relative safety of the Guardians, Elle was never more than a step away from her assassin's rifle.

Flea and Sam went inside after watching the boys jump on their horses and race off. Elle returned her gaze to the rain, remembering the first time, and grinned. She then looked at Jinni. At least Noah had been correct about the replica. It had started to sign six months ago and had recently called Elle by her name, even mimicking her voice which Flea found hilarious. It too was growing up. Unlike some in Sweetwater, Elle did not hold out much hope that it would ever be able to explain its origin. What new-born could? In spite of her prodigious memory, she could recall nothing of her birth or much of the first five years of her life. There was no memory of her sister. The Rain Thieves had created the Guardians who had, in turn, created her and the others. Intentionally or not, in that resulting mix was the hand of her great-great-great-aunt, Scout. There would not be another replica. It was a "oncer" as Noah called it. "A gift from Scout to whoever wore the knife and ring." Elle suspected that this was so. Somewhere in those caves

Atticus' sister had devised a means to save humanity from itself. Too bad she had not lived to see her last and greatest prank. Having watched Sam and Flea earlier, Elle thought it was fitting then when she learned that her twin sister's name had been Nova, 'Chaser of Butterfly' in one of languages of the first people.

Just days before his marriage to Ruth, Noah and Elle had sat on her veranda drinking coffee, old friends, comfortable in each other's company. Elle wondered aloud, "If Scout had not died when she did perhaps the coming of the Dry could have been prevented."

Noah laughed and reached over to ruffle her hair. "Elle, nothing would have stopped the Dry or something like it from happening. The pressure to control everything back then was unrelenting." Smiling broadly at her, he said, "Like growing up, for good or ill, some things, once started, are unstoppable." Not missing the irony, he continued, "What happened was as natural as rain." When he was about to leave, he turned and was not smiling. "Be careful with your new sense of power."

She toyed with the ring suspended around her neck, fingering the nick left by the Scavenger's blade. Its job done, the stone was as clear as a flawless crystal, a sign perhaps of her contentment? The best guess so far was a refinement of her thoughts while still in the bowels of the mountain. It was believed that both the ring and the knife handle contained some a kind of a catalyst, an agent, likely a retro virus, that had interacted with the Guardians, altering their internal configuration, which in turn altered everyone they came into contact with. It really did act as though it was a contagious infection. How this was done was one of thousands of as yet unanswered questions pertaining to the Guardians and the science of the Before Times. Noah said that he would be long dead before any but a very few were answered. Elle suspected, considering what had been lost, even her own grandchildren would be long dead before there was anything like a full understanding of what had gone on in the depths of those mountains.

Pulling the big watch from her vest pocket, she read the time. Noah had presented it to her shortly after his wedding day. He told her that the changes wrought by the Guardians made the world's future unknowable; however, his time and that of his generation had passed. It was now her turn. Putting the watch back into her vest pocket, she spoke to Jinni who was standing at the edge of the veranda watching a stream of water fall from the roof.

"Where does the time go?"

The replica did not answer that particular question, instead signed "I like watching free water fall."

"Me too," said Elle in reply. Then they both turned and followed the others. There was a lot of packing to do before tomorrow.

Later, in spite of her previous insistence on urgency, the sounds of a harmonica drifted out from the bedroom, soon accompanied by a high clear voice of a young woman.

THE END